THE STRUGGLE FOR AUTHORITY
THE STONE CYCLE BOOK 4

THE STONE CYCLE SERIES

The Stone of Knowing (The Stone Cycle Book 1)
The Cost of Knowing (The Stone Cycle Book 2)
The Stone of Authority (The Stone Cycle Book 3)
The Struggle for Authority (The Stone Cycle Book 4)
The Stone of Vitality (The Stone Cycle Book 5)
...with more to come

Companion Novelettes
The Seer: A Prequel to The Stone of Knowing (The Stone Cycle)
The Rending: A Prequel to The Cost of Knowing (The Stone Cycle)

THE STRUGGLE FOR AUTHORITY

THE STONE CYCLE BOOK 4

ALLAN N. PACKER

LUMINANT PUBLICATIONS

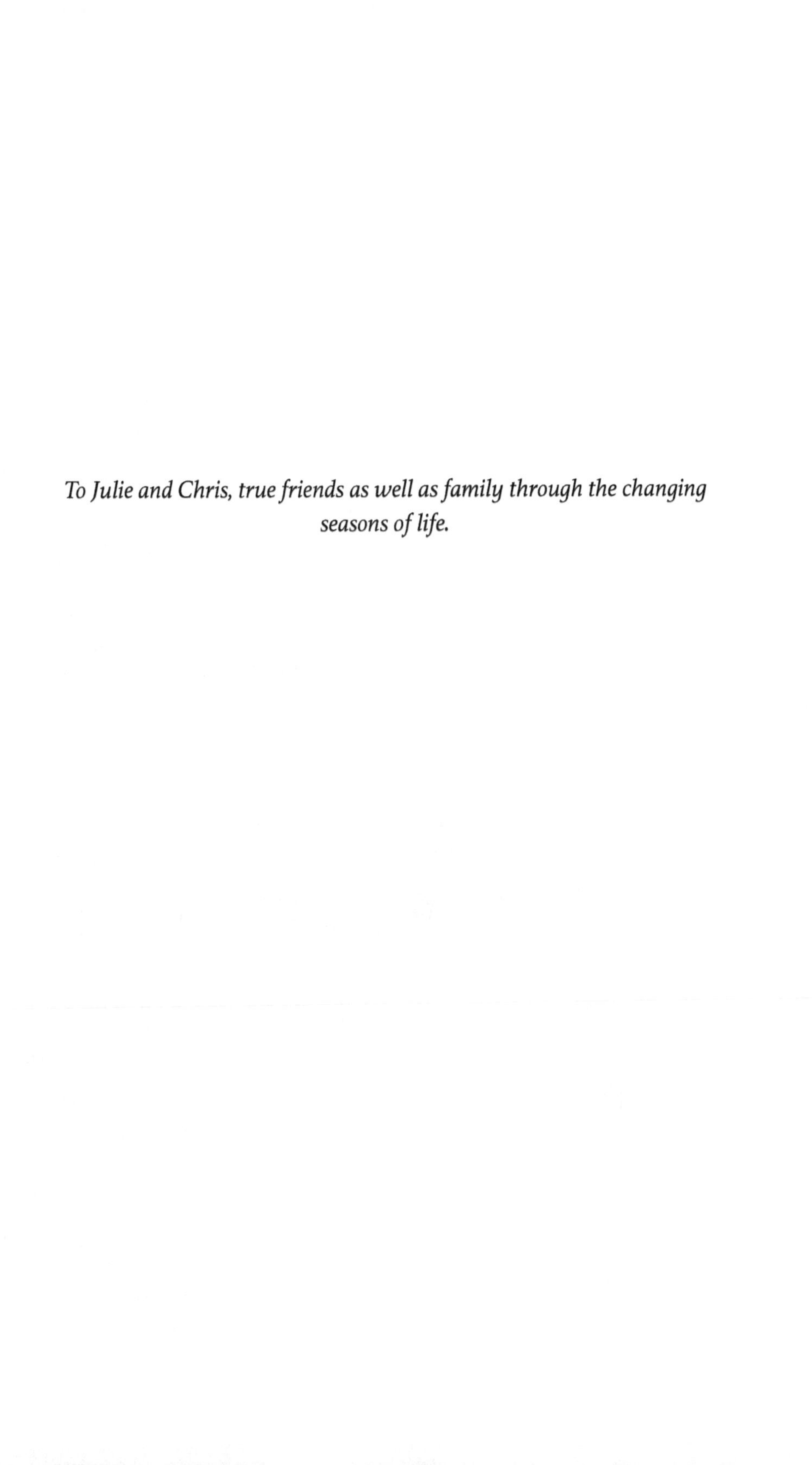

To Julie and Chris, true friends as well as family through the changing seasons of life.

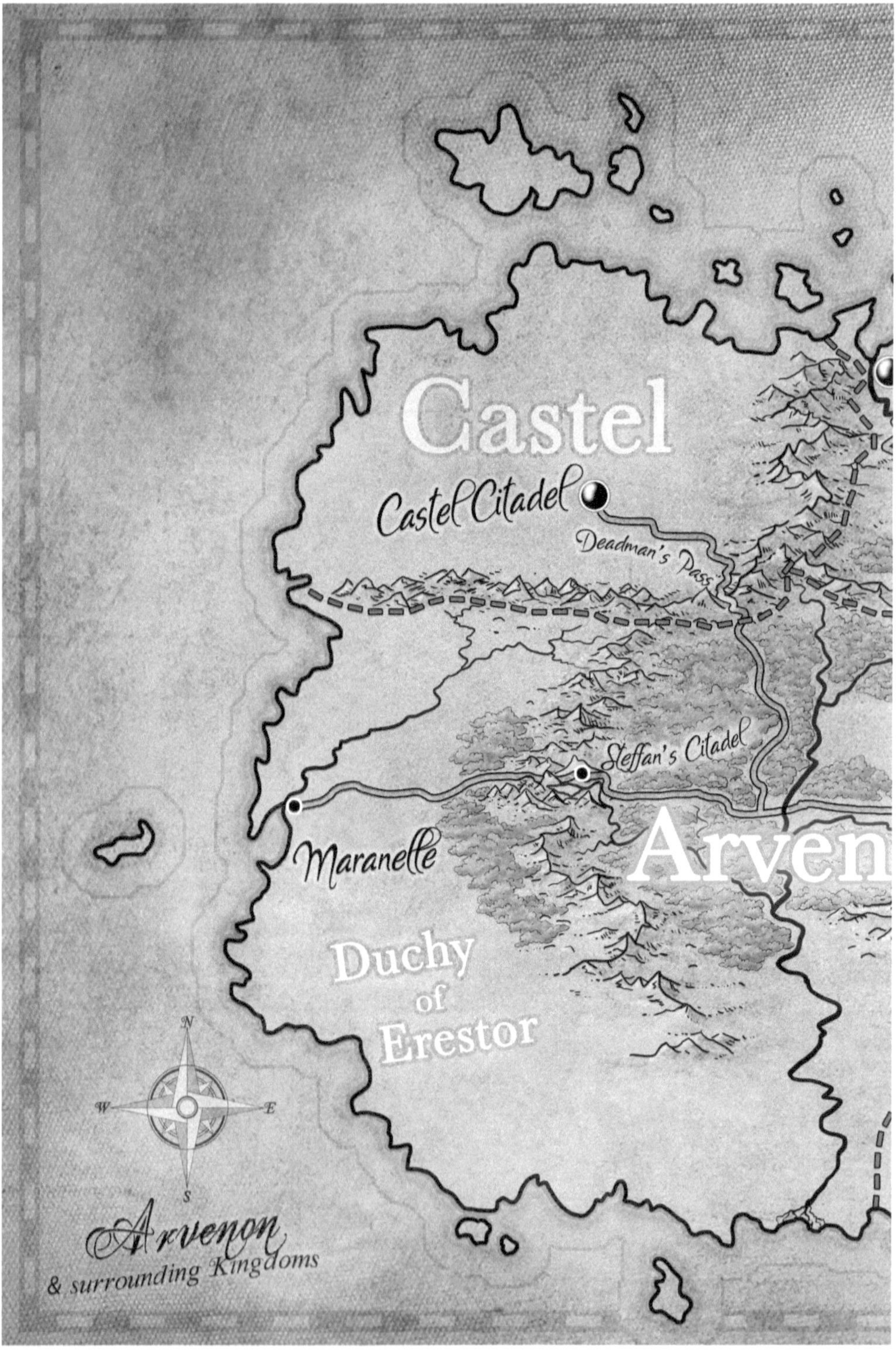

Castel
Castel Citadel
Deadman's Pass
Steffan's Citadel
Arven
Maranelle
Duchy
of
Erestor
N
W
E
S
Arvenon
& surrounding Kingdoms

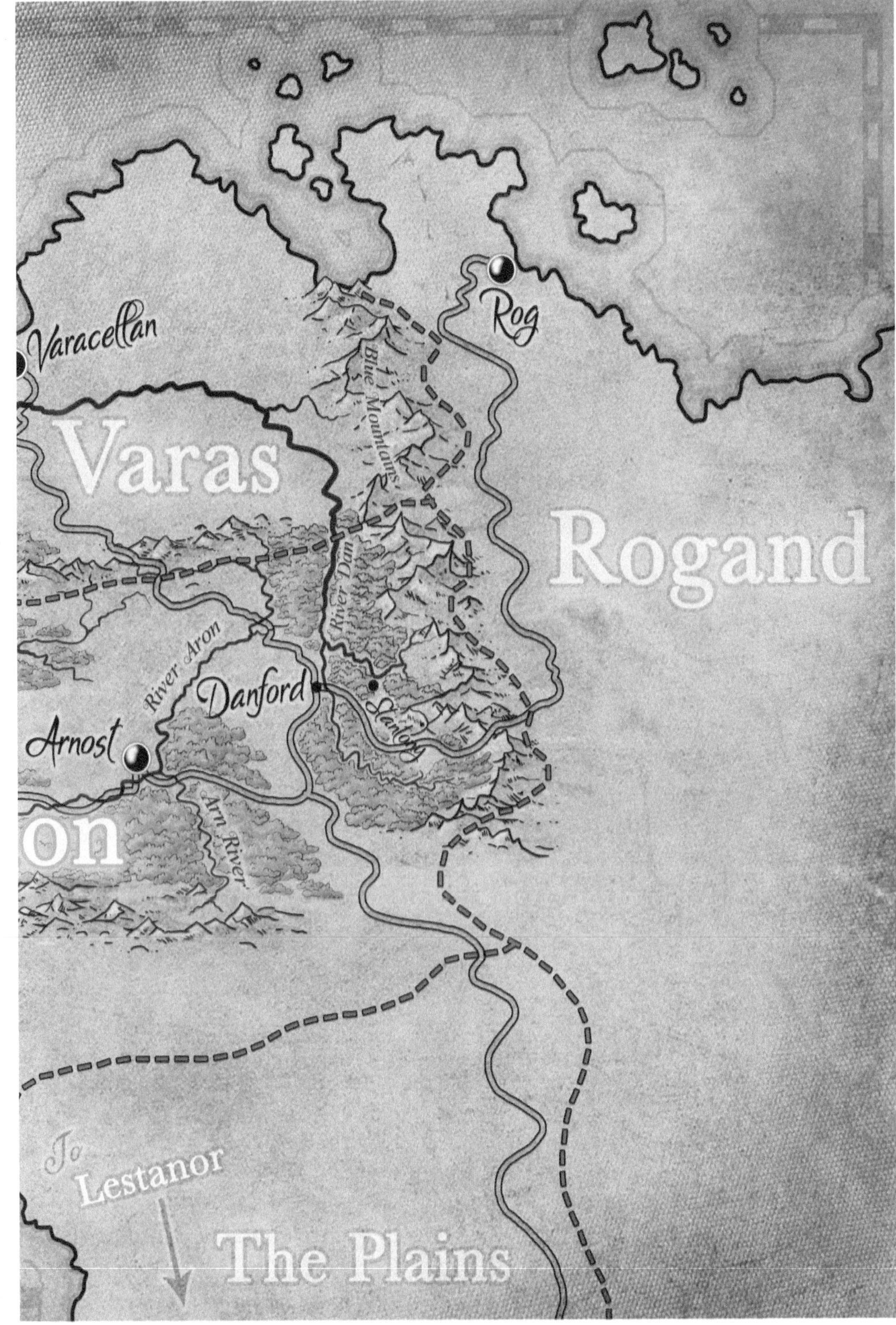

Varacellan
Rog
Varas
Rogand
Blue Mountains
River Dan
River Aron
Danford
Arnost
Arm River
on
To Lestanor
The Plains

VOLUME 1—THE SWELL BEGINS TO BUILD

PROLOGUE

Heaving up a final sack of turnips, Carnwill clambered onto the cart.

"Move!" he growled. The crack of a whip sounded, and the horse took up the strain, rolling its burden slowly forward.

To outward observation, Carnwill and his two companions were traders, selling vegetables to the army camped outside Steffan's Citadel on the border of Erestor. A shrewd observer might have called them an unlikely group of produce merchants.

For a man of Carnwill's talents, his current occupation was incongruous. Competent and accomplished, he was an Arvenian native who spoke Rogandan fluently. From early beginnings as a farmer and a trader, he had made his mark as a sailor and a soldier.

Carnwill was dangerous and relentless. As a tracker he was second to none, and his skill had led to a covert role in the employ of King Agon of Rogand. Agon trusted him implicitly, which made Carnwill the rarest of the rare.

He now had a single purpose—to find Thomas Stablehand. He would have been willing to drag him before King Agon as well, but his employer made it clear he intended to use other resources for that purpose. Carnwill's brief was to hunt him down and inform the king of his whereabouts.

His quarry had been traced to Carnwill's current location, and the tracker needed a way to explore the region without attracting attention. Trading vegetables provided a perfect cover.

The work was boring—mind-numbingly so—but Carnwill was a patient man.

1

Six days after Hazor's mercenary force was destroyed in Will's ambush

The sun had disappeared below the tree line, and darkness was creeping slowly in to take its place, settling over the forest like a heavy mantle. Breysen knew he should be grateful for the protective cover of night, but the forest felt alien and hostile to him in the gloom. Each night his discomfort had grown as the hours stretched away beneath the somber boughs. At times he imagined the low hanging branches were reaching down to strangle him. His head told him sternly that any such notion was ridiculous, but his heart wasn't convinced.

Campfires burned brightly just beyond the edge of the forest, and delicious smells often wafted toward him when the wind shifted in the right direction. There was no welcome for him there. Will Prentis's men were vigilant, and every fugitive who emerged from the forest had been dealt with ruthlessly.

He wondered once more what had possessed him to sign on as a mercenary. Hazor, his recruiter, had sought Breysen out, somehow aware that he had fought at Torbury Scarp and that he needed coin. The mercenary leader insisted he was not looking for paid killers; he had been commissioned to rapidly build a force of irregular soldiers with the sole purpose of maintaining order throughout the kingdom.

The wages on offer should have given sufficient warning, but Breysen chose to ignore the signs, lured by the size of the promised payout. A bag bulging with coins had been dangled before him as a reward for signing on, and he had hesitated for barely a moment before taking hold of it. He saw now that he had been a fool, and a credulous fool at that.

At first Hazor's group had done little more than canter about the countryside. Everything had changed when they set off in pursuit of a group of armed men. Hazor's hunters enjoyed an overwhelming advantage in numbers and most of them were hungry for a fight, but their apparent superiority proved illusory.

The ferocity of their quarry beggared belief—Breysen had once hunted a wounded bear that seemed genial by comparison. The hunters were never allowed to rest. Arrows descended from the sky at any time of the day or night, and always when least expected. The size of Hazor's band rapidly diminished; the deadly rain eventually accounted for hundreds of the mercenaries. The men had fallen with barely a glimpse of their enemies.

Rumors began to surface. A few of the mercenaries whispered that their targets were the king and his pregnant queen. The idea hadn't troubled most of them, but Breysen had been appalled. He hadn't signed on for treason, and he wasted no time in confronting Hazor directly with the rumors. The mercenary leader reacted with fury, and Breysen had hastily withdrawn without answers and in fear for his life.

Then came the rumor that their invisible enemies were being led by Will Prentis.

A veil had finally been lifted from Breysen's eyes the moment this latest rumor reached his ears. Everything suddenly made sense. He had served under Will and his deputy Rufe, and it no longer came as any surprise that the fighting had been so one-sided.

From that moment he had abandoned hope. Hazor was doomed, and all of his men with him.

The mercenary leader apparently couldn't see it coming. Hazor could reasonably boast his share of animal cunning, but he clearly lacked the wit to grasp what lay in store for him and his men.

The unequal struggle continued until Will finally lured Hazor into the forest. The mercenary's entire force had been wiped out in the disastrous battle that followed. Breysen had been one of the few who survived.

Almost a week had passed since the battle. The forest still smoldered from the fire that raged through it during the fighting, and bodies lay scattered among the charred undergrowth, many of them burned beyond recognition. The stench had become almost unbearable. Bird song echoed through any normal forest; the trees here were as silent as the grave.

Breysen knew how to survive on his own in the wild, but he could find precious little that was safe to eat in this scorched wasteland. Streams still flowed freely, and he was largely reduced to satisfying himself with fresh water.

Other mercenaries had survived, although none so far had matched Breysen's patience. One by one the ragged fugitives had appeared at the forest's edge, hungry and miserable as they waited for nightfall. He had watched as they abandoned the cover of the trees, willing to risk discovery in their desperation. Not one had survived.

Every night the bright moonlight had conspired with the sentries against the fugitives. Nature itself seemed set on bringing the mercenaries to final ruin.

On that particular night, Breysen's luck appeared to have turned. Thick clouds covered the moon completely. His moment had arrived.

Making his way carefully to the very edge of the forest, he positioned himself behind a large tree and peered out at the sentries. As usual, very few of them were sitting around the campfires. Most of them were out patrolling in the darkness.

His reserves of stamina had long since been depleted, but he wasn't planning a desperate sprint to freedom. He was willing to content himself with an undignified crawl on his belly.

As he steeled himself to go, a branch cracked behind him in the forest. Spinning around, he dimly saw another man creeping stealthily toward him. He drew his sword frantically, his heart racing, dismayed at having been exposed at last. When the other man made no move to attack him, Breysen belatedly realized he was facing another fugitive like himself. As the figure drew closer it became obvious that he was in an equally miserable condition.

Breysen sheathed his sword, frowning at the intruder. His chances of survival were poor enough as it was. He hadn't planned on being burdened down with another helpless runaway.

The wiry newcomer drew alongside, contenting himself with a nod in the direction of Breysen. His face was drawn, and his arm had been bandaged crudely. From the stains on the bandage he had been losing blood, although he seemed unperturbed by the injury.

Breysen didn't mince his words. "Don't expect me to look out for you," he whispered roughly. "I won't be expecting help from you, and I have nothing to offer myself."

The other shrugged in the darkness. "No quarrel with me," he replied. "Our chances are better on our own."

With that the stranger touched his forehead in a simple salute, then slipped away from the shelter of the trees and disappeared into the darkness.

Breysen forced down his annoyance. He didn't need distractions. Now he had to choose whether to set off immediately or to wait until the other man was long gone. The sentries were undoubtedly on high alert given the moonless night. If the other man was caught, they would be doubly cautious.

He quickly decided that his best option was to leave immediately. If one of the two fugitives was detected, the other might have a better chance of slipping away in the confusion. He took a breath, then headed out into the open.

Dark as it was, Breysen knew where he was heading. He had not entirely wasted the days of enforced inaction that lay behind him.

Climbing repeatedly into a tall tree during daylight hours to assess the topography of the area, he had plotted his escape route carefully. A broad stretch of undulating land lay before him, and he intended to avoid exposed ridges and take full advantage of every available depression. His journey would proceed in four stages, with a pause as soon as he reached each landmark. He hoped that the dense cloud cover would reduce the likelihood of him being spotted.

Breysen scurried forward in a low crouch until he reached a natural hollow in the ground. The first and easiest part of his journey was now behind him.

The next stage was the most dangerous. A long stretch of exposed ground lay ahead with no natural protection. Every other fugitive had been run to ground in this area. Most of them had tried to run as quickly as possible across the open space. Now that he was there himself, the temptation to run like a rabbit was almost overwhelming. He thrust such urges aside. He had a plan, and he intended to stick to it. He would crawl.

Lowering himself onto his belly, Breysen squirmed out into the open.

Progress felt painfully slow, and he forced down the panic that threatened to overwhelm him, concentrating instead on the patch of ground immediately before him. He had plenty of time. Night had barely begun, and he expected to be long gone when daylight dawned.

After a few nervous minutes Breysen had made slow but steady progress. Then he came to a sudden halt—his surroundings were slowly becoming visible. His heart began to pound, even as his eyes widened with alarm. A quick glance into the heavens confirmed that the clouds covering the face of the moon were beginning to dissipate.

Acting instinctively, Breysen dropped to the ground to conceal himself. As he did so, a dark figure rose up behind him, closer to the forest. Breysen had passed his fellow fugitive in the dark. Apparently spooked by the sudden change in the conditions, the other man decided to run for it. It was a poor decision, because it exposed him to one of the patrolling soldiers. The sentry spurred his horse toward the fleeing figure.

From his prone position on the ground, Breysen saw that the speeding horse was heading directly toward him.

There wasn't time to think. As the rider approached, Breysen leaped to his feet, directly in front of the animal. The horse reared up, squealing in fright. Its rider was thrown to the ground. Before the man could get up, Breysen threw himself forward and punched him hard in the face. The sentry went down and didn't move.

Shouts sounded from the direction of the campfires. Other sentries must have become aware of the disturbance—he had very little time. Hurrying to the horse, Breysen grabbed its reins and swung himself into the saddle. His feet had barely settled into the stirrups when the horse reared up again. The other mercenary had reappeared.

Breysen struggled to calm the animal. Then he turned to his fellow fugitive. "Quickly! Get up behind me!"

The other man ignored him at first, pulling a knife as he turned away. Bending low, he plunged his blade several times into the unconscious sentry before turning away and clambering onto the horse's back. The knife disappeared again into his clothing. He hadn't bothered to wipe the blade clean.

Breysen sat frozen in the saddle, shocked at the cold-blooded execution of a defenseless man. "Go!" the other man demanded. Snapping out of his daze, Breysen urged the horse forward.

Their attempt at escape might have been short-lived, except that heavy cloud cover once more blanketed the moon, plunging their surroundings into total darkness. Breysen steered the horse away from the forest, trying to roughly follow the path he had planned. Voices called out behind them, but the darkness shielded them as they raced toward freedom.

They continued to ride with only short breaks until the sky began to lighten with the coming of the dawn.

By then the horse was almost spent. Neither of the riders were in any better condition. Breysen was barely able to stay in the saddle.

For much of the night they had ridden across grasslands and rolling hills. The open ground had disappeared just before dawn, and the trees of a vast forest again surrounded them. To hide their tracks they sought out a suitable stream and rode along it for the best part of an hour. Finally they guided the horse out of the water onto rocky ground where its hoof prints would not be visible. Then they sought out a quiet clearing hidden among the towering trees.

Both of them were utterly exhausted. Breysen managed to find some strips of dried meat and some stale bread in a saddlebag. He shared it with his companion, who chewed it unthinkingly before lying down. He was asleep almost immediately.

In defiance of his depleted state, Breysen somehow found the energy to remove the saddle and bridle from the horse before slumping to the ground. Rich green grass flourished in the clearing, and the last thing he remembered before falling asleep was the sight of the animal quietly cropping the grass.

It was the cold that eventually woke him. Daylight had almost faded away. The cloud cover had disappeared entirely, and stars were already winking in the open sky above the clearing.

The other fugitive was still sleeping, and Breysen grasped the opportunity to take a searching look at his companion. The mercenary looked emaciated—hardly surprising given the circumstances of the last few days—and his face was drawn and haggard. He had a hard face.

Breysen got up and stretched, wincing at the tightness in his muscles. Every part of him ached.

Glancing across at his companion, he noticed that he had woken.

"I'm Breysen," he said with a cautious nod.

"Kantor," the other replied. He peered around him in the gloom. There was no sign of pursuit or any kind of threat. "Looks like we've beaten the odds," he grunted. "We're probably the only ones who managed to escape that death trap."

"We're not out of this yet," said Breysen. "They'll track us. They seemed determined to keep the king's location secret."

Kantor snorted. "You think that's their reason for killing every person who tried to escape?" He shook his head dismissively. "They're butchers. No other explanation is necessary."

"Is that why you killed the sentry?"

"Did I need a reason?" snarled Kantor, glowering at him. "He would have killed me without blinking. Or you, for that matter."

Breysen shrugged. "He was helpless," he said. "He had no way of harming us."

"And if I'd been lying helpless? Do you think that would have saved me?" Kantor looked at him in scorn. "Have you gone soft in the head? It's us or them. It's that simple."

Kantor was right, of course—the sentry would have killed them without a second thought. Somehow it seemed different to Breysen though. Was it because he saw himself as a traitor, and therefore deserving of death? Either way, Kantor clearly wasn't interested in discussing the rights and wrongs of it. Breysen said nothing further.

His companion got up, stretching as uncomfortably as Breysen had. He placed a hand gingerly on his neck, screwing up his face as he briefly massaged the muscles on his shoulders. Then he turned his attention to his injured arm. He unwrapped the bandages, wincing with pain as he pulled the cloth away from the wound.

Even in the gathering dark the wound looked ugly. "That needs to be stitched," Breysen told him. "Would you like me to do it?"

The mercenary looked doubtful, but he didn't refuse.

Breysen led him to a nearby stream and did his best to clean the wound. It was becoming increasingly difficult to see what he was doing, but he managed to retrieve a small cloth bundle from the pouch at his belt and unfolded it. Within it was a tiny piece of wood, roughly the thickness of his little finger but only two thirds the length. He tugged at the wood with both hands, and it fell apart into two pieces, revealing a long piece of thread and a thin needle.

Kantor eyed it curiously. "Where did you get that?"

"I made it," Breysen replied. "It's been useful on occasion," he added simply.

He had fashioned the needle himself from the bone of a bird, carefully sharpening one end and boring an eye into the other.

Constructing the little wooden box to house it had taken many hours.

It took him many attempts before he succeeded in threading the needle. Deciding to act quickly before the light faded entirely, he pulled Kantor's arm closer and began pushing the needle through his skin as if mending a garment. The mercenary grimaced but said nothing.

Breysen sewed the flesh together quickly and efficiently. When he had finished, he squinted down at the arm before nodding once in satisfaction. Then he cleaned the needle and wiped it dry on his tunic before returning it to its wooden box. Finally he instructed Kantor to lower his arm into the water to wash it clean.

The light had faded away completely by the time they had finished.

"It's time we were gone," Kantor grunted.

Breysen nodded in the dark. They couldn't afford to wait for the dawn. "Where to?"

"West, toward Erestor," grunted Kantor. "I've heard there's an army camped outside Steffan's Citadel. It isn't far from here. We know roughly where the king is hiding out, and that information will be worth a lot of money to the right people."

Rejoining an army didn't appeal to Breysen at all. All he wanted was to slink away, as far from here as possible. Somehow he had survived where so many others had died, and he had no interest in tempting fate any further.

Beyond that, selling out the king didn't sit right with him at all. He'd lost interest in being a mercenary from the moment he realized that Hazor's orders were to kill the royals.

It was obvious to him that his reservations would make no sense to Kantor. What could he say?

He decided to say nothing. He would bide his time.

Breysen bent down briefly and drank from the stream. Doing so made him realize how hungry he was. It was time to divide up any food remaining in the saddlebags and refill the water skin.

"Where did you leave the horse?" asked Kantor.

"I don't remember exactly," Breysen replied.

Kantor gave a low growl in response, then he ignored Breysen, whistling for the horse as he crossed the clearing.

After many minutes of increasingly frantic searching, it became clear that the horse was nowhere in the area.

Kantor came to Breysen. "You took off the saddle and bridle," he spat. "Did you think to put a halter on it?" Even in the dark Breysen felt his fury.

"I can't be certain," he grunted.

"You incompetent idiot!" roared Kantor. He grabbed Breysen's clothing with his good arm. "This will be the death of both of us! You understand that, don't you?"

"And what did you do to secure the horse?" Breysen asked, struggling to stay calm.

Kantor shook with anger for a moment, then he seemed to master himself. He released Breysen and stepped back, spitting on the ground. "I should just knife you and be done with it. I'd do it right now if you hadn't sewn up my arm. If you cause me trouble again I won't hesitate. You've been warned."

With that he stepped into the stream and began wading along it.

Breysen stood undecided, staring after Kantor in the dark. Finally he shook his head and stepped into the stream after him.

2

W

ill frowned in exasperation at the two sentries brought to him by Rufe. "A mercenary escaped? After all this time? And stole one of our horses? How is that possible?"

The men stared at the ground. "There was heavy cloud cover last night, My Lord," one of them replied. "The mercenary took advantage of it. One of our men still spotted him and ran him down. There was a fight, and the guard was killed. The mercenary took his horse."

"How did a fugitive manage to kill a soldier on horseback?"

"The tracks indicate there were two of them," the other sentry replied, his face downcast. "That's the only reason they managed to overwhelm the guard."

"Are they being followed?" demanded Will.

Rufe nodded. "I've sent ten men after them, including our best trackers."

"We can't afford to have any of these men on the loose," said Will. "If they report our whereabouts, the king and queen will be exposed. The next time we see mercenaries here, they'll have brought a real army."

He shook his head grimly. "Gather the men," he told Rufe. "All of them. I want a sweep done through the forest. Today. If anyone's still alive in there it's time they were hunted down."

LATE THAT AFTERNOON Thomas and Elena were summoned by Will to a conference. Having been directed to a large hut where the meeting was to be held, they hurried there to discover they were the first arrivals.

Ten seats had been positioned around a huge wooden table in the center of the hut. The table dominated the space. It had been constructed from a solid slab of wood hewn from a single tree of great girth, with striking knots and swirls in the grain highlighting its smooth polished surface.

Thomas gazed at it in awe, admiring its rugged beauty. Being both sturdy and refined at the same time, the table somehow captured the spirit of Newhaven.

The next arrival was Will, soon followed by Anneka and Rellan, Rufe, Jonas, Count Ranauld, and finally the king and queen. Thomas noticed immediately that no other children had been brought to the conference, and he shot a wide-eyed glance at Elena, relieved that she had arranged at short notice to leave their little daughter Tammi with Elena's father, Rubin.

As soon as the king and queen were seated, the others took their seats as well. Only Will remained on his feet, his face somber.

"Your Majesties," he began, bowing to the king and queen. "Yesterday our men carefully searched the forest where the battle took place. It was harrowing work—the battleground is not a pleasant place to visit right now." His expression showed his distaste. "We were looking for survivors. We found none."

"That's encouraging news," offered the king.

"I wish it were so, Your Majesty," Will replied grimly. "Unfortunately, our search was prompted by an incident." He nodded to Rufe.

Rufe got to his feet, bowing to the king and queen before speaking. "Since the battle, Your Majesty," he said, addressing the king, "our men have been patrolling the fringes of the forest, alert for any sign of survivors. The conditions have favored us, with a full moon making our task much easier. A small number of mercenaries tried to escape during that time, and our men successfully intercepted them all. Until last night."

Rufe's face appeared flushed. "Two men managed to escape after killing one of our guards and taking his horse." He bowed to the king. "There is no appropriate way to apologize, Your Majesty. We have failed you."

The king shook his head firmly. "Preventing every surviving mercenary from escaping was never going to be easy. I know how hard your men have been working to secure the area, and from what you've said they did intercept these men last night, even though they were unable to stop them.

"I fully understand the likely implications. But I haven't lost sight of the bigger picture, Rufe. We are here today only because of the extraordinary efforts you and others made to bring us to safety. We could never have survived without you. I will not allow you to berate yourself."

Rufe bowed low again.

"Have men been sent after these mercenaries?" asked the king.

"Yes, Your Majesty," Rufe replied. "And they were ordered not to return until they find them."

The king nodded, and Rufe sat down.

The king directed his attention to Anneka and Rellan. "If word of our location leaks out, we will not be the only ones affected. The community at Newhaven will be at risk as well if another army is sent against us." He turned to Will. "We must take that into account in whatever we decide to do."

Will acknowledged the king's statement with a bow. "As you are all aware," Will said, addressing the entire assembled group, "we have been conferring with the king for some time, considering a range of options. The potential consequences of this escape now force us to act immediately.

"We have not been entirely idle during our time here at

Newhaven. Our scouts have traveled widely throughout Arvenon, and all of them have now returned. We know that Pisander has assigned a number of smaller mercenary forces to patrol the countryside. A couple of those groups pursued us when we left Paradise Valley after the assassination attempt. We ambushed and destroyed them not far from here. The two mercenaries who just escaped appear to be the last remnant of that combined force.

"When Pisander took control of Arnost, he arranged for Arvenon's standing army to be split into two forces. Both are now commanded by unknown mercenaries appointed by him. Other mercenaries loyal to Pisander have undoubtedly infiltrated their ranks. We need to regain control of those two armies."

"What do you propose?" asked the king.

"We have limited resources, Your Majesty," Will replied. "We will need to stretch them as far as we can." His face became grave. "We have four immediate problems to address. First, Pisander has sent one of the two armies westward to blockade Erestor, after spreading the story that I have been fomenting a revolt against Your Majesty." Snorts sounded around the table, and Will waited for the noise to die down before he continued. "That western army is currently camped outside Steffan's Citadel, at the gateway to Erestor. Your uncle, the duke, closed the border with Erestor at the time Pisander took over. We know that the duke remains loyal to you as always, and he will be able to assemble a formidable army on our behalf from within Erestor. We need to contact the duke and let him know that the king and queen are alive and well. We need his army."

"I might be able to help with that," said Rellan. All eyes turned to him. "I know how to get through to Erestor without going through the pass at Steffan's Citadel—I've done it before. And Lord Burtelen knows me. He will get me access to the duke." He looked at his wife. "I can imagine what you're thinking, Anneka," he said, acknowledging the alarm on her face. "No one else can do this," he said gently. "I'll be careful."

Anneka didn't look at all happy. But she said nothing.

Will glanced at the king, who dipped his head silently in approval.

"Thank you for your offer, Rellan," said Will. "I wish I could promise that no one will suffer loss in the days that lie ahead. But all of you understand the realities as well as I do."

Rellan simply nodded.

Will addressed Anneka. "If Rellan were to go, would you be willing to oversee the defenses of Newhaven on your own until he returns?"

"I bore that responsibility on my own for many years," she replied grimly. "I can do it again."

Will thanked her before continuing. "Contacting the duke is only part of the solution," he said. "The duke's forces can't move out of Erestor while Pisander's western army is blockading the citadel and the pass that runs through it. Pisander's appointees might command that army today, but most of the soldiers in it are likely to still be loyal to the king. Their original leaders know me, and I need to find a way to communicate with them. If we can regain control of that army, we can assign some of the men to protect the approaches to Newhaven. The rest can be deployed along with the duke's army from Erestor. Lord Burtelen will be able to help provide leadership."

"You can't just show up there, Will," growled the king. "You're supposed to be a rebel. The mercenary commander will have you killed before any questions can be asked. I'm not going to throw away your life on a risky adventure."

"I don't deny that there will be risks, Your Majesty," Will replied calmly. "But what other options are available to us? I assure you that I have no desire to throw my life away. I will take Rufe and Jonas with me, and we will do nothing rash."

The king was clearly not satisfied with this answer. "We will speak more about this," he warned.

"I understand," Will acknowledged, moving immediately to the next topic. "The second problem is the remainder of Arvenon's standing army. It is also currently commanded by mercenaries that are not known to us. Pisander sent it north to the borders of Castel, supposedly to forestall a Castelan attack on Arvenon. I expect this northern army to be stationed outside Deadman's Pass. We need to make contact with the loyal soldiers in that army. We also need to find a way to make direct contact with the Castelans. Queen Essanda's young brother, King Rupert, is reigning in Castel now, and he needs to know that King Steffan and Queen Essanda are still alive, and that they have a son and heir. He also needs to know that the army threatening his borders was not sent there by King Steffan."

"These are tasks for me to attempt," Count Ranauld said, rising from his seat. "I know many of the original leaders of the army—I worked closely with them after the Battle of Torbury Scarp. I don't doubt they would have been demoted when Pisander's mercenaries took control, but hopefully they are still with the army. I can also try to make contact with the Castelans. I have connections with some of King Rupert's senior noblemen."

The king assented with a grateful nod to the count.

"Thank you, Ranauld," Will replied. "I can think of no one better suited. Unfortunately we cannot send a force with you. You will need to rely entirely on diplomacy."

"I understand," said Count Ranauld with a nod, sitting down once more.

"The third problem presents us with a more difficult challenge," said Will. "It won't be easy to find an effective way to deal with Pisander and his lackeys in Arnost."

No one immediately commented or offered to help. Thomas had been the one who brought back information from Arnost about Pisander. Was it possible that Will and the king might expect him to volunteer? Surely not. He simply couldn't imagine anything useful he could do to unseat the traitor. Nevertheless he kept his eyes down, sweating uncomfortably.

Thankfully it quickly became apparent that Will had ideas of his own on the topic. "The key to resolving this problem is regaining control of the western army on the border with Erestor, and the northern army on the border with Castel," he said. "If we are able to do that, those armies, along with the duke's army from Erestor, will readily be able to block any attempt Pisander might make to deploy more men throughout Arvenon. Retaking Arnost will follow, sooner or later."

He glanced around the table. When no one offered comment, he continued. "The final problem is the most difficult of all," he said. "Thomas discovered previously that Pisander's maneuvering has been funded by King Agon of Rogand, and that Agon has been scheming to annex Arvenon, Castel, and Varas. Some of you might not be aware that Thomas also learned that Pisander intends to invite King Agon to Arnost."

"That's madness! Why would Pisander do that?" asked Rellan in consternation. "Surely it wouldn't be in his own interests to allow Agon anywhere near Arnost."

Will shrugged. "Perhaps he had no choice. Agon might have made it a condition of helping him."

Rellan slowly shook his head, his brows creased.

Thomas felt sure there was a different explanation. If Agon had the Stone of Authority, Pisander might be acting under some kind of compulsion. Thomas had no way of knowing for certain, though, and he could hardly speak openly about the stones. He needed to keep his guesses to himself. He could discuss his suspicions with Will later if the need arose.

"Is Agon planning a short visit, or does he intend to base himself in Arnost while he attempts to subdue the kingdom completely?" Will wondered. "We can only guess. But he won't leave Rog until he is confident that his own kingdom will remain secure in his absence. Either way, he will want to arrive before winter sets in. So we don't have a lot of time."

As Will paused to scan the faces around him, Thomas glanced around the table himself. Everyone was looking grim. He had no need of the Stone of Knowing to tell him what people were thinking.

Will's expression was grave, yet he somehow managed to project a calm confidence. Thomas could only admire his composure. He had no idea how Will did it.

"We cannot afford to let Agon get established in Arnost," Will said. "He'll undoubtedly bring an army of his own with him from Rogand, and it won't be easy to displace them. We know ourselves that Arnost is well able to withstand both an assault and a siege."

"How can we stop him?" asked the king.

"I propose that we send a force to secure our border with Rogand," Will replied.

"We'd need a big force to do that," said the king, "and we don't have one available."

"You're right, Your Majesty," said Will. "Right now we cannot spare even one hundred men. We will need the western army currently camped outside Steffan's Citadel, combined with the duke's army from Erestor."

"If these men are sent to the border, how can we bottle up Pisander? And how can we retake Arnost?" asked the king.

"I am hoping that Count Ranauld will also eventually be able to bring us the northern army camped outside Castel," Will replied. "It's all a question of timing. Denying Agon access to Arvenon is the crucial first step. The other steps will need to follow at an appropriate time."

The king hesitated for a moment, but he soon nodded his agreement. "What you're proposing makes sense, Will. All of it. Implement it as you see fit."

Will bowed his thanks to the king. Then he turned to the others. "Each of us knows what we need to do," he said. "Those of us leaving Newhaven will set out at dawn the day after tomorrow."

"There's no point in delaying the journey to Maranelle to meet with the duke," Rellan said abruptly. "I'll be ready to leave at dawn tomorrow."

Anneka glared at him, but his face was set stubbornly.

"You need to come to a conclusion together," Will told them.

Neither commented, but they both nodded tightly. Thomas found himself thinking that the discussion was likely to be animated.

Anneka and Rellan rose first and left the building. Rufe, Jonas, and Count Ranauld followed closely behind them. As they did so, the king moved closer to Will and began conversing quietly with him. The queen joined them, listening attentively.

Thomas and Elena were about to leave the hut when Thomas noticed Will's hand go up to forestall them. Having caught their attention, Will waved them over to join the conversation.

As they approached, the king nodded a welcome, and Queen Essanda beamed them a friendly smile.

"Thomas has an unusual ability to ferret out information from people, Your Majesties," said Will. Thomas felt his face redden. Will was clearly referring to the stone, although it seemed apparent that he had not told the king or queen about it.

Not for the first time, Thomas wondered what the king might say if he learned of the stone and its powers. Would he demand that Thomas hand it over to him? Kings could issue whatever commands they chose, and their subjects were expected to obey. If anyone refused, a king had ways of forcing them to comply.

A jumble of thoughts went through Thomas's mind as he settled himself after the king waved them both to their seats. Uppermost in his thoughts was the awareness that he had no interest in giving up the stone. It was curious that Will had never suggested that Thomas needed to surrender it to the king. Nor had he ever asked for the stone for himself, even though there must surely have been times when he would have found it invaluable. Will had instead consistently protected Thomas's secret, accepting from the beginning that Thomas was the custodian of the stone. Thomas had no idea what Will's reasons were.

Thomas didn't fully understand his own unwillingness to give it up either—it was one of many mysteries surrounding the stone. It had certainly brought him far more than his share of trouble. And the ripples had since spread to encompass his family.

He told himself that he felt responsible for the stone. Was it as simple as that though? He set aside his musings to focus on what Will was saying.

"I am going to need your help when I go to the army outside Steffan's Citadel, Thomas. I'll need to know where the leaders stand."

Thomas suppressed a shudder. Will's request—and it clearly wasn't a request—showed how far out of reach a normal life had become for him. He nodded, not trusting himself to speak.

"If Thomas is going, I will go too," said Elena abruptly.

All eyes turned in her direction. Will and the king both began speaking at the same time, expressing alarm at any such idea.

Elena simply stared back, her beautiful face unyielding.

The king raised a hand, and Will fell silent.

"I greatly admire your pluck, Elena," said the king. "But I would never forgive myself if I allowed you to put yourself at risk in such a manner."

Elena's expression did not waver, although Thomas saw her lips trembling.

Finding the boldness to speak up in such exalted company was no easier for Thomas than it was for Elena, and even the idea of challenging the king unnerved him. But he could not allow his wife to stand alone. "Elena has proven herself many times," he said quietly, "and in situations that would overwhelm most people. I would not be alive today without her resourcefulness."

The queen smiled at his words. "I might add that I too was sternly discouraged from joining my husband when he traveled to Paradise Valley," she said. "Yet when all of us were put to the test, I like to think that I gave a good account of myself. Even though I am a woman, and even though I was well advanced in my pregnancy. I don't think we should deny Thomas and Elena the final say in deciding whether she should go."

"My comments were intended only to spare Elena whatever trouble might lie ahead," the king replied. "I had no desire to call her capabilities into question." He gazed at his wife. "No one could question the significance of your contribution on behalf of the kingdom. Your influence has been decisive on more than one occasion."

Essanda smiled, grasping Steffan's hand and squeezing it. The king smiled back at her affectionately.

Then he turned to Elena. "I don't claim to know you well, Elena, but all of us have caught glimpses of your determination. I don't doubt that you might have a part to play that I cannot foresee. Nevertheless, I am still not convinced about the wisdom of you accompanying Will and Thomas."

"I have a proposal," said Will. "It would strengthen the resolve of the soldiers greatly if they could catch a glimpse of their king and queen. It would be even better if they have an opportunity to see the baby prince with their own eyes. I know that sounds extremely risky," he added quickly, "but I am not proposing that Your Majesties join us when we make initial contact. Only when we are absolutely certain that we have won over the soldiers and their leaders, and dealt with any traitors among them. If you are waiting nearby we can send for you to join us. If you hear nothing from us by an agreed time, you can withdraw to safety."

He turned to Elena. "I would like to suggest you wait with the king and queen, and join Thomas when they meet us."

She looked uncertain.

Will looked at her frankly. "May I be direct, Elena? If you're with us when we meet with the soldiers, none of them will pay attention to a single word we say!" The king stifled a laugh, and the queen put a hand to her mouth to hide a smile.

Elena blushed deeply. But she looked at Will and nodded her head to indicate her acquiescence.

Thomas expelled a breath, discovering in the process how tense he had been feeling. He reached out and took Elena's delicate hand in his own.

"Does my proposal meet with your approval, Your Majesty?" Will asked the king.

"It does," King Steffan replied. "Your plans are bold given our slender resources. But I cannot offer better options, and you always seem to find a way through."

"We will do our best," said Will in response. "It hardly needs to be said that you will be left largely unprotected if we fail."

"We will not speak of failure," declared the king firmly.

3
—————

Ashar drew his horse to a halt beneath the spreading boughs of a huge tree. The canopy above offered limited protection from the incessant rain, but any respite was welcome.

He studied his surroundings carefully. He could reasonably claim to be widely traveled, but this part of Lestanor was entirely unknown to him.

The sun had almost touched the horizon, and the cold had begun to gnaw at his bones. Shivering in his sodden garments, he reminded himself of the size of the payout once he'd delivered the package.

If he didn't reach a village soon he'd need to find a place to camp. The thought held no appeal, and he decided to ride on for a few more minutes.

Ashar had almost given up hope when he caught a distant glimpse of a cluster of dwellings. Peering through the driving rain in the fading light he couldn't be certain of the size of the village, but it might be large enough to boast an inn. He urged his horse forward in eager anticipation of hot food and a bed.

No one was abroad in the village by the time Ashar reached the first of the low huts. Even without a glimpse of the inhabitants, though, the appearance of the dwellings in the gathering gloom told him everything he needed to know about this place.

Fully alert, Ashar took careful note of his surroundings. He did it effortlessly and almost without conscious thought. He knew how to take care of himself. His employers had chosen well, but he didn't waste energy congratulating himself with the knowledge.

When a modestly sized inn appeared before him, he dismounted and tied his horse to a post. Then he pushed open the door and stepped inside. He removed his dripping cloak and hat and hung them on hooks on the wall, scanning the room as he did so.

He found himself in a large room filled with a number of small tables. Upwards of twenty men sat around the tables holding mugs of ale. The low rumble of conversation had ceased abruptly at his appearance. Every person in the room was now eyeing him warily.

Ignoring their stares, Ashar made his way to the serving counter. The innkeeper nodded a guarded greeting.

"Do you have hot food and a room?" Ashar asked, slipping easily into the local language. "And can you stable my horse?" His fluency in the language of Lestanor had already proven invaluable.

The innkeeper looked his visitor up and down, his eyes lingering on Ashar's sword and knives. "If you have the coin," the man finally returned.

Ashar pushed a few silver pieces onto the counter, and the innkeeper nodded once more. "Find yourself a table," he said. "I'll bring the food over. My boy will see to your animal."

Ashar located a table off to one side of the room and took a seat. Conversation had resumed in the room, but many eyes remained fixed on him.

The innkeeper arrived with a mug brimming with ale and a bowl filled with steaming meat and a few scrawny vegetables. He put it down and left without a word.

Ashar paused long enough to place a long-bladed knife within easy reach on the table. Then he wasted no time getting into the food.

A small group of men at a nearby table watched him closely. After a few moments one of them swung his chair deliberately around to face him. He aimed a scowl first at the new arrival, then at his knife.

Ashar spared the man a glance between mouthfuls, noting the way the firelight picked out the prominent scars on his face.

"What brings scum like you to our village?" demanded Scarface.

Ashar paused in the action of chewing and looked up, his eyes narrowing. If this fool wanted to die, Ashar would be happy to oblige him.

He hadn't come looking for trouble though. All he wanted was a meal and a good night's rest.

"Just passing through," he replied evenly, ignoring the provocation.

He added a question of his own. "I'm looking for someone—perhaps you know him."

Scarface glowered at him. "Who?"

"A man by the name of Jace."

The room went instantly silent. Nobody moved except Ashar, who resumed his assault on the food.

Scarface laughed—a harsh and grating sound. "You have no idea who you're dealing with," he said contemptuously.

Ashar stared back at him. "The same could be said of you," he observed casually.

Scarface's eyes hardened. But he turned away and moved to a different table.

Conversation in the room was still muted when Ashar decided to turn in for the night. The innkeeper led him up a flight of stairs to a room above the public room. Ashar poked his head in and looked around, then returned to the passage and examined the approaches to the room.

The innkeeper watched him for a minute before stating adamantly, "I don't allow trouble in my inn. Keep to yourself, and others will do the same."

Ashar shrugged. There would be trouble. If not in the inn, then after he left it.

He had no reason to doubt the innkeeper. Nevertheless he slept lightly, as he always did.

Ashar appeared in the public room at sunrise to find the proprietor already hard at work. "Food is cooking if you want some," the innkeeper told him.

Ashar shook his head. He never broke his fast until later in the day. "I'll be on my way."

He handed over more silver pieces to pay for his stay. His host was clearly more than satisfied. "Are you still determined to continue your search?" he asked.

Ashar nodded. He couldn't fail to notice the innkeeper's unwillingness to speak the name of the man he was seeking.

The man shrugged. "It's your funeral then. Follow the road out of the village. In a couple of leagues it forks. Take the left fork. It heads southeast. He'll find you before you find him."

Ashar dug into his pouch for another silver coin and handed it to the innkeeper.

Glancing at the pouch, the proprietor added, "You might find some company waiting for you down the road."

The warning wasn't necessary, but the innkeeper couldn't know that. Ashar palmed him a final coin, then headed outside for his horse.

He emerged into the open to find that the rain had cleared. As he mounted, a rider galloped away on the road ahead of him. No doubt the rider was a sentry charged with warning the ambushers that Ashar was about to set out.

Ashar took the road out of the village, remaining on it until the buildings were out of sight. Then he turned aside into the trees. When the road lay two bowshots behind him, he resumed his journey.

As he picked his way through the undergrowth he pondered the likely motives of his ambushers. Scarface was undoubtedly blinded by his wounded pride. And his friends would have noticed the silver coins Ashar handed to the innkeeper. Perhaps they'd guessed—correctly in this case—that he had plenty more.

Whatever their reasons, they were fools if they thought he would simply blunder into their trap.

After a while he heard the soft nickering of horses. Dismounting, he tied his horse to a branch and crept forward. Four horses stood in a huddle, tied up with halters.

Ashar snorted to himself. Scarface and his friends had a lofty opinion of themselves if they thought four of them were enough to bring him down. He considered turning aside to kill them all. It would bring a satisfying end to the foolishness. But there wouldn't be a payout, so it wasn't worth the time or the effort.

He untied the horses instead and led them to his own animal. Remounting, he set off with the four horses in tow.

As soon as he was well clear of the area he rejoined the road, urging his horse into a trot. After two hours of steady riding, he spotted a small stream near the road and brought the animals to a halt. Removing the halters from the other horses, he released them. They soon moved away from the road and began cropping the plentiful grass beside the stream.

If the horses were stupid enough, they might eventually find their way back to their owners. Ashar was content to let them decide for themselves. Either way, he didn't expect he'd ever see Scarface or his friends again.

When the sun set he found a place to camp for the night. Having chosen a sheltered location well away from the road, he saw no reason not to build a small fire. He retrieved some dried meat and stale bread from his saddlebags and sat down to warm himself by the fire while he ate it.

He had barely finished his meager meal when a sharp object stabbed into the back of his neck.

"Get up. Slowly," said a cold voice.

He complied, berating himself for his carelessness.

"Remove your sword and knives. Put them on the ground, then step away from them."

He did as he was told, slowly and deliberately.

"The knife in your boot as well."

This man didn't miss much.

"Now stand with your back to that tree, facing the fire."

He eased back to the tree and stood unmoving with a sword at his throat.

He finally had an opportunity to observe his captor. The man's face was turned away from the fire, but the captive could see cold eyes glinting dimly in his face. They were remorseless eyes—the eyes of a killer. A cold chill ran up Ashar's spine.

"I am Jace. You've been looking for me. You found me." The killer's voice was as cold as his eyes.

Someone had sent Jace a warning. The innkeeper?

"I was hired to bring you a package," said Ashar, succeeding at keeping his voice steady.

"Where is it?"

Ashar reached for his chest.

"Careful," warned Jace.

Ashar reached carefully into his clothing and withdrew a small parcel. He held it out.

Jace took it and unwrapped it with one hand, his eyes never leaving his captive.

A sheet of parchment appeared in his hand, and a bright object fell to the ground. Ashar shifted his eyes downward to look at it. It was a golden dagger, its hilt encrusted with jewels. He'd been carrying around a small fortune inside his vest.

Jace glanced briefly down at it, letting it lie where it had fallen.

The killer scanned the parchment, his eyes flicking up frequently to ensure his captive hadn't moved.

Ashar forced himself to relax. He was nothing more than a messenger. Jace had no quarrel with him.

"Did you open this package?" the killer demanded.

"No," Ashar replied truthfully.

"Have you read the message?"

"No." Ashar paused for a moment before adding, "I can't read."

Jace nodded. "That must be why you weren't worried about the final instruction."

Ashar had no idea what Jace meant. He wasn't granted an opportunity to find out.

JACE MOMENTARILY CONSIDERED TOSSING the parchment into the fire started by his victim and letting the flames reduce it to ash. Then, deciding abruptly to keep it instead, he tucked it into his clothing.

The message was from Lord Drettroth. The nobleman had been the highest profile casualty of the disastrous Rogandan invasion of Arvenon, and Jace was well aware that he was dead. Receiving a message from beyond the grave was therefore unexpected and disconcerting.

When he first heard of Drettroth's death, the assassin had felt something akin to regret. The Rogandan nobleman was a rare individual—one of the few men Jace respected as a peer. As a result, Jace was more than willing to undertake an assignment on his behalf, whether or not he was still alive.

It seemed that before his death Lord Drettroth had left a package with a trusted retainer. In the event of Drettroth's demise, the retainer had been instructed to wait for five years, then to arrange for the package to be delivered to Jace.

The five years had now elapsed. Following his late master's instructions, the retainer had engaged a messenger to deliver the package.

The commission described in the parchment was for an assassination on the usual terms: payment in full in advance, buried in a secure location; freedom for Jace to choose his own means and his own timing; and no suggestion of returning the payment if the target was no longer alive when the commission was delivered. The message even used a secret code devised by Jace to describe the location where the payment had been hidden.

The Rogandan nobleman, as always, had done his preparation thoroughly.

Jace threw a casual glance down at the body lying in the dirt before the fire. Drettroth had never liked loose ends, and it came as no surprise to Jace that the parchment ended by instructing him to dispose of the messenger.

He located the ornate dagger and retrieved it from the dirt, dusting it off before turning it over in his hand. The weapon itself was worth almost as much as the promised reward.

Beyond its intrinsic value, the dagger was a signature that clearly identified the author of the parchment. It further confirmed Drettroth's seal. Jace recognized the dagger, because years earlier Drettroth had given him its twin, part of the reward for a similar assignment he had carried out on behalf of the nobleman.

Jace ignored the body of the messenger. Sooner or later someone would find it, and as far as he was concerned they were welcome to loot it. However he did thoughtfully remove the saddle and the bridle from the messenger's horse before setting it free.

His next move would be to retrieve Drettroth's payment. Not that he needed it—he was already wealthy beyond imagining. But a workman was worthy of his hire.

After that he would begin his planning. It would need to be careful planning indeed. Assassinating a king involved the highest level of risk and danger.

He was not deterred. As usual, Drettroth had not stinted on the payment. But Jace had another more compelling reason for accepting the commission. He had always risen to a challenge, and he had been lacking a worthy challenge for far too long.

4

King Agon of Rogand sat sullenly on his throne in the audience chamber adjoining his private apartments, waiting for Pisander's envoy to arrive. The king was not in a good mood. His body ached all over, and the padded cushion beneath him felt hard and lumpy. The discomfort did little to improve his temper.

Agon had slept badly. His head had been pounding before he rose for the day; he felt certain he was coming down with some kind of illness. After examining him carefully, his doctors had assured him nervously that it was nothing worse than a cold. One of the imbeciles had almost referred to it as a common cold—from the look on the fool's face he had barely caught himself in time. It would have been a fatal mistake, and Agon could only scowl at the leech's lucky escape. Whatever name might be attached to his malady, the doctors apparently also expected to find the ailment lurking among the most wretched of his subjects. The king could only rail at a universe with the audacity to behave so indiscriminately.

A goblet of wine on a table beside him caught his eye, and an entirely different thought came abruptly into his mind. Would anyone be stupid enough to risk poisoning him?

Chaotic thoughts tumbled about in his head, and for one delicious moment it occurred to him to execute his current food and wine taster. He shrugged off the idea indolently.

A servant entered and bowed low, waiting to be acknowledged before daring to stand upright in Agon's presence. As he stood bent in an awkward posture, the king studied him casually, much as a spider might study a fly struggling feebly in its web.

After a while Agon tired of the amusement. "Well?" he asked imperiously.

The servant attempted to conceal a wince of pain as he straightened. Agon was not sympathetic. If the king wasn't well, it was only right that others should suffer too.

"The envoy has arrived from Arnost, Your Majesty."

"Show him in," growled the king.

The envoy also bowed low as he entered, although he did not wait for permission before standing upright again. Agon reminded himself with difficulty that he needed to exercise restraint.

"Speak," the king commanded.

"I bring greetings from your loyal servant, the Earl of Pisander, Your Majesty. He eagerly awaits the pleasure of your arrival in Arnost."

The envoy had a great deal more to say on Pisander's behalf, although the words danced around all of the issues that most interested Agon.

"What of the former king and queen?" the king asked bluntly.

"His lordship has been reliably informed that they are dead, Your Majesty. He is daily expecting final confirmation."

"And what of Erestor?"

"The old duke is still hiding there, trapped by one of his lordship's armies. He can be dealt with at any time."

Agon scowled with annoyance. This latest message from his pet noble in Arvenon gave no more answers than the one that preceded it. As usual, if Agon wanted things finished off properly, he would be forced to do it himself. The pace would change considerably once he arrived in Arnost.

Tiring of words and needing to get the man out of his sight before he lost control of himself, Agon decided to call the audience to a close. "Scurry back to your master," he told the envoy dismissively, "and tell him I demand to see the heads of Steffan and Essanda. I've given Pisander enough money to buy two kingdoms, and I'm tired of promises and excuses."

In fact the entire exercise had barely troubled Agon's coffers. But the king wasn't about to acknowledge that to Pisander or anyone else.

The Arvenian hurried away, and Agon grasped the opportunity to swallow a potion prescribed by his doctors. He'd used it before at such times, and it had helped with his aches and pains.

He had no opportunity for a real break before his next visitor arrived. His servant introduced a person very familiar to Agon. She entered with little ceremony.

Since the demise of Drettroth, Ona had gradually emerged as the most effective of his subjects. She had somehow wormed her way into this status almost before he was aware it was happening. Once he saw what she was capable of, though, he offered her unstinting encouragement. He had already promoted her to more than one formal role, and he would continue to expand her responsibilities for as long as she proved loyal and reliable. Officially she had administrative responsibility for trade, both local and foreign, and for tax collection. Unofficially he had recently given her oversight of his network of foreign agents. Perhaps most usefully of all, she kept an eye on his nobles for him.

Agon never failed to make time for Ona whenever she wanted to see him. She had never yet wasted his time.

He eyed her hungrily as she entered the room. Seeing his reaction, she leered provocatively at him. She had never made a secret of the fact that she dressed and presented herself specifically to provoke such a reaction. No other woman had ever dared to flaunt herself in his presence in this way.

The truth was that she fascinated him. The woman was commanding, beautiful, sophisticated, and utterly ruthless. In short, Agon found her positively delectable.

Mouthwatering though she might be, he had never been seriously tempted to make her his plaything. She wasn't a person to be toyed with, and unlike so many of her victims, he saw from the beginning that he could never afford to let his guard down with her. King or not, she wouldn't hesitate to find a way to take advantage of him if he offered her half a chance.

That didn't mean he couldn't appreciate from a distance the assets she flaunted with such self-assurance.

Ona was far beneath him, of course, as every other mortal creature must inevitably be. She was noble born—she would never have been able to make her way so effortlessly among his nobility if she was not—but she also had the common touch. She knew how to dress and carry herself like a peasant, and she could move among them as if she were one of their own.

Possibly Ona's most striking quality was her single-mindedness. And she was almost as callous as he was—he admired that in a person.

"Your Majesty," she simpered, offering him a mock curtsy.

"My Lady Ona. What havoc have you been wreaking in my kingdom?" he wondered idly.

"I've been poking around here and there," she replied. Her face turned suddenly serious. "You have problems in your outlying provinces, Your Majesty."

His smirk instantly became a scowl. "What problems?"

She waved her hands vaguely. "Grumbling about taxes. And about your continuing fascination with foreign adventures."

A frown furrowed his face. She needn't think that her impertinence was guaranteed to amuse him. Perhaps he should remove her pretty head after all.

"I found I was able to...divert the energies of some of them," she continued pertly. "Once I had captured their full attention, I offered very sweetly to bring their concerns to the direct attention of their sovereign." Her lip curled. "For some reason, none of them seemed enraptured at the prospect," she added with her usual flair for understatement.

He nodded with satisfaction. Lady Ona was good. And she'd wasted no time in reminding him why he valued her so highly.

"Krasmir?" he asked.

A delicate frown flitted across her bewitching features, as a cloud might briefly shroud the sun. "Lord Krasmir is a man who's never been frightened to state his opinions. It's been suggested in some quarters that he has more reason than most for discontent. But he seems surprisingly untroubled by these issues."

She raised her hands heavenward. "I can't make him out," she acknowledged helplessly.

Agon grunted. Krasmir's unlikely compliance came as no surprise to him, thanks to the small stone concealed on his person. He had chosen Krasmir as the first important test of the Stone of Authority, and the results had far exceeded his expectations.

"I want names, and every detail of their mutterings," he growled, moving quickly to change the subject away from Krasmir.

She smiled indulgently back at him. "I have no doubt that Your Majesty will use the information...carefully," she offered.

"You will not be exposed as the source," he assured her in a bored tone.

He gazed at her steadily for a moment. "Keep me informed of your whereabouts," he said. "I might have need of you again very soon."

She bowed briefly and delivered an immodest curtsy before sweeping elegantly from the audience chamber.

He'd never used the stone on her. In recent times he'd considered it more than once. But there was something raw and unpredictable about her. As long as she continued to serve his interests, he saw no reason to risk dulling her razor edge.

Agon's servant made another appearance almost the moment she had left the room.

"No more audiences!" snapped Agon.

The servant fled while attempting to execute a hasty bow.

Agon got up slowly and headed into his private apartments. Without the distraction of Lady Ona his symptoms were quickly reasserting themselves, and he suppressed a moan, determined to pay no attention to the discomfort. If he didn't improve soon, he might find it necessary to distribute some pain among his doctors.

Ennawi, Agon's mute slave with no hands, was occupying his usual position by the balcony. Approaching the slave casually, the king peered into his habitually unresponsive face. "I wonder if Lady Ona might be able to get a reaction out of you," he said thoughtfully.

Ennawi's face didn't twitch.

Agon shrugged. "My plans have progressed well in Arvenon," he said. "Pisander has almost outlived his usefulness, but not quite. Once I'm properly established in Arnost I'll find a less willful local to rule in my name. Someone without expectations should be appropriately grateful for the opportunity."

His expression turned to a scowl. "And yet the moment an opportunity arises to cross the border, new obstacles appear in my path. My barons have the effrontery to whine about me. Behind my back! The fools will learn there is a price to pay for saying what they think.

"And that isn't the worst of my difficulties. Who can I leave in charge of Rogand when I am gone? I have no heir, and none of my aides are suitable."

The uncomfortable truth was that Agon never retained competent administrators for long. Before long he always found a reason to thrust them aside.

At least he was no longer executing every administrator or agent who disappointed him. Not usually, anyway. He had been working hard on exercising restraint. Summary execution might have offered a satisfying resolution for his disappointment, but it had proven counterproductive as a long term policy. It completely unnerved whoever he tried to bring in as a replacement.

Now he once more found himself needing someone competent—more so than ever before.

"None of my barons can be trusted," he grumbled.

His conversation with Lady Ona about Lord Krasmir came suddenly to mind. "I wonder..." he said, musing aloud. "Is it possible that Krasmir could do the job? He certainly wouldn't be frightened to apply a heavy hand when it's called for."

Could Krasmir be trusted to act on Agon's behalf? Lady Ona had confirmed that he remained compliant. Perhaps the Stone of Authority had provided an unlikely ally.

"Krasmir," murmured the king thoughtfully.

There was no way he could just announce such an appointment of course. It would be necessary to acquaint the nobleman with any responsibilities that couldn't be deferred during the king's absence. The handover would take time—at least a month. That period would give him further opportunity to focus the stone on Krasmir. It would also allow him to decide whether the arrangement might work.

He stood before his slave and examined his face. "What do you think about Lord Krasmir as regent, Ennawi? Any concerns with the notion?" He paused for a few moments. "From your silence I take it that you approve. You are very wise."

Agon snorted. He was never backward in enjoying his own cleverness.

"I like this idea of a regent," he continued more seriously. "I can see the benefit of allowing someone else to take the heat for a while."

Even if Krasmir solved Agon's problem of appointing a regent, the king would still be faced with an irritating delay before he could follow through on Pisander's invitation. Moving into Arvenon would not be possible anytime soon.

As he turned the issue over in his mind an intriguing possibility occurred to him.

"I promised you a trip to Arnost, Ennawi," he told the slave. "I'm sorry to say I need to delay it further. But there's no reason I can't send a representative ahead of me. It has to be someone I trust implicitly—I need an accurate assessment of what's really going on there. So much the better if it's someone capable of unsettling the Arvenian rabble who call themselves nobility."

He smirked at the slave. "I've just realized that I have the ideal person—Lady Ona."

The idea was delicious. He would be sending a fox among lambs.

After she'd finished with them, they'd welcome Agon as a deliverer when he arrived. They'd find out too late that the fox had been replaced by a wolf.

"What do you think, Ennawi? I know she speaks Arvenian." The king's lips peeled back in a smile of satisfaction.

No response was forthcoming, exactly as Agon expected. He nodded solemnly. "I'll order her to set out as soon as she can make herself ready."

The king knew he could not delay lying down for much longer. He'd still done nothing about his recalcitrant nobles, but that would have to wait. Deferring his response didn't mean he'd decided to tolerate their sedition. He was simply allowing himself time to dream up a truly gratifying way of abasing them.

5

———

The unusual isolation of Newhaven had ensured that Anneka's community had remained small. Nevertheless, Brother Ander had been searching for his fellow monk for some time before he located him beyond the cultivated fields that surrounded the settlement. His friend was sitting quietly on a log, peering into the gathering dusk.

"There you are, Brother Gerome. You're a hard man to track down."

"Newhaven offers a number of perfect scenic outlooks," the monk replied contentedly. "I've been relaxing here enjoying the sunset."

"The sunset?" replied Brother Ander, glancing belatedly up at the sky. "I hadn't noticed it."

Brother Gerome sighed. "Perhaps you see things the same way as Brother Kaylis. His view is that nothing in nature matters if it doesn't have a clear purpose. For the most part it is obvious how natural elements and living creatures are useful. For example, a mighty river and a lowly dung beetle each fulfill a role. However Brother Kaylis sees no possible benefit from sunsets, so he ignores them."

"Do Brother Kaylis's ideas have a useful purpose?" asked Brother

Ander with a shrug. "I never paid much attention to him. His head is in the clouds."

"Very apt, since we're discussing sunsets," said Brother Gerome dryly.

Brother Ander groaned. He opened his mouth to change the subject, but his friend got in first.

"Sunsets are remarkable," said Brother Gerome. "They're never the same from day to day. And I'm told that the same sunset looks different from different locations."

"And that tells you what?" asked Brother Ander. He knew his friend would get to the point sooner if he humored him, but it didn't stop him feeling restless.

"It tells me that the Creator is incredibly extravagant," said Brother Gerome. "He isn't solely interested in utility, whatever Brother Kaylis says. I have the feeling that sunsets are designed mostly to delight us."

He looked up at Brother Ander with a knowing smile. "But you didn't come here to talk about the wonders of nature. Something is bothering you," he said.

Brother Ander nodded impatiently. "Will...Lord Torbury I mean...wants me to leave. He says that the king and queen will be going somewhere with their baby son, and he thinks they might benefit from having me with them." He shook his head.

"And why is that a problem?"

He looked at Brother Gerome in surprise. "I was just getting settled here. For the first time I'm starting to understand how my calling as a monk and as a healer might work in practice. That's only been possible because I came to this community."

"And why can't you exercise your calling with the king and queen?"

"You've seen what life is like around them. Their lives are a never-ending drama of intrigue and battles. Fighting was my life once, but all I want now is to escape from it. I've put all of that behind me. The king needs warriors, not monks."

"You saved the king's life. It isn't hard to understand why they might want a healer on hand."

"That wasn't just me. And anyway, I didn't become a monk so I could spend my days as medic to the royal family." He shot a glance around them before adding, "I mean no disrespect to Their Majesties."

Brother Gerome offered no immediate response, and both of them gazed for a time out into the gathering gloom.

"What about you? What will you do?" Brother Ander eventually asked.

"I have been giving that question much thought and prayer," Brother Gerome replied. "Anneka and Rellan have told me how much they've appreciated having us both here at Newhaven. Anneka remembers fondly the priest from her estate in Erestor—Father Bryan I believe he was called. She said the Newhaven community had nowhere to turn for spiritual guidance before we arrived."

He gazed up at Brother Ander. "I've been thinking that I will stay here. Brother Elias spoke with me at Paradise Valley, before he sent us off with the king and queen. He told me then that the future was uncertain, and that I should be willing to follow God's leading, wherever it might take me."

"He had a similar conversation with me," replied Brother Ander. "I think he suspected at the time that we might not return."

"So what are you going to do?" Brother Gerome asked.

Brother Ander shrugged. "I will go with the king and queen. I'm not sure that refusing them is an option, even if I wanted to."

Brother Gerome nodded. "You could ask God to show you a way to wiggle out of it, but I'm not sure it would do any good. I have a feeling it's what he wants you to do."

As Thomas was leaving the conference, Will had asked Thomas to meet him later that day. The commander had suggested a quiet location overlooking Newhaven. Thomas arrived early to gather wood and light a fire. He now sat watching the flickering glow while he waited for Will to arrive.

The light was slowly fading from the sky as Will hobbled toward him and took his place before the fire. Thomas peered curiously at his friend in the semidarkness, wondering what he wanted to talk about.

The commander wasted no time in getting to the point. "Why is Elena so set on joining you, Thomas? I can understand that she doesn't want to be parted from you, but this assignment will be dangerous."

"There's a lot I haven't told you, Will," Thomas replied awkwardly. "Everything was frantic when we first saw you again after we'd left Arnost to search for the king. Then we were all on the run for so long, and you've been busy since we arrived here."

"I understand," Will told him. "I don't have a lot of time right now, either, but I'm listening."

"After we fled our home in the forest, I was badly injured, and Elena needed to use the stone to get us out of a dangerous situation. The way she handled it was astonishing. And we discovered that the stone reveals different things to her. Or rather she discovers different things from what it reveals. Since then we've been handing it back and forth between us as the need arises."

Will looked surprised. "I would never have guessed that sharing the stone was even a possibility," he said.

Thomas shrugged. "There's so much we still don't understand about it. But I have to admit that Elena's insights are sometimes more useful than mine."

Will raised an eyebrow. "Jonas?"

Thomas winced. "That's a particularly embarrassing example," he said. "I can't believe that I ever thought him capable of treachery. I never managed to get a good enough look at him at the time. It was only ever fleeting glimpses. After it was all over I asked Elena to do a check of her own. She saw right through to the heart of it. As always."

Will laughed. "Don't worry, Thomas. You don't have anything to be ashamed about. Without you the kingdom would have been in big trouble on more than one occasion."

"Thanks, Will. The reason I'm telling you this is that Elena is much more resourceful than people think, and unusually insightful as well."

"There is a great deal more to Elena than meets the eye," said Will with a wry smile. "And the stone can be shared..." He fell to musing for a while.

Thomas began to feel uneasy. What was Will thinking?

Will studied Thomas's face knowingly. "I'm sure you're wondering about the possible consequences of having told me that. Let me assure you that I've never wanted your stone, and knowing that it can be shared doesn't change that."

He stared into the fire. "You've chosen to be open with me about the stone, Thomas, and I appreciate that. I've never had designs on it, though. My life is complicated enough already." He laughed, although there was no humor in it.

"I'm very grateful that you've always protected my secret," Thomas told him.

"I haven't always protected it as well as I should have. That council of lords meeting in Arnost during the siege comes to mind. I haven't hesitated to drag you into some dangerous situations so you could use it to help me out. So I owe you something."

"You don't owe me anything, Will," Thomas replied. "The debt lies much more heavily on my side."

They both went silent for a time. Thomas had known for some time that he needed to share his suspicions with Will. Now that a perfect opportunity had presented itself, he didn't quite know how to begin. After a few moments of fruitless rumination, he shook his head, frustrated at his own hesitancy. He decided he just needed to speak.

"There's something else I need to tell you, Will."

Will's face turned serious. "Why do I get a bad feeling about this?" he murmured.

"You know that after Elbruhe died, Brother Vangellis and I went to a monastery," Thomas said.

"Up in the mountains?"

"Yes. They have a huge library there, with a lot of old scrolls. We asked the monk who was their librarian if he'd ever heard of anything like the stone. He did a search and found an old scroll."

"You've never mentioned this," said Will.

"I did set out to tell you on one occasion," Thomas replied. "When we were at Hazelwood Ford, after the battle. You were too busy. You couldn't spare the time, so I decided not to bother you with it."

"I'm sorry I shut you out, Thomas. I was completely overwhelmed. Even after the fighting was over there was so much to think about. The kingdom was devastated after the Rogandan invasion, and we needed to shift our energies to rebuilding. It was hard to know where to start."

"I could see the pressure you were under," Thomas said, "and my news didn't seem pressing. The scroll raised as many questions as it answered. But I've started to wonder if some of it might be important now, even though it didn't seem especially relevant at the time."

"Tell me," said Will.

"The writer of the scroll knew about the stone I have—he called it the Stone of Knowing. What he said about the stone was accurate, so it seemed to me he must have known what he was talking about. But I was surprised to learn that there are two other stones. One of them apparently grants long life. He called that the Stone of Vitality. The other one he referred to as the Stone of Authority."

"What did the scroll say about this Stone of Authority?" asked Will, listening intently.

"It was only a brief mention, because the scroll had been torn and maybe half of it was missing. But it said that the stone granted power and influence. Only the Stone of Knowing was described in any detail in the fragment the librarian found."

Will's brows were furrowed, but he said nothing.

"There were times when I wondered if you had the Stone of

Authority," Thomas said with a self-conscious laugh. "You're such an effective leader."

Will shook his head. "I know nothing of any other stones," he said.

"I'm not actually serious," said Thomas. "But I did find myself thinking about the scroll again when I discovered that Pisander was planning to invite Agon to Arnost. I can't imagine Pisander wanting to share power, much less hand power to anyone else. It seems so out of character. If Agon has the Stone of Authority though, he might have been able to use it to influence Pisander. Could that be why Pisander agreed to something he wouldn't normally consider?"

Will frowned. "Very possibly. This information raises questions about the attack at Paradise Valley. One person was almost certainly behind the attacks. The obvious candidate is Agon, but I haven't been able to see how he could make it happen. Someone needed to get Pisander working effectively with people from Castel and Varas on a goal that's bigger than any of their own personal agendas."

As always, Will's mind quickly led him to the broader implications.

"I haven't been able to understand why Pisander would plan such an attack," Will continued. "Why would he try to kill all three kings at once? It would increase the risk significantly. And even if he succeeded, he wouldn't be in a position to receive any direct benefit. But if Agon has found a way to impose his will on individuals from all three kingdoms..." He shook his head. "That would make him very dangerous indeed."

An important question was weighing on Thomas. "Are you going to tell the king about this?" he asked. He wasn't able to keep the anxiety from his voice.

Will smiled grimly at Thomas for a moment before shaking his head. "Your suggestion about this Stone of Authority would sound preposterous to anyone who hadn't already seen you in action with your Stone of Knowing. And I'm not eager to expose your stone more widely."

Thomas tried not to let his relief appear too obvious, but Will looked at him shrewdly. "I'm sure you must have wondered why I've been so willing to keep quiet about it," Will suggested.

Thomas hesitated for a moment before deciding there was nothing to be gained by pretending. "Yes, I have," he said frankly. "Many times."

"You once promised that you would never use the stone on me," Will reminded him. "Have you kept that promise?"

The question sounded casual, but Thomas was not deceived for a moment. He could never forget the day on the riverbank, and the fury in Will's eyes as he slapped the stone from Thomas's hand.

"I've kept the promise," Thomas assured him. "I long ago decided not to use the stone on anyone I have regular contact with. Elena can confirm that I have followed through on that decision."

Will simply nodded. "And that's a key reason why I've been content to leave the stone with you, hidden from the world. There's more to it than that, of course, and I'm happy to explain if you like. I'm sure that the subject is of considerable interest to you." He gave Thomas a knowing look.

Thomas nodded. He quietly took a deep breath, then released it slowly in an effort to calm himself.

"A leader faces many challenges," Will began. "There are so many things to consider. Leaders must represent the interests of whoever appointed them. They also need to anticipate the likely ways that powerful people might react to whatever they do. It doesn't end there, either—in my view no leader is worthy of respect unless they also consider the interests of the powerless."

"I have no idea how you balance all these things," Thomas said, shaking his head.

Will sighed. "It isn't easy," he said. "I'm surrounded by intrigue, and there are times when I would be very pleased to have a way of finding out what others are thinking. If I tried to base my decisions on what other people think, though, I'd invariably end up confused and frustrated."

"I can believe that," Thomas replied. "I'm sure it's impossible to please everyone."

"Completely impossible," Will agreed. "Always knowing what others think would become a distraction. That isn't a distraction I need."

Will creased his forehead, adding new lines to his scarred visage. "And that isn't the only complication. What if you knew the secret thoughts of everyone around you, and you also had the power to prevent them from ever acting on the worst of those thoughts? It would become very tempting to deal with possible threats before they could be carried out. When you knew that someone had become a potential threat, you wouldn't give them the benefit of the doubt, because there wouldn't be any doubt—not about what they were thinking, anyway. The more powerful you were, the more dangerous such an ability would become."

Thomas understood completely. Drettroth had lusted after this power, and there was no doubt in Thomas's mind about how the Rogandan commander would have used it.

"People don't always put their thoughts into action though," said Will. "Sometimes fear of the consequences holds them back. Sometimes they simply change their minds. None of that would matter—they could be condemned before they ever had a chance to exercise restraint. Normally people are punished for what they do. Now they'd be punished for what they think."

As always, Will had seen the bigger picture clearly and completely.

A grim smile came over Will's face. "Who can be trusted with this kind of knowledge? I'm not confident that I can be trusted with it. It's safer in your hands, Thomas."

Was it truly safe to entrust the stone into his hands? Thomas had misused it terribly when he first found it, with dire consequences for him and for others. But so much had changed since then. And now Elena bore it with him—both its revelations and its burden. Thomas was only beginning to understand how much of a relief that was for him.

Fortunately, Thomas's status limited his ability to act on the stone's revelations. That was also a very good thing.

"I think I understand what you mean," Thomas replied. "Whenever I've discovered anything truly alarming, I've come to you, because you have the power to do something about it. I don't have that power myself, and it's safer that way."

"Exactly," said Will. "Jonas is a perfect example. You shared your concerns with me, then left it to me to decide how to respond."

"And it would have been a terrible mistake if you'd taken me too seriously," said Thomas, shamefacedly.

"No harm was done," Will replied. "Both of us did what we needed to do."

Will clapped him on the back. "This has been a very enlightening conversation, Thomas," he said.

"For me as well," agreed Thomas.

"I'm happy for Elena to join the king and queen," Will said. "You'll need to make arrangements for your daughter."

Thomas raised his eyebrows in surprise. "It sounds like you're expecting we'll be gone for some time. Would it be possible for Rubin to come—to help with Tammi? That means that Haldek will want to come as well, of course."

Will pondered a moment before nodding. "If they're willing to take the risks, I'm willing to let them come too. In fact it might prove useful at some point to have Haldek along," he added thoughtfully.

"We have some preparation to do," said Thomas, suddenly anxious to be gone.

"We leave at dawn," Will reminded him as they parted. "Don't be late!"

6

———————

The morning after the conference Will rose early to see Rellan off. Anneka and Rellan had already arrived with their two children, and they stood huddled together. A small party that included the king, Rufe, and Brother Gerome joined Will just before dawn.

The king approached Anneka and Rellan and gravely expressed his thanks to them both, offering his best wishes to Rellan for his journey. They bowed in response, and he moved away to allow Rellan to say his goodbyes.

Anneka held their two-year old daughter, Bella, in her arms. Rellan stood beside her, stomping his feet restlessly as he cradled Bella's twin brother, Kuper. Neither of the twins were awake. Brother Gerome stood beside them.

Rellan was poised like an arrow ready for release. He was waiting only for the first glimmer of sunrise, determined to set off for Erestor as soon as the light allowed it. He would not be traveling alone. Petar, an exceptional hunter and tracker from Newhaven who was also an unusually capable archer, had agreed to accompany him. Petar waited patiently nearby, holding their horses.

Rellan handed little Kuper to Brother Gerome before briefly

embracing Anneka. He then took the reins of his horse from Petar and mounted, turning back once to wave farewell as he rode away.

Anneka, her face a mask, stared after him until long after he had vanished from sight.

SOON AFTER RELLAN and Petar had left, Rellan noticed his companion guiding his horse closer. Petar's face held a question. Rellan could guess what was coming.

"Are we heading where I think we're heading?" asked Petar.

"There's no other option," Rellan replied. "The journey will take long enough even going the quick way."

Petar grimaced. "The 'quick way', as you put it, won't help anyone if we end up floating face down in the lake. You know better than anyone how unstable that slope can be."

"What's the alternative?"

Petar pointed behind them. "We could head south, around the mountains."

Rellan shook his head. "That would take weeks. We don't have that kind of time."

"Did Anneka know you were going to risk the lake?"

"We didn't discuss details—we didn't need to. She understands the situation."

Rellan slowed his horse and turned to his companion. "It isn't too late to change your mind, Petar. You don't have to come with me. You didn't volunteer for this, and there'll be no shame if you decide to head back."

Petar shook his head firmly. "Forget it," he replied. "I'm not going to let you do this on your own, Rellan." With that he clicked his tongue and moved his horse forward again.

Rellan accepted Petar's response at face value and put the matter from his mind. He knew that they wouldn't reach the lake until the following day at least. Once they had crossed into Erestor, an even longer journey lay ahead of them before they reached Maranelle.

Everything would depend on finding a way past the lake.

A SMALL GROUP had already gathered on the outskirts of the Newhaven community when Thomas arrived with his little party the following morning. They stood shivering in the cold air as they watched the sky for any sign of the coming dawn.

Will stood off to one side talking quietly with Count Ranauld. Rufe and Jonas waited nearby with their horses, longbows slung across their backs and quivers bristling with arrows.

The king and queen arrived just as the first hint of the sun brightened the sky. Ava, the queen's handmaid, hurried along with them, holding the baby prince. Brother Ander followed close behind. Brother Gerome had also accompanied them, Anneka at his side.

Will ended his conversation with Ranauld and turned to face the group. "Everyone ready?" he called. Without waiting for an answer he added, "Time to go."

Count Ranauld set off first with two soldiers, heading north. Thomas knew that Will had offered him more men, but Ranauld felt that a small party was less likely to attract unwanted attention.

Thomas had been holding Tammi. As Will mounted his own horse, Thomas handed the toddler to Elena, kissing his wife lightly on the lips.

"Be careful," she whispered to him.

Thomas nodded to Rubin and Haldek, then mounted up. Clicking his tongue, he guided his horse over to Will, who waited with Rufe and Jonas.

Thomas's stomach had begun to clench uncomfortably—it was hard to leave Elena and Tammi. As he rode away, he looked back in time to see the rising sun light up the scene behind him. Elena clutched Tammi almost defiantly, her attention fixed unwaveringly on her departing husband. Rubin had wrapped his arm around her shoulder. Anneka stood to one side of them, her expression unreadable. Brother Gerome's head tilted upward to the heavens. His eyes were lightly closed, and he seemed to be mouthing a prayer of blessing over the departing men. Brother Ander towered beside him, his head bowed. The king's face wore a stern look. Only the queen seemed calm.

The future held no guarantees for any of them. Only danger and uncertainty lay ahead, and each of them would need to face it as best they could.

Long after the scene had disappeared behind him, it remained etched in Thomas's memory.

A SENSE of foreboding descended over Elena as she watched Thomas ride away. Their brief period of peace at Newhaven had ended so abruptly. When would they enjoy such tranquility again?

The Stone of Knowing had gone with Thomas, and she experienced nothing but relief to know it was so far from her reach.

She was not free of it, though. It had been the stone, and only the stone, that made Thomas so necessary to Will. Thanks to the tiny object her beloved was heading into danger. As long as Thomas retained the stone, it could upend her world at any time.

Would they ever be free from its unsettling influence? She could not pretend herself ignorant of the stone's potential for good, though the power of its insights held no lasting allure for her. She would cheerfully cast it off the edge of the world if she could be certain it would never be found again. But she knew of no effective way to conceal it. As long as the stone remained accessible, it would forever be at risk of discovery by the unscrupulous.

Like Thomas before her, she had acquired a sense of responsibility for the stone. She sighed and shook her head.

With an effort, she put the subject from her mind.

WILL'S small group had long disappeared from sight, and Elena saw that the king and queen were about to mount their steeds. Rubin had offered to make a sling for Prince Aiden—a smaller version of the one he had fashioned to allow Tamara to be carried safely and comfortably while on horseback. The sling had been positioned around the queen's neck, and the little prince was now nestled snugly within it.

Before the queen could climb into the saddle, Ava ran to her, wringing her hands. "Please let me come with you, Your Majesty," she pleaded. "I don't want to leave you. Who will serve you?"

"You've been a wonderful and a faithful companion, Ava," the queen replied quietly, "and I'll miss you very much. I can't know what the coming days might bring. I only know that there will be danger and uncertainty. I want you to stay here—to make a life for yourself in Newhaven. I release you from my service."

At her words Ava began to weep inconsolably, covering her face with her hands. Clearly moved by her former handmaid's distress, the queen drew her into a lingering embrace. She caught Brother Gerome's eye and nodded to him, and the monk moved quickly to Ava's side to comfort her.

Tears glinting in her own eyes, the queen turned away and mounted her horse, guiding it alongside the king's animal. The monarchs moved forward, surrounded by a dozen guards hand selected by Rufe.

Elena and Tamara, along with Rubin and Haldek, intended to accompany the royals and their guards, and they also mounted. Brother Ander completed the party, and he stood ready nearby with his horse.

All of them would ride toward Steffan's Citadel and position themselves near the western army camped outside the citadel without getting close enough for their presence to be detected. They would not see Will again until he called for them. That request would not come until Will was certain it was safe for them to rejoin him. What might happen after that, Elena had no idea.

When the soldiers began to move out, the king and the queen among them, Elena nudged her horse forward to join the column. Rubin guided his horse alongside her. Tammi rode with him, settled into her sling and still sleepy from the early start. Haldek swung in behind them.

Brother Ander brought up the rear, his face somber. He appeared lost in thought. Elena had no way of knowing what he might be thinking, but his mood matched her own if his expression offered any indication.

RELLAN AND PETAR rose at dawn and set out immediately. They rode hard throughout the day, with the result that they reached the lake that afternoon. Roughly three hours remained before the sun would reach the western horizon. The question facing them was whether to risk the slope immediately or wait for the following morning.

They stood beside each other, scanning the landscape before them apprehensively.

"How many times have you crossed that slope?" Petar asked.

"Twice," Rellan replied. "Once in each direction. I also partially crossed it with Anneka the day of the landslide."

He fell silent as the memories flooded through his mind. He relived his horror as the slope slid away before his eyes, carrying Anneka with it. Somehow he'd reached her in time. Never would he forget clinging to her as they dangled on the end of a rope, watching wide-eyed as the tidal wave swept inexorably toward them.

He returned to the present with an effort. "What about you?" he asked.

Petar stared into the distance. "Only once. When we first came here with Anneka. Somehow we all made it across from Erestor. The men hunting us were another matter. They deserved everything they got and more, but watching them sliding helplessly into the lake with their horses...it wasn't pretty." He gazed into the lake with obvious distaste.

Rellan nodded, his head down. "Anneka has told me about it. You did well to defeat those men."

The lake stretched out before them, no breeze ruffling its surface.

The scene was one of complete tranquility, although both Rellan and Petar knew how deceptive appearances could be.

"Should we attempt it before sunset?" Rellan asked. "A good night's sleep would be welcome. But time is against us, and I'm not sure that the crossing will seem any easier after a whole night thinking about it."

Petar looked down at the slope before glancing across to the trees on the far side of the lake. "We might as well do it now," he said.

Rellan gave a sharp nod. "I agree. Let's not carry anything we don't need. Just in case." He dismounted, removing his sword, his bow, and his cloak, and securing them to the saddle. Petar did the same. Both men had brought ropes with them, and they placed them within easy reach, loosely attached to their saddles.

Rellan led his horse out onto the slope above the lake. Petar followed a couple of horse lengths behind.

The slope beside the lake seemed stable enough; Rellan knew from experience that the most dangerous section lay ahead of them. He moved carefully forward, the horse between him and the lake. The animal seemed jittery, perhaps sensing his mood, and he spoke to it quietly to calm it.

An hour had passed by the time Rellan finally reached the part of the slope that he knew to be most unstable. This was the spot where Yosef and Jon had set out to trigger a landslide, succeeding beyond their wildest imaginings and losing their own lives in the process.

He paused and peered forward intently. Several years had gone by since the fateful day when a thick layer of soil had flowed down into the lake, but the slope appeared little altered. If anything, it looked steeper and more treacherous.

Rellan glanced back at Petar. His companion's face was pale but determined. Taking a deep breath, Rellan led his horse slowly onto the slope. His feet slid downhill with every step, making forward progress extremely hazardous. His horse plodded slowly beside him, snorting nervously.

A part of Rellan wanted to abandon caution and common sense, and sprint across the slope until the unstable section lay safely behind him. He knew such an approach would end badly, so he paused for a moment to allow his heart to stop racing.

Rellan began to breathe more freely once he caught his first glimpse of more stable ground, only a few horse lengths away. Anxious not to make a mistake with safety so close at hand, he stepped out more warily than ever.

A sharp cry sounded behind him, and he swung his head around to see that Petar had lost his footing and was sliding under his horse's legs. He was clutching desperately to the reins, but before Rellan could react he lost his grip and began sliding down toward the lake.

Rellan responded instantly, reaching for his rope and quickly tying one end of it to his saddle. He turned to throw the other end of the rope to Petar, but the hapless rider was already out of reach. Keeping hold of his own rope, Rellan moved as quickly as he dared to Petar's horse and grabbed the other rope, tying one end of it to his own rope. Making a loop in the other end of the rope, he placed it over his shoulders, tightening it under his arms.

Then he allowed himself to slide downward, playing out the rope as he went. He tried to tell himself that he had done this before, but it wasn't the same. This time everything depended on his horse remaining in position at the top of the slope and supporting his weight.

Rellan looked down and saw Petar at the edge of the lake, trying to pull himself out of the water and onto the bank. At every attempt the edge of the bank simply crumbled away.

"Swim to me," Rellan called.

Petar saw him coming. Abandoning his attempts to climb out of the lake, he swam awkwardly to where Rellan was heading. Petar's condition was rapidly becoming critical. He was shivering uncontrollably in the icy cold water.

As soon as Rellan reached the edge of the lake he allowed the rope to tighten, hoping desperately that his horse would not lose its footing. The animal whinnied, but seemed to take up the strain.

Rellan reached down just as Petar strained an arm up to him. Grabbing hold of Petar's arm, Rellan dragged him bodily from the water. The rope stayed taut, but there was no telling how much the horse could take.

They needed to get back up the slope. With a mighty effort Rellan took a step upward, dragging Petar with him. It was obvious immediately that this approach was doomed to failure. The slope was simply too long and too slippery, and the effort was beyond them both. Even if the horse was somehow able to keep supporting their weight, Rellan would never manage to climb all that distance with Petar hanging on as little more than a dead weight.

Rellan planted his feet and held his current position, his mind whirling. He needed to find an alternative, and find it quickly.

The hint of an idea came to him. Whistling to the horse, Rellan urged it forward. The horse didn't respond, so he whistled again, louder this time. The animal took a step forward, then another. Keeping the rope taut, Rellan began to shuffle along the slope, barely above the waterline, dragging Petar along behind him. Once or twice the horse almost lost its footing, slipping down a short distance, but it recovered, and Rellan took up the slack on the rope, hanging on grimly. He called out a continual stream of encouragement as the horse continued to struggle forward.

Refusing to dwell on the odds of success or failure, Rellan narrowed his entire world to the next step before him. Slowly, laboriously, they moved across the slope.

It felt as though an eternity had passed by the time they finally reached more stable ground, although it surely must have only been a few minutes. The slope around them now consisted of firm soil interspersed with rocks. It showed little sign of giving way beneath them.

Rellan allowed the rope to go slack, and encouraged Petar to sit. Then he carefully climbed up to the horse and untied the rope. Petar's horse had trailed along behind his mount and he went to it and retrieved Petar's cloak. Then he climbed back down to Petar.

His companion was trembling violently. The first priority was to get him dry and warm.

"We need to get you to your horse, Petar," he said. "Come on, I'll help you."

On many occasions throughout his eventful life, Rellan had faced physical challenges. The final climb back up the slope with Petar surely ranked as his greatest feat of endurance. By the time they reached the horses, both men were utterly spent. But Rellan could not afford to rest.

Somehow he got Petar onto his horse, then he remounted as well and led them both forward until the lake lay behind them. The light was fading quickly. The moment he found a sheltered location under some trees, Rellan retrieved every available blanket and left Petar to struggle out of his wet clothes. Then he set about building a fire. Once it was crackling heartily, he positioned some branches near it and spread Petar's sodden clothes across them. Then at last, weary beyond words, he slumped down himself before the fire.

A couple of hours after the sun had set, Rellan felt able to bestir himself. He prepared food and managed to get Petar to eat some of it.

Petar, too, was showing tentative signs of recovery. He was no longer shivering violently, he had hot food in him, and some of his clothes were almost dry.

After seeing to the horses and gathering an impressive pile of wood to keep the fire burning throughout the night, Rellan finally allowed himself to relax. He sat down before the fire and released a heavy sigh.

"Why did you do it?" asked Petar.

"Do what?" asked Rellan, puzzled by the question.

"Come down for me. It was madness! I'm not sorry you saved me, of course. I'll forever be in your debt. But it's a miracle that either one of us survived. What were you thinking?"

Rellan glanced briefly at him. "I remembered you saying what it had been like to watch the men and their horses sliding helplessly into the lake. The memory was clearly horrific, even though they were your enemies."

Rellan stared back into the fire. "You risked the slope anyway. I couldn't leave you in the lake when it happened to you."

He fell silent, and Petar found nothing further to say either.

Before another hour had passed, Petar's clothes were almost dry. Rellan woke him from his doze, and he dressed again and returned Rellan's blankets. Rellan banked the fire, and both men settled down to sleep.

When the sun rose once more, Petar felt able to continue their journey. They saddled their horses, mounted up, and headed for Maranelle.

Nothing now prevented them from reaching the duke. They would let him know that the king and queen were alive and well and on the move. And they would convey how urgently the monarchs needed the army he commanded in Erestor.

Before long the lake was lost to sight. Rellan prayed fervently that he would never clap eyes on it again.

7

———————

Thomas stood huddled with Will, Rufe, and Jonas as the sun rose on a new day. Two days ago they had left Newhaven. It had taken much of the day to travel upriver and trek through the ruined forest. They had camped in the forest beyond the battleground, and ridden northwest for much of another day. They halted as soon as the western army, camped outside Steffan's Citadel, lay within reach. They spent the rest of the afternoon watching it from a safe distance. When the sun set, they tried to sleep, knowing that the following day would decide their future, one way or another.

When the sun rose Will called them together. "Are you all clear about what you need to do?" he asked.

They nodded in unison.

Jonas needed to leave immediately, and he accordingly mounted his horse, preparing to ride away.

Will preempted him, hobbling over and reaching up to clasp Jonas's forearm in a salute. "We're indebted to you once more, Jonas," said Will soberly.

Jonas shrugged. "All of us are doing what we can."

Will nodded, releasing his arm.

"I have no way of knowing when I'll be back," Jonas told them, "but it might be sooner than you expect."

"We'll be ready," Rufe promised.

Jonas called to his horse, and it sprang away.

Thomas watched him leave with trepidation. His own turn would be coming soon, very soon.

Will's plan was bold and risky. Thomas tried to assure himself that Will knew what he was doing—no one was better equipped than Will to successfully navigate a situation like this. But cheering on the commander from the sidelines was very different from playing a part as an active participant.

Thomas thought of Elena. She wouldn't be as terrified as he felt—he was certain of it. He could almost see her smile of encouragement, assuring him that he could do it.

He sighed, trying not to sweat too much while he waited for Rufe to say it was time to go.

***

"WHO ARE YOU, and what's your purpose here?"

The tone of the sentry was rude and aggressive, but Jonas ignored it. "I'm here to speak with your commander. Hazor sent me."

The sentry grunted, clearly unimpressed, but he nevertheless sent another soldier to pass on the request.

"What have you all been doing?" Jonas asked, keeping his tone light.

The sentry paused, considering whether to reply. "Sitting. Always sitting," he finally replied, spitting on the ground beside him to underscore his frustration. He eyed Jonas narrowly for a while before his curiosity apparently overcame his brusqueness. "What's going on in the rest of the kingdom?" he ventured.

Jonas gazed down at him casually. "The usual kinds of things," he said.

The sentry frowned up at him, clearly annoyed at the evasive reply. Then he turned away, ignoring Jonas entirely.

At least thirty minutes passed before the soldier reappeared. "Come with me," he said curtly.

Jonas dismounted, leaving his horse with the sentry. He smiled to himself as he followed the soldier. From his perspective it was as promising a beginning as he could reasonably have hoped for.

As they made their way through the camp, Jonas took careful note of the mood of the soldiers he passed. The men seemed restless and disaffected. He wasn't surprised. Soldiers never coped well with idleness. By now they were undoubtedly spoiling for some action. He dared to hope that some of them might also be disillusioned with their current leaders.

Yes, the tone of the camp was definitely encouraging.

Jonas found himself ushered into a hut. Three men were sitting behind a table, apparently waiting for him. They didn't offer him a chair.

"You claim that Hazor sent you." So they knew who he was. Perhaps the various mercenary leaders were known to each other.

The scowl on the speaker's face and the way he spoke Hazor's name made it clear that Jonas need not expect a warm welcome. Jonas was not daunted by their cold reaction.

"Describe Hazor," the man demanded.

Jonas raised his eyebrows in mild surprise at the request. Nevertheless he was not alarmed. He might have only clapped eyes on the mercenary leader once—apart from when he killed him—but he remembered him well enough.

He described Hazor as requested.

The grunt from his inquisitor offered little indication of his reaction, but Jonas could see that he was satisfied.

"Who are you?" the man demanded.

"My name is Jonas. Hazor recruited me because I fought under Prentis, and I know how he thinks."

The commander eyed him silently.

Jonas stared back at him. "And who are you?" he asked bluntly. It wouldn't serve his purpose if they thought he was soft.

The commander's eyes narrowed for a moment, then his expression cleared. "I'm Lord Redfass," he said silkily. "These are my senior commanders—Kernon, and Namor," he added, stabbing a finger toward the men beside him.

Jonas bowed deeply. "My Lord," he said respectfully.

He had never heard of any of them, and he didn't doubt for a minute that 'Lord Redfass' was no more a nobleman than he was. He wondered where Pisander and Lygell and their cronies managed to dredge up such trash. Now these men had the temerity to command one of the king's armies. This was not just any army, either—it was part of the renowned force that had crushed the Rogandan invasion. Redfass dared to pretend he was acting in the king's interests, supposedly to quash a rebellion stirred up by none other than Will Prentis, the former commander of this same army. The effrontery of it made him sick to his stomach.

"So Hazor sent you, did he? What does that ambitious mongrel want?" growled Lord Redfass.

"Hazor would wish to return your compliments, I'm sure, My Lord," said Jonas dryly.

"If you have something to say, then say it," said Kernon.

"Hazor needs your help," began Jonas.

"Why am I not surprised?" said Lord Redfass, turning to his companions and raising his hands heavenward. "He should have come here himself if he wanted to beg for help."

"He couldn't risk it," returned Jonas. "He has the king and queen trapped, and he isn't going to let them out of his sight."

"I thought the king was dead," said Namor suspiciously.

"I never believe anyone's dead until someone I trust has seen the body," replied Jonas.

"If he has them trapped, why doesn't he go in and finish them off?" asked Lord Redfass contemptuously.

"Because the king and queen are defended by Prentis," said Jonas.

All three of the mercenaries raised their eyebrows at that.

"How many men does Prentis have?" asked Kernon.

"No more than a hundred," Jonas told him.

"And how many does Hazor have?"

"Three times that," Jonas replied.

"What's he waiting for then?" sneered Lord Redfass. "I've always known he was a coward."

"This is Prentis we're talking about," said Jonas seriously. "I'm sure you know his reputation as well as I do. No one in their right mind makes a move against him unless they have overwhelming force to back them up."

"Three to one isn't overwhelming?" sneered Kernon.

"Not with Prentis," returned Jonas stubbornly.

"So why should we trust you?" Kernon persisted.

Jonas shrugged. "It's your choice. The royals won't be going anywhere—Hazor will make sure of that. If you're not interested I'll head for Arnost. I imagine Lord Lygell might show a bit more interest than you have." He raised an eyebrow. "He might also be curious to know why you turned the opportunity down."

Kernon sneered in response, but his silence was telling.

"The king, the queen...and Prentis," mused Lord Redfass. "Taking them down is an attractive idea. It could be very rewarding indeed."

Jonas nodded. "Hazor is willing to share the spoils as well as the glory. Half to him, half to you."

Guffaws of scoffing laughter immediately sounded from all three of them. "So he wants us to do the dirty work while he gets the glory?"

"He's the one who has the royals bottled up," Jonas pointed out.

"I presume you know the location yourself," Lord Redfass said smoothly. "We can make it worth your while if you tell us where it is. Or, if you prefer, we could just squeeze the information out of you right now at no cost to ourselves."

"I do know where they are," said Jonas calmly. "But I also know something Hazor doesn't know. While I was on the way here I caught sight of Prentis. I saw him at the edge of a forest, alone and a long way from his main group."

"Why should we care?" asked Kernon.

"He didn't see me, and I can lead you to him."

"It'd be a waste of time," said Kernon dismissively. "He'll be long gone by the time we get there."

Jonas shook his head. "I don't think so. I watched him for a while. He was examining the hoof and front leg of his horse. It showed all the signs of being lame. After he finished with the horse Prentis sat down, apparently to wait. If he's expecting someone to join him, he'll be stuck there until they arrive. If we leave now, we can deal with him before moving on to the royals. They'll be a lot easier to manage without him."

The men still looked doubtful.

Jonas shook his head in frustration. "What do you have to lose? It's on the way to Hazor anyway. If Prentis is gone, we'll simply continue on and help Hazor finish off the royals."

"And share the spoils with Hazor?" scoffed Namor.

"I'm sure you'll find a way to satisfy him."

He made no comment about the smug smiles that appeared on the faces of the three men.

"Namor, go get a couple hundred men," said Lord Redfass.

"Wait!" said Jonas. "We haven't agreed on terms." He paused before coolly offering them a proposal. "Why not split the spoils four ways? I'm not greedy—I'm willing to settle for a quarter share."

"Done," said Lord Redfass.

Out of the corner of his eye Jonas saw Kernon and Namor exchanging smirks. He pretended not to have noticed.

Jonas addressed Lord Redfass. "I don't know who you're planning to take with us, My Lord, but I hope it's not the regulars."

"Why not?" Redfass demanded.

"They've fought for Prentis and for the royals. The outcome is going to be very unpredictable if you give them an assignment like this. Take men you're sure you can rely on."

"He's got a point," Namor conceded.

Lord Redfass nodded. "Bring our own people."

"What about the regulars?" asked Kernon.

"What about them?" Redfass waved a hand dismissively. "They

can stay here. They won't be going anywhere." He turned to Kernon. "Make sure our insiders stay with the rabble to keep an eye on them."

So the mercenaries had planted their own people among the soldiers. That was no surprise. Leaving them with the soldiers wasn't what Jonas had been hoping for, but there was nothing he could do about it.

He followed Lord Redfass to the edge of the camp and retrieved his horse. Then he waited, becoming increasingly impatient as he watched the mercenaries assemble. He couldn't afford to reach Will too quickly, but he'd expected to be long gone from the camp by now.

Jonas counted almost three hundred by the time the force was finally ready to depart. He led the men out.

"Where are we heading?" Lord Redfass asked him.

"We're taking a roundabout path, My Lord," Jonas replied. "Prentis is positioned at the edge of a forest. If we approach head on, he'll see us coming long before we arrive, and he'll try to disappear into the forest. I'm going to lead us in from a different direction— we'll approach him from the side. He won't know we're there until we're on top of him."

Redfass nodded. "Lead on, then. But you'd better be aware that we'll be watching you."

AFTER THEY HAD BEEN RIDING for two hours, Lord Redfass pulled his horse alongside Jonas's mount, his face twisted in a scowl. "How much further?"

"Another hour or two I expect, My Lord," replied Jonas. "It's frustrating, but there's no way to get there more quickly."

A perverse desire came over him to take a poke at the so-called nobleman.

"Do you ever find yourself envying the endurance of lesser creatures?" he asked innocently. "Just the other day I saw a spider sitting on its web for hours, waiting for an insect to happen by."

Redfass glowered at Jonas. "So who's the spider, and who's the fly?" he growled. "Get your head out of the clouds, and concentrate on getting us there!"

Jonas made no further comment, but he smiled to himself. Redfass hadn't entirely missed his meaning, and he had responded with a telling question.

Four hours eventually passed before Jonas slowed his horse to a halt, holding up a hand. The column came to a stop behind him.

Lord Redfass rode up, Kernon and Namor beside him.

"We've arrived," said Jonas. "If all is going to plan, we should spot him as soon as we round those trees ahead."

"Well get on with it," snapped Redfass.

Jonas kicked his horse in the flanks, and it sprang away. He rounded the trees at speed, the other horsemen following hard behind him. Once he was in the open he halted his horse again, facing the forest. Lord Redfass's mercenaries flowed around him, spreading out on either side.

Ahead of him, no more than a furlong away, stood Will Prentis. He was standing among the trees on the outskirts of the forest. He was entirely alone. He slowly mounted his horse, seemingly untroubled by the sight of the large body of soldiers swinging around to take up positions around Jonas.

Will Prentis made no attempt to flee. Silent and unmoving, the solitary figure faced Redfass's hundreds.

BREYSEN HAD HIDDEN in the forest for days, overwhelmed by the stench of decay and stumbling over the detritus of battle before risking everything on a desperate escape in the dark. Since then he had been trudging on foot for several days through an unfamiliar landscape, without food, and accompanied only by a dangerous and highly strung killer. Life had not been easy for him, but never had he faced a more grueling experience.

Quiet despair washed over him as he considered his situation. What would become of him? And what of his wife and little ones back home? He thought of the two children they hadn't so far needed to bury. Even if he survived and made it back to his family, he had no idea how he could provide for them.

The only thing he knew for certain was that he would never again sign up as a mercenary.

He couldn't be sure if anyone was still tracking the two fugitives, but a considerable amount of time had now elapsed since their escape from the forest, and every hour surely made it less likely that they would be found.

For much of the day he had been wondering if he should continue to follow Kantor or head off on his own. Neither of them would ever have selected the other as a companion—they had been thrown together. He didn't trust Kantor even slightly, and the idea of parting company with him was extremely appealing.

The only reason he hadn't done it already was in response to a strange sense of duty. The more he thought about it, the greater his misgivings about having helped Kantor to escape. A sense of impending doom hovered about the man. Breysen hoped his premonitions were wrong, but he decided to stick around, at least for a while.

His musing was interrupted by the sight of Kantor's hand raised in warning. His companion moved quickly to conceal himself behind a tree. After creeping closer, Breysen did the same.

Voices sounded ahead, not far away. Were they about to be discovered at last?

As Breysen peered around the tree, listening intently, he was reassured to hear the voice of a woman. He couldn't imagine a woman among their pursuers.

She laughed, and the simple sound was almost enough to undo him. It evoked memories of home, of family, of companionship. Memories of joy and of laughter.

He had given it up. And for what?

He had become a mercenary for the promise of money. Poor as he was, he saw now that what he left behind was worth much more than any payout offered by Hazor. He swallowed against a lump in his throat.

The woman's voice pulled him back to his current situation. "No need to worry about me," she was calling. "I won't be gone for long."

It wasn't difficult to guess why she might need a few moments' privacy, and she had no reason to suppose that stepping away from her companions might place her in danger.

Her voice was drawing closer, and Breysen's heart began to race when he realized that she was heading directly toward Kantor.

Kantor waited until the woman had almost reached his tree. Then he drew his knife in one fluid motion and leaped forward. Grabbing her, he spun her around before him, one hand smothering her mouth and the other holding a knife to her throat.

"Easy now!" he said quietly to the woman. Seeing Breysen hurrying toward him, he scowled. "You have no part in this. This woman is my free pass out of here. I'm getting me a horse, and she's coming as a hostage. Do whatever you like, but stay well away if you value your skin."

Anger rose up in Breysen as he glared at Kantor, his unease about his companion hardening into an unshakable determination to resist him at any cost. He'd seen for himself the mercenary's casual cruelty, and he was ready to do whatever it took to prevent him from harming an innocent victim.

Then he glanced at the woman and stopped in his tracks. Something about her seemed familiar, and his mind raced as he tried to figure it out.

All of a sudden it came to him, and the blood drained from his face. Kantor had made a hostage of the queen.

8

"Are you ready, Thomas?" asked Rufe.

The two men waited on their horses. The camp of the western army was in sight, but no one appeared to have spotted them yet.

"I'm ready," Thomas replied, trying to hide his nerves. "I'll let you know whenever I spot someone I don't think we can trust. And I'll also keep an eye out for anyone likely to be especially sympathetic to our cause."

Rufe looked at him strangely, but he nodded. "Let's go," he said, setting off toward the camp.

Thomas followed him in, twisting the clasp suspended beneath his vest to bring the stone into contact with his skin. He wondered if his friend truly believed he could do as he'd promised. If so, what did he make of it?

More soldiers were coming into sight now, and a tidal wave of impressions began to sweep over him, pushing Rufe from his mind. Thomas tried to narrow his focus, to sift out anything irrelevant to their situation.

One man stood out at once. He needed to warn Rufe.

Thomas urged his horse alongside the big soldier. "Rufe! Over there." He nodded toward the man, realizing at once there was little chance that Rufe knew who he meant.

The man headed away from them, hurrying back into the camp. Rufe did appear to have noticed him, but he seemed unconcerned. Other men were hurrying forward, some with weapons drawn. Open shock showed on many faces when they saw who was approaching.

Rufe drew his horse to a halt, Thomas pulling up beside him. The milling soldiers also came to a standstill immediately before them.

"It's Rufe!" a number of voices called. Men crowded closer. Thomas had no idea what might be about to happen.

"Who's that with him? Is it Thomas, the horse master?"

Startled, Thomas cast his eyes to identify the speaker. One of his former students must have recognized him. Thomas had been in hiding for years. He was surprised—and gratified too if he was honest—to discover that he hadn't been entirely forgotten.

His musings came to an abrupt end with the arrival of a group of mounted men. The soldiers had drawn their weapons, and their faces showed they meant business. They were led by the man Thomas had singled out previously. The stone showed him exactly what they had in mind, and the weight of their malice took his breath away.

Thomas turned to Rufe in alarm. The big soldier caught his eye as Thomas nodded urgently toward the group of men. Rufe followed his glance, but he didn't react at all. To Thomas's bemusement, he seemed neither surprised nor concerned.

What should he do? Thomas's misguided warnings to Will about Jonas came abruptly into his mind, and a flush of embarrassment washed over him. This was surely different though—a further glance at the approaching horsemen left no doubt about their intentions.

Had Will told Rufe about Thomas's mistake with Jonas? Surely not—Will had promised not to expose his secret. Perhaps Rufe was simply unconvinced that Thomas could help in a situation like this.

His consternation grew as the men drew closer.

NOT ALL OF the mercenaries had ridden away with Lord Redfass from the camp of the western army. The commander had intentionally left behind a few of the men he had placed in the ranks to inform on the regular soldiers.

The most senior of the informers was Belac, and he watched with narrowed eyes as the two men rode in. One of them didn't appear to be armed, and he immediately dismissed him as any kind of threat. The other rider was imposing and vaguely recognizable. Belac identified Prentis's right hand man before anyone else seemed to. Rufe Sarjant meant trouble, and Belac hurried away to get support.

As he ran, he cursed Redfass for disappearing with most of the reliable people. None of them could have known that Rufe Sarjant would show up the minute they'd gone of course, but it was spectacularly bad timing. Now it was up to Belac to retrieve the situation. He comforted himself with the knowledge that Redfass would make it worth his while when he returned. The mercenary commander had always come through in the past.

After locating another of the men Redfass had inserted into the ranks, Belac sent him off to help gather the others. In an impressively short time a group had assembled. All of them were mounted and fully armed. Belac led them back to the outskirts of the camp to deal with the big interloper.

Sarjant's unarmed companion saw them coming, and he was clearly terrified. He had reason to be. Sarjant also spotted them, but he seemed content to ignore them. Belac chuckled to himself. By the time he learned his mistake it would be too late.

Sarjant was standing up in the saddle. "Will Prentis needs your help," he called. "The king and queen are nearby too, and they're counting on you to help them deal with these mercenaries."

"Move aside!" Belac roared as his men tried to push through the press of soldiers. "Don't listen to these men—they're traitors to the king!"

Normally horses could be relied upon to force their way through any crowd, but soldiers were not the common rabble. They weren't intimidated by the animals, and their densely packed ranks made forward progress almost impossible.

Sarjant sat on his mount watching them calmly. "The real traitors are here before you," he called to the men. "Take a good look at them so you know who they are."

Belac's face twisted into a scowl as all eyes turned on him and his men.

"He's a snake!" someone shouted, pointing at Belac. "He goes slithering to Lord Ratface—I've seen him!"

Another soldier pointed at one of Belac's companions. "He had my friend arrested for no reason!"

Angry voices began to be heard until a voice bellowed above them all. "It's their turn!"

Loud cries sprang up all around, and Belac and his men were set upon from every side. Horses reared in the confusion, throwing some of Belac's men. Others were dragged from their saddles.

After a few minutes of chaos, the mercenaries were all disarmed. Several of them were dead.

Belac was dragged before Sarjant.

"What's your name?" the burly soldier asked him harshly.

He said nothing, but someone called, "His name is Belac."

"Well, Belac, this is your lucky day. I'm going to let you and your fellow reptiles slither away. You can keep your horses, but you won't be taking weapons or provisions. If you're anywhere near this camp in the next few minutes, consider yourself fair game."

The men around him stripped Belac of his weapons and pushed him to his horse. Only four others were able to mount up behind him. They rode out accompanied by loud jeering from the soldiers. A few of the men pelted them with rocks as they left.

As soon as they were clear of the camp, they reined in their horses.

"What are we going to do?" asked one of the men. "We need to find Redfass. Where did he go?"

"I have no idea," Belac replied, "but it makes no difference. Joining him is pointless. Sarjant has the whole army licking his boots now, and Lord Redfass doesn't have anything like enough men to bring them back into line. We'll head for Arnost. Like as not Lord Redfass will be following us before long."

He squinted off into the east. "Someone needs to get to Lord Lygell and tell him what happened here. When he finds out, he'll sort out this rabble for good."

He clicked his tongue and pointed his horse in the direction of Arnost.

THOMAS SAT on his mount watching the frenzied preparations as soldiers collected their weapons and saddled their horses. He had no idea why he was there. The stone had been almost useless in such a vast crowd, and although he had managed to focus his attention on one bad apple in the barrel, it had made no difference to the outcome. His efforts to warn Rufe about Belac were neither effective nor necessary.

He had been hunting an unknown number of adversaries among a multitude. Rufe had employed the simplest of strategies to flush out the lot of them.

Thomas had never felt more useless.

After dismissing Belac and his companions, Rufe ordered the men to prepare urgently to ride to the aid of Will. Word spread quickly—"Will needs our help!"—and the soldiers sprang immediately into action.

Now Rufe was waiting quietly, watching the men assemble. From the look on Rufe's face, they were taking far too long.

"Why did you let Belac go?" Thomas asked. "He'll take the news back to Pisander and Lygell in Arnost."

"It was Will's idea," Rufe replied. "Pisander and Lygell have had it all their own way so far, and he wanted them to know we've taken control of their army. It's about time they took a turn at guessing and worrying. People make mistakes when they're anxious."

As he was speaking, Rufe's attention was drawn to a soldier he knew. He called the man over. "Where are the other leaders, Timo?" he asked. "And why aren't you with your men?"

"All of us were either dismissed or demoted," Timo replied. "You can thank Lord Ratface for that," he added, spitting contemptuously into the dirt.

It wasn't the first time Thomas had heard the nickname. The soldiers delivered the title like an obscenity, invariably spitting whenever they used it. Ratface wasn't his real name of course—one of the soldiers had told them that the western army was commanded by Lord Redfass. He spat twice after speaking the name.

"Ratface appointed new leaders from his own people," Timo continued. "They called themselves leaders, anyway—most of them were useless. They all went off with him earlier."

"How many of the original leaders are still here?" Rufe asked.

"A reasonable number," came the reply.

Rufe nodded. "Round them up! I need to speak with them."

Timo hurried away.

No more than two or three minutes passed before men began to present themselves to Rufe. He greeted several by name. He waited impatiently until a sizable group had gathered.

"How can we help, Rufe?" one of them asked.

"All of you have your old responsibilities back," Rufe told them. "If any of the soldiers argue, send them to me. Round everyone up! We can't wait any longer."

While they were gone, Rufe moved among the soldiers who had already gathered. He pointed to about a dozen men that he seemed to recognize and drew them aside. "I've seen all of you in action," he told them. "We're missing too many of our leaders, so consider yourself appointed." He pointed off to one side. "Go over there and spread yourselves out," he ordered.

Some of the men looked startled, others looked delighted. All of them moved immediately to the place he indicated.

Rufe faced the soldiers already gathered. "If you don't have a captain, go attach yourselves to one of these men," he said, pointing to his new appointees. "They're your new captains. No more than fifty men to each. Move!"

Soldiers who had already reconnected with a captain remained where they were, but others surged across to the new appointees.

Ignoring the chaos of jostling men and horses, Rufe called Timo aside. When he had finished speaking, Timo nodded once and positioned his horse beside Rufe's.

Even before order had entirely emerged, Rufe decided it was time to go.

"We can't wait any longer," he bellowed, "we're moving out. New captains can follow Timo. The rest can follow me."

Thomas didn't stay with Rufe. He had nothing to offer in the fighting that lay ahead. Feeling like useless baggage, he allowed the men to ride by, drifting to the rear of the column.

As the soldiers surged past, Thomas tried to estimate the size of the troop. It was impossible to be certain, but he suspected more than eight hundred were following Rufe.

The thunder of hooves shook the ground as the soldiers rode away in a seemingly endless stream.

***

CARNWILL and his vegetable traders watched the men ride out with considerable interest.

The person trailing behind the giant leader had especially captured Carnwill's attention. He closely fit the description of Thomas Stablehand.

There was a simple way to be certain. Carnwill had learned from King Agon that Thomas's wife was reported to be unusually beautiful. If this was Thomas, his wife wouldn't be far away.

"I'm going to find out where they're headed," Carnwill told his men. "You stay here."

He raced away in pursuit of the soldiers, staying close enough to remain in touch, and far enough away not to be noticed.

Something was happening at last.

THE SENTRIES on the walls of Steffan's Citadel watched curiously as the camp below them slowly emptied. The citadel commander arrived on the battlements as the last of the men disappeared from sight.

"A smaller group—maybe two or three hundred—left earlier, Commander," he was told. "The camp seems empty now, although they haven't packed it up."

The commander looked on silently. "Where are they going?" he wondered aloud. "They've left for a reason, and they're expecting to return."

He turned to an aide. "Get an errand rider. Something's happening, and the duke needs to know."

9

"Let her go!" demanded Breysen.

Kantor sneered at him. "Go find your own hostage."

Something snapped in Breysen. He stepped in front of Kantor menacingly, pulling his knife and bending low in a fighting crouch.

"Get out of my way," growled Kantor.

"Or what?" asked Breysen. "If you slit her throat, your only free pass will be to your grave." He moved closer. "And you'll have to deal with me before you try anything with her."

"That's easily done," snorted Kantor. He hurled his hostage roughly to the ground and lunged at his challenger, his flashing knife almost finishing the fight before it had begun.

Breysen barely managed to lurch out of the way. He'd been in good condition once. But the deprivations of recent days had weakened him, and his reactions had slowed considerably. As Breysen slowly circled, his opponent lunged again. Kantor was weaker himself, though. Breysen swayed out of danger, stretching out with his own knife and nicking Kantor's arm as he withdrew it, drawing blood.

Overcome with fury, Kantor slid forward, sweeping Breysen's feet out from under him. Breysen fell heavily, landing hard on his back. Kantor was astride him in a moment, his knife raised high for a killing thrust.

Before the knife could descend, Breysen grabbed Kantor's arm, desperate to keep the blade away. Kantor drove the knife downward with all his might, bringing it ever closer to his enemy's chest. Breysen's eyes bulged as he struggled to prevent it. He couldn't keep it up for much longer.

Kantor tumbled suddenly forward, a startled look on his face. He collapsed on Breysen, his knife barely missing Breysen on its way down.

Heaving his attacker aside, Breysen stumbled to his feet. Bemused and panting heavily, he peered around anxiously for the queen.

The queen was on her feet, shaken and dusty, but apparently unhurt. Her would-be abductor lay unmoving in the dirt, a knife protruding from his back.

"He isn't the first mercenary to die by my hand," she said shakily, glancing down at her victim with a haunted look in her eyes. "It doesn't get any easier." Her face was pale, and she was trembling.

Hurrying across to her, he offered his arm, and she took it gratefully, leaning heavily on him as she attempted to steady herself.

A robed monk appeared from among the trees. He moved quickly toward them, his eyes flicking from the queen to Breysen and finally to Kantor's body.

"Your Majesty?" he asked, a deep frown upon his face.

Breysen stepped away from the queen as the big man approached, surprisingly apprehensive. He'd never been anxious around monks before, but this man was no ordinary monk. His face might radiate calm, but there was something perilous about him.

The queen shook her head as the monk took her arm. "You needn't be concerned about him, Brother Ander," she said, nodding at Breysen. "He nearly lost his life defending me from the other one."

The monk turned briefly away. "Her Majesty needs help!" he called loudly. Then he returned his attention to the queen.

Soldiers raced toward them, a more lavishly dressed man not far behind. Breysen realized at once that he was looking at the king.

When King Steffan reached his wife, the monk also relinquished her arm and positioned himself beside Breysen.

The king took his wife by the shoulders and drew her into a quick embrace. Then he stood back, examining her carefully.

"Are you hurt?" he asked, his voice shaking with agitation.

"I'm fine," she assured him.

The king glanced at Breysen, then locked eyes with the monk, his eyebrows raised questioningly.

The monk seemed to understand the unspoken request. He bowed. "I will join you shortly, Your Majesty," he said.

The king nodded once. Then he turned back to his wife and ushered her quickly away.

A couple of soldiers moved to the body of Kantor. After removing the queen's knife, they turned him over to examine him. Others headed into the surrounding trees. No doubt those protecting the king and queen would be doubly alert after what had happened.

Ignoring the soldiers, the big monk placed a hand on Breysen's shoulder. Breysen started at the touch, but the monk's grip was surprisingly gentle as he steered him away.

"I'm Brother Ander," said the monk.

"My name is Breysen," he returned nervously.

"Where are you from, Breysen?" Brother Ander asked in a friendly tone.

"From a small village near Danford."

The monk nodded. He jerked his head toward Breysen's former companion. "Who was he?" he asked.

"His name was Kantor. I didn't really know him—we stumbled upon each other a couple of days ago." He passed a hand across his face. Had it really been only a couple of days?

"And what brings you here to the forest?" asked the monk.

Breysen's heart skipped a beat. What could he say that wouldn't betray his role as a mercenary? If these people discovered what he had been doing, he would be finished. His brain seemed frozen. He couldn't find an answer to the monk's question.

After an awkward silence, Brother Ander looked him up and down. "You look famished," he said cheerfully.

Breysen nodded dumbly. He hadn't answered the monk's question, and the possible consequences of that omission filled him with apprehension. Nevertheless, the thought of food drove all else from his mind.

The monk led him to a clearing occupied by the king and queen. They were accompanied by a woman of unusual beauty, a couple of men, and several soldiers. The beautiful woman had been holding a small baby, and she was in the act of handing it to the queen. An older man cuddled a small child. Beside him stood a man whose features suggested he was foreign, possibly even Rogandan.

A delicious smell drew Breysen's attention to a pot of hot food, apparently prepared over a fire by some of the soldiers. He tried to restrain his eagerness, but having spotted the food he couldn't keep his eyes off it.

Brother Ander introduced him around. He bowed to the king and queen and tried with limited success to pay attention to the other faces and the names that went with them.

The queen was the first to speak. "I haven't thanked you for defending me," she said, looking at Breysen earnestly.

He felt his face redden. "You were the one who saved me, Your Majesty," he managed, bowing low once more.

The queen waved off his comment. "You look hungry," she said. "Please, take as much food as you want."

He thanked her sincerely, and she rewarded him with a gentle smile that reached to her eyes.

A soldier handed him a plate laden with stew, and he accepted it wide-eyed. How long had it been since he last enjoyed a proper meal?

Sitting down, he directed his full attention to the food. It occurred to him that he shouldn't embarrass himself, but before long he abandoned all restraint, shoveling down the stew with a zeal that bordered on desperation. When the plate was empty, he sat back and closed his eyes. An involuntary sigh of deep contentment escaped his lips.

A stifled laugh startled him back to reality. He opened his eyes to discover every single person staring at him, many of them grinning broadly.

"You haven't eaten for a while," observed the king.

He blushed deeply again.

"I'm sure we all have things to do," said the king pointedly, and the clearing abruptly filled with bustle.

Another plate laden with food was offered to Breysen. He took it gratefully, trying not to feel too ashamed.

He managed to show a measure of restraint as he ate this time. As he methodically chewed and swallowed, he noticed the king conversing quietly with Brother Ander. The king was doing most of the talking, the monk mostly contributing an occasional nod.

His attention was drawn irresistibly back to the food though, and he soon ignored everything else as he focused on eating.

Before long Breysen was startled out of his absorption. Both men joined him, sitting on the ground before him. He froze, his mouth full of half chewed food.

"Thank you for defending the queen," began the king. "We owe you a debt of gratitude."

Breysen dipped his head awkwardly.

"You've stumbled upon us at a sensitive time," the king continued. "We cannot afford for our whereabouts to become known." He looked Breysen in the eye. "We're going to need you to remain with us for the moment. I hope you will understand."

Breysen nodded, not sure if a response was expected. He sincerely hoped not—he had no idea what to say, and he could hardly speak with his mouth stuffed full of food.

The king fell silent. Breysen glanced at Brother Ander, and the monk caught his eye.

He couldn't look away. His eyes grew wide, and his heart skipped a beat, a wave of panic threatening to overwhelm him. The monk could see right through him—he was certain of it. Those eyes seemed to penetrate his defenses, laying bare his every secret.

Breysen swallowed convulsively, grimacing as the partially chewed food made its slow and painful journey down his throat. His hand trembled as he put down the plate, his eyes flicking to the king as he did so. The monarch was studying him with a thoughtful expression on his face.

Breysen stole another glance at Brother Ander. The monk too was gazing intensely at him, although nothing now seemed unusual about his regard. Had Breysen just imagined his earlier impression?

He felt exposed and vulnerable. Surely these men must have pieced together where he'd come from. Someone might have told the king that a pair of mercenaries had slipped through the patrols at the edge of the forest. If so, he would also know that one of his guards had been butchered during the escape. Breysen felt the blood drain from his face.

And yet the king hadn't called for his immediate execution. Not yet, anyway. When Kantor had taken the queen, Breysen had leaped instinctively to her defense. Had that act saved him?

He managed to look more calmly at the two men again, lowering his head respectfully after little more than a glance at the king.

"You've clearly been through some difficult times," said the king. "I've asked Brother Ander to look after you. He will make sure you get whatever you need." He nodded to the monk. "Thank you, Brother Ander," he said. Then he got to his feet and moved away, leaving Breysen alone with the monk.

A couple of soldiers swung in behind him as he left. They had been hovering protectively nearby the whole time. Breysen hadn't noticed.

The moment the king had gone, Breysen discovered that his body had been almost rigid with tension. He abruptly went limp, feeling as though he had just emerged from a physical pummeling. A long, shuddering sigh escaped from his lungs.

Brother Ander looked at him calmly. He gave Breysen a few moments to settle himself, then he asked, "How do you earn your living?" His tone was friendly rather than accusatory, but Breysen guessed that a great deal might be riding on his answers.

"I'm a blacksmith," Breysen replied without conscious thought. He was relieved to note that it hadn't even occurred to him to say he was a mercenary.

"At least I've been a blacksmith since I married. I was a sailor before that."

The monk raised his eyebrows in curiosity. "A sailor? Did you grow up in Maranelle?"

"No, although I've been there many times. My mother was Arvenian, but my father was originally from Varas. I was born in Varacellan, the capital of Varas. It's a major seaport—ships of all sizes go there. I grew up around ships, and I went to sea with my father from the time I was a child. I expected to become a sailor myself. Then he was badly injured and couldn't sail anymore. We moved to Danford."

"And you became a blacksmith?"

"Not at first. The mouth of the River Dan is at Varacellan, but the river flows all the way from Danford to the sea. When we arrived in Danford I spent my time on river boats at first. I only became a blacksmith after I married and moved to my wife's village."

Brother Ander pondered this information silently. After a couple of minutes he pointed off into the trees. "One of the horses seems to have a problem with its shoe," he said. "Would you be willing to take a look?"

"Certainly," Breysen replied. He guessed that the monk was testing his story, but he didn't care. He was desperate to do anything that might make him useful to these people.

He followed Brother Ander to where the horses were tethered. For a brief moment he was almost overwhelmed by a wild urge to jump on a horse and flee, but he mastered the impulse. Quite apart from the soldier guarding the horses, something told him that the monk might not stand by and watch him gallop away.

He allowed himself to be led to a horse that was clearly favoring one leg. The animal seemed uncomfortable whenever the leg touched the ground.

Lifting the leg, he thoroughly examined the hoof. His attention was immediately drawn to a telltale white spot on the hoof. Both the monk and the soldier came closer and watched over his shoulder.

"It appears to be an abscess," he said, looking up at them. "It doesn't look too serious. Do you have any cloth I can use to wrap the hoof?"

"I'll get some," the soldier replied, and hurried off to the main campsite.

"Can you please soak it in water?" Breysen called after him.

The soldier soon returned and handed Breysen a large piece of cloth, dripping wet.

Breysen tore off a long strip of the cloth, intending to use it to secure the cloth to the horse's leg.

Pulling out his knife, he carefully exposed the pus. "It will drain away when the horse lowers its foot," he explained. Then he folded the moist cloth several times and placed it over the hoof, tying it into position with the long strip.

"This will act as a poultice to encourage the pus to drain," he said. "It will also prevent dirt or other material from getting into the hole while it's healing. The horse shouldn't be ridden for a few days."

Brother Ander thanked him and led him away from the horses. When they came to a quiet place they both sat down.

"You appear to know what you're doing," said the monk.

The comment came with a smile of encouragement, but Breysen shrugged uncomfortably. "I enjoy my work," he said. "I just wish I could still do it."

Brother Ander looked puzzled. "What do you mean?"

He sighed. "My wife comes from a small village. It's big enough to support a blacksmith, but only barely. I was able to support my wife and children. We never had any coin to spare, but we got by. Then the Rogandans invaded. Our local baron came to our village to collect men to join the king's army. He told me the army needed blacksmiths. He didn't offer me a choice of course—I had to go with him." He shook his head. "I soon discovered that the army already had plenty of blacksmiths."

Brother Ander nodded. "We had more skilled people than we needed. Those who weren't needed ended up as soldiers."

Breysen looked at him with raised eyebrows. "You were in the army?" He wasn't entirely surprised at the thought. He'd sensed from the beginning that there was more to this monk than met the eye.

"Yes," confirmed Brother Ander with a nod. "I haven't been a monk all my life. How did your family manage while you were away?"

The question poked at painful memories, and Breysen closed his eyes for a moment in an attempt to control his emotions. "Without me there to provide for them, they struggled to survive. When I returned, after the fighting was over, my wife was so thin it scared me. She'd almost wasted away. She looked like she'd aged ten years. There was nowhere near enough food for the children either. In the time I was gone, two of them had weakened and died." Tears welled up in his eyes, and he dashed them away with his arm.

"Did you return to your blacksmithing?"

"I intended to, but while I was gone a young man had started out on his own. He'd been my apprentice when the Rogandans came. He'd injured his leg, so the baron didn't take him as a soldier. As soon as his leg recovered he married, so he had a wife to support as well. There wasn't enough work for both of us."

"Why didn't one of you move?" asked the monk. "Surely other villages could have used a blacksmith."

Breysen looked at him blankly. "How could we do that? My wife's family has lived in that village for generations. Where would I take her? And who'd want strangers moving into their village anyway?"

Brother Ander nodded slowly. "I understand. It was like that where I grew up too. People thought that moving to the next village was migrating to a foreign country. I left to become a soldier when I was still young, and my father was completely baffled when I left. He could never understand why I stayed away." He shrugged, then redirected his attention to Breysen. "What did you do?" he asked.

"Both my wife and I turned our hands to anything that came along. None of it was enough though."

"So you agreed to become a mercenary?"

The abrupt question shocked Breysen, and he stiffened, staring back at the monk out of startled eyes. So the monk really could see right through him. His shoulders slumped in defeat. There was no use pretending. He was exposed now, and he had nowhere to go.

"Yes, it's true. Hazor sent out scouts around the countryside. Once he heard I'd fought at Torbury Scarp he wanted to recruit me. He offered money—a lot of it. He told me our role would be to keep the peace, nothing more, and I believed him." He paused for a moment, stealing a glance at the monk. "I suppose it would be more honest to say I chose to believe him." Breysen shook his head. "It did start out innocently enough."

He sighed deeply. "I gave my wife the initial payment before I left. She'd never seen that much money before. For the first time in years I saw a glimmer of hope in her eyes again, and it convinced me I was doing the right thing. I told her there would be a lot more when I got back. There won't be any more now of course—maybe there never would have been." He ran a shaky hand through his hair. "She won't have used it all yet—she's incredibly thrifty—but when it does run out she'll be destitute again. It will be worse than ever."

He buried his face in his hands.

"You said it started out innocently," said Brother Ander. "What went wrong?"

"After we'd been out on patrol a while we started pursuing a group of armed men. It went very badly for us. After a while I heard a rumor that our real targets were the king and the queen." He nodded in the direction of the campfire.

"I confronted Hazor with the rumor. He was furious with me, but he didn't deny it. I lost all interest in fighting for him then, but what could I do? I couldn't just ride away. Or maybe I didn't have the courage to do it." He hung his head.

He fell silent. As the moments dragged slowly by he discovered, somewhat to his own surprise, that he didn't care about being exposed as much as he'd expected. He was sick to his stomach of feeling conflicted. His unease had grown stronger the longer he worked for Hazor, and he was bone weary of it.

A minor commotion at the campsite distracted his attention. One of the soldiers seemed to have brought in a couple of men to speak with the king. They conversed in low voices for a couple of minutes, then all eyes turned in his direction. The interaction continued for a while longer, before the king appeared to dismiss them. The soldier led them away.

As soon as they were gone, the king headed over to Breysen and the monk, flanked by two of his soldiers.

He faced Breysen, his countenance stern and unyielding. "It seems that you've had trackers on your trail, Breysen. Why are you here?" he asked bluntly. "And why were you traveling with a man who took the queen hostage and threatened her life?"

Breysen's heart sank. He opened his mouth to speak, but nothing came out.

"He originally came here with a group of mercenaries, Your Majesty, led by a man named Hazor," said Brother Ander calmly.

"I am now aware of that," the king replied. "You need to explain yourself," he said to Breysen. He spoke severely, but he appeared willing to listen.

Breysen swallowed. "I was a mercenary, Your Majesty, and I won't pretend otherwise," he said miserably. "I'm only here by accident. Several days ago we were led into battle not far from here. There were plenty of rumors flying, and they said we'd be fighting men led by Will Prentis. We'd been told he was a traitor, but I never believed it. I fought under him at Torbury Scarp, and there was no way I was going to fight him or kill any of his men. I didn't know when I joined that we would ever be asked to fight our own people. As soon as the battle started I concealed myself. I knew it would be seen as the act of a coward, but I didn't care.

"Almost all of Hazor's men were killed. The only reason I survived was because I avoided the fighting. I hid in the forest and waited a few days until the moon was covered with clouds. Kantor, the man who attacked the queen, showed up as I was about to leave. I'd never met him before. Both of us got away on a sentry's horse. Kantor knifed the sentry as we were leaving. There was no need to kill him— I'd knocked the man unconscious."

He stared off in the direction of the campfire. "Kantor would have killed the queen as well if he thought it would benefit him. I think he enjoyed killing. He was never my friend, and I regret having played any part in helping him escape."

The king made no immediate response, and Breysen lowered his head in despair.

Of all the people he could have stumbled upon, why did it have to be the royal party?

10

Lady Ona sat calmly on the windowsill of her suite, gazing down across the rooftops of Arnost. She liked almost every-thing she had seen of this city.

The day she arrived she had dressed as a commoner and hidden her face, then she had wandered among the markets and mingled with the people. Two things were immediately obvious to her. First, the grinding poverty so prevalent in Rog was much less evident in the capital of Arvenon. Second, a mantle of fear had settled over the city. She was used to that in Rog, but somehow it felt out of place in Arnost.

Her inquiries indicated that the mood of the city had changed the moment Pisander and his minions took control. The new masters intended to stamp their authority from the very beginning, and enough people had been hanged for one reason or another to ensure that the populace got the point.

Pisander had based himself in the castle, and it came as no surprise that the biggest changes had taken place there. Many of the former castle servants had quickly abandoned their posts, and by all accounts the people brought in to replace them left much to be desired. The kitchens had clearly been affected—thus far the quality of her food had been disappointing. Cold seemed to ooze out of the walls of any castle, and she'd needed to get angry before fires were lit and properly maintained in her suite.

Even so, she had noticed a cheerful straightforwardness about the people in the markets that hadn't been entirely stifled by the city's new masters. She wondered whether such buoyancy could long survive the arrival of Agon.

Standing up, she stretched luxuriously, delighted at the prospect of an extended period out of the saddle. Her second morning in Arnost had dawned, and it was time she began to stir the pot. An impressive wardrobe had accompanied her on the long journey from Rogand, and she picked her way through the finery, selecting garments in her usual calculated way. On this occasion she wanted to strike a balance between intimidating and provocative. Having arrived with a clear strategy, she intended to waste no time implementing it.

A large mirror had been provided for her use, and she positioned herself before it while her maid fussed around her.

When finally she was satisfied, she sent her maid to fetch a servant who could lead her to Pisander.

The former earl was occupied with one of his soldiers when she arrived. He nevertheless waved her to a chair.

"Where was this disturbance?" he demanded of the soldier.

"In the markets, My Lord," the man replied. "Two of the merchants were complaining loudly about the policies of the current administration."

"Hang them both," Pisander said coldly. "Leave their bodies dangling on the edge of the market square for a few days. The other merchants will benefit from the example."

He dismissed the soldier curtly, and the man departed after a quick bow.

Lady Ona observed the interaction with interest. The punishment might have been excessive considering the offense, but it was consistent with what she knew of Pisander's approach. She couldn't help wondering if the extreme response was partly for her benefit.

The former earl turned to her. "Lady Ona, this is Lord Lygell," he said, nodding toward the official who stood beside him. "I have entrusted him with oversight of Arvenon."

Lygell nodded stiffly. He appeared restless.

Pisander stared at her dispassionately for a moment. "You seem to have made yourself comfortable, My Lady," he observed dryly. He pointed at a parchment that had traveled with her from Rog. "I see that King Agon has requested me to grant you extraordinary powers during your stay in Arnost."

She smiled to herself. Agon wasn't the kind of man who 'requested' anything, and she had no doubt that Pisander understood that as well as she did. "I am sure you and your aides will support me wholeheartedly in my endeavors," she said, fixing both men with a steely gaze.

Pisander seemed bored. "Of course," he replied languidly. "Lygell will provide you with anything you need."

She nodded slowly, redirecting her attention to Lygell. "Tomorrow I will confer with the official responsible for collecting taxes, and also the person who manages the central market. But today I want to meet whoever oversees garbage collection in Arnost. The entire city stinks!" she declared, screwing up her nose in disgust.

Before her comment, Lygell had already been looking uncomfortable. His face now colored red, whether from anger or embarrassment she couldn't tell.

She stared back at him. "You will attend of course," she informed him. "We will meet as soon as I have broken my fast."

With that she gave both men a curt nod, and left the room.

HAVING ESTABLISHED herself in a meeting room provided for her personal use, Lady Ona waited impatiently for Lygell and his underling to arrive.

King Agon had granted her sweeping powers, but she was well aware that respect could not be granted by decree—she needed to build respect herself. She would establish her authority by her actions. She wasn't concerned. She was an ambitious and capable leader with no compunction about manipulating people whenever the need arose.

She needed to start somewhere, and the issue she had seized upon would serve her purposes as well as any. It would give her insight into how administration was handled in the city. And observing how Pisander's people reacted to her intervention would also be very revealing.

Lygell marched into the room, annoyance showing plainly on his face. Having become expert at reading the signs, she could see that he was strongly attracted to her. He was probably irritated by his own response, which would undoubtedly contribute to his frustration. She suppressed a smile. She had no doubt she would win his enthusiastic cooperation before long, one way or another.

The minor official ushered into her presence by Lygell appeared terrified. He had no need to be. Not yet, anyway.

"I am told you are responsible for keeping the streets clean," she told him, keeping her tone neutral.

He shot a glance in the direction of Lygell before nodding once.

"How many people work for you?"

"Fifty," he replied.

She raised her eyebrows. "How many of them actually do their job?"

"Maybe five or six," he replied bitterly.

"And what have you done about it?" she asked patiently.

He looked baffled. "I've threatened to dismiss them. But it hasn't helped."

She nodded. The man was clearly incompetent. The only question that remained was whether he was capable of improvement.

"Here's what you're going to do..." she told him.

Two hours later Lady Ona looked on as the official stood before a small crowd of scruffy men and women in the courtyard.

"Everything is about to change," he told them importantly.

"Beginning right now. I pay you to clean the streets, and you will spend the rest of the day doing it. Then I will assess your work. We will meet here again tomorrow at the same time. If you're not here, you will be hunted down and punished. You are dismissed! Get to work!"

Once they had gone he looked toward Lady Ona expectantly. She nodded her approval.

The following day the official once again met his workers in the courtyard. A count was carried out, and two of them were missing.

A group of guards waited nearby. The official called four of them aside and gave them names and descriptions of the malingerers. "Search for them," he instructed the guards loudly. "When you find them, hang them. They're lazy incompetents, and I've given them too many chances already."

The guards glanced at Lygell. He nodded once, and they hurried away.

Lady Ona rolled her eyes at the garbage official's response. She had no real complaint though—he'd grasped the general idea even if he was a little enthusiastic.

The other workers now watched wide-eyed as the official turned to them. He called one of them forward. It was a woman, and she was trembling uncontrollably as she came to him.

"You've done your job well," he told her. "Your section was the cleanest in the city. Here's your reward." He pressed a couple of coins into her hands. She returned to her place with a look of delighted astonishment on her face.

He called ten other names, and the men and women he had named stepped forward eagerly, all with greed written across their faces. The official glared at them. "Good-for-nothing layabouts!" he yelled. He turned to the remaining guards. "Throw them into the dungeons!" he ordered. "Don't release them until this time tomorrow."

The ten were dragged away screaming and pleading. When they were gone, the official turned to the remaining workers. He had their undivided attention. "You've all seen how things are going to work from now on. You will be paid if you do your jobs properly. Anyone who is lazy will receive a more appropriate reward. Now go and do what you were hired to do!"

When he dismissed them they scurried away, eager to be gone.

Lady Ona was impressed. She approached the official and ruffled his hair indulgently. "Well done," she told him with a little smile. He beamed back at her happily.

Lord Lygell had watched the process silently. As soon as the official had gone, Lygell approached her boldly. Executing a sweeping bow, he invited her to join him for dinner.

The man was pitifully transparent. She kept him hanging for a few moments before accepting his invitation.

She walked away shaking her head. These people weren't going to know what hit them when Agon arrived.

LADY ONA'S initiative with the garbage collection official was just the beginning. Not all of the officials proved to be equally cooperative or teachable, and her efforts yielded mixed outcomes. A few had conspicuously failed to produce results, and she made sure that Lygell threw the worst of them into the dungeons. She didn't offer him a choice. He had appointed the officials, and she suspected that many were personal friends or even relatives. If so, he had no one to blame but himself.

Lygell had exclusively appointed men to positions of authority. Capable women were surely available, and he was the loser by overlooking them.

Ona was a woman with many talents, and she had never limited herself to administration. From the moment of her arrival in Arnost she had begun preparing for more interesting pursuits, and it suited her just fine that Lygell's officials were all men. It made her task that much easier.

Her restless energies had soon been directed along a familiar path. As usual, her endeavors were rewarded with success. As a conspicuously attractive and blatantly available woman, she received attention from a long line of hopefuls among the officials below Pisander. She made no attempt to discourage them.

A few days had now passed since her arrival, and she had set the whole castle buzzing. She had every intention of ensuring it stayed that way.

On that particular afternoon, she followed her usual practice after a meeting, returning to her apartments to change her garments.

As the special envoy of King Agon, Lady Ona had been assigned a lavishly appointed suite in the castle. In the days since her arrival in Arnost she had already added to the imposing array of fine clothing that traveled with her from Rog. Her wardrobe could only be described as formidable. Having selected a dazzling outfit, she occupied her usual position in front of the mirror while her maid prepared her to return to the fray.

Satisfied with her appearance at last, she stepped into the passageway and made her stately way down to the lower levels of the castle.

Having reached ground level, she stepped out into the courtyard to find herself confronted with a heated argument between two men. They abruptly fell silent the moment she appeared, the flush on their faces making it obvious that she had been the subject of their disagreement.

Someone abruptly took her arm, and she looked up into the smiling and handsome features of another of Lygell's self-appointed noblemen. As he led her away from the quarrelers, she aimed a wink in their direction. She couldn't tell if they noticed or not—they were too busy glaring at their supplanter.

Lady Ona shook her head as she turned away. Men could be such babies.

The upheaval was entirely her doing of course. Since her arrival she had been stoking the flames tirelessly. Arnost had provided her with a marvelous new stage on which to strut. None of Pisander's men had any inkling of her existence, and they greeted her arrival with the same open mouthed wonder that a simple shepherd boy might afford a meteor as it flashed across the evening sky.

She boldly flaunted both herself and the authority she enjoyed as Agon's representative. Physical allure and raw power made for a heady mixture, and it was hardly surprising that few could resist.

She never hesitated to take the initiative, although her actions were always understated and indirect.

In Arvenon no less than in Rogand, men and women used subtle hints to communicate availability and degree of interest. Such communication transcended language and custom, and Lady Ona had attained unrivaled mastery at the delicate dance.

The man now at her side had first approached her at a banquet the previous night. They had exchanged a series of charged glances that spoke more eloquently than words. Ona had been anticipating the outcome with considerable interest ever since.

Not everyone succumbed to her glittering intensity. As she glided along beside her new admirer she caught sight of one of the few men who had chosen to ignore her charms. His eyes slid across her as they passed, and she gazed thoughtfully at his retreating back.

She had glimpsed him with a woman of his own hanging on his arm. The woman could not have been called a beauty. Nevertheless it seemed apparent that he had made promises to her, and it was even possible he intended to keep them.

While Lady Ona respected the man's self-restraint, she had no more interest in him than he had in her. People like him bored her.

She returned her attention to her latest paramour. Before they managed to leave the castle grounds their progress was interrupted by the arrival of Lord Lygell. Moving at once to intercept the couple, he approached with chin held high, not deigning even to spare her companion a glance.

"My Lady Ona," he sniffed, thrusting out an arm possessively.

"My Lord Lygell," she replied coldly. "Perhaps you hadn't noticed that my attentions are otherwise engaged at the moment."

Lygell stared back at her dumbfounded. She deftly steered her companion around him.

She didn't bother to glance back to see Lygell's reaction. After her arrival she had allowed the puppet ruler of Arvenon to wine and dine her. He hoped to lure her to his bedchamber as well, but she had declined haughtily. She nevertheless kept him dangling, allowing him to parade about with her on his arm. As a result Lygell dared to imagine he had made a conquest. The fool was about to make the painful discovery that she wasn't the one conquered.

Lady Ona leaned closer to the man at her side. "I trust you are willing to brave the displeasure of your master," she ventured.

His reply was a dismissive snort, and she patted his arm approvingly.

A FEW DAYS later Lady Ona retired to her apartments to review her progress. She had made considerable inroads in her efforts to understand the fledgling power structures of the new Arvenon. Pisander had dredged up officials who were eager to lead, and given them the appearance of credibility by allowing many of them to call themselves nobles. All of them excelled at infighting. Beyond that, the vast majority had little or no idea about effective administration. She had poked and prodded them into action, managing to spearhead a few worthwhile changes in the process, but her view was that many officials were beyond help, from her or anyone else.

The former earl was an obvious exception. To begin with, he was a capable and effective leader much of the time, unlike the majority of his underlings. He was, of course, twisted and unscrupulous, and his methods were frequently inhuman. She could see why Agon had recruited him.

He also seemed immune to her charms. She couldn't quite put her finger on the reason, but if she was reading him correctly it had nothing to do with his proclivities.

His disinterest in her was by no means the strangest thing about him though. There were ways in which he seemed completely vacant, as if portions of his thinking process had gone missing entirely.

For the most part Pisander had reasons for everything he did, and he was both willing and able to articulate those reasons clearly.

When it had anything to do with Agon though, Pisander planned and took action without ever articulating reasons for his behavior.

She shook her head. That wasn't quite right. It wasn't just that Pisander never articulated his reasons—he behaved as if he didn't have reasons. That made no sense.

It brought to mind an experience on a recent visit to the coast near Rog. As a child she had stayed in a pretty cottage perched at the top of a cliff. Finding herself in the area she had sought out the location, eager to savor again the fresh sea air and spectacular views.

Upon arrival she was baffled to find no sign of the cottage. The sea still sparkled and the cliff still towered above it, but something wasn't right. After inquiring of the locals, she was astonished to learn that a large section of cliff had crumbled into the sea, carrying the house with it.

In the same way, some parts of Pisander's thinking processes had seemingly disappeared. Curiously, she'd noticed very similar behavior from Lord Krasmir in Rogand the last time she met with him.

Something strange was going on. Was it possible that Agon had a hand in it? She decided to make an extra effort to keep her eyes and ears open.

Her attention had by no means been focused entirely on Pisander of course. She had cut a swath through the new nobility of Arvenon, most of them proving powerless in the face of her beguilement.

Privately she held her starry eyed admirers in contempt. Bedding them held no interest for her and hadn't proven necessary even once; most of her admirers would have been astonished if they knew how disinclined she had been in that regard. She had been amused to discover that a number of the hopefuls believed they alone had missed out. Perhaps over time they would learn, as she had, that reputation should never be confused with reality.

Her most important conquest had been Lord Lygell, the vain peacock placed in authority over the kingdom by Pisander. She had used him shamelessly to rapidly expand both her influence and her notoriety.

Lygell was a devious man with grand ideas. The real question was whether he could follow through successfully. She had been singularly unimpressed by most of what she had witnessed.

The man had a vicious streak and had taken prodigious advantage of it. After sufficient exposure to him she concluded that he was unwittingly compensating for a deeply rooted lack of confidence. Once or twice she'd been tempted to croon in his ear, "There, there. Didn't daddy take you seriously?"

She smiled wryly to herself, trying to imagine how he might react to such behavior. Violently, if she knew anything. She'd have been forced to kill him, and that might have led to misunderstandings.

No, she was better off humoring him. She'd be doing it from a distance in future. Sooner or later he'd get over the humiliation of being dumped by her.

A servant appeared at her doorway. "The Earl of Pisander requests that you join him," he said with a bow.

Her curiosity aroused, she left her apartments and followed the man to the upper reaches of the castle. On the way they passed Lord Lygell. Peering at her inquisitively, he swung in behind her and followed tentatively in her wake.

She soon arrived at a small meeting room to find Pisander standing beside the window waiting for her. The servant bowed and excused himself.

Lygell had followed her to the entrance of the room, and he stood peering in with a look of mingled envy and annoyance. Adopting a prim smile, she moved serenely to the door and closed it in his startled face.

She turned back to Pisander. "My Lord Earl, I believe you requested to see me. What is your pleasure?" she asked boldly.

He stared at her for a moment, an unreadable expression on his face.

"I have found you to be...accomplished," he said. "You get things done. You have a way of drawing the best from people, even as you manipulate them. And you don't hesitate to fully use your...formidable assets."

The unexpected compliments brought a pert smile to her face. She offered him a slight bow.

Pisander continued. "I have a task I wish to offer you, one that requires unusual delicacy. A successful outcome would lead to further opportunities. I am sure I don't need to state that the inducements would be considerable."

She stared back at him coolly. "You have people of your own. Assign the task to one of them."

His brows drew together in a deep frown. "Far too many of my subordinates disappoint me," he said. He shook his head. He mumbled, almost to himself, "I have need of a Will Prentis, or someone very like him."

Her eyebrows rose at once. "There's that name again," she said thoughtfully. "I would very much like to meet this Will Prentis. I have heard a great deal about him, and he sounds uncommonly promising." She twirled a finger around a loose strand of her dangling hair, lost in her imaginings.

Pisander glowered at her. "Are you refusing my offer?"

"I am," she told him bluntly. "King Agon didn't send me here to become one of your paid lackeys. You have been appointed by the king to act on his behalf, and I am here to report on your effectiveness. I plan to do just that. No more, and no less."

She turned on her heel and glided from the room without bothering to wait for Pisander's reaction.

Lygell was skulking in the corridor, and he reached out hesitantly to her as she approached. Lady Ona ignored him, sweeping past without a backward glance.

11

———

Pleasant as Arnost might be, Lady Ona soon decided she was ready to leave. She quickly wearied of the men who fawned incessantly upon her. Some of them boasted openly to anyone who would listen about their supposed exploits with the foreign beauty. She shook her head in disdain. They were equally pathetic. It would be refreshing just for once to meet a real man in this former kingdom.

Pisander was the only reasonably capable leader among them, even if she couldn't entirely figure him out. As for Lygell, although he wielded significant authority, he was heavily reliant on his underlings to make him look good, and most of them were not delivering.

Agon had reason to be gravely concerned.

Pisander's attempt to recruit her had also made her curious. What were the crucial tasks he needed her to carry out? She immediately began digging. The results were revealing.

Pisander controlled Arnost and the surrounding countryside. She was not aware of any organized resistance. She had briefly visited the dungeons to observe Lord Bottren, the man placed in charge of Arnost by King Steffan when he left for Paradise Valley. She didn't understand the reasons why Pisander kept him alive, but whatever they might be it was clear that Bottren offered no threat. He was a shell of the man he must once have been.

Two Arvenian armies still existed, both under the control of men appointed by Pisander. One was camped to the west outside Erestor, and the other to the north on the border with Castel. She had learned that these armies largely consisted of veterans of the war with Rogand, which suggested they were formidable fighting units. However, since they had been given no recent tasks to perform, it was impossible to form any assessment of their new leadership or their current effectiveness.

One very serious concern had emerged. The attempt to assassinate the rulers of Arvenon, Castel, and Varas had met with limited success, with the king of Castel the only confirmed kill. No one could state with certainty that either King Steffan or Queen Essanda was dead.

In view of that, Lygell had sent two large squads to Paradise Valley with orders to finish off the Arvenian king and queen. Neither squad had reported back.

Unconfirmed reports suggested that a large body of men had been seen riding in the opposite direction, away from Paradise Valley. No reports of any kind had been received since then. Lygell's men had apparently vanished from the face of the earth.

If Lady Ona had been placed in charge of Arvenon, she would have found this information very disturbing indeed. She would have placed the highest priority on getting to the bottom of it.

Decisive action was clearly needed in a number of crucial areas. Lygell held the reins of power, but the man was paralyzed. He seemed more concerned about Lady Ona's indifference toward him than about fulfilling his responsibilities.

Pisander clearly harbored many frustrations about his underlings, and with good reason. It wasn't difficult to see why he had tried to recruit her.

In spite of the challenges faced by Pisander, Lady Ona could only marvel at how much the disgraced exile had achieved. It was true that King Steffan and Queen Essanda had not yet been accounted for, but

Pisander's accomplishments were nevertheless remarkable. He had wrested control of Arvenon, or at least Arnost and most of Arvenon, from the ruling monarchs. The assassination attempt had been accompanied by a smooth and rapid takeover of the capital. The entire Arvenian army had quickly been placed under the command of men loyal to Pisander. The magnitude of these achievements should not be understated.

At the same time, it was equally obvious that after seizing power so effectively, Pisander was finding the task of wielding power considerably more challenging.

To function well, a kingdom required more than just willing leaders. An endless list of routine but essential roles needed to be carried out by competent people. The garbage disposal system in Arnost offered a perfect example. Until her intervention, it had been heading for collapse. Sooner or later the result would have been disease and death, with the rich and powerful suffering along with the poor.

There was a limit to how much she could achieve, and it had become obvious to Lady Ona that little could be gained by remaining in Arnost. She accordingly began making preparations to return to Rog. Pisander offered no response of any kind when she notified him of her plans. She didn't bother even to inform Lygell.

King Agon had sent her to review the overall strategic situation in Arvenon, and to get the measure of Pisander and his henchmen. She had done what she came to do.

The king wasn't going to be at all happy when he heard her report.

KING AGON STARED WILDLY at Ennawi, his eyes almost popping out of his head. Agon's heart was pounding, and he could feel his veins standing out. He ground his teeth noisily before tilting his head back and shouting at the top of his voice.

The king turned away without bothering to see if his mute

servant had registered a reaction. A response of any kind was so unlikely it wasn't worth checking for.

A small figurine lay on a side table in his apartments. Reaching down for it, the king hurled it across the room. The sight of the ornament hitting the wall and shattering into pieces felt intensely satisfying. His breathing began to slow, and his heart gradually stopped racing.

When he was almost feeling normal again he turned back to his servant. "Did you know who summoned Krasmir to Rog?" he asked calmly. "It was me! I wanted to brief him on the practicalities of ruling. I can't hand over power without some kind of preparation."

He threw up his hands. "I even thought I might pass on some of the subtleties. What made me think it was going to be straightforward?"

Agon drew closer to Ennawi and peered into his eyes. "Krasmir's a complete idiot. Why didn't any of my servants warn me?" He jabbed a finger into Ennawi's chest. "Why didn't *you* warn me?"

The king released a huge sigh. "I'm meeting with the fool again in the morning. Did you know I've been avoiding my sword, Ennawi?" he asked. "Sometimes I feel my hand twitching for it." He reached out a trembling hand and examined it.

"I can't trust myself with a sword. It wouldn't matter if I decapitated one of my servants—you, for instance. No one would care. But I'd end up lopping off Krasmir's head, and that would make the last three weeks a complete waste of my time. Worse, I'd be leaving for Arnost without a regent."

He clenched and unclenched his fists. Then he closed his eyes and took another deep breath. Finally he left his apartments, still struggling to keep his composure.

Two agents were brought to the king as soon as he had settled himself into the small reception chamber adjoining his private apartments. The king came immediately to the point. "Well? What have you learned about Krasmir?" he asked bluntly.

"He has a reputation for brutality, Your Majesty," one of them said.

"I know that," snapped the king.

The agent hesitated. "It seems that the reputation is not well founded," he finally added.

Agon frowned. "What? Impossible! What are you talking about?"

"Our sources suggest that Lord Krasmir has encouraged false rumors to reinforce his reputation for barbarity. One of his servants claims he even intentionally dresses like a brute to support the idea."

"Why would he do that?" demanded Agon.

"Apparently to discourage people from daring to challenge his authority, Your Majesty."

The king shook his head dismissively. His own opinion of Krasmir was nothing new—he had believed for many years that Krasmir was little better than a beast. Other members of the Rogandan nobility saw it the same way. His agents had more than once reported comments to that effect. It was impossible to believe that Krasmir had been putting on an act all along.

"What of his wife and children?"

"None of them have ever uttered a word on the subject, Your Majesty. But we secretly observed him with his family. He appears to treat them with great gentleness. And he has an old mother. All of his servants claim that the two of them dote on each other."

The king fell silent.

"Not one of his household servants has ever been heard whispering about the way their lord treats them. We learned that positions among his household servants are greatly coveted. Once he appoints a servant, they never want to leave."

The king's brows were furrowed. "What about his intelligence?"

"He is regarded as sharp-witted and shrewd, Your Majesty. Those who know him best all agree on that."

"And his estates?"

"Well managed by all accounts."

The king dismissed his agents, struggling to fully grasp the implications of all they had said.

Their reports had shaken him. Was it actually possible that Krasmir's reputation was nothing more than a clever pretense? Had the nobleman truly succeeded in deceiving everyone, including the king?

The most important question was whether Krasmir could be trusted. Was he a danger to Agon or his interests? He quickly dismissed any such notion—without the Stone of Authority he might have considerable cause for concern. Having subjected Krasmir to the stone, he had no doubt that the nobleman could be trusted to act in the royal interest.

As he pondered it further, he reminded himself that the nobleman had never been known to act in either an aggressive or a duplicitous manner. He was wealthy and powerful, but he had not attained that status at the expense of his peers among the nobility. His deception—assuming that's what it truly was—seemed primarily defensive in nature. He apparently wanted to make others think twice before moving against him.

It did give the king pause. He had spent a lot of time with Krasmir in recent weeks, and he had witnessed the stupidity of the nobleman for himself. It now occurred to him that other explanations could also be offered.

Was it possible that he had misjudged Krasmir? He instantly discarded the thought. No king worthy of the name doubted himself.

"I HAVE ALREADY EXPLAINED THAT, My Lord," snapped Agon, eyeing Krasmir closely as he said it.

Krasmir gazed back at him, his eyes glazed.

There was no fight at all in the nobleman, and Agon knew he could thank the Stone of Authority for that. But Krasmir appeared obtuse and uncomprehending, and if the reports of Agon's agents were to be believed, the man was anything but dull-witted. The stone was surely not to blame either. According to the scroll, the stone neither diminished nor enhanced the intelligence of the people it influenced.

Was Krasmir putting on another act?

Agon groaned. Whether Krasmir was dull-witted or not, the king had little choice but to persevere with these briefings in the hope that the nobleman would finally begin to make sense of it all.

"I will explain it again," said the king irritably. "Pay attention this time!"

* * *

LORD KRASMIR WALKED beside the king, working hard to conceal his boredom. The last few weeks had felt like the longest of his life. The king intended to bring Arvenon finally to heel, and he expected it to involve a long absence from Rogand. With that in mind he had approached Krasmir to explore the possibility of appointing the nobleman as regent.

Krasmir supposed he should have felt honored, but it increasingly felt like a bad dream. The regency itself wasn't the problem. It was the time preparing for it with the king.

"As my representative, you will be expected to attend the solstice festivals at the temple," the king was saying.

Krasmir was familiar with the solstice festivals, but on the rare occasions he attended he had paid no attention at all to the role of the king. He therefore found himself wondering what he would be expected to say, what symbolic acts he might need to perform, when he should arrive, and how long he would need to stay at the festival.

If only he dared ask.

Krasmir knew that the king believed he was providing a detailed briefing. As far as the nobleman was concerned, Agon did little more than ramble on endlessly, usually without addressing the most important questions. His long-winded explanations were rarely useful, yet he apparently felt the need to repeat himself over and over again. More often than not, Krasmir found it almost impossible to make sense of any of it. Worse, any request for the tiniest clarification inevitably led to Agon rolling his eyes and repeating everything again with exaggerated patience, each time without making it any clearer.

The king wasn't stupid. He just wasn't naturally gifted as a tutor.

And having always done whatever he pleased without question, he'd never developed the skill of explaining himself.

Even when Krasmir did understand the king's ways of doing things, they didn't always make sense to him. Every one of Krasmir's peers on the Great Council had recognized for years that the king was often his own worst enemy. No one was more practiced than Agon at working against his own best interests.

Not one of the nobles was foolish enough to say so. The king derived far too much delight from ordering executions.

It was frustrating, because Krasmir intended well. He didn't at all understand why he had the king's best interests at heart, especially in light of their shared history, but the truth was that the king could trust him completely.

Krasmir could only carry on in the hope that it would all work out somehow.

12

———

Kernon peered toward the lone figure of Will Prentis standing on the outskirts of the forest. "That's him all right," he said.

Lord Redfass looked at Jonas. "So you were on the level," he said.

"We had our doubts," Namor added coolly.

Jonas shrugged.

Kernon ignored them. He had eyes only for Will Prentis. "He's making no attempt to flee," he observed, shaking his head.

"That makes no sense," said Namor, frowning. "If he's entirely alone, why is he so calm?" He began peering around uneasily.

"I have no idea," Kernon replied. "But we need to take him down before he decides to make a run for it."

Jonas pulled his sword. "Who said he's entirely alone?" he asked fiercely. Kernon looked at him blankly.

Swinging his horse around, Jonas dug in his heels and charged at Redfass. The expression of the mercenary leader changed in an instant from puzzlement to fury. He raised his sword defensively, but Jonas drove furiously through his guard and sent him crashing from the saddle. Both Kernon and Namor watched open-mouthed. Before they could react, Jonas turned away and galloped toward the lone figure among the trees.

With a cry of rage, Kernon rose in his stirrups, calling the men forward. A shout arose, and the entire line of horsemen charged after Jonas.

As Kernon galloped forward, he noticed something happening along the line of trees. His eyes went wide as horsemen streamed out from between the trees, surging past both Jonas and Will Prentis.

A huge soldier rode at their head, and Kernon's heart abruptly missed a beat when he realized who it was. Rufe Sarjant was leading the charge. Where had he come from?

A hunting horn sounded from somewhere behind them, then another. They were surrounded. Kernon saw then that they had been outwitted and deceived.

It made no difference. Victory or death, there was no backing out now.

Kernon galloped forward, screaming his defiance.

The lines crashed together, and Kernon's world descended into a confusion of shouting men and screaming horses. He had fought before, but the fury of the men before him was unlike anything he had encountered. His attackers were literally howling for blood. And there were so many of them.

Assaulted from two sides, Kernon cast his eyes around frantically, searching for support. No help would be coming. All of the mercenaries were equally beset, and men went down even as his glance fell on them.

Taking advantage of his distraction, his attackers broke through his defenses. He toppled to the ground, agonizing pain overwhelming him. Before everything went dark a face he recognized flashed briefly into view. His fading thought was the realization that he had been brought low by his own soldiers—the men he had left waiting in the camp below Steffan's Citadel.

THOMAS REMAINED among the trees when the fighting started. He had never witnessed a battle on this scale before, and even as a distant observer he found the experience confronting. The chaos bewildered him—how could any commander make sense of what was happening?—and the harrowing cries of men and horses oppressed him.

To his untrained eye there was little to distinguish between the two sides, and when the fighting eventually ended he wasn't at first certain who had won. It was with enormous relief that he eventually spotted Will. The commander stood on a low mound surveying the scene, Rufe and Jonas beside him. All of them appeared unharmed and in control of the situation.

Thomas eventually mustered the courage to approach them, although he stayed out of the way, both to avoid distracting them and because he felt completely out of place.

After the battle, soldiers collapsed to the ground in exhaustion. Others tended to the wounded. No one seemed to notice his arrival, and he was happy to remain inconspicuous.

Thomas's attention was soon drawn to Will. The commander mounted his horse and rode slowly among the men, greeting them and thanking them for their efforts. A murmur of voices rose in anticipation as he drew near. Hands reached out to touch his horse as he passed. Even the faces of gravely wounded men lit up when he turned their way, his regard somehow dulling their pain for a time.

Was it always like this after a battle? Thomas had heard about Will's reputation, but he'd always assumed it arose from his uncanny strategic abilities. He saw now that there was more to the commander than he'd ever imagined.

"They claimed you were a traitor," one of the soldiers called to Will, shaking his head.

"Yeah. Supposedly you'd run off to Varas!" scoffed another. "Rufe too."

"None of us believed it. Not for a minute," said a soldier. Loud grunts of assent accompanied the remark.

"I am grateful to you all," Will told them. "After the lies you'd been told, we didn't know what to expect," he said frankly.

Many of the soldiers looked baffled at the idea there could be any uncertainty about their response. "'Will needs your help,'" one of them said simply. "That's what Rufe told us." He said it as if no further explanation was necessary.

The men around him grunted their affirmation.

Will nodded gravely, and moved on.

Thomas looked on in astonishment. How could any leader inspire such devotion from battle-hardened warriors? He felt like he was seeing Will properly for the first time.

These men called him 'Will', not Lord Torbury, and Will made no move to correct them. Thomas guessed that many of the soldiers had served under him at Torbury Scarp. Will was the kind of man to value the bond he shared with his men far above any formal title.

After spending time moving among the soldiers, Will made his way to a large group of men off to one side. The survivors from Lord Redfass's mercenary force—perhaps eighty men—had been herded together and stripped of their weapons. They gave him a very different kind of response. Most of them had been sprawling listlessly on the ground. They sat up at once when they saw who was approaching. Some faces showed defiance. Others simply showed fear.

Will sat on his horse for a considerable time, regarding them silently. "What's that symbol tattooed onto your right arms?" he finally asked.

At first no one responded, but eventually one of the men said, "It's Lord Redfass's mark. He required every man who signed on with him to have it."

The commander studied the men thoughtfully. "It would be simplest just to kill you all. You deserve it after your treason."

Many faces paled at his remark. But he had more to say.

"I'm going to give you a second chance. You can leave and go wherever you want. You'll be going without your weapons and without your horses. Take a water skin and food from your saddle-bags—nothing more. Every one of you can be identified by your tattoo. If you ever sign on as mercenaries again, you won't receive mercy a second time."

The men were led to their horses to collect a few provisions, then they were escorted away. Thomas noticed a few of them scowling, but most seemed grateful to have escaped with their lives.

The men had been gone for only a few minutes when Thomas noticed a commotion off in the distance. Most of the mercenaries were still striding away, shadowed by a mounted escort. But about twenty men had broken away from the main group and stopped entirely. Two of the soldiers escorting the group had remained with them, and a third was riding back toward Will.

"What's the holdup?" Will asked when the soldier arrived.

"Some of the men insist they want to join your army, Will," he replied. "What do you want us to do with them?"

Will turned to Rufe and raised his eyebrows.

Rufe nodded. "I'll check them out," he said. "Where's Thomas?" he asked.

Thomas rode forward. "Over here, Rufe," he called.

The two of them rode together to the smaller group. Thomas tried to look casual, but it brightened him enormously to know that Rufe thought he might have something to offer.

"Tell me if you see anything unusual," Rufe said as they approached the men.

Bringing the stone into contact with his skin, Thomas scanned the men. In most of them he saw regret and a desire to set things right. Two of the men were concealing a very different set of motives.

Rufe glanced in his direction, and without saying a word Thomas pointed the two men out.

Seeing that the game was up, both of them immediately turned and sprinted off after the main group.

"The others?" asked Rufe.

Thomas furrowed his brows for a moment, then nodded slowly.

"Come with us," Rufe told them. "The final decision lies with Will."

Thomas quietly exhaled a sigh of relief as they rode back to the commander. He'd finally been able to make a contribution of his own. Until that moment he'd felt completely useless.

When they reached Will, the commander turned a questioning look on the men.

"We didn't sign up to fight you or the king, Will," one of them told him. "I was with you at Torbury Scarp!"

Will eyed him for a moment, then cast his eyes across the whole group. "I'm willing to give you a chance," he told them. "Don't make me regret it."

Unable to contain their delight, they all began talking at once, their faces glowing.

"Shall I spread them throughout the ranks?" asked Rufe.

Will shook his head. "No. The other men will give them a hard time. Find them a captain of their own. They'll do better if they stay together."

Rufe nodded and headed off with Timo to find someone suitable to lead them.

They returned with a grizzled veteran who looked as if he wouldn't take any nonsense. But he spoke to the men reasonably enough as he led them away.

Will never seemed able to relax. He called Timo to his side. "Rufe told me you were leading half of the men today," he said. "You did well."

"Thanks, Will," Timo replied. "It was an honor."

"I'm going to need to ask much more of you," Will told him. "I want you to lead this army."

His request clearly took Timo by surprise. "What about you? And Rufe?"

"We're needed elsewhere. We can talk more about it later. Are you willing to lead?"

Timo nodded.

"Then you can make a start almost immediately. I'm expecting a couple of visitors soon. When they arrive I'll need you to call the men together."

Timo nodded once more. "I'll be ready."

Thomas could readily guess who the visitors might be, and he was not surprised when the king and queen rode in, escorted by Jonas and a sizable group of soldiers.

Timo gathered the troops together, and a ripple of anticipation passed through them when they realized who stood before them.

Will led the king to a mound, and he climbed upon it and faced the troops.

Every head was turned to him as he addressed them in a loud voice. "You have been reunited with your commander today." Loud whoops of jubilation broke out across the throng. "You have fought at his side once more, and you have won!" The king had to wait for some time before the cheering subsided.

"You have cast aside the traitors who claimed to be acting in my name. The kingdom is not yet safe, though. The traitors are led by the former Earl of Pisander, the man who plotted to turn Arnost over to the Rogandan commander during the invasion. At the time your commander exposed him and prevented him from carrying out his plan. Then you crushed the Rogandan army at Torbury Scarp!" Deafening cheers broke out.

The king continued when the din subsided a little. "We thought that the war was over. But King Agon of Rogand paid Pisander to hire assassins. They tried to kill me and the queen, along with our allies, King Istel of Castel and King Delmar of Varas. It grieves me to say that King Istel, my father-in-law, was killed. I was gravely wounded, but your queen fought back vigorously, and with the help of others the assassins were driven off."

More cheering broke out. The queen waved to them, and the men roared in response.

The king continued as soon as the noise abated. "I wish I could tell you that the kingdom is now secure. But it is not. Pisander has taken control of Arnost, and he intends to repay his debt to King Agon of Rogand by inviting him to Arnost. The king of Rogand expects to take control of Arvenon."

The king's news was initially met by stunned silence, but a howl of anger quickly went up at the suggestion of a Rogandan king taking control of Arnost. Only a few years had passed since these men and their comrades had suffered and died to prevent exactly that outcome.

The king waited until the clamor died down. "We will need you to secure our border with Rogand. Agon must be prevented from entering Arvenon." A growl of affirmation rose at this statement.

"There is a great deal at stake still, and I must borrow your commander for a while longer. I promise that you will be capably led by trustworthy men, though." Without waiting for the grunts of dismay to die down, the king called out more loudly than ever, "But I can leave you with some exceedingly good news!" At this, Queen Essanda stepped up beside him, holding a bundle in her arms. "Your queen has given birth to our son and heir! I present to you Prince Aiden!"

The king took the baby from his wrappings and thrust him into the air above the multitude.

His news was greeted with a thunderous roar of acclamation. Thomas joined in at the top of his lungs. The cheering continued until the king gave a final wave and stepped down with the queen and baby prince.

Will quickly took their place, holding up his hands for silence. The din gradually died away.

"As you have heard, I need to accompany the king and queen for a while longer. In the meantime, you will be led by one of your own— Timo." As he was speaking, he waved Timo up beside him.

The appointment was greeted by more muted applause, but Thomas noticed many heads nodding in silent approval. It appeared that Timo would begin with the cautious support of his men. Whether or not the support matured into enthusiasm would be up to him.

Thomas had little doubt about the outcome. Will would never have appointed Timo if he didn't already hold him in high regard, and Thomas had witnessed Will's ability as a judge of character. He also knew from personal experience that Will had a way of drawing out the potential in a person.

Spotting Elena among the royal party, Thomas eagerly set out to join her.

HIDDEN AMONG THE TREES, Carnwill watched with fascination as the ascendancy of Redfass and his cronies came to a sudden and decisive end.

The appearance of the king and queen of Arvenon ought to have been enough to capture Carnwill's full attention, but his eyes were drawn only to a young woman of rare beauty. He was not at all surprised when the companion of the big soldier sought her out after the battle. The way they embraced settled once and for all the question of their identity.

Carnwill was looking at Thomas Stablehand and his wife, and a gloating smile came over his face as he eyed his prize. King Agon would be very pleased indeed.

Wresting Thomas away from the soldiers would present a worthy challenge, but it was someone else's problem.

13

The commander of Steffan's Citadel stood on the battlements gazing down at the camp below him. Soldiers had returned to it the previous day, but tents were now being taken down and the men showed every sign of preparing to leave. Something significant had clearly happened down there. He wanted answers, but he was not willing to risk sending any of his men.

He was about to turn away when he noticed a small group of men riding up from the camp toward the citadel. He peered down curiously at them until they disappeared from sight as they reached the gates.

A soldier soon climbed to the battlements and approached him. "A visitor has arrived at the gates of the citadel, Commander," he said. "He claims he has permission to enter."

The commander frowned. "Who is it?" he demanded. He had been commanded to close the border between Erestor and the rest of Arvenon, and to deny access to all comers, with just two exceptions: Lord Burtelen, who had already passed through the gates, and Lord Torbury, better known as Will Prentis.

"It's Will Prentis."

The commander glanced at the soldier in amazement. "You mean Lord Torbury. How do you know for certain it's him?"

"A number of the men recognized him."

"Well don't just stand there, man! Let him in!"

THE FOLLOWING morning the commander sat in his private quarters pondering the events of the last couple of days. The brief contact with Lord Torbury the previous day had raised many questions while providing few answers. A conference had been arranged, though, and it was due to begin in a little over two hours. To the commander's astonishment, Lord Torbury had announced that the king and queen would be attending.

Since then the citadel had been buzzing with activity. The commander's men were scurrying about the citadel, scrubbing, tidying, and preparing refreshments. Now, with most of the work done, the commander finally felt able to relax. He was anticipating the meeting with considerable interest.

His musing was interrupted by one of his aides. "The duke has arrived and wishes to see you, Commander."

"The duke? Already?" The commander raised his eyebrows. "It's surely only a couple of days since we sent him a message. Show him to our best guest chambers and make sure he is comfortable. I will come down directly."

The aide hurried away to do his bidding.

The citadel had never been in better condition for a surprise visit by the duke. The timing of Lord Torbury's meeting was fortuitous indeed. The commander put on his best uniform and headed down the stairs.

He entered the guest chambers to find the duke sipping on a goblet of wine. "My Lord Duke—this is an unexpected pleasure! I sent a message to alert you to some changes, but I didn't expect you would even receive it before today."

The duke smiled. "Yes, I encountered the messenger on my way here. It seems to have been excellent timing on my part."

"To what do we owe the honor of your visit?" the commander asked.

"Two men—one of whom is known to me—arrived with a message from Lord Torbury," the duke replied. "I rode here with the messengers," he concluded with a smile.

The commander's eyebrows rose in surprise. How had these messengers reached Maranelle if they came from Lord Torbury? The only way into Erestor was through the citadel, and no one at all had been admitted in recent days.

The commander thrust aside his own questions. "As it happens I will be meeting with Lord Torbury in little over an hour. He is planning to bring the king and queen with him. Perhaps you would be willing to join us?"

"It would be my pleasure, Commander. Perhaps you would be kind enough to send the king and queen to my quarters when they first arrive."

"As you wish, My Lord Duke."

The commander bowed and departed.

THE DUKE RELEASED a deep sigh of satisfaction. It was good to relax for a moment before Will Prentis arrived with the king and queen.

He had been taking his ease in a comfortable armchair in the private chamber set aside by the commander for his use whenever he visited the citadel. The journey from Maranelle to the citadel took longer than he'd remembered, and his old bones had felt thoroughly shaken up by the time he arrived. It had become obvious to him on the first day of riding that he should have taken the advice of his aides and used a carriage. Riding was so much faster than a carriage, though, and the information provided by Rellan convinced him that timing was important. The imminent meeting with Will, and especially with the king and queen, provided an ample demonstration of the benefits of moving quickly.

"Uncle! What an unexpected pleasure!" King Steffan beamed a smile as he burst through the door.

The duke rose to his feet. "Your Majesty!" he replied with a smile of delight. "I hadn't expected to see you when I came here. I've been hearing such alarming rumors about you in recent weeks."

"Probably most of them are true," the king replied grimly.

"And Queen Essanda!" said the duke as she appeared in the doorway. "Just look at you!"

He favored Essanda with a wink, and she flew across the room into his open arms. As he embraced her warmly, he peered at the king from over her head. "You're fortunate I'm not forty years younger, Steffan," he said, "or you might have had some serious competition for the hand of this beautiful young woman."

Steffan laughed. "You're far too late," he said. "She's all mine!"

Essanda pulled back from the duke and tossed the hair from her face. "We have a surprise for you, Uncle," she said with a twinkle in her eye. She turned away and hurried from the room.

He shook his head in admiration as he gazed at her retreating back. His quips to his nephew might have been flippant, but she truly was captivating.

He locked eyes with Steffan, raising an eyebrow as he nodded in the direction she had gone. "She's quite something, isn't she?" he asked with a wink.

Steffan grinned back at him.

She soon returned with a bundle in her arms. "I would like to present to you Crown Prince Aiden," she said, lifting her chin proudly.

The duke's eyes widened. "This is wonderful news!" he said with a beaming smile. "Congratulations to you both!"

The baby let out a lusty squawk as Essanda handed him to her uncle. The old duke held him awkwardly for a moment, then hastily handed him back, exhaling with relief as Essanda took the baby in her arms. She jigged the little prince up and down for a few moments until he settled.

The duke shook his head. "There's a reason why such delights are entrusted to the young," he said, pointing at the infant.

"He does bring us great delight," said the king. "And he arrived hard on the heels of the most difficult time of our lives." His face grew serious. "There's a lot we have to tell you, Uncle. But it can wait a while longer. We are planning to discuss the future with Will. I can't tell you how pleased I am that we'll be able to include you in the conversation."

"Well let's get to it," said the duke, clapping the king on the shoulder and heading out the door. One of the soldiers stationed outside his private room led them all to the reception hall.

As they walked the duke leaned over to the king. "It's only fair to let you know that none of your news came as a complete surprise," he said. "Rellan reached me a couple of days ago with his friend Petar and briefed me fully. You have him to thank for my presence at the citadel. The three of us traveled here together."

They entered the hall to find Rellan talking energetically with Will, Rufe, and Jonas. The commander of the citadel sat nearby, although he wasn't participating in the conversation. Brother Ander sat off to one side, looking as if he felt a little out of place.

When the king and queen entered with the duke, everyone immediately pushed back their chairs and rose to their feet.

"Please, there's no need to get up," protested the queen.

All of them sat down again except the citadel commander, who made to leave. The king waved him to a seat. "Please stay, Commander. You are most welcome to join us." he said graciously.

"We face some difficult challenges," the king began. "Arnost is under the control of the former Earl of Pisander. I'm sure you are all aware of his history. It isn't good news for anyone in the kingdom, especially the long-suffering people of Arnost."

The duke hung his head. It had been his responsibility to execute Pisander, and he would never forgive himself for having allowed the traitor to slip through his fingers.

"We have regained control of the western army stationed here at Steffan's Citadel," the king continued. "And once we can combine forces with reinforcements from Erestor we will have a sizable force available to us."

"Several thousand soldiers under arms are stationed nearby," the duke told him. "I expected that you would need them sooner or later."

"Thank you," the king replied. "Even with your soldiers, our task will be far from easy. We know that Pisander has invited Agon of Rogand to join him in Arnost. If Agon is allowed to establish himself there, it will not be easy to remove him. We must make every effort to prevent that from happening. Closing our border with Rogand is the first step."

"Based on what the duke has told us, we should have enough men to do that once the army from Erestor joins us," said Will.

The king nodded. "Retaking Arnost from Pisander is also a key priority. We don't have enough men to do both though." He nodded to the duke. "My uncle did an excellent job of repairing Arnost's defenses only a few years ago. That is not going to work in our favor on this occasion."

"You are right, Your Majesty," agreed Will. "A great deal will also hinge on whether Count Ranauld is able to regain control of the northern army camped outside Castel at Deadman's Pass."

"Yes. If the number of men camped outside the citadel offers any indication, I imagine that the army on the Castelan border must be considerably larger than the one here," said the king. "Even with those men we won't have the strength both to secure the border and retake Arnost. Without them, we will struggle simply to maintain our position."

"Perhaps it's time to consider other options," offered the duke.

All heads turned in his direction.

"I imagine that King Delmar would believe himself to be in your debt," he said. "And Varas seems to be the one kingdom that has largely been spared upheaval. Perhaps he would be willing to help."

"That has occurred to me," the king replied cautiously.

"Would you approach King Delmar yourself, or send a representative?" asked the duke.

King Steffan did not hesitate before responding. "What we need from Delmar is an army. He can't send an army into Arvenon without my direct involvement—it would be an act of aggression."

The king shook his head decisively. "No, I need to be there in person."

"The major challenge, Your Majesty," said Will, "would be getting you to Varacellan safely. It's a grueling ride that would take more time than we can easily afford—it's a very long journey. We know because we've already ridden much of the way not long ago.

"It's likely to be dangerous too. We can't predict when we might encounter mercenaries from the northern army camped outside Castel or other men controlled by Pisander. To properly protect you and the queen we would need to divide our available force, weakening the army we send to the border."

"That isn't the only way to get to Varacellan," said the duke.

Everyone looked at him questioningly.

"Varacellan is a seaport," he reminded them. "You could board a ship from Maranelle with a small escort and be in the Varasan capital in just a few days."

The duke could not resist smiling at their faces. From their reaction, he might have been suggesting they all take poison.

"Shortening the journey is an attractive idea, My Lord Duke," said Will evenly. "But we mustn't overlook the risks."

"Sea monsters?" asked the duke innocently.

Will did not respond, but he was clearly not excited by the duke's proposal.

Only the commander of the citadel seemed to take the suggestion seriously. "I have taken more than one sea voyage," he said, "and I found it less difficult than I expected."

"I can certainly echo the sentiments of the good commander," the duke offered with a smile.

"Have any of the rest of you been on a ship?" asked the king, looking around the group. "I've traveled on small river craft on occasion, but I've never been to sea."

Every one of the others shook their heads, a few of them emphatically.

"We have one person among us with extensive experience at sea," said Brother Ander.

All eyes turned to the monk.

"Who is that, Brother Ander?" asked the king.

"Breysen," he replied.

The king's immediate response was a disdainful grunt.

The queen was not satisfied to leave it at that. "I don't think we should be so quick to dismiss him," she said.

"I believe Your Majesty is wise as well as gracious," said Brother Ander, dipping his head respectfully in the direction of the queen. "Listening to Breysen's story gave me a new perspective on his actions."

"How can we trust him?" asked the king. Seeing the look on his wife's face, he added placatingly, "I haven't forgotten that he risked his life to defend you. That is worth a great deal to me."

"I am willing to do some further investigations," said Rufe. "I'll take Thomas with me," he added, with a glance at Will.

Will's face was unreadable, but he added, "A good idea, Rufe. Take Elena too."

The duke looked curiously at Will. The mention of Thomas abruptly reminded him of the momentous meeting in Arnost during the Rogandan invasion—the council of lords meeting where Pisander had been exposed. Thomas had been no more than a tousle haired youth. He had been brought to the meeting by Will, and the duke remembered him standing awkwardly off to one side.

Will had never explained why he had invited Thomas or exactly what role he had played in identifying the traitor. Thomas had been fingering something in his pouch—what was it? The duke wasn't the only person present at the meeting who had asked such questions.

Thomas had gone with Will when he left Arnost, and the chatter had gradually died away.

Now there was talk of an Elena. Who was she?

"All of us need time to consider these matters further before we make any decision," the king was saying. "Please stay within the citadel, at least for the rest of the day. I might need to consult with you again."

With that the king called the meeting to a close.

Before anyone could leave, the commander stood up. "May I speak, Your Majesty?" he asked.

The king nodded. "Of course."

"I'm sure you are all hungry," the commander suggested. "Food will be served in the adjacent room in thirty minutes."

The duke slipped away quietly and headed for his private chamber, determined to take a few minutes to relax in peace.

———

BREYSEN HAD BEEN STANDING beside Brother Ander when the king addressed the soldiers. It would have seemed like a good speech if it had been directed at him. But he couldn't claim to be one of the king's loyal soldiers. Not anymore.

Based on what he had seen of the king, both at the campsite and before the soldiers, he could only admire him. He hadn't seemed lofty and distant—not at all like Breysen might have expected. And the queen had treated him almost like a friend. He wished he'd never set eyes upon them though, not under these circumstances. The king had left him alive, at least for now, but that said nothing about the future. Breysen's wife and children were so vulnerable. How could they ever hope to survive without him?

Will had released the surviving mercenaries, even allowing some of them to join his army. But it wasn't Will who would decide about him. His future would be settled by the king, and he didn't have the slightest idea of the king's intentions.

Brother Ander had barely left his side—perhaps at the king's request. He didn't mind at all. He had grown to appreciate the monk's calm demeanor, and he had the feeling the monk felt a degree of sympathy for him. That couldn't hurt.

Then the king and Will left for the citadel, taking Brother Ander with them. Breysen was left in the charge of two soldiers. They didn't treat him harshly—they basically ignored him—so he couldn't complain. But he missed the easy companionship of the monk.

One of the people he'd briefly met at the king's campsite was

Elena, and before long he discovered that she hadn't forgotten about him. Not long after the monk had gone, she came to visit him, bringing her husband Thomas with her as well. At first they had each looked at him a little strangely, but they soon seemed to relax. The soldiers left in charge of him didn't seem to object to their presence, and spending time with them and their little daughter Tammi lifted his spirits enormously. He was sorry to see them go when they eventually excused themselves and slipped away.

At least there was no shortage of food anymore. The soldiers ate simply, but every meal still seemed like an unexpected feast to him. He gradually felt his strength returning.

Thomas and Elena at last found the opportunity to enjoy some relaxed time with Tammi.

Elena had been darting strange looks at Thomas for some time. "What's on your mind, Thomas?" she eventually asked him.

Thomas put Tammi down and watched her as she ambled off to look at the horses. Did he really want to speak his thoughts? Some part of him worried that his fears might gain strength if he brought them into the open and named them. Glancing at the calm and untroubled face of Elena, he knew at once that such thinking was foolishness.

"I'm wondering what will happen to us," he told her. "Since we joined the king and queen, it's as if we have no control over our own future."

Elena nodded. She didn't seem surprised. "What would you like to do—if you had a choice?" she asked.

"I'd go and live somewhere far away," he said. "Like we were doing before. I miss our old life. I'm a simple person—I don't want the constant challenges Will and the king have to face."

She gazed at him knowingly. "And you're afraid that the stone will prevent that from ever happening."

He nodded unhappily. "Will and Rufe and the others are valuable to the king because of their skills and abilities. I'm only useful because of the stone. If I didn't have it, he would have released us long ago."

"Do you ever think about giving it up?"

"I used to. I often wondered if I was only keeping it out of selfishness. I thought that handing it to someone like Will or the king would be the most responsible thing to do. Then I had that conversation with Will—the one I told you about. I realized that it wouldn't be doing either of them a favor."

She nodded.

"According to the scroll," he continued, "the first person who had the stone, or the rock as it was then, gave it to his king. It didn't end well."

"So you've decided you're stuck with it."

"We're stuck with it," he reminded her.

She came to him, putting her hands on his waist and looking up into his eyes. "I know that heavy burdens have been placed on your shoulders ever since we were forced to leave our home—I've experienced it with you. I'd also be happy if we could leave it all behind and disappear into the wilderness again. Maybe that can't happen anymore. Maybe for as long as the stone is with us it won't be possible to take responsibility only for ourselves. But whatever happens, I want you to know that I'm willing to share the burden. We'll manage. We'll do it together."

He gazed down into her beautiful face. He felt bad about having dragged Elena into his troubles, but he acknowledged to himself that being able to share the stone with her was a huge relief.

She put her arm around him and nestled into his shoulder. "I admire the king and queen very much, and I think Will is amazing. But I'd leave all of them behind in a heartbeat. You and Tammi, my father, your parents, and Haldek. You're all I need."

He bent down and kissed her on the forehead. "What would I do without you?" he murmured.

Putting kings and conferences out of his mind, he turned his attention back to Tammi. A few minutes in her company helped settle him. He had discovered that his little daughter drew something out of him that found no other expression. He wasn't sure if he was entertaining her or she was entertaining him, but she was soon giggling uncontrollably as he tipped her upside down and waved her through the air.

Elena watched them for a while, a smile playing across her face. Finally she reminded him that Tammi was overdue for a nap, and he reluctantly redirected his efforts toward calming her down. Their little toddler soon fell fast asleep, completely exhausted.

Almost at the same moment, Rufe appeared.

"I've just been spending time with the former mercenary, Breysen," Rufe told them. "I'd like to know what both of you think of him. I believe you've already met him, Elena."

"We spent some time with him earlier today," Thomas told him, wondering what lay behind Rufe's request. It seemed ironic that Rufe should appear so soon after Thomas had been wishing he wasn't an ongoing part of Will's world.

"Do you think he's what he seems to be?" Rufe asked.

"Yes, I do," Thomas replied. "I have no doubt about it."

Rufe turned to Elena, an eyebrow raised questioningly.

"I believe he's genuine too," she said seriously. "He's very worried about his wife and children, and he joined the mercenaries mainly out of a desire to provide for them. It breaks my heart to see what's happened to him as a result."

"Now that he's spent time as a mercenary, do you think there's any doubt about his loyalty to the king and queen if things get difficult?" Rufe asked.

"I don't think he's ever intentionally done anything disloyal to the king and queen," Elena replied.

Thomas nodded. "I agree," he said without hesitation. "As soon as he realized who the mercenaries were fighting, he avoided fighting himself."

"Thank you," Rufe said. And without further comment he mounted his horse and returned to the citadel.

When they received an invitation to meet with the king early the following morning, Elena gazed at Thomas with a resigned smile on her face. It was obvious to him that she felt no more desire to belong to the king's inner circle than he did. He shrugged.

It seemed likely that their immediate future would be decided for them. He found it overwhelming even to imagine what it would be like to determine the futures of so many people. Who would ever want to be king?

And who would want to bear the burden of advising and protecting him? King Steffan had almost been killed when his enemies tried to wrench his kingdom away from him, and the task of preventing them from succeeding had fallen to people like Will and Rufe and Jonas. Not to mention the queen and Brother Ander. He shook his head.

The stone had also played its part. A small part, to be sure, but he knew it had made a difference. If he and Elena had remained hidden away in the forest, he wouldn't have met Will on his return from Erestor. He wouldn't have been able to alert Will to what was happening with the king at Paradise Valley.

He couldn't ignore the responsibility that came with the stone. Would a normal life ever be possible for Thomas and his family again?

He shrugged off such gloomy thoughts, deciding instead to spend some time with his father-in-law and Haldek.

Thomas and Elena rose at dawn the next day and once again left Tammi with Rubin. They found themselves riding to the citadel with Brother Ander and Breysen. The former mercenary looked nervous, but he managed a weak smile when they greeted him.

The four of them made their way to the reception hall together.

They arrived to find Will, Rufe, Jonas, and Rellan already there and engaged in a quiet but animated discussion.

The king, the queen, and the duke arrived immediately after them, and all conversation ceased at once. Every eye turned to the king.

"Agon plans to establish himself in Arnost, with the intention of annexing Arvenon, then Castel and Varas. The Rogandan invasion made it clear what we can expect if he succeeds."

He glanced around the group. "You are here because each of you will be affected by the decisions I have made. I am going to need your full support to have any hope of thwarting the plans of Agon and his henchmen."

Thomas couldn't guess what was coming next, but it didn't sound promising.

"I have decided to travel to Varas to seek the support of King Delmar," the king continued. "We defeated the Rogandans at the time of the invasion because the three kingdoms stood firmly together. We will need to do so again."

From the look on the king's face, he was about to say something that even he found distasteful. Thomas held his breath involuntarily.

"I have decided to travel by ship from Maranelle to Varacellan. And I need all of you to join me on the voyage."

Thomas was too stunned to do more than stare wide-eyed at the king. A quick glance around the room showed him that he, Elena, and Breysen were the only people surprised by this announcement.

The king nodded to the duke. "There will be two exceptions. The first is Rellan, who will help lead the army stationed below us and the reinforcements from Erestor. The second will be my good uncle, who has graciously agreed to remain here to act as regent once more in my absence."

King Steffan turned to Breysen. The former mercenary was staring at him open mouthed, apparently relieved and alarmed in equal measure. "I imagine you might not have been expecting this, Breysen," said the king. "Do you have any questions?"

Breysen managed to close his mouth. "I am grateful to Your

Majesty," he said. "I am just..." Then he hesitated, seemingly unable to find the courage to continue.

"Concerned about what it might mean for your wife and children if you disappear off on a sea voyage," Brother Ander finished for him.

The haunted look Thomas could see in Breysen's eyes confirmed the monk's assessment.

"There are ways we can help," Brother Ander told him. "I have just made contact with a traveling monk who comes to this region from time to time. I asked him if he would be willing to go to your village near Danford, and to do whatever he can to assist your family. The monk agreed, and the king has entrusted to him a gift of money for your wife. You can provide the monk with directions before we leave."

Hope and relief flashed across Breysen's face before being displaced by a look of such pathetic gratitude that Thomas turned away feeling awkward.

The king's attention had already turned elsewhere. "Brother Ander and Breysen will set out for Maranelle as soon as Breysen has spoken to the monk, accompanying the duke and Rufe. The rest of us will leave later today. Thank you all."

The people around Thomas stood up and moved to the door. He was in the act of pushing back his own chair when the king addressed him and Elena directly. "Please stay a moment longer."

Thomas and Elena obediently resumed their seats. Soon only the king and the queen remained in the room with them.

"Perhaps you are wondering why I have asked you to join us on this voyage," he told them frankly. "I felt that you would provide useful companionship to the queen, Elena—she holds you in high regard." Seeing the look on the queen's face, he quickly added, "I must make it clear that Queen Essanda had no desire to see you caught up in our troubles."

"I would very much appreciate your company, Elena," added the queen. "But I tried very hard to talk the king out of involving you. Being dragged around the world with us would not be your first choice I'm sure, especially with a small child in your care."

The king didn't wait for Elena to respond. "Will was insistent, Thomas. He pointed out that you have a way of ferreting out information. He told me you took the risk of visiting the castle in Arnost, and you were almost caught by Lygell's men as a result. You did much more than escape though. You managed to get wind of Lygell and Pisander's plans. And Will has told me that this is not the first time you've provided him with information that proved significant. Rufe supported him strongly."

Rufe's involvement surprised Thomas. A long forgotten interaction came abruptly to his mind. When Rogandan soldiers had appeared at the gates of Arnost, the stone had exposed their intent. After Thomas had alerted Will, his friend had immediately called for Rufe and given him urgent instructions to kill the men at the gates identified by Thomas. *"Can Thomas really be certain who deserves to be put to death?"* Rufe had asked Will. *"He can,"* Will had replied. *"There's no time to explain now. Don't fail me in this, Rufe!"*

Rufe had never spoken about it after the fight at the gates, although Thomas had sometimes wondered what he must have thought. Since then the big soldier had seen for himself, more than once, that Thomas knew things—things that no one should rightly be able to know. Was Rufe beginning at last to guess at Thomas's secret?

"How you manage it is a mystery to me," the king was saying. "But all of us would value your insights."

The king didn't realize it of course, but it wasn't Thomas's insights he needed. It was the revelations from the stone.

Thomas bowed his head in acceptance of the king's decision. It wasn't as if he had a choice.

"We would be happy to help however we can, Your Majesties," he replied evenly. "I hope it will be possible for Rubin and Haldek to come with us."

"Yes, of course," said the king. "Will also felt that it might prove useful for Haldek in particular to join us."

As soon as the king released them they returned to their horses.

"I'm so sorry, Elena," Thomas said as they rode back to their campsite. "This is all because of the stone. Where will it end?"

"I don't know," Elena replied with a gentle smile. "But nothing happens without a reason. If it weren't for the stone I would never have met you."

She was right. The stone had brought so much trouble into his life. But gazing into her lovely eyes he had to acknowledge that it had brought him a great deal of good as well.

Rubin and Haldek accepted the news about the upcoming sea voyage calmly. The two men exchanged a look that indicated they understood perfectly how this had come about. Rubin directed a searching look at both Thomas and Elena, but he didn't comment.

Thomas felt uncomfortable. He sensed that something more was needed, but he wasn't sure whether to apologize or to attempt a more complete explanation. He needn't have worried, because Elena knew exactly what to do. Moving to her father, she embraced him, nestling comfortably into his shoulder. He held her tightly for a long moment, then he placed his hands on her shoulders and held her at arm's-length, gazing steadily into her face.

No shadow troubled her smile, and he seemed to relax as he recognized the peace and contentment that so readily defined her. A tender smile came to Rubin's lips and reached to his eyes. After a while he released his daughter and busied himself gathering up their meager possessions.

Bundling Tammi up once more, the four of them mounted up and rode to the citadel to join the party traveling to Maranelle with the king.

EVERY MOVEMENT of Thomas had been observed closely by Carnwill. When Thomas disappeared into Steffan's Citadel with his daughter as well as his wife and failed to return before nightfall, it became apparent that they intended to remain in Erestor. Most likely they were heading for Maranelle.

Carnwill took a parchment and penned a brief note to the Rogandan king. It simply read,

'Fugitive located near Erestor, but now on the move.
In pursuit.
C.'

He arranged for it to be delivered to a trusted courier who would take it to King Agon in Rog.

No longer needing a cover, he paid and dismissed his two associates. They could do whatever they pleased with the cartloads of vegetables they had accumulated.

The next challenge was to gain admittance to Erestor. Deciding on a bold and simple approach, he rode up to Steffan's Citadel and demanded to speak with the commander.

Two hours passed before the commander arrived. "Well?" he demanded, looking Carnwill up and down with indifference.

Carnwill handed him a parchment. He did not offer comment.

"This is the Duke of Erestor's seal," said the commander in surprise. He opened it and scanned its contents before looking uncertainly at Carnwill. Then he dismissed the guards.

The tracker waited until they were alone. "I need to enter Erestor," he said.

"The border is closed," the commander replied flatly. "It will remain closed until the king orders otherwise."

"You've seen the document," Carnwill replied calmly.

The commander hesitated. "The duke only left a while ago. You could have appealed to him in person if you'd come earlier."

"You mean *you* could have appealed to him in person," growled Carnwill. He pointed at the parchment. "The duke's instructions are clear and unambiguous. If that's not good enough for you, send a messenger after him. Be ready to explain why you ignored his orders and hindered one of his agents."

"What is your purpose in Erestor?" asked the commander stiffly, trying to sound like he was still in command of the situation.

Carnwill bristled. "You said yourself the duke has been here at the citadel. If he chose not to tell you, then it isn't your concern. He won't thank you for prying into his business."

The commander frowned. Two options lay before him, and he was clearly comfortable with neither of them. Carnwill folded his arms, silent while he waited for the inevitable conclusion.

"The guards will let you through," the commander finally said, returning the parchment to him. "If you hurry you might catch the duke before he reaches Maranelle. Now get out of my sight before I change my mind."

EMERGING IN ERESTOR, Carnwill rode away from the citadel without a backward glance. In the duke's absence, the parchment had been unanswerable. Things would have ended very differently if he had called on the commander while the duke was still present at the citadel.

When the tracker had left Rog after two bizarre weeks in the presence of Agon, the king had given him a number of valuable gifts. The parchment was chief among them. Carnwill had no idea how King Agon had acquired the parchment, but the gift highlighted the significance of the mission the king had entrusted to him.

The message on the parchment was simple and clear. It read, "The Duke of Erestor commands that every requested assistance be provided to the bearer."

Whether the seal was genuine, Carnwill couldn't say. But the citadel commander had been convinced, and he must surely have seen the seal many times before.

Carnwill turned his mind to his reason for entering Erestor. Locating Thomas had been a major achievement, but his quarry was on the move. King Agon had known that Thomas was in hiding, and expected to be able to send in men to retrieve him as soon as the location had been identified. All that had now changed. Carnwill's efforts would have been completely wasted if he failed to keep Thomas in sight.

Based on his observations, a number of key people were heading for Maranelle, including the king and queen, Will Prentis, his deputy Rufe, and Thomas Stablehand with his family. They could be taking refuge with the duke in Maranelle, but it seemed unlikely.

The king had just taken control of an army, and his key commander was not staying behind to lead it. That must surely mean the king had something more important in mind.

Carnwill nodded with satisfaction. The king must be planning to travel by sea, almost certainly to Varas, and he was taking the most important of his subjects with him. The heirloom stolen by Thomas was clearly of great significance if he had been able to use it to gain the attention and favor of King Steffan.

Carnwill urged his horse forward. If Thomas was sailing to Varas with the king, Carnwill intended to make sure he sailed with them.

15

The sun cleared the treetops, flooding the grounds of Agon's palace with misty light. The king stood sullenly on his balcony peering out across the vista before him. Some might have called the scenery spectacular, but he wasn't in the mood.

Life would have felt a lot less frustrating for him if he'd managed to choose a regent who showed more aptitude as a student. Yet the grindingly slow progress with Krasmir was not the only thing that kept him awake at night.

Since the death of Lord Drettroth, Agon had become aware that two goals consumed much of the attention of his late army commander. The first was his quest to find and take possession of the Stone of Knowing. The second was his mission to attain unending life by sealing a bargain with the dark gods. His planned conquest of Arvenon, Varas, and Castel had been devised primarily in support of these purposes.

Once he fully understood what Drettroth had intended, Agon did not hesitate to adopt these goals as his own. And he was determined to succeed where his commander had failed. To his intense annoyance, both matters were yet to be resolved.

Agon spotted movement in the corner of his eye and turned to see a servant hovering fearfully near the door. Seeing that the king had spotted him, the man bowed deeply. "Great King, may you live forever…"

Agon eyed him impatiently. "Well?" he snarled.

"Your visit, Your Majesty."

The king glared back at him, trying to guess what visit he might be referring to.

"You wished to see the mystic…"

Agon flew into an instant rage. "Do you think I need to be told? Am I stupid?"

The man bowed and fled, almost tripping over himself in his haste to be gone from the king's presence.

The king left his private chambers immediately, heading for his horse. A guide was waiting for him, and he led the king out of Rog after explaining that the mystic lived about two hours' ride away.

The extended period in the saddle gave Agon an opportunity to reflect on his situation. After learning of Drettroth's plans he had at first decided to focus on finding the Stone of Knowing, both because it promised immediate benefits and because organizing a search seemed relatively straightforward.

As time went by, though, his attention had increasingly shifted to Drettroth's search for unending life. The lifespan allotted to him would come to an end sooner or later, however much his subjects might intone, "Great King, may you live forever." Without an effective bargain with the dark gods, none of the stones would be able to deliver lasting value to him. With such a bargain in place, his prospects would change dramatically. Perhaps he could even find patience for the time it was taking to add the Stone of Knowing to his arsenal.

Agon had found a scroll among Drettroth's effects that spoke of his plans to forge a deal with the dark gods. The problem had been to find a compliant priest who might be willing to shed light on the scroll and its vague references to the practical considerations involved in striking a suitable deal. No progress whatever had been made in finding such a person.

Rumors had long persisted that Drettroth once trained secretly to become a priest. The king dismissed such rumors, if only because he was certain Drettroth could never have found the time. Even so, Agon had wondered at times if he might be forced to undertake such training himself. He knew the idea was preposterous of course. Apart from the fact that he would find it abhorrent, he knew it would be no more realistic for him than it had been for Drettroth.

None of it would matter if only he could have made sense of the ramblings in Drettroth's scroll. With no hope of understanding it on his own, Agon's only other resort was to find someone who could.

He needed to make a copy of the scroll before letting another person anywhere near it. Given the supreme importance of protecting it from other eyes, Agon briefly considered doing the copy himself. Knowing he lacked the necessary patience, he took a more realistic approach and commissioned a scribe to do it on his behalf.

The moment the task had been completed, Agon snatched the duplicate from the scribe and examined it eagerly. The king had promised a handsome reward if the job was properly done, and he was as good as his word. The scholar had applied an exacting standard to the task, and the payment was thoroughly deserved.

The scribe left delighted, naively unaware that he would be executed the moment he left the king's presence. Disposing of the workman seemed to Agon an obvious necessity given the pressing need to keep the contents of the scroll secret. A side benefit was that the copy would cost him nothing once he retrieved his payment to the scribe.

With an exact duplicate now available, the king immediately secured the original scroll in a safe place. Agon would allow the mystic to peruse the copy. He was eagerly awaiting the assessment.

THE DWELLING OCCUPIED by the mystic was located deep within the forest, far from any other human habitation. When Agon first caught sight of it, he spat onto the ground in disgust, gesturing with his right hand to ward away evil. He hadn't expected a palace, but the hovel before him seemed scarcely fit for swine.

Before he could ride away, a grizzled figure in a dirty robe appeared in the entranceway. Although the man appeared old, he bent over in a surprisingly fluid bow. "Welcome to my humble dwelling, Great King," he said calmly, his bright eyes staring up at the king. "My name is Chalno."

Agon was taken by surprise. He realized he'd half expected the man to be completely insane. The mystic was merely disgusting. His teeth were rotten, and pus oozed from an open ulcer on his leg.

The king reluctantly decided he could tolerate disgusting, at least for a short time. The only question that mattered was whether this Chalno could shed light on Drettroth's scroll.

Two of Agon's guards checked the man for weapons before nodding to the king.

Agon had previously instructed his men to position themselves near at hand while remaining out of hearing range. He now waved them back.

Dismounting, he approached the mystic. "Read this," he commanded. "I want to know if you can make any sense of it."

The man studied the king quietly for a moment, his face a blank mask. Then he nodded once. Reaching for the scroll, he received it from the king's hand.

Chalno read the document slowly from start to end. "It is a scholarly text," he observed respectfully. He read it again thoroughly before finally gazing at the king.

"You wish to extend your life, Your Majesty. You wish to extend it indefinitely."

Since the mystic had not asked a question, the king did not bother to respond.

"The writer anticipates a heavy price. Are you able to pay it?"

"The payment is my business," the king replied testily. "What of the scroll? What sense do you make of it?"

Chalno again regarded him silently for a moment. "The author is a madman. Else a genius."

"Which is it?" demanded the king.

The mystic shrugged. "Either. Or both." He gazed into the heavens, and his eyes glazed over. The silence seemed to stretch out endlessly before he spoke again, his voice solemn. "The ravening she-wolf—is she a dangerous monster, or a nurturing mother?" he droned. "Her prey squeals one answer; her pups howl a different tune. What is the truth?"

Agon frowned. He had no interest in riddles. "Does the scroll offer a way of extending life indefinitely?"

"It does," purred the mystic, nodding wisely. "As it must."

"How is it to be done?"

"Slowly, and with great caution. How else can one make a captive of the wind?"

Agon clenched and unclenched his fists, working hard at containing his anger.

"What...do I need to do...to make it happen?" he demanded through gritted teeth.

"The stars of heaven shout an explanation, and the scroll echoes a reply: the spirit must grovel so the body can soar."

The king's patience ran out. "Don't dare to play word games with me," he roared. "Disappoint me and I'll have your heart ripped out! Once you find yourself in the clutches of Malzakh you can try your riddles on him!"

Chalno showed no concern whatever at the threat. He stared at the king thoughtfully. "I myself was a priest of the dark gods. It was long ago. But I have the knowledge still. Everything I once learned is in here." He tapped his skull. "The dark gods wanted everything." He slowly tapped his chest. "I fought for independence. The path was bitter—there is no easy road."

Agon scowled at him. He had no idea what the mystic was raving about. He opened his mouth to renew his threats, but Chalno got in first.

"You invoke the dread name of Malzakh, King Agon," said the mystic, apparently deciding to speak plainly at last. "But what do you really know of the Destroyer? And what do you know of Nehrvina, his Awful Sister?"

Agon shuddered involuntarily. He made no reply.

"I see you know no more than I guessed. These are not the right questions to ask you then," Chalno concluded with a shake of his head.

The mystic stood silently, peering at Agon with his penetrating eyes. The man seemed oblivious to the certain demise of anyone who dared talk down to the king. Finally he nodded to himself. "Here are the questions I must ask the king of Rogand."

He pointed at his chest. "What am I? Madman? Or genius?" He jabbed a finger at Agon. "And what are you? Wolf? Or prey?"

He nodded slyly. "You offer to separate my heart from my body. You suggest that the Destroyer will feast endlessly on my soul." He paused. "Perhaps you are wrong. Perhaps Nehrvina will take me."

Eyeing the king conspiratorially, he lowered his voice almost to a whisper. "Or perhaps neither destiny awaits me. Perhaps I have already made different arrangements of my own."

Agon stared wide-eyed at Chalno, completely bemused. What did the mystic mean? Was he suggesting he had some kind of leverage of his own with the dark gods?

The king ground his teeth in frustration. What could he do? He had threatened the mystic, and it had made no impact. Where could he go next? He saw that he had lost the initiative. Having done so, he found he had no idea how to regain it.

The king couldn't rule out the possibility that the fool knew something. He might even have the knowledge that Agon needed. Much as it galled him, he knew his only option for now was to exercise restraint.

"Four weeks," said the mystic abruptly, handing the scroll back to Agon.

Agon stared at him blankly.

"Come back in four weeks," the man repeated. Then he disappeared into his dwelling.

The king stood dazed for a moment. He had been dismissed. Turning meekly away, he headed for his horse.

Agon couldn't decide what to think of Chalno and his strange behavior. The mystic made no promises, but he had hinted he would have something further to say to the king in another four weeks.

A future meeting with Chalno would delay Agon's planned move to Arnost. It would also force him to extend his time in the company of Krasmir. Neither outcome was acceptable to him, and it was galling to find himself in such a position. As the king, Agon was the one who called the tune and settled the dates.

Nevertheless, he intended to do as he had been told.

As he rode back to Rog, he could not shake from his mind the mystic's question. What am I? Madman? Or genius? It would be so easy to conclude that Chalno was mad. But the mystic had taken the scroll seriously. And he was a former priest.

Agon had always been the one in command. Was he being played for a fool? He shook his head grimly. He would return in four weeks, and when he did all of the questions would be answered.

Chalno had asked another question. What are you? Wolf? Or prey?

If Agon didn't like the mystic's answers, Chalno would swiftly discover the answer to his question.

LONG BEFORE HE arrived back at the palace, Agon's mind had veered in a different direction. Drettroth's scroll had long baffled him. Now that he nurtured at least a faint hope of its mysteries being unraveled, his thoughts turned once more to the quest for the Stone of Knowing.

Drettroth had come tantalizingly close to achieving the goal. The Stone of Knowing had been almost within his grasp, and only his murder had denied him the prize. Agon had initiated his own search for the elusive stone as soon as he learned of Drettroth's actions. By then the trail had gone cold. After many months and more than one group of investigators, he was only now beginning to see progress.

Carnwill was the best of the best among trackers, and luring him to Rog was something Agon should have done much sooner. Two weeks under the influence of the Stone of Authority had been enough to ensure Carnwill's loyalty. Agon passed on every piece of information his previous agents had uncovered, then sent out his new tracker to resume the search.

Walking into his private suite in the palace, Agon found Ennawi standing near the balcony.

"It isn't all bad news," the king told the slave. "I've just heard from my newest agent. He's a tracker, and he's been searching for Thomas, the person who dared to take possession of the Stone of Knowing. He has him in sight at last."

Accustomed to a total lack of response from his slave, the king continued. "I'm sure you're asking where this Thomas has been hiding. It's an astute question, Ennawi, and no less than I've come to expect from you."

He nodded wisely at his slave. "All will be revealed before long. In the meantime, Ennawi, don't give in to impatience. No fugitive can hide forever, and the time is fast approaching when we'll run this one to ground."

16
____

The morning was not entirely spent when Breysen arrived at Maranelle with Brother Ander and Rufe, accompanied by the duke and his escort. A series of foothills overlooked the seaport, and he had stared down with astonishment at the panorama that opened before him as his weary horse crested the final ridge. A citadel built from white stone crowned the gleaming city that lay below him, and pennants of every color fluttered from the tall towers that climbed boldly into the blue sky. White sands shone on the broad beach that fringed the bay below the city, and fishing boats bobbed peacefully in the bay or sat proudly up on the sands. The scene could only be described as idyllic. And if that hadn't been enough, the smell of sea air filled his nostrils.

Noticing his expression, the duke had regarded him with amusement. "It's beautiful, isn't it?" the duke had asked.

"I never imagined that Maranelle could be described as beautiful," Breysen had replied. "I visited the port many times in my youth, but I don't recognize anything I'm seeing down there at all."

"You probably never left the port when you were here before," the duke suggested.

The duke was right.

The port at Maranelle was seedy and squalid, just like the ports in every city he had ever sailed to. No one could have described it as idyllic. And on his previous visits, Breysen had never found occasion to leave the dockside.

The duke pointed to a headland that jutted into the sea at one end of the wide bay below the city. "The port was built on the far side of Maranelle Head," he explained. "Fishing boats are always working the bay and the waters beyond it, so oceangoing ships are prohibited from sailing across the fishing grounds when they approach Maranelle. Ships heading for the port approach from the far side of Maranelle Head, and always from well out at sea. So you probably never even caught a glimpse of the city from the seaward side."

Breysen could only nod in wonder. As a lowly sailor, he'd never shown interest in such subtleties. He suddenly wondered how many other cities he'd visited without ever seeing them.

The duke led them to the citadel. After giving them an opportunity to wash off the dust of the road, he offered them refreshments. Breysen had surveyed the feast laid out by the duke's servants for no more than a moment before setting upon the food energetically. He noticed the duke eyeing him with a grin, but decided he didn't care. He'd never eaten this well. Who could guess how long it might last?

Even before all of them had eaten their fill, Rufe had become impatient. "We are grateful for your hospitality, My Lord Duke," he said. "Our pressing need now is to find a suitable ship."

"It isn't safe for you to wander around the docks on your own," the duke told him. "One of my men will escort you there." He called at once for one of his retainers, then added, "Speak to me before you make a final decision on a ship. I know something of most of the captains."

They thanked the duke gratefully.

The duke's man arrived and spent several minutes in quiet conversation with the duke.

Breysen watched them curiously. The duke's choice of a guide seemed eminently appropriate. The man's hard-bitten appearance and well worn clothing appeared more in keeping with a dockhand than a duke's retainer.

"This is Jaxin," the duke told them. "He will help you find what you're looking for."

Jaxin nodded to them sternly, then led them away without a word.

As they headed for the docks, Breysen noticed that Rufe seemed even more reserved than usual.

"Have either of you ever been to a port before?" he asked.

Both Rufe and Brother Ander shook their heads.

"Don't wander off anywhere," Breysen warned them. "The dock-side district is controlled by a person known as the Peerless Mariner; there's one in every port I've ever visited. His men keep an eye out for strangers. Sailors are left alone if they mind their own business. But if you have no business in the docks you'll very quickly find yourself in trouble."

"Will they leave you alone?" asked the monk.

Breysen shrugged. "Maybe. Maybe not. If they decide any one of us is here without a good reason, we'll probably end up floating face down in the harbor before long."

Rufe raised his eyebrows. Brother Ander seemed unconcerned.

Many years had passed since Breysen last visited the docks of Maranelle. He quickly saw that very little had changed.

Jaxin clearly knew his way around. He led them to a large tavern with a narrow door. A couple of burly men stood just inside the entranceway. The sounds of loud conversation punctuated by raucous laughter issued from within.

Jaxin eyed them all closely, then nodded to Breysen. "You're with me."

He turned to Rufe and Brother Ander. "Wait here," he instructed them. "Don't follow us in. And stay out of trouble."

The men at the door admitted Jaxin without comment. They eyed Breysen briefly before stepping aside to let him in as well.

Breysen followed Jaxin into a large and dimly lit room dotted with tables. A haze of smoke filled the air, and sailors slouched on large stools around most of the tables. Many of the customers were loud and boisterous, and most of them were clearly tipsy.

Jaxin went to the bar and exchanged a few words with the bartender, who poked a finger at a couple of tables across the room. Many eyes turned in their direction as Jaxin headed for the first of the tables, Breysen close behind him.

A grizzled sailor with a long silver beard sat alone at the table, a large tankard of ale before him. He was chewing on the stem of a well worn pipe.

"Captain Yordin of the Nomad Lady?"

"Aye, that's my name and that's my ship. I know your face," he told Jaxin. He turned to Breysen. "Who might you be?"

"This is Breysen," said Jaxin, jabbing a thumb in Breysen's direction. "And in case you've forgotten, I'm Jaxin, and I work for the Duke of Erestor."

"The duke is known to me," the captain said noncommittally. He waved them to stools opposite him.

"The duke is looking for someone reliable to deliver some cargo for him," Jaxin said.

Captain Yordin grunted. "What's the nature of this cargo?"

"Passengers mostly. Thirty or so."

The captain's bushy eyebrows raised in mild surprise. "Where do they want to go?"

"Varacellan."

The captain grunted again. "The Lady is fast—she's a two master, a proper oceangoing ship—and she carries a bigger cargo than most vessels. What about the fee?"

Jaxin frowned. "Has the duke ever defaulted on payment?"

"He's reliable enough, and he knows the rate," the captain acknowledged with a nod. "When are these passengers wanting to depart?"

"As soon as you're ready to sail."

"My crew is short two or three men, but the mate should be able to find replacements today," the captain said. "We can sail with the tide tomorrow."

"The duke will want a say in any final decision," Jaxin told him. "If you don't hear otherwise by nightfall, you can assume that he has engaged your services."

The captain nodded. "Make sure your passengers are ready to board the Lady at sunrise," he said.

Jaxin shook his head. "Discretion is required in this particular case," he said. "You'll need to stand to as soon as the Nomad Lady has cleared the harbor. The passengers will be delivered to you by fishing boat."

Captain Yordin showed no sign of surprise. "Discretion costs more," he told them bluntly.

"You'll get your gold," growled Jaxin.

The captain pulled tobacco from a pouch and carefully began packing it into the bowl of his pipe. He appeared to have lost interest in them entirely.

Jaxin and Breysen stood up together and headed for the door. The noise level dropped momentarily, and Breysen noticed many pairs of eyes darting between them and Captain Yordin as they left.

Brother Ander glanced around him. No more than a few minutes had elapsed since Jaxin and Breysen disappeared inside the tavern. In that time a small group of men had gathered. They were staring at Rufe and the monk with undisguised disdain.

"We seem to have attracted some attention," Brother Ander observed.

Rufe didn't respond.

A wizened man stepped out from the group, looking them up and down contemptuously. "I don't like you," he said, jabbing a finger at the monk. "You don't belong here."

Brother Ander gazed back at him. "You and I have something important in common," he said calmly.

"Do we now?" snarled the wizened man, his fingers twitching around a knife that had appeared suddenly in his hand. "I live in the devil's backyard, and you live in a monastery. What could the likes of you possibly have in common with me?"

"We both draw breath from the same Creator," said the monk. He swept his arm around the group that had gathered. "It's true of all of us."

The knife man spat into the dirt. "Is that so?" he sneered. "I might just cut out your lungs. Then we can see for ourselves where your breath comes from."

The attacker lunged at the big monk with his knife extended. Brother Ander twisted easily aside, grabbing the man's wrist before he could withdraw it and squeezing hard. His assailant cried out with pain and dropped the knife.

Other men stepped forward, all of them armed with knives or clubs.

Rufe positioned himself beside the monk. He had picked up a large lump of wood, and he thumped it rhythmically into his other hand. The attackers drew back warily, sensing that the two strangers might not be the easy pickings they had first imagined.

At that moment Jaxin reappeared from inside the tavern, taking in the scene at a glance. He frowned at the semicircle of armed men hovering just out of reach. "Mess with them," he growled, jerking his head toward his companions, "and you'll have the duke down on you."

The monk's attacker stood cradling his crushed hand and wincing uncomfortably. "You don't rule here, Jaxin," he sneered, "and neither does your precious duke."

"Really?" asked Jaxin, raising his eyebrows. "Are you speaking on behalf of the Peerless Mariner or on behalf of yourself? Because I have a feeling that the duke would find that remark very interesting."

Another voice broke in. "We don't want no trouble." In little more than a heartbeat the other men had melted away. Brother Ander's attacker stood entirely alone.

"Perhaps we should continue this conversation in the city lock-up," Jaxin suggested.

"No harm done," mumbled the man sulkily before he too turned and scurried away.

"It's time we were gone," said Jaxin.

BREYSEN HURRIED AFTER JAXIN. Having witnessed a few too many dockside brawls in his past life, he had no desire to participate in one. Rufe and Brother Ander followed hard on his heels. They needed no urging either.

As they left the docks Breysen pondered the scene he had just glimpsed. The monk had faced down a hostile crowd, apparently without fear. Breysen had never met a monk quite like him. Rufe had seemed equally calm and untroubled—he was a good person to have around in a crisis.

All that aside, it was abundantly clear that they would have achieved nothing useful without Jaxin.

He thought about Captain Yordin. Breysen had served under many captains, and he knew how to read the signs. His instincts told him this man could be trusted, provided he was paid fairly and his ship wasn't put at risk.

Breysen was no untrained novice when it came to the sea though. Even with a reliable captain and a seaworthy vessel, nothing was ever certain the moment you stepped across the gangplank and said goodbye to solid ground.

CAPTAIN YORDIN'S interaction in the tavern with Jaxin had attracted the interest of one sailor in particular. Carnwill sat quietly sipping his ale and listening intently to all that was said.

As soon as Jaxin left, Carnwill sought out the mate of the Nomad Lady. Before the day was out he had boarded the ship as a new hand. He was soon hard at work with the other sailors preparing for departure the following morning.

He had no doubt that Thomas would be boarding the following day. The king and queen and a number of others would be sailing as well. Carnwill would need to be careful.

Caution was needed for another reason. King Agon had given him a very specific instruction before sending him away from Rog. *This Thomas must never be allowed to see you—not even to glimpse you,* the king had said. *Do you understand?*

Baffling as the instruction had been, the king must have said it for a reason, and Carnwill had taken careful note.

How he would manage to complete a voyage on the same ship without being noticed by Thomas he had yet to figure out. But he would find a way.

———

RANAULD HAD LAIN HIDDEN on a ridge with his two companions for several hours, peering down at the Arvenian army encamped below. It would be dark in little more than an hour. They would need to find a sheltered place to camp soon. He would use the hours of darkness to rest before he made his move.

It had taken several days of steady riding to reach this region and three more days to find the place where the northern army had camped. Army patrols seemed to be everywhere, and they had been forced to move cautiously to avoid being discovered. Eventually they had found an ideal location where they could observe the campsite undetected.

Ranauld had set out before Will made his attempt to regain control of the western army outside Steffan's Citadel. Even without knowing whether Will had been successful, though, Ranauld was confident that the vast majority of the regular soldiers in both locations were loyal to the king.

Ranauld's intent was to find a soldier he could trust, and ask that person to put him in touch with one of the original leaders of the army. Ranauld would have connected personally with many of them at one time or another.

The task shouldn't be difficult; in his role as a senior commander he had rubbed shoulders with a considerable number of soldiers after the Battle of Torbury Scarp. This army camp was vast, which made his job more challenging, but he only needed one person to start the process.

Sounds of restlessness from their tethered horses put Ranauld on sudden alert. He spun around to find that five mounted men had come between them and their horses. All of the riders held drawn weapons.

Ranauld's mind raced. The furtive nature of his behavior must have made it obvious that he was not connected with the army below. He and his men had been distracted with their observations, and therefore unusually vulnerable, yet the five men had not raised the alarm or moved against them while they held the advantage. The new arrivals had not even challenged them.

The most likely conclusion was that the newcomers were no more connected to the army below than Ranauld and his men were.

He stood up slowly and carefully, keeping his hands well away from his sword. "Who might you be?" he asked.

Several of the newcomers flicked a glance at one of their number, a wiry man with a confident demeanor. He was clearly the leader. "We could ask you the same question," he said. "What are you doing spying on the army?"

These men must surely be Castelan soldiers. Ranauld decided to take a risk. "You're Castelans, aren't you?"

The wiry leader offered no immediate response. But he didn't deny it. Then he spoke abruptly. "I know you," he said. "You were with Will Prentis at Torbury Scarp."

Ranauld gave a slight bow. "Count Ranauld at your service," he confirmed. "Did you fight there?"

"I did," the wiry man told him. After a pause, he added, "You're right. We are Castelans."

Ranauld nodded. "You asked why we are here. Enemies of King Steffan have taken control of the capital, Arnost, and placed mercenaries in charge of the king's armies. The army below has come here on their orders. Most of the regular soldiers are loyal to the king. Our goal is to make contact with them, and regain control of the army on behalf of the king."

He peered at the Castelan leader. "Why are you here?"

"I can tell you that we're not in any way associated with your mercenaries," the stranger returned. After a moment's consideration, he added decisively, "You need to come with us. Details can wait until we're back at our base."

Should he go with them? If he did it would almost certainly prevent him from making contact with the army anytime soon.

However, Ranauld's other key purpose was to communicate directly with the Castelans on King Steffan's behalf. It appeared he was being offered an unusual opportunity to do just that. Having just left the king he was in a unique position to explain to the Castelans that his monarch had no hostile intentions toward them.

Peaceful intentions made little difference, of course, while King Steffan was not in control of the Arvenian forces. But Ranauld could also make the Castelans aware of the king's fierce determination to do whatever was necessary to regain control of his country and his armies.

He would have preferred not to be faced with achieving only one of his two goals. Nevertheless he soon reached his decision. "We'll come with you," he said.

The wiry man shook his head. "Just you, Count Ranauld. Your friends can do as they please."

Ranauld hesitated, frowning. Then he nodded reluctantly. He turned to his companions. "You know why we're here. Do anything you can," he told them.

The men looked bewildered, but he had no real choice but to leave them to take their own initiative. They were reliable men, but he knew they had little chance of achieving anything useful without him.

He walked to his horse and mounted, then with a wave to his companions he rode away with the Castelans.

The men carefully worked their way around the encamped

northern army until they came to open ground, then they rode swiftly in a northerly direction.

Even before they reached their destination, it became obvious to Ranauld that they were heading for Deadman's Pass, the only accessible pass through the mountains that marked the border between Arvenon and Castel. His guides were clearly Castelan scouts, sent to observe the Arvenian army.

When they arrived at the entrance to Deadman's Pass, the leader gave a password, and a path was opened wide enough to admit one horse at a time. The barrier was replaced as soon as the last of the men had ridden through.

The leader of the scouts disappeared for a few minutes. The moment he returned he approached Ranauld.

"Please come with me, Count Ranauld," he said. "Our commander has requested that you leave your weapons with us." He nodded toward one of his men. "Purely in view of the current uncertainties between our armies. I hope you understand. We will take good care of them until they can be returned to you."

Ranauld hesitated only briefly. Quickly deciding that he would probably make the same request if the roles were reversed, he removed his sword belt and his knife and handed them over.

The scout led him to a tent. The guards standing outside nodded to the scout, and he ushered Ranauld inside. A thick set man sat in an elaborate chair. His face appeared neutral at best.

"Count Ranauld, this is Lord Kaebon. He commands the Castelan army here."

Ranauld bowed, and the commander nodded stiffly in return before waving him to a seat.

"Why are you here?" Lord Kaebon asked him bluntly.

"Your men insisted I return with them to your base," Ranauld replied evenly. "Fighting Castelan soldiers was never on my agenda, so I agreed to join them."

Lord Kaebon made no response.

Ranauld decided to be more direct. "I have recently come from

King Steffan. It occurred to me that there might be an unexpected opportunity for dialogue between our two kingdoms."

The commander grunted. "I will send to Castel Citadel for instructions," he said. "In the meantime I will arrange for you to be offered refreshments and somewhere to sleep. I will also assign two soldiers to you for security."

When Ranauld raised his eyebrows, Lord Kaebon added, "Purely for your own protection, of course. Given recent provocations, I'm sure you will understand that not all of our men are inclined to view Arvenians in a favorable light."

The commander nodded stiffly once more, and Ranauld was ushered from the tent.

17

—————

Thomas and Elena had gathered with the other members of the party heading for Varacellan.

"Yordin's boat, the 'Nomad Lady', is eminently seaworthy. And the man himself is dependable, Your Majesty," the duke was saying. "He's as solid as any of the captains out there."

"None of that sounds like a ringing endorsement," the king told him. His brows drew together. "I hope we're doing the right thing."

The duke didn't seem at all concerned. "It will all turn out well in the end," he said with a smile. "I have a very good feeling about it."

"I hope you're right, Uncle," the king replied. He raised his arms in a gesture of resignation. "We're in your hands. When do we need to head for the port?"

"Yes...," said the duke, looking a little uneasy. "About that..." Glancing first at Jaxin, then at Breysen, he squared his shoulders. "You won't be boarding from the port," he announced.

The king stared at him blankly.

The duke looked the king squarely in the eye. "If you appear on the docks with your retinue, Your Majesty," he said, "you might as well proclaim your intentions from the rooftops. Within twenty-four hours the entire world will know that the king has fled Arvenon for Varas."

The king threw up his arms again. "So how do we board?"

"We'll wait until the ship has left port, then we'll board you from fishing boats."

"From fishing boats? In the middle of the ocean? How do you expect to get a baby on board? And what about the queen?"

"It won't be entirely straightforward," admitted the duke. "But the captain and his crew are resourceful people, and none of you are in any way disabled. The queen has proven herself capable of managing in much more challenging circumstances."

"No one so much as hinted at any such necessity when I was considering the options," grumbled the king.

The duke winced a little, but he said nothing further.

"What do you think about this, Breysen?" the king asked.

"The transfer won't be straightforward, Your Majesty," Breysen told him frankly. "But I'm sure we will manage it." He hesitated for a moment, then he added, "Provided the seas aren't too rough of course." He glanced at the duke before quickly adding, "I believe that My Lord Duke is right about what will happen if you board at the port."

The king ran a hand across his face. Then he shook his head. "I suppose we're committed now," he said. "Somehow we'll have to find a way to make it work."

* * *

BREYSEN STOOD on the pitching deck of the Nomad Lady, peering down at Rufe as he steadily climbed the rope net to the deck. Little Tamara was carried along as well, secured to him in her riding sling.

After a few minutes of nervous deliberation, Elena and Thomas had agreed to entrust their little daughter to Rufe. Now they stood beside Breysen on the deck, looking on anxiously as the ship swung erratically back and forth, threatening to pitch the burly soldier and his little passenger into the rolling seas. They were visibly relieved when he safely completed the climb.

King Steffan had been one of the first to clamber aboard, and he monitored Rufe's progress closely. Seeing that the journey had proceeded without incident, the king waved his permission for little Prince Aiden to be transported in the same way, secured to Brother Ander. The queen watched from a fishing boat below as the monk took his turn on the rope net, her face noticeably pale even from a distance.

The prince reached the deck safely and without incident as well.

With the exception of the queen and two final soldiers, the rest of the party had already braved the hazardous climb. Although the swell was by no means mountainous, the boat rocked back and forth constantly, occasionally lurching violently as it rolled after cresting a wave. The unpredictable movement made the climb up the ship's side extremely challenging, and Breysen was both amazed and relieved to see person after person complete the journey without incident.

The time had now come for the queen to take her turn. The fishing boat that had brought her to the ship was also pitching and rolling in the swell, and like those who had preceded her she had to wait for the right moment to launch herself forward onto the coarse rope netting.

The king gasped audibly as his wife leaped from the fishing boat and grasped hold of the net. She began to climb steadily upward, pausing whenever the ship's movement made it unsafe to continue. She appeared to be in no danger of falling, and the king began to relax a little as she crossed the halfway mark.

Below her the first of the remaining two soldiers made the leap and began scaling the rope net. He had barely begun his upward journey when a larger than usual wave caused the ship to roll viciously. The netting swung outward before crashing back into the side of the ship. The queen, higher up the net and less affected by its movement, managed to cling on. The soldier was not so fortunate. After swinging far away from the ship, he came smashing back into its side as the Lady rolled the other way. The force of the shock dislodged his grip on the rope, and he fell backward toward the sea. As he fell, one of his legs caught in the netting. Breysen heard a sickening crack as the force of his fall snapped his leg. The soldier cried out in agony.

Every watcher on board gasped. Without a moment's hesitation, the queen climbed back down to him. A moment later, one of the sailors on the fishing boat grabbed a hatchet and jumped for the netting.

"Can you lift him, Your Majesty?" the sailor cried over the loud groans of the injured man.

"He's too heavy for me," she called back. "Give me the hatchet!"

The sailor hesitated at first, but seeing no alternative, he yielded to her demand and handed it over.

"Don't let him go!" she called as she began hacking away at the rope around his leg.

Whenever she hesitated, the sailor offered directions. "That piece next!"

She continued chopping with all her might.

As the last piece of rope parted, the sailor grasped the injured man tightly as he fell free. Another cry of agony came from the soldier, causing Breysen to wince again.

Other sailors on the fishing boat had retrieved a piece of fishing net, and they prepared to throw it across to their fellow crewman.

"Support him, Your Majesty!" the sailor called as the net was thrown across to him.

The queen took hold of the man while the sailor wrapped the net around him.

Lengths of rope stretched from each end of the new net back to the fishing boat, and the sailors took in the slack. Another of the sailors jumped into the water holding a large wooden plank and swam it across to the ship, drawing as close as he dared to the pitching vessel. Assisted by the queen, the sailor beside her lowered the injured man onto the wood as carefully as they could manage in the rolling seas, the sailor in the water holding him steady.

The first sailor retrieved his hatchet from the queen and slipped into the water on the other side of the wooden plank. The queen watched from her position on the rope netting as the men on the fishing boat steadily pulled on the ropes, drawing in the sailors with the soldier floating between them. When they reached the side of the boat, the net was lifted on board, bringing its human cargo with it.

The two swimmers were pulled from the water.

The first sailor waved to the queen. "We'll get him back to shore," he called.

She waved back, then once again began climbing upward, soon followed by the final soldier.

The king began to pace restlessly along the deck, almost frantic with worry whenever the ship rolled more vigorously than usual. When the queen finally appeared over the side of the deck, he ran to her and embraced her fiercely, completely oblivious to the stares of everyone on board.

The queen quickly detached herself and hurried to her infant son. Only once she had satisfied herself that he was well did she allow herself to relax. Heaving a slow sigh of relief, she beamed a smile at the people around her.

Thirty handpicked soldiers from the army of Erestor had accompanied the king and his party, every one of them expert with both the bow and the sword. They had long since climbed aboard. Another fishing boat had transported their supplies, and swords, bows, thick bundles of arrows, and additional food supplies were now hauled up to the deck.

Captain Yordin had insisted on giving up his own cabin to the king and queen, and Breysen noticed him showing them to their quarters. He was not absent for long. The ship was now under sail, and the captain soon hurried back to the helm, shouting orders as he went.

With the drama of the boarding behind them, Breysen was soon busy helping the soldiers and the other members of the king's party find hammocks below decks. Few of them had ever sailed before, and it was obvious to Breysen that many of them would be emptying their stomachs before long. He was determined to return to the deck as soon as he possibly could. Experience had taught him the wisdom of staying well clear of first time passengers when things started to get messy.

THE WIND HAD PICKED up noticeably, and the crew of the Lady were reefing the sails. Spotting Will leaning over the railing, Breysen hurried to his side.

"Careful you don't fall in," he said, speaking loudly enough to be heard over the wind and the creaking of the timbers. He was only half joking.

Will glanced at him with heavy lidded eyes. Seeing the look on his face, Breysen's first instinct was to burst out laughing. But he quickly choked it back. He hadn't forgotten how kindly he had been treated when he was at his lowest point.

"You look a little green about the gills there," he said.

"Do you...enjoy this?" Will managed, waving a hand vaguely about him.

Breysen took hold of the rails and tilted back his head, closing his eyes as he filled his lungs with the cold salty air. "Yes!" he replied with feeling. "It's been far too long."

Will risked a glance over the railing. "Even in these mountainous seas?"

Breysen's eyebrows went up in surprise. "These seas are by no means mountainous. Wait until you experience a real storm!"

Seeing the look on Will's face, he hastily added, "You needn't worry. Unless I've completely lost my weather sense, the wind is much more likely to ease off."

Will turned away to retch helplessly once more over the side. Then he pushed himself back from the rail and headed unsteadily for the hatch and the ladder that led below.

As he left, the king and queen appeared on deck. Swaying in an effort to compensate for the motion of the deck, they wended their way to Breysen's side. The queen held her baby firmly in one arm.

With the other she had locked arms with the king to steady herself against the constant rolling of the ship. Neither of them seemed at all troubled by seasickness.

The three of them watched together as Will stumbled down the steps on his way below.

"Poor Will," said the queen. "He doesn't look at all well."

"No, he doesn't," said the king. "It seems we've finally found something that doesn't come naturally to our worthy commander," he added with a wry smile.

"He has the first stage of seasickness, Your Majesty," Breysen noted dryly.

"What's that?" asked the king.

"It's when someone feels so ill they're afraid they're going to die," Breysen replied.

"Is there a second stage?" asked the queen.

Breysen nodded. "The second stage is when they're afraid they're going to live," he told her.

The queen burst out laughing.

Noticing that the king's only response was a raised eyebrow, Breysen turned quickly to the queen to change the subject. "How is the baby coping, Your Majesty?" he asked.

"Surprisingly well," she replied, gazing down tenderly at the infant. "He's mostly been asleep since he came on board."

Seeing the way she responded to her son brought to mind his own wife and children, and Breysen shifted his attention to his feet in an attempt to recover himself.

Queen Essanda must have guessed what was on his mind. "Brother Ander tells me that the monk is very reliable. I mean the one you spoke to, who's planning to search out your wife and children."

"Thank you, Your Majesty," he replied. He managed to master himself again, but the silence still felt awkward.

"Do you know these waters, Breysen?" asked the king briskly.

Breysen nodded. "I have traveled them many times before, Your Majesty. We're currently sailing north along the coast of Arvenon.

Depending on the winds, we should cross into Castelan waters sometime tomorrow. We'll continue north until we sight Point Turtan. Captain Yordin will then have a choice. He can steer a northeasterly course through Savage Strait, between the mainland and Baron Island. Or he could head north for a while longer and sail right around the island. The strait is quicker to navigate, but it has many shoals. Traveling around Baron Island would allow us to avoid the shoals entirely. It's a longer journey, though, and it would take us into open sea, well away from coastal waters."

"Savage Strait doesn't sound promising," the king observed.

"It can certainly be true to its name if the weather is bad," Breysen told him. "But the passage isn't usually difficult provided the weather is good. And the scenery is quite unique."

"And will we reach Varacellan once we navigate the strait?"

"Not quite. There will be more small islands to sail past and more shoals to avoid. But those waters are more protected. As long as we navigate those seas during daylight hours there should be little risk. If the captain decides to use Savage Strait, he'll try to enter it soon after dawn. If the winds are fair, we should be able to reach Varacellan by nightfall."

"Have you ever been shipwrecked, Breysen?" asked the queen.

"Yes, once. If you are interested I would be happy to tell you about it sometime, Your Majesty. Perhaps after our voyage is over," he said with a smile.

A particularly large wave loomed ahead, seeming to tower above them. The ship rose high on the wave before plunging down again as it rolled past.

"I don't want to hear anything about shipwrecks until I'm back on solid ground," said the king emphatically.

18

Pisander wandered along the battlements of Arnost castle, head down and with his hands clasped behind his back. He avoided eye contact with the soldiers on the walls; they took the hint and ignored him.

He needed the fresh air—it cleared his senses. These days he spent far too long in his office trying to administer Arvenon. Even his own private schemes had largely been pushed into the background.

Lady Ona had ridden out the previous day, and he was glad to see the last of her. There was no denying the woman had stirred a few of Lygell's people into action, but she'd also exposed the incompetence of many among his new nobility.

She'd even forced Lygell to send some of his officials to the dungeons. Pisander supposed he should be grateful to her—sooner or later he would have needed to execute some of them himself, and she'd helpfully identified the most likely contenders for the hangman's noose.

She'd become a problem only when she refused to let him recruit her. He wasn't lying when he told her he needed her skills, but putting her to work wasn't his sole motivation. She was going to report back to Agon, and he'd counted on having her in his employ when that happened. She would have been much more likely to deliver a sympathetic report if he'd been lining her pockets.

There was no use worrying about it. He would figure out how to handle Agon when he arrived.

He was still waiting for clear information about the date. The Rogandan king had deferred his trip more than once already, and Pisander couldn't help wondering why.

There were benefits to the delay—it gave him more time to get his own house in order.

The robed figure of Lygell was trudging in his direction, and Pisander paused from his pacing to observe his progress. His deputy was joining him on the battlements in response to Pisander's summons. Lygell didn't look happy. This meeting wasn't going to improve his mood.

Pisander waited until Lygell reached him. "You've got work ahead of you," he said bluntly. "Lady Ona hasn't made either of us look good. Fixing that is your problem, because you appointed the incompetent idiots she flushed out."

Lygell made no immediate reply, but his face darkened at the mention of Lady Ona.

Pisander saw his reaction and was not impressed by it. "Wake up to yourself, Lygell!" he snapped. "You were a fool to let her get to you. She never had any interest in you—she was only ever using you from the beginning."

Seeing Lygell's brow darkening with anger, Pisander reached out and slapped him hard on the face.

Before his deputy could react, Pisander leaned in and jabbed a finger painfully into his shoulder. "Don't think you can behave like a child around me, Lygell! I'm not here to coddle you. You'd better sharpen up! Agon is coming, and Lady Ona will have delivered her report before he gets here. If you haven't turned things around dramatically by the time he arrives, he'll separate your head from your shoulders in a heartbeat."

Lygell stared at Pisander with startled eyes.

Pisander glared back at him. "You wanted power, didn't you? Is that what you thought this position was about? Getting a chance to throw your weight around? If that's what you thought, you'd better think again. I've given you plenty of chances, and this will be the last. I want a plan on my desk by sunset tomorrow. You're going to show me how and when you're planning to fix everything that's broken. You'll hand me a list of every one of your people who hasn't been performing. I don't care if you send them to the dungeons or the gallows, but a lot of your precious friends won't be here next week. It'll be them or you. Your choice."

Lygell's cheeks were flushed, and he couldn't meet Pisander's eyes. "Get out of here!" growled the former earl.

He shook his head in disgust as Lygell retreated in disarray from the battlements. It remained to be seen whether Lygell would be able to extricate himself from his predicament. If not, Pisander would be finding himself a new deputy.

He cursed under his breath. Good people weren't easy to find. If they were, he wouldn't be in this position.

He largely had himself to blame though, and he knew it. Appointing Lygell was shaping up as a major blunder.

He thought he'd recognized something of himself in his deputy. Lygell had the same hunger for power, the same ruthlessness, the same ability to focus, and the same ability to strike fear into both subordinates and enemies.

He seemed to have begun well. However it was becoming clear that he lacked the ability to see the bigger picture. Since he seemed unable to focus on the overarching goals, his failures were hardly surprising. He hadn't initiated the actions needed to achieve his goals, nor had he identified likely barriers to his success. If Lygell couldn't do it himself, he had no hope of effectively mobilizing the people below him.

Pisander headed back down to his office. He had troubles of his own to attend to.

One of his aides intercepted him. "Jarah has arrived and wishes to speak with you, My Lord."

Pisander nodded. "Send him to my office."

As he returned to his office, it occurred to Pisander that Jarah's arrival might be timely. If things turned ugly, Pisander was going to need a few reliable people on hand who weren't frightened to knock heads together.

He'd worked with some good people over the years, and he wished he could still call on some of them. During his early years in Erestor—when he was still known as Lord Dunnridge and before he became the Earl of Pisander—he'd employed an enforcer named Fowkes. Of all his associates over the years, he missed Fowkes the most. The man had been reliable, dedicated, effective, and utterly ruthless.

No one had unlimited luck though. Having sent Fowkes to finish off a noblewoman called Lady Neave, there had been no further word from him. It later became apparent that Fowkes and his men hadn't succeeded in finishing the job, since Lady Neave, or Anneka as she now called herself, had resurfaced during the Rogandan invasion.

It was long past time Pisander did something about her. He had never tolerated unfinished business. At the same time, he had never allowed his need for revenge to blind him to more important priorities. He would deal with Anneka when he had his house in order.

Jarah appeared at the door of his office not long after he arrived himself.

Pisander waved him to a seat. "Have you made any progress? I'm overdue for some good news."

Jarah had been gone a long time. The grim look on his face ruled out good news, but he didn't look entirely discomforted. That suggested he had at least something to report.

Before Jarah started, Pisander added, "You fed me a lot of information when you last reported, and I've had far too much on my mind since then. Give me a simple summary to refresh my memory."

"Certainly, My Lord," Jarah replied. "You might remember that after a considerable amount of effort we eventually identified the boy who showed up at your council of lords meeting. His name is Thomas. He wasn't easy to track down—he's moved around a lot, and he mostly kept well out of sight. He did come back to Arnost a few years ago to get married, and some very interesting people attended the wedding. Will Prentis was there. And the queen."

Pisander nodded. These details weren't easy to forget.

"After the wedding they disappeared. The young woman he married was unusually beautiful though, and that helped a lot in tracking them. It's much harder to hide someone who stands out. They hid themselves away in a remote location in a forest with two or three others. We eventually found the location, but it had been abandoned. Either they burned their own dwellings to the ground, or someone got there before us."

"Who else would be going after them?" Pisander asked skeptically.

Jarah shrugged. "I don't know. Probably no one. The trail led back to Arnost. We found out that his parents had been living right next to the castle the whole time. His father, Axel, was the stable master. When we went to get the parents we discovered they'd fled as well. We only just missed them. That's a summary of my last report."

"So what have you been doing since?"

"It seemed likely that this Thomas and Elena had gone with his parents, so we set off after them. Then we received word that they had parted company and headed in the direction of Erestor. So we stopped trailing the parents and went after them instead.

"We didn't find them, but there were indications they'd joined up with Will Prentis. As I'm sure you know, Will Prentis vanished around that time. They apparently vanished along with him."

Pisander glowered at Jarah. He was not in the mood to be presented with the latest in a growing list of failures.

Jarah apparently decided it was time to change the subject. "There's more, My Lord," he added hastily. "As you know, Lord Redfass has been commanding the western army camped on the borders of Erestor, just outside Steffan's Citadel, with the support of a large number of mercenaries. On our way here we unexpectedly met some of Lord Redfass's men. They told us that Will Prentis has reappeared. With help from Rufe Sarjant, he's taken control of the army. Lord Redfass and almost all of the other mercenaries have been killed. Prentis let some of the survivors go, without horses or weapons, and they're on their way here now. A few of them even begged Prentis to let them join his army."

Pisander scowled.

"The Thomas and Elena we've been searching for are probably there as well, assuming they remained with Will Prentis. And that's not all. When the mercenaries were leaving, they saw someone ride up and address the soldiers. They were a long way off by then, but a few of them swear it was the king."

Pisander narrowed his eyes. The situation had deteriorated more than he could have imagined possible.

"Your search for Thomas is on hold, as of now," he told Jarah. "For the immediate future I'm going to have more pressing tasks for you to do. Get your men settled in at the castle, and make sure I know where to find you at all times."

Having dismissed Jarah, he located one of his aides. "Find Lygell, and bring him here. Now!"

The aide hurried away immediately.

Jarah's report had shaken Pisander from his lethargy. Having begun with real energy, the former earl saw now that he had allowed his focus to wander since taking control of Arnost. Apparently Will Prentis had not made the same mistake.

Everything was about to change. Pisander had clawed his way into a position of strength, and he wasn't about to give it up. The king might have an army now, but without control of Arnost, his options were limited.

Pisander did not waste a moment. He located a quill and a blank parchment and sat down to write a note to King Agon. He debated with himself for several minutes before deciding he needed to keep it brief and to the point. Eventually he simply urged the king to come to Arnost as soon as possible, and to bring an army with him. Agon would have come with an army anyway, but Pisander's request should cause him to be especially alert.

By the time Lygell arrived, Pisander's messenger was already on his way to Rog with the dispatch.

As Lygell entered the room, Pisander was pleased to see anger prominent in the mixture of emotions revealed on his deputy's face. Now was not the time to search out a replacement for Lygell. Pisander needed to work with what he had.

"The king is back," he told Lygell bluntly. "And Will Prentis is with him. They have taken control of Redfass's army. Close the gates of Arnost immediately, and get men onto the city walls. From now on the gate will be opened briefly twice a day, and anyone entering or leaving will be questioned and searched. Send armed men into the surrounding countryside to requisition supplies. I want the city fully stocked in preparation for a siege. As of now we're effectively at war."

He stared grimly at his dumbfounded deputy. "Your opportunity to redeem yourself has just arrived."

Without waiting for a response, he added, "Send messengers to the northern army camped at the borders of Castel and find out who's commanding it. If it's our people, tell them to break camp and return to Arnost. We won't bring them into the city—they'll be needed to keep Prentis away from the border with Rogand. I don't want King Agon forced to fight his way into Arvenon. And tell them to find anyone in the ranks who used to be a captain under Prentis. Any leaders who served under the king should be executed immediately."

He shook his head. "Redfass was a fool. He demoted the original leaders to the ranks. Prentis probably has them all reinstated by now."

Lygell's mouth had been hanging open, but his eyes had narrowed and his face had set. His features now showed nothing but determination. "There's a lot I need to do. With your permission, I'll withdraw and get started."

Pisander nodded. He watched in satisfaction as Lygell strode from the room.

All of them, himself included, had been asleep at the helm. Lady Ona had attempted to shake them out of their stupor, but it had taken Will Prentis to fully wake them.

Now they were alert at last. Prentis had poked his stick into the viper's den, and the serpent was about to slither out, fully aroused. Will Prentis would have no one but himself to blame.

19

———

Thus far little Tammi was not coping at all well with life at sea, and neither Rubin nor Haldek was doing much better. Thomas and Elena found themselves tending to all three. Thomas insisted that Elena should take a break, and when she returned he made his way onto the deck for some fresh air.

Seeing Brother Ander standing alone by the rail, Thomas joined him.

The two of them stood in companionable silence for a time, watching a large pod of dolphins frolicking beside the ship. There was something captivating about the exuberance of the animals as they glided through the water, slicing effortlessly through the bow wave before diving and reappearing alongside.

Thomas stole occasional glances at his friend. The monk seemed relaxed and content, so different from the man Thomas had known before the fight in the village where Ander almost lost his life. So much had changed for all of them since then.

"Do you think about Brother Vangellis much?" Thomas asked.

The monk glanced briefly at him, then nodded. "Yes. Often."

Thomas had once put a question to Brother Vangellis that his late friend had not been able to answer. The question related to Brother

Ander, and it struck Thomas that now might be the perfect opportunity to resolve a matter he had long wondered about.

"I know you came to respect Brother Vangellis as much as I did," said Thomas. "But why did you dislike him so much at first?"

The stone could readily have provided a detailed answer, of course, but Thomas refused to consider using it for such a purpose.

Brother Ander gazed out over the waves for some time without speaking.

The silence stretched out for long enough that Thomas felt uncomfortable. He began to wonder if his bluntness had been offensive. "Forgive me if I was too intrusive," he said awkwardly. "Just ignore the question."

After a further short silence Brother Ander turned to look at him. He didn't look upset. "I don't mind talking about it," he said. "It brings back painful memories, and that's the only reason I've been slow to answer."

The monk sighed. "I had a younger sister when I was growing up. We all agreed she was made of sunshine and laughter." He nodded toward the bow where the dolphins were still playing. "Those creatures make me think of her—they're all carefree energy and playfulness."

He stared off into the horizon. "Sickness came to our village from time to time. The very old and the very young were always vulnerable, but one of the contagions took my sister. She was her normal happy self in the morning, and by the time the sun had set she was dead.

"All of us were devastated. My parents went to the priest to arrange her burial. He was well known to be an evil man—it's obvious to me now that he didn't know God at all, in spite of his profession. He demanded money to do burials, and in my sister's case the amount was much more than my parents could afford. He said if they didn't pay he would bury her outside the graveyard with the murderers. We'd been told that anyone buried there was doomed to spend eternity in hell.

"My mother was horrified. The very thought of her precious

daughter being condemned for eternity was more than she could bear. She somehow came up with the money and paid the priest, against my father's wishes. My father knew our family was being plunged into poverty, and he told the priest exactly what he thought of him.

"The priest carried out the ceremony, then told the gravedigger to bury her outside the fence. It was his way of hitting back at my father. My mother never recovered—the horror of it sent her to an early grave herself."

Thomas was appalled.

"My father refused to have anything more to do with the priest," Brother Ander continued, "so my mother was buried outside the fence as well, beside my sister."

He shook his head. "My father was never the same. He became consumed with anger—he was difficult to be around. I came to hate the priest bitterly.

"The priest spent the money he extorted on wine, and one day I came upon him when he was drunk. I railed at him to his face. I would have killed him if I dared. He cursed me in return. He told me I was destined for an eternity in hell with my sister and mother.

"The moment I was old enough, I left the village to become a soldier. I had a deep well of anger inside me, and the army gave me an outlet for it.

"Eventually we all joined Will when he left Arnost, and he led us to the monastery to collect our new guide. I hated Brother Vangellis from the moment I clapped eyes on him. I was blinded by my bitterness—all I could see was the drunken priest from my village. If he'd died when I slashed his wineskins, I wouldn't have cared a bit."

Thomas listened wide-eyed, horrified at the chain of events that had brought Ander to such a state.

"As you know, I was soon on the brink of death myself after the battle with Baron Rudungen's men. I had no idea that Brother Vangellis was fighting for my life, refusing to rest for days on end. I could never have imagined any man doing that for a person who hated him so much." He shook his head.

Brother Ander looked Thomas in the eye. "I've never told anyone else about this, Thomas, but I had a vision while I was lying there wounded. I know it was a vision now, but it felt completely real to me at the time.

"I woke to find myself in hell. It was horror beyond description. I was absolutely terrified. And who should be there to greet me but the priest from my village? I knew he'd died since I joined the army. He was in torment himself, but he was delighted when he saw me arrive. He shouted at me, 'You finally got what you deserve!'

"I was in dread of him and turned away to look for my sister and my mother. When he saw what I was doing, he just laughed at me. 'They're not here, you fool! It makes no difference what side of the fence you're buried on!' He started gloating. 'I was the one who taught you to hate. Now you're condemned for all time! You'll spend eternity here, with *me!*'"

Brother Ander passed a hand across his face. "I know it wasn't real, but I've never forgotten the sound of him mocking me."

The look in the monk's eyes unnerved Thomas. "What happened?" he asked.

"I was completely without hope. Then Brother Vangellis called me. I can't really explain what happened—all I know is I woke up to find him tending me, along with Elbruhe."

"So your sister and mother didn't end up in hell?" Having blurted out the question, Thomas immediately berated himself for his insensitivity in asking.

Brother Ander didn't mind. "That isn't for me to say. God decides a person's destiny." He shrugged. "It might have felt real, but it was just a vision. It's true that the location of a person's grave makes no difference though."

"Was the vision the reason you became a monk?" asked Thomas.

Brother Ander shook his head. "No." A wry smile came to his face. "Some people probably think I became a monk out of guilt, or because I needed to repay a debt. They weren't the reasons.

"I hated Brother Vangellis, and I knew from experience that hate is more infectious than the plague. Yet he wasn't infected by it.

"In the end he did a lot more than dress my wounds when I was lying there. I wasn't in a good state, even before the fight in the village. My anger was never far from the surface—hatred oozed out of every pore. The weird thing was that Brother Vangellis might have had his own flaws, but grace oozed out of him.

"You asked why I decided to become a monk. When he pulled me out of hell—and I don't just mean in my vision—it undid me completely.

"All my life I'd wanted to lead men into battle. I finally got my chance at Torbury Scarp, and it didn't satisfy me at all. After a while I realized I wanted to do what he'd done." He raised his arms helplessly. "So I decided I needed to become a monk."

"And now you've become a healer as well." Thomas gazed at the monk in wonder. "I remember what you were like before," he said. "You're different. You seem more content."

Brother Ander said nothing in response, but he returned a smile.

Realizing that he needed to return to his duties, Thomas said a reluctant farewell to the monk and headed below deck again.

The impact of Brother Ander's words remained with him long after the conversation had ended.

A STIFF BREEZE pushed the hair from Breysen's eyes as he stood on the deck basking in the sunshine. No matter how many years he might have spent on dry land, the sea was in his blood.

The king stood beside him, gazing around in wonder and peering up at the squawking gulls that wheeled overhead. "It's stunning!" He pointed to a land mass rising out of the sea off to one side. "What's that ahead? Given the direction we're sailing, I suppose it must be an island, but if so it seems surprisingly big."

"That's Baron Island off the port bow," Breysen told him. "Captain Yordin must have decided to navigate the strait." He slowly turned full circle, staring at the horizon and glancing up at the sky. "There seems little likelihood of a storm right now. We're probably more at risk of losing the wind altogether."

"Why is that a risk?" asked the king.

"Any ship that's becalmed is at the mercy of the tide. When you're near land, you might drift onto some rocks."

"Why would the captain risk that happening?"

"Nothing is ever certain at sea," Breysen said with a shrug. "There's always risk, no matter where you steer the ship." He glanced again at the sky. "Sometimes when the weather looks calm, squalls blow up out of nowhere. At other times the sky looks threatening, but conditions turn out to be perfect. You have to trust your experience. And your instinct."

Breysen nodded toward the helm. "Captain Yordin has a good reputation. I'm willing to trust his judgment."

There was no sign of the queen. "How is the little prince coping with the conditions, Your Majesty?" asked Breysen.

The king's brows drew together. "He's managing, although I won't be sorry to get him back on land again. The queen had a restless night with him."

Other soldiers had been spilling onto the deck. Seeing Will emerge with Rufe and Jonas, the king waved them over.

"You look a little better, Will," the king offered. "Have you found your way to the galley?" he asked with a grin.

Will screwed up his face. "I'm not ready to eat just yet, Your Majesty," he replied. He adopted a more cheerful look. "I didn't get much sleep last night, but I'm feeling more normal now. Hammocks are surprisingly comfortable."

Will's attempt at brightness didn't fool Breysen.

Even in the current mild conditions the commander didn't seem entirely himself. He appeared to be adjusting to the rhythmic motion of the ship, but his stomach was still very unsettled if his face offered any indication.

"Keep your eye on the horizon," Breysen suggested. "That helps when the ground won't stop moving under your feet."

Will took his advice, returning a nod of thanks.

It did seem to help. Over the next few minutes the gaunt look gradually began to fade from the commander's face.

As the sun climbed slowly in the sky, the breeze became fitful, and the forward movement of the ship began to slow noticeably.

Thomas and Elena joined them. Elena looked concerned, and a glance at little Tamara was enough to explain the reason. The toddler was clearly not coping well at all.

Breysen had seen children sicken and die on longer journeys. Memories still haunted him of parents watching helplessly as the bodies of their little ones were committed to the deep.

He comforted himself with the knowledge that this particular voyage would be brief.

20

B reysen's musing was interrupted by an exclamation from Thomas. "What is that sailor doing?"

He followed Thomas's gaze to a sailor perched high in the riggings. The sailor appeared to be stuffing something into his clothing. The brief glimpse revealed nothing particularly unusual to Breysen about the man's behavior. He glanced back at Thomas, frowning in puzzlement at the alarm on his face.

At the same moment a voice rang out from the crow's nest above, "Sail ahead!"

"Another ship!" No ship sighting had been announced since the Nomad Lady left the harbor at Maranelle, and the soldiers ran to the railing, peering ahead curiously in hope of a sighting.

Thomas stared up at the sailor above, though, his brows drawn together in concern. He turned to Will and spoke quietly into his ear.

Will at once became alert, any queasiness thrust aside. "Breysen, go ask the captain what he knows about that sailor." He pointed aloft. "Hurry! And ask him if he's expecting trouble from that ship ahead."

Surprised by Will's request, Breysen opened his mouth to question him, but the look on the commander's face changed his mind. He turned and sprinted to the helm.

"Captain Yordin, how well do you know that sailor? Will Prentis sent me to ask you." He pointed to the man, who was now climbing down from the rigging.

The captain peered up at him. "I don't know him at all. He's one of the men we took on at Maranelle." He turned to the mate who stood beside him at the wheel. "He had the necessary experience," the mate said defensively. "He ain't no saint, I imagine, but how many of 'em are?" He waved his hand in the direction of the crew.

"And the ship ahead?" Breysen pointed to the distant sails, now noticeably closer.

The captain frowned at him. "What are you suggesting?"

He raised his hands helplessly. "I know nothing more than you."

"What is she?" Captain Yordin asked the mate.

The mate peered forward. "She's too far off to say anything for certain. But she appears to have three masts—isn't that a square-rigged foresail?" He added darkly, "Pirates like fast vessels."

The captain frowned, glancing up at the two lateen-rigged masts towering above his own ship.

Looking down at the deck below him, Breysen saw that Will had not waited for the captain's response. His men had seized the sailor the moment he reached the deck.

The captain had seen it as well. A look of thunder came to his face. "King's commander or not, this is my ship!" He stormed down onto the foredeck.

"What's the meaning of this?" he roared, approaching Will belligerently.

"The same question I was going to put to you," Will replied calmly. "Was this man signaling from the rigging on your orders?"

"Signaling? What are you talking about?" The captain glared at the sailor. "Well?"

The sailor squirmed uncomfortably. "It ain't true, Cap'n!" he said sulkily. "It's all lies."

Thomas whispered in Will's ear, and the commander reached out and in one smooth motion hoisted up the sailor's vest. Two pieces of brightly colored cloth fell to the deck.

The captain stared at him in disbelief. "Tie the cur to the mast!" he shouted.

Several sailors pinned him against the mast and tied him securely in place. A never ending stream of abuse and curses spewed from him until someone shoved a rag into his mouth and tied it in place.

"Never before has one of my men betrayed his own ship," the captain said gruffly, shaking his head.

"Are pirates common in these waters?" asked Will.

The captain shook his head. "Not at all. It's only twice I've been boarded. No one yet has taken my ship, and it won't happen today neither."

"The target might be the king and queen rather than your ship," Will told him.

"I don't care what the target is," replied the captain. "If they try to board us we'll slit their throats." He glanced ahead at the sails drawing ever closer. "They'll have to catch us first. I have the fastest ship in Arvenon. Even with only two masts."

He called to his men as he hurried back to the helm, "All hands! Prepare to defend the ship!"

The sailors scurried about the ship, arming themselves with swords, knives, and long gaffs tipped with vicious hooks.

"Will we be able to get past them?" Will asked Breysen, nodding toward the approaching ship. "And if we do get past, can we outrun them?"

The former sailor looked up at the sails of the Lady, flapping listlessly in the gentle breeze. "Perhaps. If we had wind." He shook his head. "Even with wind, they have three masts. More likely it will come to a fight."

Will's face turned grim. "Make sure the men are fully armed," he told Rufe. "We're told they're all capable with the bow and the sword. They're about to have an opportunity to demonstrate it."

The commander called to Jonas. "Get the king and queen below. And Thomas and Elena too. Make sure they're properly defended."

Rufe and Jonas left immediately to carry out his orders.

"What are these pirates likely to do?" Will asked Breysen.

"I've only been boarded once," he replied. "It turned ugly quicker than you could blink." He saw again in his mind's eye the deck slippery with blood. He pushed the memories aside. "They'll row over in longboats. Then they'll climb aboard any way they can. Pirates get creative—I've heard some tales."

"We need our archers to take them out before they get here then."

"That sounds easier than it's likely to be," Breysen murmured grimly.

Rufe hurried up, and the commander turned away to speak with him. Breysen took the chance to do some preparations of his own.

Noticing a sailor hurrying past, Breysen strode across to him. "Where do you keep your supplies of pitch?" he asked.

The sailor pointed vaguely down into the hold, then turned to hasten away.

Breysen grabbed his arm. "You need to show me. Now!"

The sailor scowled down at the hand restraining his arm, and Breysen hastily released him. "It's important," he added gruffly. "The safety of the Lady could depend on it."

The sailor glared at him for a moment, then seeing the confusion of people dashing in every direction, he shrugged. "Come with me."

The hatch was already guarded by Jonas and several soldiers. The sailor led Breysen past them, down the steps, and deep into the hold. After pointing to a few barrels in a corner, he left without comment.

Blocks of pitch had been stacked in the barrels, and Breysen hunted around for something to carry it in. Finding a sack, he upended its contents and began stuffing lumps of pitch into it. Once the sack was bulging, he headed for the galley.

The cook was nowhere to be seen. Glancing around, Breysen noticed a large metal pot filled with potatoes. Dumping the potatoes unceremoniously onto the floor, he filled the pot with pitch.

The galley boasted two metal ovens that saw constant use for cooking. Satisfying himself that the fires were still alight, Breysen set the pot on one of the ovens. While he was waiting for the pitch to melt, he hurried off to find a few torches and a flint.

Long before Breysen was satisfied that the pitch had liquefied sufficiently, he had begun pacing the floor restlessly. When he was finally convinced that the liquid was ready, he grabbed a bundle of rags and used it to protect his hands as he lifted the metal handle of the pot. He tucked the unlit torches into his belt, then he headed up to the deck, working hard to keep the pot upright as he carried it across a surface that was rolling unpredictably.

The ship was pitching much less than usual and he discovered the reason why as soon as he arrived on deck. The wind had died away almost completely, and the ship was rolling only in response to the gentle swell of the ocean.

Men lined the rails, many of them armed with bows. When he looked past the prow of the Lady his eyes opened wide in shock. He had expected to see three or four longboats heading toward them, but he counted eight, each of them crammed with armed men who were jeering and shouting as they watched the preparations on the Lady.

Even given the size of the other ship, it was difficult for Breysen to imagine how so many longboats had been safely secured and so many men accommodated. Clearly this was no ordinary pirate vessel.

Spotting Will near the bow, Breysen set down the pot of hot liquid in a safe location and made his way forward.

"Wait until they are much closer!" Rufe called to the archers. At the rate the longboats were moving, they would be in range very soon.

"Target the rowers in the leading boat," Breysen urged Will. "On the starboard side."

Both Will and Rufe turned to him, puzzled looks on their faces. "Which side is that?" Will asked. "And why?"

"Their right side. Our left," Breysen replied. "Try it—you'll see."

Will nodded to Rufe.

Rufe selected four of his men. "Target the rowers in the nearest boat," he told them. He pointed left. "Only the ones on our left side."

Firing arrows on land could not compare with firing from on deck, due to the movement of the boat. But the swell was gentle, and there was no wind to speak of. Arrows sliced into the water around the longboat, but some found their mark. Two of the rowers slumped over their oars unmoving, and a third cried out in pain, dropping his oar. With fewer men now rowing on one side of the boat, the bow of the longboat swung abruptly around. The boat was no longer drawing closer. It sat in the path of other boats, and shouts of annoyance came from the men forced to row around it.

Splashes sounded as lifeless bodies were dumped overboard, and other men took the place of the rowers. The boat slowly faced forward again and began to move.

"Keep at it!" Breysen urged.

Rufe nodded. "Don't stop!" he called to his four archers. "More of the same!"

Other boats were now well within bowshot, and Rufe selected other groups of four and ordered them to apply the same strategy to different boats. Loud curses could be heard from the longboats as a continuous treatment of arrows now flew through the air toward them.

Breysen hurried away and returned with his pot of pitch. Men in the longboats were becoming noticeably reluctant to take the place of rowers on the starboard side. Nevertheless, all of the boats had drawn slowly closer.

Putting down his pot, he took up the rags he had used to carry it and tore them into strips. Then he dipped them carefully into the hot pitch.

"Rufe!" he called. "Wrap these around some arrows. We'll light them before they're fired."

Rufe nodded. He decided to try it himself first. While he wound a strip onto an arrowhead, Breysen lit a torch. Rufe drew the bow, Breysen touched the torch to the arrowhead, and Rufe released the arrow. It landed in the closest longboat, and men frantically moved to smother the flames before they could spread. No damage was done, but the distraction added to the confusion.

Rufe's next arrow sank into the arm of a rower, setting his clothing alight. The man screamed and jumped overboard to douse the flames. Unable to swim with his injured arm, he clung onto the longboat with the other hand. With the extra drag of his body in the water, the forward progress of the boat was slowed further, and the wounded man cried out in pain and anger as others in the boat shoved him away from the boat with their oars.

Rufe quickly called aside several other archers, and a steady stream of flaming arrows soon filled the air.

All this time the other ship had slowly drifted nearer.

"Can any of your archers reach that ship?" Breysen asked Will.

The commander turned to him at once, clearly willing to receive any suggestion Breysen might offer. "Why?" he asked curiously.

"When we try to get away from here we need to make sure they can't follow us," Breysen replied. "If we can get some flaming arrows into their sails..."

Will nodded. "Jonas!" he called.

Jonas came running across the deck.

Will pointed to the other ship. "Can you put arrows into their sails? The arrowheads will have burning rags wrapped around them. That will reduce their range."

Jonas squinted across at the other ship. "Maybe. I can try."

"We'll only get one attempt," said Breysen, frowning. "They'll withdraw as soon as they see what we're up to."

Will nodded. "Wait until you can be certain, Jonas."

Jonas prepared several arrows, then waited.

The first longboats were almost upon the Lady. The archers had now abandoned their earlier strategy. Their only goal now was to reduce the number of attackers.

Breysen caught Will's eye. He pointed down at the longboats. "If we burn their sails, this lot will have even more reason to take our ship."

Will nodded grimly. "I understand. We'll do it anyway." He turned to Jonas. "Can you do it?"

Jonas took a calculating look at the other ship. Then he selected an arrow and drew back his bow. Breysen touched the torch to the tip of the arrow.

Jonas released the arrow. It flew truly and buried itself into the sail. But the flames had gone out before it struck.

Faint shouts could be heard from the other ship. Sailors began reefing the sails.

"Quickly!" urged Breysen.

Jonas chose another arrow with more rag on it. He dipped it once more into the pitch and Breysen lit it. This time the flame was still burning when it struck the lateen sail on the main-mast opposite. The canvas around it slowly began to ignite. Sailors climbed into the rigging in an attempt to smother the flames. They were too late. Both the square-rigged foresail and the sail on the mizzen-mast were quickly alight as Jonas continued his onslaught.

The only possible way of limiting the damage now seemed to be to reef the sails, and sailors were frantically attempting it. Burning debris was falling all around them though, and they were hard pressed to prevent the flames from spreading further on the deck.

Breysen's satisfaction was short-lived. Cries of warning around him alerted him to a new danger.

Longboats had reached the Lady.

21

One of the longboats had disappeared behind the stern, and two more had pulled in close under the prow of the Lady where it was difficult for the defenders to reach them. Ropes with grappling hooks had already been thrown over the prow.

Other boats had come alongside the ship, and men were climbing up ropes toward the deck or attempting to smash their way into the ship through portholes.

Jonas had returned to the hatch to oversee the defense of the king and queen and little prince, and Rufe was fully occupied directing archers and preparing men for hand-to-hand fighting.

The unlit torches were still tucked into Breysen's belt. Thrusting the burning torch into Will's hand, he said to him urgently, "Come with me!"

The pot had cooled, but its contents were still liquid. Breysen picked it up and carried it to the side of the ship. He tipped it over the side, half of its contents spilling onto a longboat that had just pulled alongside. Grabbing an unlit torch from his belt, he touched it to the burning torch in Will's other hand and dropped it over the side. Seeing it coming, one of the men in the longboat swatted it aside, but

Breysen had already sent two more torches after it, and he only managed to intercept one of them. The other landed squarely among the pitch, spreading flames across the boat. After a frantic attempt to smother the flames, men leaped into the sea, some of them with their clothing on fire.

Breysen didn't stay to watch. Calling for Will to follow him, he hurried to the other side of the ship in time for another longboat to arrive. Positioning himself above it, he upended the pot entirely, emptying the remainder of its contents directly onto the longboat. The men in the boat had not witnessed the earlier incident, and they were taken entirely by surprise. That longboat too was soon ablaze.

All of the pitch was now gone, and Will hurried away, no doubt seeing that he was needed elsewhere.

Breysen drew his sword just as the head and shoulders of an attacker emerged over the side of the ship. Lofting the empty pot, he raced toward him. Swinging wildly, the heavy metal pot connected with the head of the man just as he bent to step over the rails. The man fell backward over the side of the ship. On his way down he collided with another attacker, dislodging him from the rope he was climbing. Both men crashed heavily onto the near side of the long-boat, causing it to capsize. The other occupants were pitched into the water.

In spite of the best efforts of Breysen and the archers, men had scrambled onto the Lady, and vicious fighting had broken out across the deck. He glanced around, trying to decide what to do next.

Muffled cries from the hatchway suggested that a deadly struggle was underway below deck. Remembering his debt to the king and queen, Breysen made his choice.

Hurrying to the hatchway, he found it entirely unguarded. Jonas and his men must have been drawn away in defense of the royals. Even as he peered down the stairs, he heard the sound of running feet behind him. He spun around to face two attackers making directly for him.

Determined to deny them access below deck, he stood before the hatch and prepared to defend it.

His mind was quickly consumed with a frenzied struggle to stay alive. He knew he could not long defend himself against two determined opponents, but he fought with every ounce of determination he could muster.

Ducking under a furious sword swipe, Breysen stumbled into the entranceway of the hatch. Somehow he managed to plant his feet on the ladder, but he knew he had neither the strength nor the skill to force his way back onto the deck. And if he retreated further down the ladder, it would quickly become impossible to prevent his attackers from leaping down after him.

Abruptly he was seized from behind and pulled off the stairs. Before he could react in any way, the hatch cover was slammed shut above him and fastened with a beam of wood used to secure the hatch in heavy weather. The shouts of anger from the men above were instantly reduced to muffled yells. Feet began to stomp on the hatch cover above, but it had been made to withstand the elements, and it held firm.

Lying on the floor at the base of the stairs as the hatch was being sealed, Breysen saw that his rescuer was Brother Ander.

"Thank you," he said breathlessly.

The monk nodded. "That will hold them for a while."

Cries and the clash of weapons drew his attention away from the hatch.

"You're needed below," the monk told him.

"Lead the way," Breysen said, scrambling to his feet.

The big monk hastened through narrow walkways and down another level before they burst into a large hold. A quick glance revealed Jonas and another soldier fending off four attackers. The king and queen, both armed with swords, faced two more together.

The attackers fought with their backs to Breysen. Heads turned as they belatedly registered his arrival, but they were too slow to prevent Breysen from stabbing forward, once, twice—killing one man and injuring another.

His arrival tilted the balance, completely changing the

momentum of the struggle. In just a few moments, all of the attackers lay dead.

Both King Steffan and Queen Essanda turned to their baby son who lay in a basket behind them. He appeared to be unscathed.

The monk turned to Breysen. "I couldn't...I couldn't do it," he said, raising his hands helplessly.

Breysen stared at him for a moment, uncomprehending. Then suddenly he understood. Unable to bring himself to fight, the monk had gone for help and found Breysen. What would he have done if Breysen hadn't been there, and he had instead found himself facing two more attackers coming down the hatchway?

Brother Ander's relieved face stared down at him. "Thank you," he said.

Before Breysen could respond, Jonas joined the monk, echoing his thanks. The king and queen were not far behind him.

Their appreciation overwhelmed Breysen, and he could do no more than dip his head awkwardly in response. He wasn't fighting for money now—he was defending people worthy of his respect. Everything had changed so rapidly.

"Get them somewhere safe," Brother Ander was telling Jonas, "somewhere defensible."

"I'll see if Will can send reinforcements," said Breysen.

Jonas nodded, and Breysen set off to retrace his steps.

He reached the hatch without encountering another soul. The hatch cover was still intact and the hatch sealed. He could hear no sound above him.

Should he risk opening the hatch? He stood silently for a couple of minutes, wrestling with the dilemma.

Eventually he climbed the steps. As silently as he could, he pulled away the beam securing the cover. Then he carefully lifted the cover a crack, ready to slam it back shut at a moment's notice. He saw no sign of another person.

Opening the cover completely, he emerged onto the deck and looked around.

Bodies, both of attackers and defenders, lay strewn around, and several small knots of men were still fighting. But something else had changed. Breysen sensed it the moment he emerged on deck. The wind had picked up, filling the sails. The ship was moving.

A loud splash sounded. Looking in the direction of the noise, he saw a man disappear over the side of the ship. Another splash soon followed. The attackers had apparently decided to get out while they still could.

Others followed, and Breysen looked down to see several heads bobbing in the water as men swam for the remaining longboats. The Lady was gradually picking up speed, and the longboats had already fallen noticeably behind.

Spotting Will and Rufe with Captain Yordin at the helm, Breysen decided to join them.

"Rufe is going to do a sweep right through the ship," Will was saying. "We'll need a few of your sailors to guide us, to make sure we don't miss anything."

The captain called four sailors by name. "Go with this man, and show him through every corner of the Lady. We don't want a single one of those pirates left on board."

The men grunted their understanding. As they were about to go, Will said to Rufe, "Find the king and queen before you do anything else."

"I've just come from them," said Breysen. "Jonas is with them, Brother Ander too. Jonas was planning to hide them away somewhere safe."

Rufe nodded and set off with the sailors and six of his surviving soldiers.

Will nodded a salute to Breysen. "If you hadn't been here, the outcome might have been different. You evened the odds considerably."

Unable to decide how to respond, Breysen said nothing.

Will left the captain and headed to the railing, waving for Breysen to join him.

"I wasn't certain we could trust you," he told Breysen frankly. "I don't doubt you any longer."

Will gazed back toward the ship and its longboats, steadily falling further behind the Lady. "Who were those men? What was their purpose?"

Breysen raised his hands helplessly.

"The man lashed to the mast might give us some answers," said Will, heading for him.

Long before they reached the mast, it was obvious that the man was no longer there. The ropes that had restrained him lay severed at the foot of the mast.

"His friends must have cut him loose," said Will, a frown of annoyance covering his face.

The commander hurried back to the helm. "Did those men seem like pirates to you?" he asked the captain.

"I've had little enough experience with pirates," Captain Yordin replied. "And I can't say I'm sorry about it."

He turned to the mate, who shrugged. "That weren't no pirate ship," he said.

"Why not?" demanded the captain.

"She was flying a Castelan flag," he replied.

"I saw no Castelan flag," said Will, frowning.

"They took it down," the mate said indifferently. "I didn't see it until after they launched the longboats. Too little wind—I only saw it when they removed it."

"Are you certain?" asked Will, clearly unconvinced.

The mate shrugged noncommittally.

Rufe appeared in the hatchway followed by the king and queen, with Jonas close behind. Thomas and Elena emerged with Brother Ander soon after them.

Will hurried over to them with Breysen in his wake.

"We're fine, Will," the king said, preempting his commander's question.

"Thanks to Jonas. And Breysen," added the queen.

Feeling himself coloring, Breysen bent his head in a bow.

Multiple conversations broke out, giving vent to the general sense of relief now that the ordeal was behind them.

Breysen noticed Will drawing aside with Thomas. After a whispered conversation, Will approached the king and queen.

"I have surprising and disturbing news, Your Majesties," he said. "The ship that attacked us was flying the Castelan flag."

The king snorted in disbelief.

"I refuse to believe it, Will," said the queen defiantly. "What makes you even consider such an idea?"

Will looked at her steadily. "The mate saw them lowering the flag."

The interaction bemused Breysen. Will had seemed no more convinced than the queen after hearing the mate's account. Yet a brief conversation with Thomas had left him with no doubt at all. He stole a quick glance at Thomas.

He wasn't the only one whose curiosity had been aroused. Rufe was also observing Thomas keenly. And the big man didn't seem at all surprised by Will's assertion.

What did it all mean?

The conversation drifted on without clear resolution to the mysteries surrounding the attackers.

Baffling as their identity and purpose might be, one thing was clear to Breysen—no question remained about his own reliability. The degree to which his situation had turned around was nothing short of astonishing.

There could be no certainty about the final outcome of the king's efforts to regain his kingdom, but Breysen had at last found himself fighting for a cause he could believe in. The king could rightly demand his full allegiance, but in Breysen's eyes he was a man who also deserved it. Close exposure to Will, Rufe, and the others surrounding the king and queen had only reinforced the reputations of them all.

***

ONE SAILOR HAD FOUGHT with special vigor against the boarders. Apart from the fact that it wasn't in Carnwill's interests for Thomas to fall into anyone else's hands, he could barely remember when he last had a good fight. Once Thomas disappeared below decks, he saw no reason to hang back.

He hadn't realized how constrained he'd been feeling until he had a chance to take out his frustrations on someone else. He must have accounted for at least six of the attackers. It had been invigorating. And if no one had especially noticed his efforts, then so much the better. He needed to stay out of sight.

Before long they would arrive in Varacellan. Once they reached the port, he would notify King Agon of Thomas's new location.

The Rogandan king would have agents in the city, and an opportunity for them to abduct Thomas would present itself before long. And Thomas would be closer to Agon than ever—only a short voyage by sea separated Varacellan from Rog.

THE GRIM TASK of committing to the deep the bodies of the slain fell to Brother Ander. Captain Yordin's sailors, the king's soldiers, and fallen attackers alike had been sewn without distinction into canvas bags.

Putting aside his habitual reticence clearly cost the monk a lot, but he nevertheless stood calmly beside the long line of canvas-wrapped corpses.

"Some of these men were friends, and some were foes," he called. "They share one thing in common, besides the watery grave that awaits their earthly remains. Each must give account to their Maker for their choices while on earth."

His eyes scanned the gathered crowd. "All of us are accustomed to receiving services in return for goods or the use of our skills. Occasionally we might benefit from an unearned service too great to be repaid. That was my experience. My own life was saved by a man who owed me nothing and received nothing in return except my gratitude."

Breysen's curiosity was aroused. He wondered who might have saved the monk's life.

"I lay mortally wounded after a battle," Brother Ander continued, "and I neither earned nor deserved the help of the man who healed me. In the same way I will rely on the mercy of my Maker when I stand before him. I won't have earned or deserved mercy any more than I did my healing."

Bodies were released as he spoke, sliding one by one into the sea and sinking slowly into its depths.

Breysen had heard many words spoken over the dead, both on land and at sea, but the monk's words stirred his interest. Perhaps it was because he had so recently received mercy from the king, in spite of having thrown his lot in with a mercenary.

Perhaps it had to do with Brother Ander himself—Breysen had never met a monk like him. Whatever the reason, Breysen wanted to know more, and he resolved to engage the monk in further conversation when he found an opportunity.

The voyage continued without further incident, and at noon on the following day they entered the broad bay into which the River Dan emptied. A forest of masts crowned the tall ships at anchor in the sheltered harbor, and many buildings sprawled across the docks and beyond them.

Above the port lay the city of Varacellan with its many fair towers. The royal castle crowned the city, bright flags fluttering from its sturdy battlements in the gentle breeze.

A pilot met them and guided them to a place among the anchored vessels—single masted, two masted, or even three masted caravels. Captain Yordin arranged for the king and his party to be transported to shore in a longboat. Finding himself sitting alongside Thomas when he climbed aboard, Breysen was unable to prevent himself from directing frequent curious glances at the young man.

Once they reached the shore, they were met by officials who arranged an escort to the castle. A messenger was sent ahead, and they were met part way by a squadron of King Delmar's personal guard who led them to guest quarters within the palace walls. Lord

Karevis appeared and greeted them warmly, bringing an invitation for the king and queen to meet with him privately at their earliest convenience. King Steffan's entire party was invited to join King Delmar at a welcome banquet that evening.

They had safely reached the capital of Varas at last.

VOLUME 2—THE BREAKERS COME CRASHING IN

22

———

Ranauld's days in the Castelan camp crawled painfully by without a second invitation to meet with Lord Kaebon. The two soldiers assigned by the commander were dour men who rarely spoke, although they stuck to Ranauld like molasses.

His boredom and the enforced inaction allowed him unlimited opportunity to repent of his decision to go with the Castelan scouts. He had done nothing whatever to carry out one of the two key tasks assigned to him on behalf of the king. It seemed unlikely in the extreme that the two men he had left behind would achieve anything useful on their own.

He had followed the scouts here with hopes of engaging in a fruitful dialogue with the leadership of Castel. He decided ruefully that any such hope was no more substantial than the morning mist that blanketed the Castelan camp each morning, dissipating slowly as the sun rose.

After almost a week had passed, a small group of men rode into the camp. After disappearing briefly into Lord Kaebon's tent, one of the men approached Ranauld.

"I have been sent by King Rupert," he said crisply. "You will ride with us to Castel Citadel." It was not a request.

The man had not extended the courtesy of introducing himself. Ranauld did not intend to show the same disrespect.

"Count Ranauld at your service," he said with a small bow. "I do not recall having had the pleasure of meeting you before."

The other man winced slightly. "I am Lord Mardone," he announced hastily, delivering a small bow of his own.

So they had sent a nobleman to escort him to the capital. Ranauld supposed that counted for something.

The two men set out for Castel Citadel within the hour, accompanied by a dozen soldiers. Ranauld was allowed to take his horse, along with the spare clothing and basic supplies in his saddlebags. His weapons were not returned to him. He was a prisoner in all but name.

His situation could have been worse. Ranauld rode with Lord Mardone in the center of the column of soldiers, and having been nudged in the general direction of civility, Lord Mardone's attitude gradually thawed. After no more than a couple of hours in the Castelan nobleman's presence, Ranauld was convinced they would have become friends had circumstances allowed it.

"Have you visited Castel Citadel, Count Ranauld?"

"I'm sorry to say I've never had the opportunity," he replied. "Count Gordan promised me a tour if I was ever able to make the journey."

A shadow passed across the face of Lord Mardone at the mention of Count Gordan, and he quickly changed the subject. Ranauld had not failed to note his reaction, and it filled him with foreboding.

"I am expecting our journey to be comfortable," Mardone said brightly. "We typically see a lot of rain in the capital throughout the year, but the weather has been unseasonably mild of late."

Ranauld accepted the change of direction in the conversation. "I understand that Castel Citadel, like Arnost, is a long way from the ocean," he replied. "That apparently makes a difference to the weather."

"So I am told. Castel has no port of any significance—only a number of seaside towns, all quite modestly sized. Our coastline does not offer the advantages of Varacellan with its well protected harbor. I understand that your own kingdom also boasts a thriving port at Maranelle. Castel does have a navy, though," he added proudly. "We may have a limited number of ships, but all of them are well equipped. We have even commissioned a three masted ship in recent times."

Count Ranauld was no expert in naval matters, but he was well versed enough to know that most vessels used either one or two masts, and he made an effort to sound suitably impressed.

Lord Mardone had arranged accommodation for them throughout their trip, and for Ranauld the journey proved to be unexpectedly relaxed, and as comfortable as his host had predicted.

As they rode through the countryside Ranauld was struck by the number and size of the orchards they passed. He also noticed the abundance of fruit in the meals served by the Castelans.

"I am impressed by the quality and variety of the fruit here in Castel," Ranauld told the nobleman.

Lord Mardone brightened. "Every Castelan, from the poorest to the most wealthy, enjoys a wide range of fruit in their diet," he said.

Apparently sensing that his visitor was interested to learn more, Lord Mardone warmed to his subject. "The cooler climate suits apples in particular, and from our earliest years we enjoy fresh apples in season, as well as stewed apples for dessert. Every farm also takes advantage of a frost proof root cellar, usually below ground, that is used to store apples for many months out of season, along with other fruit and a range of root vegetables and nuts."

It quickly became clear that on this topic the nobleman needed little encouragement. "We also use horse-powered crushing wheels to prepare a wide range of apple based beverages, including fermented cider, hot mulled cider, and sparkling cider. Some here even refer to Castel as the Apple Kingdom. Pears and stone fruit are also served fresh as well as preserved for consumption out of season."

Ranauld absorbed all of it with interest. The commoners they passed appeared healthy, and their bright clothing and attractively decorated dwellings seemed to suggest a general contentment with life. He liked everything he was seeing of Castel, and he could only wish he had found himself there in more genial circumstances.

The following day his curiosity was aroused when they rode past row upon row of what appeared to be bricks laid out on the ground. "Are those bricks? For building?" he asked Lord Mardone. "Wattle and daub is used in most of the dwellings through Arvenon, and country folk mostly thatch their roofs, but I haven't noticed buildings of that type in Castel."

The nobleman seemed pleased by his interest. "Yes, you're right. The clay in this region, and indeed throughout Castel, is ideal for brick making. The clay is ground into powder, then moistened and pressed into molds before being laid out in the sun to dry. Once the bricks have dried they are fired in a kiln.

"Every peasant is able to make bricks, and both rich and poor alike build their houses from them. Those who are wealthiest build from stone, but most other houses throughout Castel are made from clay bricks. We also use clay tiles on the roof. The dwellings are sturdy and weather proof, and not as flammable as houses made from some other materials."

"There is a great deal to admire about your country," said Ranauld, waving an arm about him. "That applies to its people too," he added. "Our queen—your former princess—is one of the most estimable people I have had the privilege of knowing."

"We have much to be grateful for," Lord Mardone replied with a nod. But Ranauld thought that the nobleman seemed troubled as he said it.

If the Castelan did indeed feel some degree of discomfort, he quickly shook it off, and the two men chatted amicably throughout the remainder of their journey.

Ranauld's first view of the capital of Castel took his breath away. The road had taken them over a ridge to reveal a broad and fertile valley below them. The sun had completed half of its journey to the western horizon, and gray clouds covered much of the sky. Afternoon light flooded through gaps in the clouds, illuminating the rich greens and blues and browns in the scene before him.

The citadel from which the capital took its name had been built upon the foothills that climbed above the plain. The fortress was built in light gray stone, and colorful flags waved from its tall battlements. The effect was both imposing and pleasing to the eye.

The city designers had taken good advantage of the topography. A huge outcrop of rock rose up behind the fortress and spread out on either side of it. The rock formed an impenetrable barrier denying access to the fortress from behind. A broad river swept in a wide arc around the outcrop, completing a natural barrier that enclosed an area large enough to host the citadel and the city spread out below it.

The natural defenses were strengthened by a city wall that stretched along the river, rising up from the opposite bank. The wall followed the line of the river, merging with the tall outcrop of rock on both sides.

The vista was stunning. Ranauld would have been able to appreciate it more had he felt hopeful about the likely outcome of his visit.

In recent times dwellings had spread across the river, and the two parts of the city were connected by a stone bridge of great size. Riding through the outer section of the city, they crossed the bridge. A huge pair of wooden gates stood open wide at the far end of the bridge at the point where it reached the city wall. The guards at the gate halted them briefly, then waved them through with a nod of acknowledgment to Lord Mardone.

The nobleman led Ranauld to a rough stone building and ushered him inside. The building was well guarded and at first glance it appeared to be a prison. However Lord Mardone led him up several flights of steps to a comfortable if simply appointed room with a small window onto the outside world. Glancing out of the window, Ranauld saw a panorama of the city. He also saw that the room was high above the ground, offering no opportunity to exit the building from the window.

"Please make yourself comfortable, Count Ranauld. Your horse will be cared for and the contents of your saddlebags brought to you. I will arrange for food to be served. I believe that the king is planning to meet with you, although he is a busy man, and I can't tell you when that might happen."

"Thank you, My Lord," Ranauld replied. "You have been most courteous. I hope we will meet again soon."

"I hope so too," Lord Mardone replied with a bow. He left the room, closing the door behind him.

As soon as the sound of his footsteps had faded away, Ranauld went to the window and gazed out at the view. He didn't bother to test the door, assuming it was locked.

The room was furnished with a bed, a comfortable armchair, and a small table that supported a pitcher filled with water and a wooden cup for drinking. A small adjoining room featured plumbing and a large jug of water for washing. Anyone occupying the room was clearly expected to be self-sufficient apart from food.

It seemed apparent that none of his usual ways of occupying himself would be available. Perhaps it was a good thing, since his most important priority was to prepare himself for his meeting with the king. He settled into an armchair, brooding.

A KNOCK at the door brought him leaping to his feet before he remembered that he had no way to unlock it. After a polite pause, the door opened. A soldier appeared in the doorway holding a tray with food and a goblet of wine.

The food looked good, and Ranauld eyed it hungrily. "Thank you," he said, before asking, "Will I be allowed to leave the room to stretch my legs?"

The soldier looked surprised at the question. He glanced behind him and saw that no key protruded from the inside of the door. "I wondered why you didn't unlock the door when I knocked," he said. "I will fetch you a key. You are welcome to lock the door whenever you choose for the sake of your own privacy."

He glanced at Ranauld strangely. "This is not a prison. We have been requested to ensure that you remain within the building at all times, so that you will be available whenever the king calls for you.

But you may wander freely throughout the building. An excellent view of the city is available from the roof."

"Thank you," said Ranauld again with a smile.

The soldier bowed and left the room, leaving the door ajar. He returned a few minutes later with a key, which he placed on the inside of the door. Then he bowed again and left without locking the door.

Ranauld allowed himself to relax. He brought the tray of food and the goblet of wine to the armchair and devoured it hungrily. After he'd finished he got up and tested the key. It did indeed lock the door.

The sunlight had almost gone by the time he climbed to the top of the roof of the building and looked out over the city. Little twinkling lights gave the place a magical feel. The thought of his friend Count Gordan and his offer of a tour prompted a sigh.

Lord Mardone's reaction to his mention of the count reminded him that a great deal had changed in Castel. The reception offered to him was a key example. In the past, a visiting senior nobleman from a key ally would have received a warm welcome and been treated as a dignitary. The soldier who brought his food had been polite and helpful, but he had not greeted Ranauld with the deference due a nobleman.

Ranauld might not exactly be a prisoner, and he hadn't been treated badly. But his hosts were keeping him on a very short leash. All of it was a reminder that he needed to remain on his guard and keep his wits about him.

Acutely aware that he was weary in both body and spirit, he headed back to his room and lay down to sleep.

23

———

As soon as Essanda and Steffan arrived at the royal castle, one of King Delmar's aides ushered them into a pleasant reception room. "King Delmar will be with you shortly," he told them.

Essanda glanced around her, struck by the contrast between her current situation and the drama that had surrounded them when last they had met.

King Delmar appeared in the doorway, his face beaming. "Your Majesties! I can't tell you how delighted I am to see you!" His eyes widened as he glanced at the baby in Essanda's arms. "And who is this?"

"This is Prince Aiden," she told him proudly.

"He shows no signs of having been adversely affected by all that his mother went through."

"Thankfully not," she assured him.

Delmar turned to King Steffan. "It's so good to see you, Steffan," he told him warmly. "I'm more relieved than I can say to see you on your feet and so obviously recovered," he added seriously. "It distressed me greatly to leave you in the condition you were in."

"You did what you needed to do," Steffan assured him. "Your first responsibility was to your kingdom. And I was well cared for."

"I was surprised and alarmed when Lord Nilsean rode in without you. But he assured me that he was playing a part assigned by your Lord Torbury."

Essanda nodded. "We were very grateful that you lent us Lord Nilsean and his men. And he spoke truly—he was very reluctant to leave us. But he carried out his role as a decoy perfectly. He bought time for Will to escort us well away from the area."

"I was much more hopeful once I knew that Will was with you. It seems that the monk—the one who was previously a soldier—did a good job of caring for you, Steffan."

"He did," Steffan agreed. "All of us have a great deal to thank him for."

"You must have quite a story to tell," said Delmar. "What happened after Will joined you?"

"The story is quickly told," Essanda replied. "Will outmaneuvered and outfought a much larger force, and got us to safety. We've been hiding away in a remote refuge near Erestor."

Delmar's face turned grim. "I imagine that the news is what brought you out into the open again."

"What news?" both of them asked at once.

"We thought the location of our hiding place had been compromised," Steffan told him. "That's the only reason we left."

"Then I'm sorry to be the bearer of bad tidings," said Delmar. "Is it true that your ship was attacked on the way here?" They nodded. "And by a Castelan vessel?"

Steffan frowned, but neither of them could confidently deny it.

"There was a reason for the attack," Delmar told them. "Castel has announced that, in view of Arvenian aggression, a state of war now exists between the two countries."

"Castel! At war with Arvenon? But that's ridiculous! It's all nothing more than a misunderstanding," cried Essanda in dismay.

Steffan's response was very different. "How can they dare to attack us?" he asked in anger. "After all we've done to support them!"

"Killing us does not appear to have been the only goal of the people who planned the assassination," Delmar told them. "That was just the beginning. Their failure to kill me set them back in Varas, but they seem to have made inroads in both Arvenon and Castel."

"Do you know who is influencing my brother in Castel?" Essanda asked him.

"Yes, I do," he said. "It's the former Lord Eisgold."

"Surely not!" she said, shaking her head in disbelief. "The man was completely discredited. Are you certain?"

Delmar returned a reluctant nod. "I trust my sources implicitly."

"So how did they come to attack us at sea?" asked Steffan. "How did they even know where we were?"

"As you know better than most, Castel has always enjoyed a well informed spy network," said King Delmar. "You were spotted in Maranelle. Castelan agents saw one of the duke's men engaging a captain in the port and arranged to place one of their own on board."

Steffan shook his head, a fierce look on his face. "Someone will pay for this!" he said.

Essanda looked at him in concern. "We mustn't forget who our real enemy is. Castel is just as much a victim as Arvenon."

"They're victims through no fault of their own, but no one forced them to become credulous fools!" he insisted.

"They're being misled," she replied. "They're like our soldiers outside Steffan's Citadel. Some might argue that they were credulous fools too. But they showed their true colors once they saw the truth."

Steffan grumbled, but he became silent.

"I must compliment you on your own spy network," Essanda said with a wry smile. "You seem to know a great deal about what's going on."

Delmar smiled, although there was no humor in it. "We certainly haven't been idle. I will be happy to make our findings available to you both."

"Thank you, Delmar," said Steffan. "We are very much in your debt."

Delmar waved his comment away. "Let us not speak of such

things. Should we ever decide to do an accounting, it will quickly become obvious that I am hopelessly in your debt." He sighed. "If it's any comfort to you, our enemies had plans for Varas as well as for Arvenon and Castel. The man planning the undoing of Varas was the same person who ruled as a Rogandan puppet during my imprisonment—the former Lord Tarestel. He was not as fortunate as his fellow conspirators. After my agents identified him, they were able to capture him while he was trying unsuccessfully to foment revolt in the provinces. They dragged him to Varacellan. He has been a guest in my dungeons for a short time."

"What have you learned from him?" growled Steffan.

"Very little, unfortunately. He has told us nothing useful. He almost appears tongue tied."

"So he is still alive?" asked Steffan.

Delmar nodded. "He is. But not for long. I made the mistake of banishing him before. This time I will leave nothing to doubt. He is under guard by men I trust completely. I haven't finally despaired of learning something useful from him. But one way or another, he will be hanged before the week is out."

Thomas and Elena had been accommodated in a section of the castle maintained for royal guests. Tammi was sharing their room, while Rubin and Haldek each had smaller rooms of their own. Both the accommodations and the food were excellent, and all of them were thoroughly enjoying the unfamiliar luxury.

Will sought out Thomas on the morning of their second day in Varacellan. "I need your help, Thomas. King Delmar has a prisoner here. I suspect there's a lot we could learn from him, but he's refusing to talk." He looked at Thomas significantly.

Thomas nodded. "I'll come with you," he assured Will.

"Bring Elena too," suggested Will. "She might discover something useful."

Thomas couldn't help wondering if Will might be hinting that his insights from the stone were not always entirely accurate. If so, he could hardly complain—he had given Will good reason to question the accuracy of his perceptions. In any event, Elena had demonstrated her own facility with the stone, and the two of them complemented each other perfectly.

They were led to a circular staircase built from stone that wound its way into the bowels of the castle. A guard with a torch preceded them, and another followed behind.

"Not too many customers down here at the moment," the first guard said conversationally. "The king only sends the worst of the worst to his dungeons."

The stairs led down to an iron door. One of the guards unlocked it and swung it open. They stepped through to find themselves in a dank corridor dimly lit by torchlight, with many iron doors stretching away into the distance on either side. No sound could be heard except the occasional dripping of water.

The guard led them to the first of the cells and inserted a key into a huge padlock. He glanced at Elena as he shoved open the door. "No need to fear," he said roughly. "The prisoner is fully restrained."

Thomas stepped into the room behind Will, gagging involuntarily as the smell of the place assaulted him. Elena followed close behind. Until the guard made his way into the cell with a blazing torch, the scene before Thomas was illuminated faintly by the guttering light of a single candle.

He saw a prisoner chained to the wall, sitting on a low bed. A small table beside the bed held nothing except a jug of water and the candle. The prisoner looked up and gazed at them vacantly.

Will turned to the guard. "Thank you," he said.

The guard shrugged as he handed him the torch. "Take as long as you like," he said. He left the cell, leaving the door ajar.

Will moved to Thomas's side, glancing at him questioningly. In response Thomas fixed his gaze on the prisoner and reached for the clasp dangling from the chain around his neck. Spinning it around, he brought the stone into contact with his skin.

A wave of impressions immediately assaulted him as the stone granted him access to the mind of the former Lord Tarestel. He braced himself, working to sift the thoughts and memories, to follow the tendrils back to the secrets denied to Tarestel's inquisitors.

The effort of wading through the murky world of Tarestel quickly exhausted Thomas. The imprisoned man had lived a hard life. From his earliest childhood he had been subjected to systematic abuse of various kinds, and he had seen no reason to restrain himself when the opportunity arrived to inflict abuse of his own. It was beyond distasteful—Thomas felt as though he was wallowing in a sewer.

Eventually he navigated his way to the assassination plot. Pisander had been the prime mover; Tarestel had played a peripheral role. Nevertheless, a great deal of information was transferred to Thomas in just a few moments—he witnessed the interactions with Alfic and understood the role of Gretchen. Above all, he understood the master plan that lay behind it all. And he knew he would be able to call upon his own memory to revisit the information at a later time.

Determined to expose any possible role of the Stone of Authority, he chased the memories back—and hit a dead end. Baffled, he tried to find a way around the blockage. Every attempt failed. Something was preventing him from gaining access to Tarestel's memories. He could follow the disgraced nobleman to Rog, and back to Arvenon. But key sections of the time in Rog seemed covered with fog.

After a few minutes of complete frustration he gave up the attempt. Taking Elena to one side, he made her aware of what she would encounter in Tarestel's mind, then he outlined his difficulty. She looked as bemused as he felt, but she took the stone when he removed the chain from around his neck.

Thomas put his arm around her as she fixed her gaze on the prisoner. She started, staggering for a moment, and he held her more tightly. He could imagine what she was seeing. Then he waited, trying to be patient.

Eventually Elena snapped her eyes shut and looked away. After slipping the stone to Thomas, she lowered her gaze until he had replaced it once more around his neck. Then she turned troubled eyes to him. She had no need to express in words her urgent need to be gone from that place.

Thomas had to restrain a desire to run as they left the dungeons. It wasn't just the setting. There was something unnerving about Tarestel. The way men looked at Elena acted as a constant irritant to Thomas. Defensiveness on behalf of his wife had become a normal part of his world since they left the safety and isolation of their home in the forest. Yet when Tarestel first caught sight of Elena, he had looked right through her.

It had nothing to do with the man's sexuality. Thomas had been holding the stone at the time, and he saw that the prisoner simply didn't register her any more than he registered his other visitors. Part of Tarestel's being had completely shut down. Thomas had no idea what might have triggered it, but the effect was profoundly disturbing.

<hr>

THOMAS AND ELENA hastened after Will, scurrying up the stone stairs that led out of the dungeon. Only when they had emerged into the open air did Thomas permit himself to relax.

A quick glance at his wife showed him she had found the visit to Tarestel equally oppressive. He put a supportive arm around her shoulder, and she leaned in and buried her face in his shoulder. He stroked her hair tenderly while she recovered herself.

Will examined their faces quietly for a few moments. He turned first to Thomas. "What did you learn?"

Thomas closed his eyes for a moment, shaking his head. "I haven't often glimpsed a mind so...so disturbing." He shuddered involuntarily. Then he steadied himself. "I learned a great deal about the plotters and how they set up the attempted assassination. Their planning was painstaking, and we're fortunate that they succeeded only in part. I also learned that assassination was merely the first step in their plans. As we already suspected, extending the power of King Agon is their real goal, even though they expect to benefit personally as well."

He outlined everything he had learned, and identified the key people hired to carry out the plans.

"You've done well, Thomas! We will track down their paid helpers, particularly Alfic and Gretchen. They must be held to account for their actions. The final goal of the plotters seems remarkably selfless. Did you discover any hint of the involvement of this other stone—the Stone of Authority?"

The final question was delivered casually, but Thomas guessed that Will was much more interested in the answer than he might appear.

"It was very strange," he replied. "Tarestel did go to Rog, but I could discover nothing at all about his time there. It was almost as if his thoughts and memories about it were blocked. I have never seen anything like it."

Will glanced at Elena, his eyebrows raised questioningly. "Did you have any success?"

She nodded cautiously. "Thomas briefly explained the situation when he gave me the stone. I knew he had explored the matter of the plotters, so I ignored that. I was also confronted by the barrier, and I couldn't find a way through it either." She closed her eyes, as if recalling the experience. "I decided to try to go around it. I went back to the young Cedric. That was his name before he became Lord Tarestel."

"Did that approach work?" asked Thomas eagerly.

"Partially. Cedric has struggled with authority figures throughout his entire life, mainly because of the influence of his father. He learned from an early age that authority figures were greatly to be feared. He could never afford the risk of trusting them. In his mind, the only guaranteed way to be safe was to gain power and exercise it himself. If he was the one holding the power, with no one else in authority over him, he had nothing to fear.

"Eventually he inherited the title of Lord Tarestel. He himself wasn't at all safe as an authority figure. All his life the young Cedric had seen what his father did, and he instinctively behaved the same way. He exercised power with little concern for the effect it might have on others. King Delmar is a very different person—he doesn't make a habit of abusing his power—but Lord Tarestel seemed unable to learn from that."

She paused in an attempt to collect herself. "I'm sorry," she said, "some of the things I saw..." She shook her head as if to clear it.

"I saw glimpses of King Agon's effect on Lord Tarestel. King Agon reminded him of his own father, only worse. It reawakened all his fears. His response was to lock himself away, deep inside, for protection."

She trembled, and Thomas moved to her side once more to offer support.

"That doesn't seem to explain why his mind is blocked, though. The cause of that might have been the Stone of Authority. It didn't seem to be anything natural."

She paused, frowning. "There's one other thing. Usually when people behave in a certain way, they're prompted by their hopes or fears, they're expressing their beliefs, or they're reacting to things that happened in their past. Some of Lord Tarestel's decisions didn't seem to come from any of those motivations. Especially decisions that involve helping King Agon. He decided to act, but he did so for no apparent reason."

Elena fell silent, and all of them stood pondering her words.

Will finally broke the silence. "There's only one way we can know for certain what Agon is planning, and whether he has the help of the Stone of Authority. We need to find a way to get access to him directly. If we can do that, the Stone of Knowing will be able to answer all of our questions."

With nothing further to say, the meeting ended. But Thomas could not get Will's parting words out of his mind. They continued to haunt him long after the conversation had ended.

STEFFAN WALKED the castle battlements with Delmar, squinting against the sun as it climbed over the horizon. Both men had clothed themselves warmly against the cool breeze from the sea.

He gazed up at the gulls as they wheeled above, shattering the stillness of the early morning with their cries.

Delmar turned to him. "I have just received confirmation that Tarestel was executed before dawn."

Steffan grunted his satisfaction.

He stared into the west in the growing light before shifting his gaze southward, almost expecting to glimpse his enemies if he strained hard enough.

Finally Steffan redirected his attention to his friend. "The challenge now is to arrange a similar fate for Pisander and Eisgold," he said.

"That is indeed the challenge," agreed Delmar.

24

———

"Count Ranauld. King Rupert commands your attendance—I am here to escort you to him."

Ranauld followed the royal aide out of the building that had become his home, conscious that he had been offered no opportunity to prepare himself. He had at least taken the precaution of abandoning his travel stained garments in favor of the most presentable of the clothing available in his saddlebags.

He had woken on his first morning in the capital of Castel with high hopes of an early audience with the king. That had been more than a week ago. In that time he had seen Lord Mardone once, and only briefly. He was bored beyond words, and ready to welcome change of any kind, be it good or bad.

A squad of royal guards fell in with them as they left the building, and they proceeded quickly to the castle. Once they had arrived, Ranauld was shown into a long reception room with a small throne at one end. With no other chairs in sight, he had no choice but to stand.

After waiting for almost an hour he heard voices, and a group of men entered the reception hall from a door off to one side. Ranauld had never met King Rupert, but it was immediately obvious who he was. More elaborately clad than all of his companions, he was also the only one younger than late middle age.

A surge of compassion rose up in Ranauld at the sight of the young king. What must it have been like, just a few short months ago, to have been thrust into the kingship at the age of seventeen after the violent murder of his father, King Istel? Ranauld knew that both Essanda and Rupert had loved and respected their father. Prince Rupert must have looked forward to many more years of observing and learning from him before his own turn came to ascend the throne. But every opportunity had been snatched away from him.

None of the men entering with the king were known to Ranauld, with one notable exception. When he saw who was whispering in the king's ear, his jaw dropped in utter astonishment. The king's confidante was none other than the disgraced former Lord Eisgold, exiled by King Rupert's father after the Battle of Torbury Scarp.

The young king's eyes sought Ranauld out and studied him evenly for a moment.

"Count Ranauld," he said. "I have granted you an audience—against the wishes of my advisors, I must say—only because I know my late father held you in high esteem."

Ranauld bowed deeply. "I am grateful, Your Majesty. This meeting may be unexpected for us all, but I know that Queen Essanda and King Steffan would wish me to pass on their warm greetings."

A frown crossed the face of the young king. "Are you loyal to King Steffan, Count Ranauld?" he asked.

"Yes, Your Majesty. Wholeheartedly."

"Then perhaps you can explain to me why my brother-in-law's forces are attacking my kingdom. That is not the action of someone who wishes me well."

"The army outside Deadman's Pass is not there on the orders of the king or queen, Your Majesty. After assassins attacked the kings in the barn at Paradise Valley, the man behind the attack took control of Arnost. The army camped at your border is acting on his orders."

"Then what were you doing there?"

"I was sent by King Steffan to attempt to take control of the army in his name. Your scouts came upon me before I had opportunity to make contact with soldiers loyal to the king."

"So one of Arvenon's most senior army commanders was present at Arvenon's largest army camp, yet he had no connection with that army?"

"Had I been commanding the army, Your Majesty, I would have been in the camp, not peering down at it from a ridge. Your scouts will confirm that they found me doing just that."

"My scouts returned immediately to the army to defend the pass, so it is pointless to appeal to them. But you should be aware, Count Ranauld, that I received a very different account of your movements."

Ranauld forced down a surge of frustration. He couldn't afford to let his anger bubble out. With Eisgold whispering in King Rupert's ear, it was hardly surprising that the king was hearing warped versions of the truth.

He decided to change tack. "King Steffan and Queen Essanda are victims like you, Your Majesty, not aggressors. King Steffan almost died of his wounds in the attack at Paradise Valley. Your sister was forced to fight for her life and for her unborn baby. I was present, and I witnessed it firsthand."

The king sighed. "I saw a great deal of Steffan during his time in Castel, and I cannot believe he would have wanted to see my father murdered," he said. "As for my sister, she is incapable even of imagining such an atrocity."

He fixed his gaze on Ranauld. "You say you were there. Where was King Delmar during this attack?"

"He was not in the barn. He had been called away briefly."

King Rupert nodded significantly. "Very convenient, I am sure."

Ranauld shook his head, struggling to remain calm. "It wasn't like that, Your Majesty. King Delmar was not involved in the attacks. His army commander, Lord Karevis, risked his life to defend Queen Essanda. She would tell you that she survived only because of his help."

The young king sighed again. "I may be young and inexperienced, but it is obvious to me that you believe what you are saying, Count Ranauld. That does not mean that you are speaking the truth."

Ranauld bristled. "One of your own noblemen was also present, Your Majesty. Lord Eravitt if I remember correctly. He can confirm my account."

"Lord Eravitt has been much occupied on his estate in recent times. After the trauma he endured, I agreed to release him from his duties in the capital. But even if he has a similar perception—and most likely he does—the facts do allow for a very different interpretation. I have been assured that our agents have uncovered compelling evidence about the attack that resulted in the murder of my father. It was planned and carried out on the orders of King Delmar."

Count Ranauld was too astonished to respond.

"Was Will Prentis present during the attack?" asked the king.

"Sadly he was not, Your Majesty. If he had been, the kings would have been better defended."

"His absence was indeed significant, although not for the reason you seem to suppose," the king replied grimly. "We have reason to believe that Prentis colluded with King Delmar in the attack. He hoped to receive as his reward the kingdom of Castel."

Ranauld furrowed his brows in disbelief. He was unable to fathom what he was hearing.

The youthful king shook his head sadly. "It doesn't end there. I wonder if you know the whereabouts of your monarchs, Count Ranauld. They are currently in Varacellan, having thrown themselves upon the mercy of King Delmar of Varas, the very man whose scheming brought about the death of my father. We tried to make contact with them during their voyage by sea, but I am told that our overtures were violently rejected. In their minds, friends have apparently become foes, and foes are friends.

"Perhaps their vulnerability has blinded them to Delmar's true intentions. Or perhaps he has managed to persuade them he avoided the assassins himself only by good fortune. You said that Delmar's army commander, Lord Karevis, intervened to help my sister. Delmar may have used that to convince them he was not involved in the attack."

The young king shrugged. "Maybe Steffan and Essanda are simply too desperate to acknowledge to themselves that he is manipulating them. By whatever means it has come about, in making common cause with Delmar they have become a danger to every kingdom that desires only peace."

Ranauld's jaw dropped again. The king's assertions were monstrous. "Who is feeding you these...these distortions, Your Majesty?" He turned his eyes upon Eisgold, glaring openly at him.

Eisgold regarded him disdainfully before turning to the king. "I warned you of the futility of trying to reason with him, did I not, Your Majesty?" he sniffed.

He turned a cold gaze upon Ranauld. "I have no need to justify myself to you," he said. "Nevertheless you yourself are well aware of the charges leveled against me. Our beloved King Istel never once accused me of treason. My only crime was to have questioned the orders of Prentis, a commoner foisted on King Istel against his better judgment. Recent events have more than vindicated my suspicions about Prentis's character and integrity. As for his abilities, they were always overblown. The huge loss of life suffered by our forces at Torbury Scarp was entirely unnecessary. In his overweening pride Prentis fancied himself a commander. He refused to listen to my advice, and the army of Castel suffered terrible losses as a result.

"And yet we have seen that granting him the title of commander was only the beginning. Your king made a mockery of nobility everywhere by elevating him to the Arvenian peerage." Eisgold threw up his hands in disgust. "Recent events have shown that, even after all of this, Prentis's greedy ambition was still not satisfied."

Ranauld stared at Eisgold dumbfounded, wide-eyed with shock at the grotesque parody of the truth peddled by the conniving deceiver. He stood paralyzed, helpless to imagine how to begin responding. What could gainfully be said while the truth was being twisted so cynically?

Eisgold shifted his attention to the king. "This Count Ranauld heaped shame upon the nobility when he abased himself so abjectly before Prentis, a commoner. And there are serious questions around his behavior at the border. Nevertheless, Your Majesty has declared him ignorant of the truth rather than intentionally duplicitous, and in doing so I believe you have once again demonstrated wisdom beyond your years. He is a pawn and nothing more. Yet even pawns can be dangerous."

At that moment an aide came to Eisgold's side and whispered urgently in his ear.

"Other more important engagements await you, Your Majesty," Eisgold announced importantly. "Please accept my apologies for failing to alert you sooner."

When King Rupert offered no protest, Eisgold bustled him from the reception chamber. The entire party hurried away without as much as a backward glance.

Count Ranauld was escorted back to his quarters. The royal aide who accompanied the count made it clear that he was not at liberty to leave the building.

Two dreary days followed, with Ranauld in constant turmoil. What should he do? What could he do? He was no closer to an answer when a soldier appeared at his door early one evening and announced that he had a visitor. He followed the soldier to the uppermost level of the building. His guide came to a halt outside the door of a room at the far end of the passageway. The soldier ran his hands carefully over Ranauld, checking for hidden weapons, then after pointing him to the door, the soldier stepped back. Ranauld noticed several other soldiers positioned nearby, all of them armed and alert.

Was he about to meet with some kind of 'accident'? After a moment's hesitation, he shrugged and opened the door. A fire crackled in the hearth and clusters of candles attached to the wall were burning brightly. He saw at a glance that the room was empty apart from a cloaked figure standing beside the window opposite him. The unknown individual was facing away from the door, apparently gazing out over the city. As Ranauld stepped into the room a guard closed the door behind him.

The figure turned toward him, and he sucked in a breath of surprise. His unexpected visitor was King Rupert.

"Count Ranauld," said the young king with a nod. He sounded weary.

"Your Majesty," Ranauld replied with a deep bow.

"I am sorry to be the one to make you aware of this, but Castel has declared war on Arvenon."

Ranauld was aghast, but the king seemed not to notice.

"This outcome is not what I ever wanted. I hope you understand that. But the Arvenian aggression at Deadman's Pass has forced it upon me. If Steffan and Essanda had remained in control of Arvenon, it would never have come to this. But for all practical purposes my brother-in-law and sister no longer rule, and my advisors have convinced me that a statement is necessary. I cannot afford to allow Castel to appear weak."

Ranauld clenched his fists. He had no doubt that Eisgold was behind this, almost certainly with the goal of undermining King Rupert's position.

The king bowed his head, covering his face with his hands and groaning softly. A long moment passed before he recovered himself and looked up again.

When he did, Ranauld saw that his eyes appeared sunken.

A feeling of dread settled over the count. "Your Majesty! Are you well?"

The young king stifled another groan. "I don't know what's wrong with me, Ranauld. My head pounds and my gut clenches tightly. At times it's so bad I can scarcely bear it. It's happening most days now. My doctors have no answers."

Ranauld stared at him uneasily. "Is someone tasting your food and wine before you consume it?"

"I had a boy. But he proved to be a sickly lad, and I had to release him. I have a young woman now. Eisgold found her for me. He tells me she's reliable." The king gritted his teeth as another wave of pain seemed to pass over him. "She mostly seems interested in relieving me of my virtue." He shook his head. "Her brazenness is beginning to weary me."

"Dismiss her, Your Majesty!" urged Ranauld, thoroughly alarmed. "Go to someone you trust, and command them to find you a new food taster!"

"You're suggesting I can't trust Eisgold." The king gazed up at him quietly. Then he shrugged. "The others are all so...so insipid. Eisgold, at least, is willing to take the risk of expressing a point of view."

"What of Count Gordan?" asked Ranauld tentatively. "Your father trusted him."

King Rupert glared at him in sudden anger. "Don't mention that name in my presence!" he hissed. He straightened himself. "I shouldn't have come here," he said, muttering angrily to himself.

Then he abruptly seemed to reconsider. He took a slow breath, struggling to regain his composure. The harsh lines in his face gradually softened.

"You have become an enemy now, thanks to our declaration of war," he told Ranauld. "But you fought beside my father's soldiers at Torbury Scarp, and I believe you are a good man. I could not allow you to find out from someone else."

He reached out and grasped Ranauld's hand firmly. "I want you to know I bear you no ill will, Count Ranauld."

Before Ranauld could respond, the king turned away, opened the door, and was gone.

Alone in the room, Ranauld's thoughts tumbled over each other as he tried to make sense of the visit. The king had sought him out—had chosen to confide in him.

Mentioning Gordan's name had broken the spell, and Ranauld berated himself for his foolishness in doing so.

Ranauld lingered for a while in case the king decided to come back. By the time he eventually gave up and trudged back to his room, his own troubles had faded entirely from his mind. The king's vulnerability alarmed him. King Rupert might be the sovereign, but he clearly had nowhere to turn, no trustworthy shoulder to lean upon.

When Ranauld finally retired to his bed, he lay awake for many hours, burdened with an overwhelming sense of hopelessness. It was obvious to him that the young king was in grave danger. And there was nothing whatever he could do about it.

As two more days dragged slowly by, Count Ranauld mastered his agitation. His frustration had not lessened a whit. Castel was steering a course that would yield benefit to no one except Eisgold. But what could he do about it? His helplessness galled him.

Soon after he had eaten in his room that evening, he heard a soft knock on the door. He hurried to open it, scarcely daring to hope that the king might be calling on him once more.

The person outside the door was hooded and cloaked. A hand reached up and removed the hood, revealing the drawn face of Lord Mardone.

"Come with me," Mardone whispered.

Ranauld followed him to the roof, and they sat together on the edge of the building in the fading light, gazing out over the city.

Lord Mardone did not long delay before speaking. "Your arrival has stirred up a hornets' nest, Count Ranauld."

The count glanced at him curiously.

"Castel is now at war with Arvenon," the Castelan continued. "And Eisgold has tightened his grip on power."

A rumble of anger burst forth from Ranauld's throat. "King Istel should never have shown mercy to that traitor!"

"Many here share your perspective. But none dare to speak it aloud."

"What happened with Count Gordan?" Ranauld couldn't restrain the question—it burst out of him.

Mardone sighed. "When Eisgold first appeared, Gordan opposed him openly, even when it became clear that the king was softening to him. Gordan spoke forcefully, but with great discretion—he has always been a diplomat by nature. When King Rupert announced that he was pardoning Eisgold, though, Gordan told the king to his face that he was dishonoring the memory of his father. He said it boldly and in public. All of the nobles and courtiers were present."

"What did the king do?"

"He flew into a rage. He was incensed at any suggestion he would dishonor his father. He was not dissembling, either—he truly did respect his father, and he reverences his memory. The king was beside himself. He shouted that Gordan would not live to see another dawn if he ever caught sight of his face again."

"What did Gordan do?"

"He didn't utter another word. He turned and left. No one has seen him since. Sadly, the incident only served to reinforce Eisgold's standing. His authority has increased since then. And he has moved swiftly to silence any who dare to speak against him. Most of the nobles are now too frightened to say a word against him, even in private."

"Did you know that the king came to see me?" asked Ranauld.

Mardone stared back at him in astonishment. He shook his head.

"I'm greatly concerned about him. From what he told me, it seems likely that he's slowly being poisoned. He can't see it, though."

"You're not the first person to raise that possibility with me," the Castelan told him grimly.

"Can't you get him a different food taster? The current incumbent was recommended by Eisgold. The king is irritated by her constant attempts to seduce him."

"Some of us are working on it," said Mardone. "I can't say more than that."

It came as a huge relief to Ranauld to hear that the Castelan nobility was neither unaware nor completely paralyzed. "I wish there was something I could do," he said.

"Perhaps there is."

Ranauld directed a sharp glance at his visitor. "What did you have in mind?"

Lord Mardone lowered his voice. "Suppose you were to find that the door to the building was left briefly unguarded? And that a horse was waiting for you just beyond the gates of the city?"

"How could I return to Arvenon with a Castelan army camped inside Deadman's Pass? And what could I do even if I could get past them? Unless something has changed dramatically, I will not be welcomed by the Arvenian army camped on the other side."

"There are other ways. There is a small fishing village called Pescadere on the coast. If you ride northeast, keeping the mountains on your right, you will eventually reach it. From there it's a short journey by sea to Varacellan. A fisherman named Carpis will take you. I can't pretend there is no risk."

"I'm willing to take my chances," said Ranauld without hesitation. "When can I leave?"

"Right now," said Lord Mardone.

Ranauld's eyes went wide. But he quickly nodded in satisfaction.

The Castelan looked relieved. "I can do nothing to guarantee your safety, but some of my men will tail you. They might be able to direct at least some trouble away from you. If you reach Varacellan, make sure that your king and queen and King Delmar understand the true situation here."

"I'll do whatever is in my power," Ranauld replied.

Lord Mardone clasped his hand firmly. "Thank you, Count Ranauld. I hope we have opportunity to meet again in more congenial circumstances."

He handed Ranauld a heavy cloak with a hood. "Put this on."

The two of them slipped out of the door and made their way quietly downstairs to the entrance of the building.

As Lord Mardone had indicated, no guards were anywhere in sight. Ranauld wondered what had become of them, and what the consequences would be for them when it was discovered that he was missing. He could only leave such considerations to his rescuer.

Lord Mardone left the building first and soon disappeared from his sight. As he was about to follow, it occurred to Ranauld to wonder if Mardone might play him false. He didn't hesitate for long. If he was any judge of character, such an outcome was not worth consideration.

He slipped through the door and headed for the gates of the city. A few people were still abroad at that hour, but none approached him. When he arrived at the gates he found them open, even though the sky was almost completely dark. He was not challenged as he left the city.

Before he had reached the other end of the bridge, a man leading a horse approached him quietly. He handed the reins to Ranauld without a word, and the count mounted the horse and rode across the bridge into the countryside surrounding the city.

As soon as he found a road that appeared to be heading roughly in the right direction, he steered his horse onto it.

Ranauld rode steadily throughout the night. When the sun rose, it found him far from the capital.

25

Count Ranauld kept an eye on the sun as he rode, remembering to use roads that headed in a northeasterly direction. By late morning he could clearly see a range of mountains in the distance. Lord Mardone had told him to keep the mountains on his right, and he soon decided to rely on the mountain range as a guide.

Lord Mardone had promised to send men to watch out for him from a distance, but thus far Ranauld had not noticed anyone tailing him. Nor had he seen any sign of pursuit from Castelan soldiers. Apart from farm wagons, Ranauld had seen no one on the road except occasional travelers heading in the direction of the capital.

He knew he would have been missed before the morning was far advanced. Ranauld's hosts—or perhaps more accurately his jailers—had routinely brought a generous breakfast to his room not long after dawn each morning, and his absence would have been discovered then if not sooner.

The count did not doubt that he would be pursued. His captors would most likely expect him to set out for Arvenon, and that gave him hope that pursuers would head in the wrong direction. But he couldn't ignore the possibility that trackers would be sent to the coast as well.

Whether or not soldiers were coming for him, at that moment he was entirely alone, and after his confinement in the capital it felt exhilarating to be riding freely under an open sky.

Grateful as he was to Lord Mardone, he couldn't help wondering how the Castelan nobleman hoped to benefit from giving him his freedom. Even if he reached Varacellan and explained the situation to King Steffan and Queen Essanda, what could they do about it? Regaining control of Arvenon presented them with more than enough of a challenge, and until they found a way to achieve that there was little they could do to help Castel. And what could King Delmar be expected to do? Invade Castel by sea?

Nevertheless Ranauld knew that if the roles had been reversed he would have done the same as Mardone. Perhaps no further explanation was necessary.

Ranauld pressed on until he was saddle sore and weary. When he paused for a break, he discovered that generous supplies of food had been placed in the saddlebags, along with skins filled with wine and water. Lord Mardone had planned the escape carefully.

The road ran through a couple of villages and one moderately sized town, and Ranauld wasted far too much time finding a way around them. Apart from these diversions, the day passed without incident, and after pushing his horse hard throughout the daylight hours Ranauld decided to rest until dawn. Turning aside into a large forest, he picked his way through the trees until he found a suitable spot to camp well away from the road.

Nothing disturbed his rest, and he set off again in the morning after breaking his fast and refilling his water skin from a stream.

None of the roads seemed to lead directly to the coast, and he often found himself heading in the wrong direction for a time. Three days passed without any sign of pursuit, and he began to weary of the effort of working his way around every settlement that appeared in his path. After riding through a couple of villages without drawing attention to himself, he began to grow more confident.

One afternoon he turned a sharp bend in the road to abruptly find himself almost in the outskirts of a small town. The road ahead of him bustled with people, and he realized at once that it would attract undue attention if he turned and rode away. Deciding he had little choice but to risk riding through the town, he kept his head down and urged his horse forward, riding as quickly as he dared.

The road led directly through the market square, and the noise and energy of a rural market soon enveloped him. Townsfolk thronged the square, wandering happily among the stalls and sampling the wide selection of food laid out to tempt them.

A few people looked curiously at the stranger as he passed, but no one made any attempt to waylay him. Nearing the far side of the market square, his attention was captured by the smell of fresh bread. Loaves steaming from the oven had been spread out beside large rounds of cheese. Ranauld reined in his horse almost without thinking, peering down at the loaves. The woman keeping the stall was busy serving a customer and seemed not to notice him.

Among the food supplies in his saddlebags, Ranauld had discovered a small pile of Castelan coins folded into a piece of cloth. He had immediately transferred the coins to his own pouch, and they were readily to hand. He knew that a single coin would be worth more than a fresh loaf and a round of cheese.

Glancing around and seeing no obvious sign of danger, Ranauld decided to take a risk. He slipped down from the horse and approached the seller.

"One of each, please," he said quietly, holding out a coin with one hand while pointing first to the loaves and then to the cheese with the other.

The woman took the coin eagerly, although she seemed in less of a hurry to hand over the goods. "I'm sure I detect an accent, good sir," she said brightly. "We don't often see visitors in these parts. Where might you be from?"

The woman had a penetrating voice, and Ranauld felt his cheeks go warm as heads everywhere turned in their direction.

"Beyond the capital," he mumbled, waving vaguely toward the south. He reached out his hand, impatient to take the bread and the cheese and be gone.

The woman shook her head slowly, her brows puckered. "I felt certain you must be from somewhere foreign," she said loudly, a tinge of wariness in her voice.

After eyeing the coin suspiciously for a moment, she selected the smallest of the loaves and the least attractive of the cheeses and held them out. She didn't offer any change.

Ranauld took the food without comment and remounted. After nodding curtly to the woman he nudged his horse forward, forcing himself to ride away slowly and steadily.

The moment he was clear of the town he urged his horse into a gallop. At the first opportunity he veered off the road onto a trail, ignoring the fact that it led west, away from the mountains. After riding for an hour he turned onto a different trail that headed north again.

He berated himself fiercely for his foolishness. He had managed to make a spectacle of himself, and he harbored little doubt that the woman, and others in the market square as well, would readily be able to describe him to any inquirers.

By the time he paused in a secluded location, he felt weary and frustrated. The bread was no longer fresh, but he tore at it hungrily anyway. The cheese was surprisingly tasty, and considering the risk he had taken to procure it, he might as well enjoy it as much as he could. When his belly was finally full, he sat back with a contented sigh, almost willing to conclude that his foolishness had been worthwhile.

Remounting, he rode hard until it was almost too dark to find a secure place to spend the night. By the time he lay down, he was tired of self-recrimination and weary from a day in the saddle. He quickly dropped into a deep sleep.

Waking with the dawn, he struggled to identify the vague sense of disquiet that washed over him as awareness returned. Memories of his visit to the market square came flooding back, and he grimaced for a moment before clambering unsteadily to his feet.

He glanced around him slowly. Something else didn't feel right. Where was his horse? He remembered slipping a halter onto the animal and securing it nearby among some grass. He could see no sign of it anywhere.

Feeling suddenly vulnerable, he concealed himself behind a tree and peered warily toward the trail he had ridden in on. No other person was anywhere in sight.

It was hard to believe that his horse could simply have wandered off. His pursuers surely hadn't caught up with him, either—he would have been recaptured immediately if they had.

After assuring himself that he was entirely alone, he headed to the place where he had left the horse. He was astonished to find a bundle wrapped tightly in cloth lying on the ground. He cautiously removed the cloth to find a generous quantity of food within it.

The situation was baffling, to say the least. After wrestling with his bemusement for some time, he finally concluded that Lord Mardone's men had taken his horse and left the food.

If Mardone's people were involved, two questions remained. If they saw a need to remove his horse, why hadn't they spoken to him directly about it? And if they didn't want to speak with him, why hadn't they left a note?

It occurred to him that the second question was probably easiest to answer—either they saw it as too risky to leave a written message, or they were unable to read and write. As to why they hadn't spoken to him, they'd probably been instructed not to.

He tried to remember exactly what Lord Mardone had told him. The nobleman had said he would send men to tail Ranauld, and that they would try to direct trouble away. He hadn't offered a reason why the men would be tailing him rather than traveling with him.

It probably wasn't difficult to understand, though. Someone would be sure to see them if they traveled together, and sooner or later Lord Mardone would be implicated in the escape. The Castelan no doubt had excellent reasons for wanting his men to remain at arm's length at all times.

Ranauld was left with a decision. Should he stay where he was and wait, or should he set out for the coast on foot? In the end he decided to stay and wait, at least until the following morning.

Remaining in one place for a whole day quickly became wearisome, especially after an extended period in the saddle. Once the sun had set he lay down as usual, but he struggled to get to sleep, spending the first few hours tossing and turning uncomfortably on the hard ground.

Eventually he must have drifted off though, because he woke to discover that his horse had been returned. The animal was grazing peacefully where he had originally left it.

A quick investigation showed that the food in his saddlebags had been replenished too, so he broke his fast before riding out.

He could only wonder if Lord Mardone's men had seen signs of danger and decided it would have been hazardous for him to travel on the previous day.

Perhaps his pursuers had been drawing close. If so, where were they now? Were they far enough ahead that it didn't matter, or had they headed in a different direction? The thought that they were ahead of him was especially alarming. If they had guessed his destination, they'd be waiting for him.

He set off immediately, intent on staying especially alert. The day passed without incident, and he began to notice signs that he was at last approaching the sea. Unfamiliar birds flew high above him, and he watched them curiously, confident that they were seabirds.

As dusk approached he spotted a lone farmer working in a field. Seeing him approach, the man stood and waited for him.

Ranauld halted his horse a few paces away. "Pescadere?" he asked simply.

After peering curiously at him for a moment, the man pointed off to the northeast.

Ranauld nodded his thanks and rode away immediately without looking back.

With night almost upon him and Pescadere apparently still some distance away, Ranauld decided he had little choice but to find a place to spend the night. Eager to put distance between him and the farmer, he rode until the light had almost faded from the sky.

Since leaving the capital he had mostly ridden beside forests and cultivated land. He now found himself among low hills covered with bushes and scrawny trees. Finding a suitable place to camp in such terrain was considerably more difficult. Coming upon a ramshackle abandoned cottage, barely visible in the deepening dark, he decided to spend the night there.

Ranauld slept restlessly and rose before dawn. The farmer had indicated that Pescadere lay to the northeast, and the inland road continued in that direction. As soon as it was light enough to travel he decided on a more indirect approach to the town. He would ride due north instead, heading for the coast. When he reached the sea he would turn right and make his way into Pescadere from its western end.

He didn't even consider circling around to the east. That would have required a longer journey, and any approach from that side was uncertain given that a mountain range lay to the east.

After traveling for a couple of hours he reached the sea. A steep cliff towered above the water, and he dismounted before approaching the edge. Waves crashed onto the rocks below, and seabirds wheeled above him, their harsh cries carried away by the stiff breeze. He caught a distant glimpse of a single boat sailing east. Expecting to find Pescadere in that direction, he remounted and headed away from the cliffs before turning east and riding parallel with the coastline. Within a couple of hours the cliffs had given way to extensive sand dunes. The sea now broke across a rocky shoreline, with the rocks punctuated by occasional stretches of sand.

A small boat, most likely a fishing vessel, stood out to sea just off one of the sandy beaches, and Ranauld paused to peer curiously at it. As he watched, the boat approached the shore, continuing until it was beached on the sand. A man climbed out of the boat and began waving furiously at him.

After a moment's hesitation, Ranauld rode down onto the beach.

"Are you Ranauld?" called the sailor.

"Who wants to know?" he called back suspiciously, bringing his mount to a halt several horse lengths from the man.

"I am a fisherman, and my name is Carpis," the man replied. "I am here to take you to Varacellan."

26

Dismounting from his horse, Ranauld approached the boat. "How did you know to find me here?" he asked.

"I didn't exactly," Carpis replied with a crooked smile. "Put it mostly down to luck."

When the fisherman smiled, Ranauld noticed that a number of teeth were missing from one side of his mouth. He had apparently lived a rough life.

"You are fortunate you stayed away from Pescadere," Carpis told him. "Yesterday especially. The place was swarming with soldiers." He raised an eyebrow, poking a finger in Ranauld's direction. "All of them looking for you."

The missing horse now began to make sense. Lord Mardone's men must have been aware that pursuers were close behind him. Perhaps realizing that he would not reach Pescadere soon enough to avoid being caught, they had decided to delay him. In the process they had made him more alert than ever. Even without making direct contact they had managed to steer him away from trouble.

"Why did you come here?" Ranauld asked the fisherman.

Carpis shrugged. "If you were stupid, you would have blundered into Pescadere and been taken. If you were smarter than that, you would have decided to approach along the coast. The coast on the eastern side of the town is rocky and inaccessible. That left the western approach. So here I am."

Ranauld nodded. "What about the horse?"

"Mardone's people won't be far away. They'll take care of it."

Ranauld peered around him. No one was visible. He could see at a glance, though, that the sand dunes and low hills in the area offered many possible points of concealment. People could be observing him from almost anywhere.

Removing the bridle from the horse, Ranauld replaced it with a halter which he tied to one of the more sturdy bushes. Then he clambered into the boat beside Carpis.

The fisherman tossed him a large coat that felt oily to the touch. "Put this on," Carpis commanded. "It will keep you dry."

As Ranauld obeyed, the fisherman began pushing them back into the swell. The count clung to the side of the boat, eyeing its frail timbers uncertainly. Pitting such a tiny vessel against the remorseless ferocity of the ocean seemed like madness, and an unreasoning dread flooded over him, coupled with a reckless desire to leap from the boat and dash for his horse.

He shook his head fiercely, determined not to give way to such craven impulses. Carpis knew what he was doing. Fishermen took to the sea every day—their livelihoods depended on it.

And what choice did he have? He knew of no other way to escape from Castel.

Carpis dipped a pair of oars rhythmically into the sea until the boat had cleared the shore, then he raised the sail and took his seat at the tiller. Spray splashed repeatedly over Ranauld as the boat plowed through the waves, and he shrank back, trembling involuntarily.

As the boat sailed further away from the land the breakers gave way to a rolling swell and the spray diminished. The waterproof coat had kept his body dry, but Ranauld's head and face were now wet enough that he began to shiver in the steady breeze. Carpis tossed him a dry piece of cloth he retrieved from somewhere, and Ranauld caught it gratefully, using it to dry his face and hair as best he could.

Carpis now headed his boat east, and the bare shoreline was soon interrupted by a town that swung slowly into view. A few boats, appearing tiny at this distance, were anchored near the shore. Other vessels had put to sea, and one or two appeared to be heading in their direction.

"Get down! Quickly!" ordered Carpis sharply, waving his hand urgently toward the middle of the boat.

Ranauld obeyed at once, lowering himself until the whole of his body was positioned below the side of the boat.

The fisherman pointed to a large piece of sail lying across the bottom of the boat. "Get under that sheet, and stay there until I tell you otherwise!"

After a few moments Ranauld heard a loud splash. He guessed that Carpis was throwing a net overboard.

"A boat is heading in our direction with a couple of soldiers in it," Carpis said, speaking quietly. "Be ready to slip over the side if I tell you to."

"But I can't swim!" hissed Ranauld.

There was a brief pause while Carpis mumbled fiercely to himself. Ranauld couldn't hear what he was saying, but the general sense of it wasn't hard to guess.

Everything went quiet for some time. Eventually a voice called roughly, "What are you doing?"

"What do you think I'm doing?" barked Carpis. "I'm a fisherman. Can't you see I have my net out?"

More anxious moments passed.

"What's under that sail in the bottom of your boat?" the voice demanded.

Sweat began to trickle down Ranauld's face. He didn't dare wipe it away.

"Too much water, and not a single fish," growled the fisherman. "Or were you hoping for a glimpse of the naked wenches I'm hiding in the bilges?" he asked, guffawing loudly.

Ranauld heard no immediate response. He scarcely dared to

breathe. Would the soldiers board the boat? Would they demand Carpis throw back the sail? If they did, all would be lost.

The voice started up again. "We're looking for a man. A foreigner. Have you seen anyone?"

"No foreigners have been fishing around here," snarled Carpis, "and they'd better not try it! Anyone who elbows in on our fishing grounds will have my gaff hook in their guts!"

Everything went quiet. Ranauld breathed shallowly, too frightened to move a muscle. Before long he started to seriously wonder if he would go mad.

When he almost thought he couldn't bear it any longer, Carpis's voice called to him. "You can come out now. But stay down out of sight!"

Relief flooded over Ranauld as he slithered out. It was difficult to resist the temptation to stand up, but he did whatever he could to stretch his aching limbs. He peered over the side. No boats could be seen anywhere nearby.

Carpis was hauling in the net. A few fish flapped helplessly in it, but the fisherman ignored them, hastily setting the sail instead. Before long they were gliding across the water once more, heading east.

They sailed on through the day, and Carpis eventually indicated to Ranauld that he no longer needed to hide. They often caught sight of other fishing vessels and occasionally ships with two masts.

The sun was drawing near to the horizon when Carpis finally steered the boat into a broad channel. Other boats were heading in the same direction, most of them undoubtedly sailing home, and peering ahead Ranauld caught sight of an expansive harbor. Tall ships lay at anchor, and many fishing boats headed for their own moorings.

Carpis sailed the boat to a largely empty pier and secured two lines at each end of his boat to metal cleats on the pier. As Carpis was climbing out of the boat a harbor official approached. The two men had a brief conversation, and Carpis handed over a couple of coins.

The official left them after waving toward the dock area. It appeared to Ranauld that they now had the freedom of the port.

"Come with me," said Carpis. "Don't say a word to anyone. If anyone approaches us, I'll do the talking."

He steered them toward the most heavily trafficked areas of the docks, although he carefully avoided the taverns that dotted the area. They began to climb, heading toward the main part of the city.

Before they had cleared the docks a couple of rough looking men approached them. One of them had a hook nose. "Not thirsty today, friends?" he asked, jerking his head toward the nearest tavern.

Carpis looked the man up and down without offering comment. Ranauld kept his mouth shut as instructed.

"Well?" the man leered at Carpis, leaning in threateningly. He was clearly daring the fisherman to challenge him.

"Any prow is improved by a painted lady," Carpis finally responded.

The hook nosed man narrowed his eyes. "You smell of fish," he sneered. "Who do you think you are to be mouthing the code? I say you overheard it."

Faster than Ranauld's eye could blink, Carpis drew his knife and had it at the man's throat. He sneered back at Hook Nose.

"And who do you think you are?" Carpis asked. "I wonder what the Peerless Mariner might have to say about your attitude. Do you think you're better than him?"

Hook Nose glared back at him, not daring to move with the knife at his throat.

Other men had begun to gather. Ranauld noticed them stealing glances at one of their number, looking for direction. Seeing who Carpis was, the leader waved his fingers. The other men dispersed immediately, leaving the leader with Hook Nose and his original companion.

"Is there some kind of problem?" the leader asked Carpis evenly. "I know who you are, but I don't take it kindly when someone holds a knife to the throat of one of my men."

Carpis nodded respectfully to him before lowering his knife and stepping back. "Ask your man here. I gave him the code, but he only seemed interested in trouble."

The newcomer directed a sharp glance at Hook Nose, who began to squirm uncomfortably. The leader then directed his attention to the other man, apparently seeking confirmation of Carpis's story.

When Hook Nose's companion inclined his head slightly, the leader's face hardened. "The Peerless Mariner would wish to extend his apologies," he told Carpis. He glared at Hook Nose. "The issue will be dealt with," he added.

Hook Nose scowled at Carpis, but Ranauld saw fear in his eyes as he followed his companions away.

No one remained to block their path, and Carpis immediately resumed their journey.

They soon cleared the docks, and Ranauld found himself walking between rows of dilapidated cottages. "What just happened there?" he asked Carpis.

Carpis looked at him for a moment as if weighing him. "The docks are controlled by a person known as the Peerless Mariner. He's someone who doesn't answer even to the king. No one can go to the docks or move through them without permission from the Peerless Mariner. I've got a passcode—a very special one—that lets me go anywhere in the docks. That's for your ears only," he added with a frown.

"How did you get the passcode?"

"Let's just say I did something for the Peerless Mariner that mattered to him."

Ranauld nodded, more grateful than ever to have Carpis as his guide. He would never have made it through the dockside without him.

After several more minutes of walking briskly they entered a broad avenue lined with stalls selling food of various kinds. Bustling crowds thronged the stalls, people spilling out onto the avenue as soon as they had made their purchases. Everywhere he looked, Ranauld saw men and women laughing and chattering happily as they strolled together.

In his brief exposure to Varacellan, the city had presented Ranauld with a curious mix of carefree exuberance and veiled menace. He knew that similar contrasts could be found in any city. One significant difference between Varacellan and Arnost stood out —not being a port, Arnost had no dockside district.

Above the avenue towered the castle, and Carpis led Ranauld to its gates. After arriving there, the fisherman named one of the king's aides, and asked the guards to send him a message.

The aide arrived surprisingly quickly, reinforcing the influence enjoyed by Carpis. After thanking the fisherman sincerely for his help, Ranauld followed the aide into the castle.

He was taken immediately to King Steffan and Queen Essanda.

They were overjoyed to see him. Having just sat down for their evening meal, the monarchs insisted that he join them. After learning that he had not eaten a solid meal for many days, the king commanded him to take his fill before attempting to pass on news of any kind.

Ranauld yielded without hesitation. Sitting down at once, he ate ravenously, paying no heed to the entertainment he was providing others at the table.

***

STEFFAN CALLED TOGETHER the entire contingent from Arvenon to hear Ranauld's report. He also invited King Delmar.

Will and Rufe's actions in regaining control of the army outside Steffan's Citadel had seemed almost effortless. That experience had raised Steffan's expectations of Ranauld achieving something similar with the larger army camped outside Castel. He was therefore frustrated at Ranauld's complete lack of progress in winning back control of those men. He needed that army. He also needed to clip Pisander's wings in every way he could.

Steffan didn't openly express his disappointment—it was obvious to him that Ranauld was embarrassed enough already. He was soon grateful for his own restraint. His chagrin was overshadowed by his growing astonishment as Ranauld laid out his visit to Castel Citadel, his insights into the growing influence of Eisgold, his meeting with King Rupert, and his subsequent escape with the active help of a dissident faction within the local nobility.

Eisgold's return to Castel came as no surprise to Steffan—the reports of King Delmar's agents were now fully confirmed. Nevertheless he was shocked to discover the extent of Eisgold's sway. And he was almost as alarmed and distressed as the queen to hear of the vulnerability of the young King Rupert.

Both Arvenon and Castel were now subject to the malign influence of men with no regard for the best interests of those kingdoms. The only possible winner would be Agon of Rogand, and time was growing short to prevent Agon from taking full advantage of the situation.

Only Varas remained truly free. Steffan knew as well as King Delmar that without decisive changes in Arvenon and Castel, Varas was unlikely to stay that way for long.

27

In the days that followed Agon's visit to Chalno, the king considered many times ordering his men to return to the mystic's dwelling to relieve the fool of his head. He restrained himself admirably.

Even the faintest possibility of achieving unending life made it worth putting up with a lot. That didn't mean Agon would ever forgive the peremptory way in which Chalno had dismissed him, instructing him to return in four weeks. No one ever treated Agon that way and got away with it. As soon as he had everything he wanted from the mystic, Agon intended to settle the score once and for all.

The four weeks had almost elapsed when Lady Ona returned to Rog and gave Agon a full report on the situation in Arnost.

"Pisander is barely holding things together," she concluded grimly. "The incompetents who surround him only make his task more difficult."

As she was speaking Agon had been slowly turning white with fury. He finally erupted. "I give the idiot every advantage! Every resource he could possibly require! And this is how he squanders my wealth?"

He stormed about the room, shouting at the top of his voice and smashing every breakable object within reach.

Lady Ona could not help but be shaken by his reaction. Her rosy cheeks were considerably more pale than usual. The king noted it with satisfaction. Nevertheless he was also impressed to see that she was largely managing to keep her poise. Lady Ona was herself an unusually valuable resource, and Agon promised himself he would not lose sight of that fact.

Having exhausted his rage at least for the moment, he resumed his seat. "I will be departing for Arnost within the week," he announced calmly.

If Lady Ona was at all taken aback by the sudden transformation, she showed no sign of it. Agon couldn't fail to be impressed by her unusual ability to tolerate his forthright expression of his passions.

"You will accompany me," he said. "I will have need of your particular talents."

She bowed her pretty head respectfully, and he dismissed her.

Lady Ona's report had demonstrated to Agon yet again that if he wanted something done properly, he needed to do it himself.

He called for one of his aides.

"I will be leaving for Arnost in seven days' time. Make sure that everything is ready for my departure by then, or suffer the consequences. And get Lord Krasmir in here. I want to speak with him."

Krasmir was not long in arriving. An aide ushered him into Agon's private apartments.

"I am calling the Great Council together," Agon told the nobleman. "We will meet in six days. I will be informing them of my departure for Arnost, and announcing your regency in my absence. I expect you to remember all of my instructions," he added in a growl.

The nobleman nodded dutifully, his face impassive. He left the moment he was dismissed.

Agon gazed scornfully at his departing back before turning to Ennawi with a frown.

"Krasmir isn't even suitable for the regency, much less ready for it," he told the slave, shaking his head. "I have no one else, though.

Lady Ona might have made for an amusing alternative, but I need her in Arnost."

He scowled. "Of all of my nobles, the only one who would ever have made a capable regent was Drettroth. I could never have trusted him of course, so it could never have happened.

"As it is, I'm only able to trust Krasmir thanks to the Stone of Authority. I can't help wondering what might have happened if I'd become aware of the stone earlier. I could have used it on Drettroth. A lot of things would have turned out very differently." He shook his head at the thought of what might have been.

The king left his apartments, aware that more pressing matters demanded his attention. He had no more time to waste on fanciful daydreams.

As he left he called back over his shoulder, "You'll be coming to Arnost with me, Ennawi." His lips twisted in the semblance of a smile. "I'm sure a change of scenery will be exactly what you've been hoping for."

Once the king had gone, Nistinaa appeared. She came to Ennawi and fed him in the usual way.

"It seems as if we'll all be going on a journey," she told him. "If the king's taking you then I need to come, as well."

She peered into his unresponsive eyes. "Not that he bothered to let me know, of course—he probably doesn't know I exist, and I can't say I'm sorry about that. One of the servants overheard him talking and passed it on to me."

She finished her work and stood back for a moment. "What will become of us, Ennawi?" she asked.

No answer was forthcoming, and she expected none.

Raising her hands in a helpless appeal to the heavens, she turned away and left the king's apartments.

EXACTLY FOUR WEEKS had elapsed when Agon arrived at Chalno's dwelling once more. He was in a foul mood.

Early that morning a dispatch had arrived from Arnost. Pisander was asking him to come as soon as possible and to bring an army. He already knew from Lady Ona's report that there were problems thanks to Pisander's mismanagement, but clearly there had been a further deterioration. Why hadn't the imbecile stated the issues directly?

Soon he would find out for himself. In the meantime, he needed to focus his attention on Chalno.

What am I? Madman? Or genius? the mystic had asked, referring to himself. The king had been wrestling with the question ever since. At that moment he was no closer to an answer, but he would not be returning to Rog without one.

The question Chalno had directed to the king had been easier to answer. *What are you? Wolf? Or prey?* Agon was the wolf, as Chalno would soon discover if he failed to deliver on the king's expectations.

The mystic appeared at the door of his rude hut moments after his royal visitor arrived. Once again the guards checked him for weapons, then discreetly moved away to allow the two men to converse undisturbed.

"Well?" Agon demanded.

Chalno bowed. "Great King, may you live forever," he said, an ironic smile curling his lips. "Perhaps we will now be able to attach an extra layer of meaning to these words," he added.

Agon frowned. Was the mystic suggesting he had made progress?

"Come with me, Your Majesty," invited the mystic, pointing into the forest behind his dwelling.

The king followed without hesitation. His guards scrambled along behind them, frantically trying to strike the right balance between protecting their monarch and respecting his demand that they maintain a discreet distance.

Chalno led the king to a small clearing in the forest. A rough pile of stones stood in the middle of the clearing, capped by a large flat rock with a smooth surface. A dark residue covered the rock and had run down its sides. A sickly sweet smell filled the air.

Agon realized that he was looking at an altar, and that the dark residue was dried blood. It reminded him of the temple in Rog, and he screwed up his nose in distaste.

"There is life in the blood," intoned Chalno.

A shiver traveled up Agon's spine at the sound of the words. "The blood. Which creature is it from?" he asked.

"A fox, a hare, and a stoat. And my blood with it of course," the mystic replied, nodding wisely.

The thought of blood spilled for sacrifice caused the king to shudder. From his earliest days he had felt uncomfortable with such rituals. He said nothing, waiting for Chalno to speak.

"The scroll you brought to me offered hints," the mystic began. "Hints that would make sense only to a priest, and even then only to a priest willing to think beyond the narrow confines of our religion's teachings. There were still pieces missing though. I spent two weeks striving to understand them."

"And did you?"

Chalno looked at him blankly.

"Did you understand them?" Agon repeated.

The mystic's eyes glazed over. "Who can plumb the unfathomable? How can the incomprehensible be understood?" he droned.

The king's eyes narrowed in anger. As always, the fool refused to be pinned down. He gritted his teeth, once more leaving it to Chalno to break the silence.

Eventually his patience was rewarded. "I found myself faced with certain...metaphysical leaps," the mystic said, speaking as much to the air as to his visitor. "I leaped across a chasm to be faced with an abyss. Spanning the abyss I was confronted with a rift. Crossing these divides brought me to where I am today."

"And where is that?" demanded the king.

"I find myself standing on the threshold of eternity," whispered the mystic, awe in his voice.

"And how do you cross that threshold?"

"It is not necessary to cross it. It is enough simply to have reached it."

A part of Agon wanted to simply dismiss the mystic as a madman. Another part of him couldn't help but be impressed.

"So you have achieved unending life?"

"I believe I have," the mystic answered simply.

"Unending life on earth?"

"For as long as earth endures."

"You believe. But are you certain?"

The mystic shrugged. "The passage of time will reveal it soon enough, Your Majesty. I am an old man. I will not need to ask you to wait long."

"You expect me to wait until you grow old?" asked the king, scowling in disbelief. "I am not young myself. Nor am I a patient man."

The mystic had unbelievable gall to claim success without offering some means of verifying his claims. Chalno might be content to bide his time, but Agon refused to wait years to see if old age made a fool of them both.

It had already occurred to the king that he might need a way to assess the effectiveness of Chalno's supposed agreement with the dark gods.

"I could kill you right now," Agon suggested with a cruel smile. "What better way to test your achievement?"

Chalno looked horrified. "Any covenant with the dark gods has its limits, Your Majesty. Do you imagine they would care about preserving my life once my head had been removed from my shoulders?" The mystic shook his head anxiously. "This ritual does not offer a way to shield a person from the consequences of violent death, whether it be by execution, misadventure, or other means. Physical protection is still a necessity, and it must be achieved by more traditional methods."

The mystic's words made sense, and they had saved his life, at least for the moment.

"I can offer one small piece of evidence, Your Majesty," the mystic asserted.

"Well?" demanded the king.

Chalno pointed to his leg. "I have long been troubled by a weeping ulcer on my leg. Since the ritual, the ulcer has healed."

Agon remembered the ulcer—it had been disgusting. There was no further sign of it. He was impressed, although he would never admit it openly.

"What is required to achieve this covenant?" he asked.

"I will explain the requirements in detail," Chalno replied. "But blood sacrifice is needed. And in your case the price will be very high indeed. Thousands of souls will be required merely to open your account."

Agon glowered at him. "You used a couple of rabbits. Why should it be so different for me?" he demanded.

The mystic shrugged. "The price is determined by the value of the service rendered, Great King. Since your life is infinitely more valuable than mine, it will cost more to preserve it."

The king understood that well enough. Nevertheless his brows drew together in a scowl. The idea of paying his fair share had never appealed to him in the slightest.

Chalno apparently saw that he wasn't satisfied. "Think of a leaf on the river, Your Majesty. It floats without assistance. Your sword, being much heavier, could never float without support. The sword is more weighty than the leaf in other ways, too, given its greater potential to impact the lives of others." Seeing that the king understood, he continued. "The life of the king of Rogand is weightier in so many ways than the life of a poor and unheralded hermit."

Agon's life was clearly valuable beyond measure, while Chalno's life counted for nothing. The mystic's words were incontestable.

Agon pondered the possibilities. Was it truly possible that with the mystic's help he would finally be able to prolong his own life indefinitely? If so, sacrificing lives would be the least of the challenges.

"I can think of a quick way to build some credit, without even leaving my own borders. And it will prove rewarding in more ways than one." Agon rubbed his hands together in anticipation. "What else will I need to do?"

Chalno lowered his voice and leaned closer, his foul breath filling the king's nostrils. The man's ulcer might be healed, but his teeth were still just as rotten as they had been on the king's previous visit. "I will explain what is needed, Your Majesty," he said.

Agon had to force himself not to draw away in disgust. He gritted his own teeth while the mystic explained in simple terms everything that would be required.

The king knew he would find the rituals harrowing, but it would be worth it. "I will be leaving Rog for a time," he told the mystic. Then his voice became a growl. "When I return I will be expecting something much more convincing than an ulcer to verify your claims. If you fail to satisfy me I will devise a test of my own."

The look on Chalno's face made it clear that he understood the king's meaning perfectly.

The king strode back to the mystic's hovel and mounted his horse, his guards trailing dutifully behind him.

Agon felt unexpectedly buoyant as he rode away. Having waited for weeks, he at last had something to show for his patience. Any possibility of a bargain with the dark gods was worth any kind of delay. Of course everything hinged on whether the mystic was offering something more than just an illusion.

Either way, it was the work of a moment to decide on his first victims. There were more than enough of them to satisfy the dark gods, and they were long overdue for eradication. The very thought of it brightened him enormously.

The day had started badly with the arrival of the missive from Pisander. Now the mystic was pointing him to a way of extending his life indefinitely. His day was definitely improving.

As the king rode away Chalno finally yielded to the trembling that had threatened to take control of his entire body. Agon terrified him.

Whenever Chalno found himself in the presence of the king, he could barely manage to keep the shaking at bay.

For a long time he had told himself that he held life loosely. He discovered the truth only when he was confronted with death. King Agon was not a man to toy with, yet Chalno had dared to do just that. He had taunted the king with word games, pretending he was far-sighted and wise beyond other mortals. Having almost paid with his life, Chalno had discovered he was not yet ready to die.

He had convinced himself that mortality held no terrors for him. It was hardly surprising. Raised in a poverty-stricken home environment, life had been a misery from his earliest years. Ejected from the priesthood because he didn't fit in, or more accurately because he didn't measure up, his situation had not improved when he returned to the secular world. Normal people soon made it clear they didn't want him around. So he had become a mystic—cut off from the world, and desperately trying to convince himself he was above the rabble.

Then, after years of barely subsisting in the forest, he had been sought out by none other than Agon, High King of Rogand. Finding himself taken seriously by the king, discovering that the king actually needed him—it had been a heady experience. So he had played along, like the fool he was.

It had been nothing short of madness to string along someone as dangerous as Agon. Miraculously, he had survived, so far at least.

He didn't honestly know what to make of Drettroth's scroll. He had not been lying when he said that only a priest would be able to make sense of its contents, or that it was missing crucial information. He had also spoken the truth when he suggested that the scroll required a mindset that would be unacceptable to any true priest.

So, as best he could, he had enacted the rituals hinted at by the scroll. Having done so, perhaps he really was now standing on the threshold of immortality.

Had the dark gods healed his ulcer? The ulcer had persisted so long that he had given up hope of ever being free of it, but he couldn't entirely rule out the possibility that it had healed of its own accord. If it had been the dark gods who healed his ulcer, did that mean they had agreed to prolong his life?

He couldn't be certain.

Could a mortal negotiate with Malzakh the Destroyer and Nehrvina the Awful? Or were they toying with him as he had toyed with the king?

Chalno had no doubt that the dark gods would be more than willing to receive any blood sacrifice that he or Agon offered. That didn't mean they would keep their end of the bargain.

Time alone would tell, much as Agon didn't want to hear that.

He needed to decide what to do in the meantime. His home wasn't much, but he would be sorry to give it up. Nevertheless, fleeing his home was the price he must pay if he couldn't come up with better proof for Agon than a healed ulcer.

He faced a bigger question. Did he have more to fear from Agon, or from the dark gods themselves?

He sat down with a weary sigh. Any attempt at answers could wait until tomorrow.

28

Agon had little opportunity to dwell further on his interaction with Chalno. Pandemonium filled the palace as he prepared to set out for Arvenon with his retinue. Given the number of people and the resources involved in the journey, a logistical nightmare was guaranteed.

The king had decided that a large detachment of mounted soldiers would set out first, followed by foot soldiers. He would come next, riding his horse or sitting in a comfortable carriage, depending on his mood. Carriages would be provided for Lady Ona and any other travelers of note. They would follow the royal carriage. Ennawi would also have a carriage of his own, since a man without hands could hardly be expected to ride a horse. Agon was proud of himself for considering such an insignificant detail.

A small army of servants would follow, with wagons laden with food and other supplies. More soldiers, both on foot and on horseback, would bring up the rear.

Whenever the column stopped for an overnight stay, servants would set up a veritable tent city, prepare food, and serve it to the other travelers. In the morning, food would again be prepared and served, the tents packed up, and the column would set out again. A lengthy break would be taken around noon to allow food to be served in portable pavilions.

The entire journey was expected to take weeks.

Agon was unwilling to ever rely upon foreign soldiers for his protection, so the large contingent of Rogandan soldiers traveling in his column would remain with him when he finally reached Arnost.

The multitude of servants accompanying the king presented an entirely different problem. A plentiful supply of servants would undoubtedly be available in Arnost when he arrived, and that left Agon with a dilemma.

The first option he considered was to send his servants home from Arnost and rely on local replacements. The difficulty was that the unwanted servants would need to be fed and guarded on the return journey. They would consume a mountain of supplies, and a contingent of his soldiers would be needed to ensure they completed the journey and returned to their duties in Rog.

The second alternative was to retain the servants once he arrived in Arnost. Housing them within the city would present a new set of logistical challenges, and locals would undoubtedly need to be turned out of their homes as a result. Pisander would need to deal with the complexities.

Agon had settled on the second alternative, not least because he expected his daily routines would proceed more smoothly with servants who understood his mother tongue and were familiar with his way of operating.

A less benevolent ruler might have simply disposed of the unwanted servants when he arrived in Arnost. Agon congratulated himself that he was too enlightened to seriously consider such an option.

None of that would matter until they reached Arnost, and the chaos surrounding the preparations was rapidly raising questions about whether they would get there at all. Finding an effective administrator to leave behind as regent had been enough of a struggle. Agon now found himself desperately in need of another one.

In the end Lady Ona's frustration with the lack of progress

bubbled over. Stepping into the heart of the confusion, she took charge herself. Agon looked on with amazement as order miraculously began to emerge from the chaos.

For reasons he couldn't articulate, her success made him extremely uncomfortable. Fortunately, he found much to criticize.

As the day progressed, he took her aside. "Lady Ona, I can't help noticing a number of glaring shortcomings in your coordination efforts," he told her loftily. "Fortunately I am able to provide guidance. Follow my instructions closely, and everything will begin to run smoothly."

He then proceeded to give her the benefit of his superior wisdom.

Lady Ona waited restlessly for his monologue to conclude, then she bowed stiffly. "Please pardon my presumption in becoming involved at all, Great King. I am more than willing to defer to your more expert judgment." With that she departed, without waiting to be dismissed.

Intensely annoying as Lady Ona's lack of cooperation might be, Agon reminded himself that he needed her in Arnost. Shrugging dismissively, he put her out of his mind. He had come up with satisfying solutions for each of the problems he had observed. It was time to step into the breach himself to implement them.

Less than an hour had passed before Agon remembered why he hated administration. Superior as his skills and insights undoubtedly were, the process of chasing down the details bored and irritated him. It suited him much better to oversee the efforts of others. He always had flawless instructions to offer. Sadly, he had never yet found an administrator capable of effectively understanding and implementing his instructions.

In the end he sent for Lady Ona, determined to ignore her provocations. She duly arrived and bowed low.

"Organization bores me," he told her. "I have decided to allow you to do it."

She offered no response, simply staring pointedly at him.

He rolled his eyes. "Do it your way," he said irritably. "I have decided to ignore your shortcomings."

She bowed again. "As you wish, Your Majesty."

He dismissed her with a lazy flick of his fingers.

Lesser mortals were such fragile creatures. Would he ever find someone truly satisfying to work with? The idea of unending life seemed almost abhorrent at times like this.

In the end two more days went by before Agon's procession was finally ready to leave for Arnost. Under Lady Ona's direction, the number of travelers and the wagonloads of supplies had diminished considerably, but Agon didn't argue. He held to his promise and remained aloof from the details.

Late one afternoon the king was informed that Lady Ona had appeared with a request for an audience. He made his way into the small audience chamber adjoining his private apartments.

"Show her in," he ordered.

Lady Ona came in and bowed low.

He stared at her through narrowed eyes. Her garments were surprisingly modest. She would never be able to hide her beauty entirely, even if she tried, but on this occasion her customary flirtatious and provocative demeanor was nowhere to be seen.

"Great King, may you live forever," she offered humbly, before bowing low again. "Your servants are ready to depart," she told him. "We await only Your Majesty's command."

So she had done it. And without his guidance. He stared at her without speaking, observing casually the telltale signs that she was beginning to squirm. It was a familiar ritual, one he had performed many times over the years with an endless stream of servants and hopeful petitioners.

When he finally decided she had sweated enough, he addressed her curtly. "We depart at dawn tomorrow. You are dismissed."

She bowed deeply and turned to leave. She glided away with stately and measured steps, but Agon was not deceived. She desperately wanted to run, and she was not successful in hiding it.

He glowered after her shapely figure as it slowly disappeared from view. It was time he lay down for a while—his head was beginning to pound.

29

———

King Steffan stood with Queen Essanda in a pleasant meeting room in Delmar's castle, gazing out beyond the city of Varacellan to the tall ships anchored in the bay. The sun was shining, and a gentle breeze caressed the king's face. The scene before him betrayed no hint whatsoever of the troubles that beset him on every side.

King Delmar joined them, and Steffan nodded a welcome, somehow conjuring up a half-hearted smile to go with it.

The Varasan monarch gazed at him steadily for a moment before clapping him on the back. "There's sure to be a way through it all, Steffan. We'll find it together."

"Thank you, Delmar. I can't imagine where we would be without your support."

Ranauld entered, with Will, Rufe, and Jonas close behind him. Steffan waved the men to a conference table in the middle of the room, and the monarchs joined them there.

Essanda looked distracted. Elena had offered to take care of Prince Aiden whenever needed, and Thomas and Brother Ander had also promised to help Elena out. On this occasion the queen had taken her up on the offer. Essanda was confident that their son was in good hands, but Steffan knew that she never found it easy to detach herself from Aiden.

Refreshments were brought in by two servants who bowed and closed the door as they left.

"I have called this conference to consider our next steps," Steffan began.

He couldn't keep a frown from his face. "Arnost and much of Arvenon is controlled by Pisander and his henchmen. Castel has declared war on Arvenon, and has increasingly come under the influence of one of the plotters behind the assassination. Thanks to Count Ranauld we now know that King Rupert believes that King Delmar and Will are responsible for the attack that led to King Istel's death.

"We have an army stationed outside Castel. Count Ranauld was prevented from making contact with the men in that northern army, so its status is unknown. But we have to assume it is still under the command of men loyal to Pisander.

"On the positive side, we have regained control of the army originally stationed outside Erestor. That western army is now led by Lord Burtelen with the help of Rellan, and we expect it to have been bolstered significantly by the addition of soldiers from Erestor. We have instructed them to close the border with Rogand."

He nodded to Delmar. "The support we have received from King Delmar is the only other thing worth celebrating in the midst of this madness."

"After the help you extended me during the Rogandan invasion, it is my pleasure to return the favor," Delmar replied. "And there is further news. I have just learned from my agents that Agon is preparing to set out for Arnost. He is apparently traveling with enough people to populate a modestly sized town, so it seems unlikely that he will be traveling quickly."

"That is significant news, Your Majesties," said Will. "In light of it I have a suggestion to offer."

The king raised an eyebrow. "Why do I always feel anxious about your well-being whenever I hear those words from your lips, Will?" he asked. "The truth is, though, we need ideas, and yours are always worth considering." He extended his palm, indicating that Will had the floor.

"We cannot allow King Agon to establish himself in Arnost," began Will. "It will be extremely difficult to remove him if that should ever happen."

Steffan nodded grimly. "I agree. But we have sent an army to prevent him crossing the border."

"That is true," Will agreed. "But what if Pisander decides to redeploy the army currently on the borders of Castel? He might send it to the Rogandan border in support of Agon. The outcome is not easy to predict if Lord Burtelen and Rellan should find themselves surrounded, with Agon's Rogandans before them and Pisander's army behind them."

"Are you suggesting that the men in Pisander's army would be willing to fight their own countrymen?" asked Steffan.

"It is difficult to predict," Will replied. "They have been fed so many lies. If they believe you and the queen are dead, it's hard to know how they might respond."

Steffan frowned. "But what can we do? If we leave the border unguarded, Agon will walk in unopposed."

"I agree, Your Majesty," said Will. "I am not proposing to withdraw our army. We just need to prevent Pisander from sending his army against them."

"What are you proposing?" Steffan asked bluntly.

"Two suggestions," said Will. He turned to King Delmar. "The first will depend on your assistance, Your Majesty."

"I'm listening, Will," Delmar told him.

"I understand that Pisander has no significant force stationed at the border with Varas," said Will.

"That is correct," confirmed Delmar. "He has scouts, but little more."

"My proposal is that you invade Arvenon, Your Majesty," Will told King Delmar. He hurried on before anyone could object. "Your men would be accompanied by King Steffan and Count Ranauld. The goal would be to force Pisander to send an army to counter the invasion.

His only available force is the northern army currently stationed outside Castel."

Steffan could scarcely believe his ears. "Pisander's army mainly consists of men loyal to me. Are you proposing we ask the Varasans to fight my own soldiers in my name?"

"Certainly not, Your Majesty," Will replied. "As soon as Pisander's army arrives, the Varasan army would withdraw to the border. Pisander is neither strong enough nor foolish enough to invade Varas. I would expect a stalemate, with both sides observing each other from a position on their own side of the border. Meanwhile the men would have come within easier reach. Count Ranauld and Rufe are well known to the men, as are you, Your Majesty. Between you all, another opportunity might present itself to turn them against Pisander."

Steffan was still frowning. "I notice that Ranauld and Rufe feature in this proposal, but not you. What is your other suggestion?" he asked.

"I propose to go to Rogand."

"For what purpose?" asked Steffan, his frown deepening.

"With the goal of distracting Agon, possibly even intercepting him."

"How do you propose to do that?" Steffan growled. He shook his head. "I've learned to take you very seriously, Will, but your boldness does border on the reckless at times. I'm sure you're honest enough to admit that."

Will offered no immediate response.

"You seem to have been drawing from a boundless well of luck," Steffan continued. "But sooner or later that well is going to run dry. Don't expect me to agree to anything that will hasten that day— you're far too valuable to me."

Will had been listening patiently, but Steffan's little speech had clearly failed to make an impression on him. Steffan had been frustrated before by the unshakable confidence his commander showed in his latest plan. Apparently this occasion would be no exception.

"I appreciate your concern for me, and I freely acknowledge that risk will be involved," Will finally conceded. "But all of us are aware of how much is at stake. Our options are likely to dwindle over time, and dwindle rapidly. We need to take our chances, however fragile those chances might appear to be. If we don't, Varas will become our final refuge. And how long can Varas stand once Arvenon and Castel are in the hands of Agon?"

Steffan passed a hand wearily across his face. Will was right of course. As always.

That didn't mean he needed to agree to Will's proposal. The king knew he should be grateful for his commander's astuteness when it came to strategy, but he could sense where this was heading. It wasn't the first time that Will had been drawn to a high risk scheme, one that dangled an impossibly big payback. Steffan was determined to avoid being maneuvered into agreeing to any such scheme. Not when he had so much to lose.

"So what is your plan?" he asked. He was aware that his voice carried an edge, but he didn't care.

Will didn't hesitate. "I have been speaking to some of King Delmar's agents. They have learned that many of Agon's noblemen are deeply unhappy about his new foray into Arvenon. All of them were required to contribute significant manpower to Drettroth's invasion force, and all of them have suffered heavily as a result of Drettroth's losses. With fewer peasants to work the land, crops have diminished greatly. Agon has already demanded a new round of soldiers, and the nobles are expected to train and equip them before releasing them. Another bad year is looming due to these distractions.

"The nobles have no desire to continue on this path, especially when they see little purpose in it beyond bolstering Agon's ego. We believe that Agon has been made aware of this unrest, although there is no sign that he is taking it seriously.

"I believe we can provide him with a nudge. Agon's likely path to the border will take him past an area I visited more than once with my uncle during my youth. Over the centuries the kings of Rogand have given the people of that region abundant reason to hate them."

"I know a little of the Aen-ur," Steffan told him. The blank faces around him confirmed Steffan's suspicion that few in Arvenon had even heard of the Aen-ur.

Clearly Will knew of them. Steffan knew he shouldn't be surprised. It was never wise to assume anything about Will, and the king had seen more evidence than most of the folly of underestimating him.

Will continued. "I plan to go to the lands of the Aen-ur and use the area as a base. Now that I know many of Agon's nobles are unhappy, I will take any available opportunity to fan the flames. If there is any way to disrupt or delay Agon's progress to the border, I will do so. That should give Rellan and Lord Burtelen as much time as they need to get their army in place to prevent Agon from crossing the border.

"If possible, I will try to create confusion behind him. Either way, I hope to give him good reason to reconsider his plan to set himself up in Arnost. It will be worth it even if it buys us a temporary reprieve."

Steffan shook his head. "The risks far outweigh any likely benefit. You would be almost unprotected—you know how few soldiers we have with us."

"I wouldn't take soldiers. I would not be going there to fight. A smaller party is much better suited to the purpose—the last thing I want is to attract attention. Haldek's mother country is Rogand, and I will take him if he is willing to go. And I will ask Thomas to accompany us. He is reasonably proficient in Rogandan now—Haldek has been teaching him."

"You can't ask Thomas to leave Elena and Tamara, Will," the queen protested. "He isn't a fighting man. It wouldn't be fair."

Steffan's brows furrowed. "Why would you want him with you anyway?" he asked. Will seemed to place a surprising reliance on Thomas, and the king had never understood the reason.

"We will avoid fighting entirely, Your Majesty," Will told the queen. Then he addressed himself to the king once more. "I value

Thomas because he is not a soldier. He often notices things—important things—that I have missed."

"I can confirm that, Your Majesty," said Rufe gravely.

The king shook his head. Even Rufe seemed willing to take Will's plan seriously. Steffan was far from convinced, but there were far more important issues to consider, and he wasn't going to allow himself to be distracted by such details.

"I can see merit in your first proposal, Will," said the king, "and I will discuss it further with King Delmar. I can't help wondering, though, if any of my predecessors ever proposed that a foreign power invade Arvenon," he added wryly.

"As for your second proposal, I see so many problems with it I'm not ready to even consider it at this point."

King Steffan thanked everyone for their participation, then he closed the conference.

He left in a grim mood. Will's proposals might be hard to stomach, but Steffan knew that his commander was only trying to make the most of the limited options available to him. The options had narrowed so severely because Steffan had become little more than a refugee, dependent on the beneficence of a foreign ruler.

***

As Will was leaving the conference, Jonas swung in beside him.

"I won't hesitate to join you on your mission to Rogand if you want me to come," said Jonas. "I hope you know that."

"Thank you, Jonas," Will replied. "That's no surprise to me. And I don't want you to think I'd leave you behind because of any lack of confidence in you. As the king immediately recognized, the mission is a fool's errand. I wouldn't be doing you any favors by asking you along. But the bigger reason is that I need you to stay with the king. He will need competent commanders by his side, and I'm trusting you and Rufe to fulfill that role in my absence."

"We will do our best," Jonas told him.

Will stopped and faced Jonas. "There's something I've been wanting to ask you, Jonas. You grew up on a farm, didn't you?"

"Yes," Jonas replied.

"When all of this is over—assuming we survive—I've been wondering if you would be willing to consider the role of steward on my holdings in Erestor. I know it would be asking a lot. It would be a very different role from being a leader in the army, but you've seen for yourself that I'm not the most popular noble in Erestor. The role calls for an organizer who understands farming, but it may well involve fighting sooner or later."

Jonas's eyes had gone wide. "I accept!" he said, without hesitation. "I can't imagine anything that would suit me better!"

Will beamed at him. "Good! That's settled, then!" he said, clapping Jonas on the back.

A meal awaited them, and they headed off together to enjoy once more the bounty of King Delmar's provision.

* * *

LATER THAT DAY Will received a summons to attend King Steffan. He arrived to find the king in a pensive mood. He bowed respectfully. "Your Majesty?"

"I have something I've decided to entrust to you, Will." The king removed something from the pouch at his belt and held it out. "Take it."

Will reached out and received from the king a small shiny object. He turned it over in his hand. It appeared to be a small glazed tile with a brightly painted surface. He guessed it had once been part of a mosaic, but he couldn't imagine what the mosaic might have depicted. Several lines of writing in a language unknown to him had been scratched on the reverse side of the tile. The lettering was so tiny it was barely distinguishable.

A story clearly lay behind the object. "What is it?" asked Will, intrigued by its mystery and curious to understand its hidden meaning.

"It was a gift from a long-dead king of the Aen-ur to one of my ancestors," the king replied. "It was given to me by my father, just as it was handed down to him by his father. My father convinced me of its value. Perhaps that's why I still carry it with me. That and its small size." He shrugged. "I've been forced to leave so much else behind."

"It's fascinating," said Will.

The king nodded. "Sadly, the details of the story have been lost over the years, but it seems that my ancestor rendered a significant service to the Aen-ur king. In return he was given this token. It might still mean something to the Aen-ur, but I can't say that with any certainty."

Will looked at the king questioningly.

The king frowned back at him. "You'll undoubtedly conclude that I'm sanctioning your visit to Rogand," the king said irritably. "I'm not happy about it, Will! Not happy at all!"

"I understand, Your Majesty," Will replied quietly. He held up the stone. "Thank you for entrusting this to me. I hope one day I will learn the story behind it."

King Steffan dismissed him abruptly. The king might have handed over the tile, but he was clearly far from persuaded about Will's proposal.

Will hurried away to begin serious preparations for the journey to Rogand.

***

"Will! We haven't seen you for a while. Come and join us." Thomas grinned a welcome.

"Thanks, Thomas," he replied. "Elena," he added, nodding in her direction. He smiled at Tammi, but the smile seemed forced. Thomas couldn't remember seeing Will so distracted before.

"You look as if you have something on your mind, Will," he offered tentatively.

Will nodded. "I need to ask you something," he said.

Glancing at Elena, Thomas saw that she had tensed. It was

unlikely that Will would have noticed any difference in her demeanor, but the change was obvious to Thomas.

Both of them waited for Will to continue.

"I am planning to go to Rogand," he told them.

Thomas frowned. "That sounds dangerous."

Will nodded. "It is. But I have little choice. Time is not on our side."

He sighed. "I'm sure I don't need to explain the realities to you both. Agon intends to annex Arvenon and Castel, and he will almost certainly succeed—unless we can find a way to stop him. Soon only Varas will remain free. King Delmar won't be able to hold out for long. The consequences for everyone in the three kingdoms are too awful to think about."

Thomas nodded mutely, stealing another glance at Elena. She caught his eye, and he noticed that her face had gone pale. Neither of them had forgotten Will's comment after their visit to the former Lord Tarestel in the dungeon. Will had said at the time that they needed to get close to Agon, because the Stone of Knowing would be able to answer all their questions about his intentions.

Both of them could undoubtedly guess what was coming next.

"I'm not sure how much I can achieve by moving against Agon," Will admitted, "although I have a few ideas. But it would help enormously if you were with me, Thomas."

Now that Will's request was out in the open, Thomas experienced a strange sense of release. The uncertainty was finally over. His momentary flicker of relief was short-lived, though. A heavy feeling of dread slowly settled over his spirit.

"I won't let Thomas go to Rogand without me," Elena said firmly.

Will lowered his eyes. He didn't speak, although Thomas could guess what he was thinking.

Thomas turned to Elena with a sigh. "I wouldn't want to go to Rogand without you either," he said. "But taking Tammi would be impossible. And I can't imagine us both going and leaving her behind."

An uncomfortable silence followed.

Will was the first to speak. "I'll leave you to discuss it," he said. "I'm sorry to have raised it at all. I wouldn't consider going myself if the need wasn't so great."

It occurred to Thomas to ask an obvious question. "Has the king agreed to this?"

"Not precisely," Will admitted. "He needs some time to think about it. I expect he'll come around before long."

So the king was no more excited about this plan than Thomas.

Will didn't linger. He said his farewells and was quickly gone.

The moment he was out of sight Elena rounded on her husband. "You can't do it, Thomas!"

"How can I say no to Will?" he asked her miserably. "He hasn't ever held himself back. He's always given everything he has."

"But he doesn't have a wife and a daughter!"

Thomas found no answer to that.

Elena's voice became steady. "We could lend him the stone."

Thomas looked at her in stunned amazement. "We can't do that!"

"We can't?" she asked, a resolute look on her face. "Or we won't?"

He could only stare wide-eyed at her.

Abruptly she softened. "I'm sorry, Thomas. It isn't fair for me to pressure you about the stone. You've shared it with me willingly, but the responsibility for it has always rested on your shoulders. That's been true since long before I met you."

Thomas shook his head firmly. "You're right to ask me to question my motives." He sighed. "We can't lend Will the stone though. Have you forgotten my conversation with him at Newhaven? I told you about it at the time. He let me know why he's so willingly left the stone with me all these years."

"I haven't forgotten," she told him. "Will has his reasons for never asking for it himself or expecting you to give it to the king. He thinks the stone is safer with you."

Thomas nodded. "Will never does anything without a reason."

"And you're right of course," she said despondently. "Even if you offered it to him he wouldn't take it."

Tears came into her eyes. "I know you'll need to go with Will. But I'm frightened, Thomas! I'm not sure if I could bear to lose you."

He reached out and drew her close. He didn't say it aloud, but he felt just as miserable and frightened as she did.

It had felt like such a relief when Will made it clear he was content to leave the stone with Thomas. But it also meant there was to be no release from the burden.

He felt trapped. The stone seemed like a monster of the deep that had wrapped its tentacles tightly around him. It was suffocating him.

How could he ever break free of it?

30

A gentle swell pushed the flat bottomed boat onto the sand. Sailors jumped out and led three restive horses onto the beach. Thomas followed, with Will and Haldek close behind, and each of them took a halter from the sailors.

The sailors had no desire to delay their departure for a moment longer than they needed to, and they wasted no time returning to their ship. They were keenly aware that it would be some considerable time before they cleared Rogandan waters on their journey back to Varacellan.

Thomas watched them go with mixed feelings. Delighted as he was that his world was no longer bucking and swaying unpredictably, he was sorry to leave the relatively safety of the Varasan vessel. The prospect of riding into Rogand filled him with unease.

Not long after Thomas and his companions waved the sailors off, they moved inland. The beach might have been deserted, but Will apparently wanted somewhere less exposed to spend their first night on Rogandan soil. The sea had long since disappeared behind them by the time the sun sank below the hills to the west.

After leaving Varacellan, the Varasan ship had headed out to sea, staying well clear of land as it sailed past Rog, not making landfall until they reached a small bay far to the southeast of the Rogandan capital. They were now planning to ride southwest across mostly barren country until they intersected the main road south from Rog. The trading route had been established along the western edge of Rogand, in the shadows of the Blue Mountains that ran from Varas in the north down into Arvenon further south. The road traced almost the entire length of the mountain range before cutting west through a pass into Arvenon.

Their destination was a region beyond the main road that reached up into the lower slopes of the mountains. Will had said they would need to ride hard for several days before they reached it.

The horses had quickly become unsettled when they were led into the hold of the ship. Thomas had remained with them throughout the voyage, and for the most part he had done a successful job in keeping them calm. No one could be sure how rough the seas would be or how the horses would cope with it, so Thomas had selected six animals to accompany them. In the end all six of the animals had arrived in good condition, and Thomas chose three of them at random. It hadn't been easy for him to leave the other horses on the ship knowing they would be forced to endure the return journey.

Back on solid ground once more, the three horses were already looking more settled. Come the morning they would be running beneath an open sky.

After a brief discussion with Haldek, Will decided to light a fire. Thomas was grateful. Warmth and hot food were more than welcome after their time at sea.

Thoughts of Elena and Tammi filled Thomas's mind as he lay down to sleep. Elena had put on a brave face when he left, but she hadn't been able to hide the fear in her eyes. He had stroked her hair as she embraced him, whispering a promise that he would try to be careful.

Then he had lifted Tammi, holding her tightly until the moment he needed to board. She had clung to him despairingly when he tried to hand her to Rubin, and the sound of her tears had chased him up the gangplank.

Determined to get some sleep, he rolled over and tried to shut it all out. He guessed he would have plenty else to worry about on this trip.

The following morning Will called a brief conference before they set off.

"Now that we're in Rogand, we need to avoid any situation that requires you to speak, Thomas," he said. "Your accent will give you away, not to mention your grammar."

"Along with the so, so many words he still must learn," said Haldek. He chuckled and gave Thomas a wink.

Haldek was right of course. The two of them had continued to work on Thomas's Rogandan, but there was still a great deal for him to master. And he didn't have Elena's ready facility with foreign languages.

"If anyone asks why you're not speaking, we'll say that you're mute," said Will. "Don't forget. It will be a problem if you suddenly start speaking."

Thomas nodded.

"How much Rogandan do you understand?" Will asked him.

"Some," Thomas replied. "I have been working on it with Haldek. I understand a lot more if people speak slowly."

"Don't expect them to speak slowly, because they won't," said Will. "But you'll get plenty of opportunity to practice. After this conversation none of us will be speaking anything except Rogandan. We'll try to remember to talk a lot, to help you get used to it."

They rode steadily across rolling hills on the first day. Vegetation was sparse, and the entire region seemed vast and barren. They found no sign of paths and no hint of habitation. Thomas saw no sign of wild animals either. If any creatures larger than rodents inhabited this area, they were keeping out of sight.

Will once again built a fire that night. "The fire is as much for protection as for warmth," he said. "You may not think so, but dangerous creatures are prowling all around us."

That seemed to be pretty much what Will had said, anyway. As promised, he was speaking only in Rogandan now. He had tried to speak slowly for the sake of Thomas, but unfamiliar words were still unfamiliar, however carefully articulated.

When they woke in the morning Will handed Thomas a small leather pouch. In it was a thick paste, oily to the touch. "Smear this on the exposed areas of your skin, Thomas," he said. "It will make you look darker, and you won't stand out as much."

Will had a pouch of his own, and he applied the paste liberally to his own skin.

When they had both finished, Haldek eyed them critically. He shook his head in disgust. "Neither of you look like Rogandans!" he exclaimed. "And as for your hair..." He pointed disdainfully at Will's red locks.

Thomas winced when he examined their leader more closely. The color of Will's hair looked strange and unnatural against his newly darkened skin.

Will pulled two larger pouches from his saddlebag and tossed one of them to Thomas. "This is for your hair," he said. "I'm afraid it isn't going to smell pleasant." By way of translation, he touched his nose before screwing it up uncomfortably.

Thomas couldn't help grinning. Opening the pouch soon wiped the grin from his face though. The smell was indeed putrid.

"We'll only need to apply it every few days," Will promised him. "As long as we don't wash."

Thomas apparently didn't look mollified, because Will added, "The smell does fade quickly."

Thankfully Will was right about the smell. And Thomas soon had plenty else to distract him anyway.

They'd been riding steadily all morning without seeing another human. Occasionally they came upon sheep that scattered in fright as the horses approached. Eventually they crested a ridge to find themselves among a group of shepherds. The men were sitting around a large fire pit, and they sprang to their feet when Will's party appeared.

Will pulled his horse to a stop, calling out a greeting. The men stared at them suspiciously at first, but to Thomas's eye their gaze soon became calculating. One of the shepherds at once invited them to dismount and join them in a meal. He spoke in a jovial tone, but he made it clear he wouldn't take no for an answer.

Haldek had said very little, but Thomas could see he was itching to be gone. Will was polite but firm. He explained that their friend—and with this he pointed to Thomas—had become very sick, to the point where he was no longer able to speak.

Claiming to be a healer, another of the shepherds loudly insisted on examining the sick man. The shepherds began to spread out around the horses, smiling and nodding eagerly. Their cheerfulness seemed forced to Thomas. He sensed a confrontation looming.

Will called a sharp command, and all three of them urged their horses forward, riding down anyone who tried to block their path.

Apparently deciding that Thomas was the easiest target, a couple of them attempted to pull him from his horse as it sprang away. They partially succeeded in dragging him from the saddle, but his horsemanship far exceeded their expectations. Breaking free, he swung effortlessly back into the saddle and quickly rode out of reach.

"Follow me!" Will called urgently, leading them over the crest of a small hill and racing across the low-lying ground beyond it.

Only when the shepherds were far behind them did Will rein in his horse. He patted its steaming neck as it snorted.

"Shepherds have a bad reputation in Rogand," he told Thomas, lapsing into Arvenian. "And they're armed with slingshots. They use them against predators of all kinds, and they're deadly with them. We were fortunate. Things might have ended very differently if we'd still been in their line of sight when they retrieved them."

After that they became much more alert. They caught glimpses of other people in the distance a couple of times but managed to avoid further contact.

After the sun set they found a sheltered place to spend the night and shared a simple meal together. As Thomas sat absently chewing his food his thoughts wandered to Elena and Tammi far away. What had they been doing that day? Were they thinking of him right now as he was thinking of them?

By the time he lay down to sleep Thomas felt exhausted, although his weariness wasn't primarily physical. His experiences were taking him back to his wandering days during the Rogandan invasion. He had witnessed his share of fighting, and it had been terrifying. That hadn't been the only thing that sapped his energy though. He had been worn down by the constant uncertainty—the feeling of never knowing what might be lurking over the crest of the next hill.

His experience of Rogand was beginning to feel uncomfortably like that.

He thought back to a simpler time when life had offered nothing more complicated than the daily chores of a stable hand. Could such a life ever satisfy him now? Challenging as his path had been at times, it had led him to Elena and to Tammi, and he could never wish them away. He knew he had a great deal to be grateful for.

At the same time he faced an uncertain future, wandering through a foreign land surrounded by enemies. Restless and on edge, he tossed and turned for several hours before finally managing to get to sleep.

LONG AFTER THE three men had ridden away from the beach, a fishing boat pulled in to the same bay. Carnwill swam ashore, annoyed at having fallen so far behind the men he was pursuing.

The stay in Varacellan had become increasingly frustrating for Carnwill. With Thomas accommodated in the royal castle, the tracker had been unable to keep him in sight at all. Then he had almost failed to notice when his target set sail at dawn on a Varasan ship with Will Prentis and a Rogandan companion.

Thomas had left Varacellan too soon for Agon's agents to abduct him. Who could say where he was headed now?

Against the odds, Carnwill managed to quickly find and hire a sleek fishing boat. It was reputed to be the fastest in Varacellan, but by the time they put to sea the Varasan ship had long since left the port.

Carnwill didn't know for certain which direction the ship had taken once it left the harbor. Following his instincts, he had instructed the fisherman to head northeast. Many hours had passed before his guess was confirmed. When the fisherman eventually caught sight of the Varasan ship far ahead of them, Carnwill could barely contain his relief.

Both vessels were far from land when they sailed past the harbor at Rog, the fishing boat staying far enough behind to avoid alerting the sailors on the Varasan ship. Eventually they approached the shore once more, the fisherman anchoring his boat behind an island while the ship unloaded its cargo.

Once ashore, Carnwill saw at once that the men had ridden away, heading inland. Where they were heading and why, he couldn't say. Without a horse of his own, all he could do was set off after them on foot, tracking the horses.

Several days passed before he finally accepted that he had lost the trail, and with it any chance of finding Thomas.

Carnwill could think of no good reason for Will Prentis and his companions to travel to Rogand and put ashore so far from human habitation. His instinct told him that Prentis planned to intercept Agon, perhaps in the hope of assassinating the king.

He had little choice but to find a horse and seek out the king himself. Changing direction, he began walking northwest, heading for Rog.

THE COUNTRYSIDE gradually changed beneath the hooves of their horses as Thomas and his friends made their way through the heart of Rogand. Increasingly they found themselves riding through farmland, with roads, villages, and even towns beginning to appear. Not surprisingly, human contact also became markedly more frequent.

Will skillfully managed any interactions that proved impossible to avoid, and they weren't threatened again.

"The farmhouses look different," Thomas said during one of their breaks from riding.

"Farmhouses in this region are mostly made of straw," Haldek told him. When Thomas looked surprised, he added, "Straw is readily available and inexpensive. The builders start with a wooden frame, then pack in straw bales. Straw thatching is used on the roofs. The straw keeps the cold out in the winter."

"Straw houses catch fire easily too," Will added dryly.

Haldek shrugged. "Accidents happen. People learn to be careful."

"Buildings in the towns don't seem to be made of straw," said Thomas.

Haldek shook his head. "They are mostly made of cob, which is a mixture of wet clay, sand, and straw. The walls are thick, so they sit on stone foundations. The buildings stay warm in winter and cool in summer."

Rogand had always seemed so alien, so menacing to Thomas. He was caught off guard by the natural beauty of the countryside around him and surprised by how familiar the crops and the farming appeared to be. The farmhouses certainly looked different, and the towns even more so. But for the most part he could easily have imagined himself to be in a remote corner of Arvenon.

He began to see that his attitude to Rogand had been skewed. It wasn't surprising, given the atrocities carried out by Rogandan soldiers during the invasion. Yet Haldek had once been a Rogandan soldier, and Thomas knew him to be a thoroughly decent person who had come to care deeply about Thomas and his family.

Now that he found himself traveling through the heart of Rogand, Thomas realized he needed the reminder that not all Rogandans were like King Agon and Lord Drettroth.

Even so, he was masquerading as a Rogandan, having come to Rogand to subvert its king. He knew he could reasonably expect no mercy if he was caught.

· · ·

THE DAYS ROLLED STEADILY by as Will and his companions rode inland. Eventually they caught sight of a distant mountain range that Will named the Blue Mountains. The border hugged the mountain range with the mountains themselves being located in Arvenon.

After they crossed a large river Will seemed to get a more accurate reading on their location. "I've led us further south than I intended," he said. "We will head north for a while as soon as we reach the main road."

By the afternoon they were heading north in the direction of Rog.

"King Agon is heading south on this road, isn't he?" Thomas asked. "What if we meet him?"

Will didn't seem at all concerned. "He'll be traveling with a very large party," he replied. "We'll see the dust from their column long before we see any of his people."

Thomas tried not to think about it, but from that point his sense of imminent danger began to increase.

When night came Will kept them moving forward for several hours. The moon was almost full, and the road was plainly visible. The conditions made it easy to continue to ride as long as the horses could reasonably carry them. They eventually stopped for the night only after Will had found a suitable sheltered location well away from the road.

They rose before first light and continued their journey north. Will was plainly eager to reach their destination well before Agon arrived there if at all possible. After almost another day's travel they paused briefly to rest the horses.

"I am beginning to recognize a few landmarks," Will told them. "We will continue to ride until dark, then we will find a place to camp. The place I am seeking cannot be far off. I expect we will reach it not long after we set off in the morning."

"Where are you taking us, Will?" asked Haldek.

"We're heading for Aen-irac," Will replied.

Haldek looked horrified. "That is a name of ill omen," he said, his voice tight.

"Its reputation is what makes it useful to us," Will said calmly.

"Are you certain you know what we will find there?" Haldek asked him.

"If you are referring to reports of phantoms and monsters, I give little credence to such things," Will replied with a shrug.

Thomas had been working hard to suppress a growing sense of alarm. "Will we be safe there?" he finally asked.

"Nowhere in Rogand is safe for us," Will told him.

No one spoke until Haldek eventually broke the silence.

"It is time for me to remind you of a conversation we had in Varacellan, Will. I spent years at Agon's castle in Rog. King Agon is an evil man, and he is bad for Rogand. For that reason I will support your efforts to bring him down. But it stops there. I will not fight my countrymen."

Will nodded. "I have not forgotten, Haldek. I would never ask you to fight your countrymen. I am just as eager as you to avoid fighting. I suspect there are a few too many of them even for me," he added with a lopsided smile.

Will became serious again. "King Steffan only agreed to let us come to Rogand on the understanding that we would take no part in any conflict," he said.

Nothing further was said. When they resumed their journey, Will once more kept them riding until it was almost dark. Then they rode their horses into the forest, picking their way among the trees until the road lay well behind them.

Haldek appeared uneasy, casting glances about him nervously. Until that moment, Thomas had been curious about the stories the others had referred to. Now he was grateful he hadn't asked.

They ate silently. When they had finished Will quietly arranged for them to take turns watching through the night. He could scarcely have found a more effective way of saying that danger now surrounded them on every side.

Thomas took the first watch. The time passed uneventfully. Nevertheless, a sense of foreboding had settled over him, and his stomach had twisted itself into knots. When he handed over the watch to Will in the small hours of the morning, he did so with considerable relief.

Late as the hour was, sleep eluded Thomas when at last he lay down. When he eventually surrendered to it, he dreamed.

Thomas found himself standing on the porch of a large cabin in a secluded section of a vast forest. A lake stood before the house, and trees stretched out behind it far into the distance. Elena stood beside him, and Tammi played nearby. There was no sign of either Rubin or Haldek.

A strange creature with an unnaturally large fish-like head emerged from the water and stood dripping for a moment on the shore of the lake. The creature transformed into a woman. To all appearances she was perfectly normal. She seemed to be about the same age as his mother. Leaving the lake, she came and stood before him. Elena seemed untroubled by her. Tammi ignored her entirely.

She captured his gaze, and as Thomas stared into her eyes he felt himself sinking rapidly into their depths. A dizzying array of scenes raced toward him, flooding his senses. He was reminded of the sensation created by the stone when it bared a person's memories before him. The only difference was that the lives of many people swirled around him now. Some scenes emanated joy, but pain and loss issued from others.

In spite of the intensity of the experience he was not frightened. Immersed as he was, he experienced it dispassionately.

The woman somehow gathered him up, blanketing him with a warm sense of compassion, and he felt himself buoyed up as he was gently ejected back to his position beside the lake.

When the woman held out a hand to him, he somehow knew what was expected of him. Without hesitation he withdrew from around his neck the chain that held the Stone of Knowing and placed it into her outstretched hand.

Nodding a simple acknowledgment, she turned and retraced her steps to the lake. As the woman waded into its depths, she transformed once more before his eyes into the creature that first emerged from the lake. He stood watching as the woman-creature slowly sank beneath its surface. He remained unmoving until the final ripples had died away.

Thomas woke from the dream with a start. Everything around him was still and quiet, and stars peeked down through the trees overhead. He lay in silence, lost in his thoughts, until the sky slowly lightened.

Haldek had taken the final watch, and a sharp cry from the Rogandan roused Thomas to sudden alertness.

Leaping to his feet, Thomas glanced around him wildly. A ring of spears surrounded the three men, and a circle of grim faces confronted them.

No way of escape remained. They had been taken.

31

———

Even before his hand reached for his sword, Will saw the futility of any such response. Twenty men had encircled them with a ring of steel, and only he and Haldek could claim to be fighters. He forced himself to relax.

Something struck him as unusual about the men surrounding them. Peering forward with a puzzled frown, he saw in the dim light of the pre-dawn that it had not been Agon's soldiers who took them by surprise.

A young woman stepped into the circle to his right. He could not make out her face in the semi-darkness, but he sensed the confidence that radiated from her. She called out a few words in a fluid language that he did not understand. He nevertheless recognized that the words had been spoken in the tongue of the Aen-ur.

He turned to face the speaker. Everything was slowly becoming more distinct in the growing light, and he saw a slim figure clad in dark earthy colors. A wicked looking knife lay strapped against her side, but she was otherwise unarmed.

"Aen-usul aen-uwe!" he called back.

Her eyes seemed to go wide for a moment, and she trained her gaze upon him. He felt unaccountably exposed as she coolly looked him up and down.

A new set of sounds escaped her lips, and he could only shrug in response. He had quickly exhausted his paltry knowledge of the language of the exiles.

She stared at him for a moment longer before redirecting her scrutiny to Haldek. Switching effortlessly to the language of Rogand, she demanded, "Why does a Rogandan trespass in the forests of Aen-irac?" Her voice betrayed no sign of an accent.

Haldek made no reply, nervously turning his gaze to Will instead.

The woman once more fixed her attention on Will, her eyes narrowing. She jerked her head in the direction of Thomas to include him. "Neither of you are Rogandan," she said, "in spite of the dye in your hair and the oil on your faces."

She was now speaking in Arvenian, and Will stared at her in surprise. Her mastery of languages was impressive. It was also obvious that very little escaped her notice.

He inclined his head to acknowledge the accuracy of her assertion, but otherwise held his peace. It seemed wisest to avoid speaking until he needed to.

One of the spearmen spoke to her in his own language, and she replied in the same tongue, bowing briefly in respect. It appeared that the spearman was leading the soldiers, and that her role was that of spokesperson and interpreter. Whatever her actual role, she was clearly possessed of unusual confidence.

The spearman jerked the head of his spear toward the forest, and his companions reformed into a loose column with the three intruders positioned in the middle. The horses were led along behind them.

As they headed deeper into the forest, Will reflected on their situation. He had set out for Aen-irac with the intention of making contact with the exiles, and they had succeeded in doing just that. It hadn't been at all clear to him how such a connection might take place, or how their arrival would be received. The likelihood of enlisting the aid of the Aen-ur against Agon was even less certain.

Many questions remained to be answered. There was always going to be risk involved in this initiative, though, and he felt no reason to be dissatisfied with the outcome thus far.

He couldn't help being curious about the young woman, and he took the opportunity to steal glances in her direction when he was confident she was looking elsewhere. Who was she? Her facility with languages made it difficult to identify her race. She didn't look like one of the Aen-ur, and her hair wasn't dark enough for her to be Rogandan.

He was no closer to an answer several hours later when the party crossed a plank bridge suspended by ropes over a swift flowing river. A small settlement lay on the far side of the bridge, nestled among the foothills that led into the mountains. Trees had been cleared to construct a small cluster of sturdy wooden buildings.

Will and his companions were led to one of the buildings and ushered inside. Food and water were brought to them, but it was very obvious to them that they were regarded as captives. Will saw no reason to be unduly alarmed, and he sat down on what appeared to be a low bed and proceeded to enjoy his food.

Thomas did not appear especially concerned. He would undoubtedly have learned a great deal about the intentions of their captors from the stone, and Will was looking forward to an opportunity for a quiet word with his friend.

Haldek looked considerably more anxious.

"I don't think you have any reason to be alarmed, Haldek," Will began. "I don't think these people intend us any harm. Not yet, anyway."

He looked at Thomas with raised eyebrows, hoping for some kind of confirmation.

Thomas nodded. "I don't think they've decided on any course of action—they mostly seem curious about us. I imagine they'll wait until they've heard what you have to say, Will."

A question about the young woman hovered on the tip of Will's tongue, but he pushed it aside, acknowledging to himself it was little more than idle curiosity.

Darkness had fallen when the door opened. The young woman was standing outside, flanked by several armed guards.

"Come with me," she commanded them sternly, speaking in Rogandan. "You must answer for your actions in trespassing on these lands."

Thomas glanced at Will nervously. Haldek was tense, but his face was calm.

Will was not unduly concerned, and he followed her without hesitation. Thomas seemed willing enough to follow his lead.

Haldek was giving nothing away. Given Rogandan attitudes to the Aen-ur, though, Will could readily guess what he might be thinking.

The woman led them to a depression in the ground that formed a natural amphitheater. Roughly fifty men and women sat around the rim of the depression, and Will and his companions found themselves positioned at the center of the gathering. Although it was dark, many torches burned brightly among the gathered throng, illuminating their faces with flickers of light.

"Do you all speak Arvenian?" the woman asked the three of them, speaking in that language.

When they nodded, she said, "That is good. I strongly advise you to avoid the Rogandan language. The people here understand it, but they use it only at great need and even then reluctantly. Out of respect for them I will translate between their language and Arvenian."

She bowed to a man in the circle who wore a simple circlet of wood on his brow. He spoke a few words, and she bowed again.

She turned back to Will and his companions. If she sensed that Will was their leader, she gave no sign of it. Turning first to Haldek, she asked him, "Who are you, and why are you here?"

"My name is Haldek. I came here at the request of my friend," he replied, nodding toward Will.

She glared at Will as she spoke in the Aen-ur tongue. Then she turned to Thomas, a frown on her face. "And who are you?"

"My name is Thomas Stablehand. I am here for the same reason."

Once more as she translated she fixed a glare upon Will. "It seems you are responsible for this intrusion," she said, finally addressing him. "What reason can you offer?"

"Where I come from it is customary for strangers to exchange names and greetings when they first meet," he told her.

She flushed slightly, but he paid no attention to it, bowing respectfully first to her, then to the gathered people around them.

"My name is Will Prentis, and I bring you the greetings and best wishes of King Steffan and Queen Essanda of Arvenon."

"And who are you, Will Prentis, to speak on behalf of kings?" she asked.

A strange sensation prickled Will's spine hearing his name on her lips. He ignored it.

"I am also known as Lord Torbury," he said with another bow. "I command the armies of King Steffan of Arvenon."

She looked around dismissively. "And where are these armies?" she asked mockingly. "Have you come to shield us behind a wall of steel?" Her eyes narrowed. "Or have you come here to beg for help?"

Will, painfully aware of how near to the truth she had come with her shrewd guess, offered no response.

Her translation had not kept pace with their interactions, and without waiting for an answer she turned away from him and spoke rapidly to the silent watchers.

Then she turned to Thomas. "My name is Amyra," she said with a graceful bow. Next she faced Haldek and bowed once more. Finally she turned to Will. After gazing expressionlessly at him for a long moment, she bowed stiffly before turning her back on him.

Facing the man with the circlet, she spoke a few words. The man was clearly a leader among these people. He spoke again, for longer this time, then went silent. She bowed respectfully, then focused her attention on Will.

"What has brought the commander of the Arvenian armies so far from his homeland?" she asked bluntly.

Taking a deep breath, Will allowed his body to relax. "I am here because King Agon is once again on the move," he began. "It is only a few years since Arvenon, with the help of its allies from Castel and

Varas, broke the power of the invading Rogandan armies. Sadly, the peace has proven to be short-lived. Agon sent assassins into Arvenon with the goal of weakening the kingdoms that had resisted him so successfully. The assassins struck when the kings of Arvenon, Castel, and Varas were meeting together to confer. The king of Castel was killed, and King Steffan of Arvenon was severely wounded. Agon is eager to take advantage of the weakness of his enemies. He is once again heading west with an army."

While Amyra was translating, he slowly pivoted until he was directly facing the leader wearing the circlet.

The moment her voice trailed off, Will began speaking again. This time he spoke in Rogandan, ignoring the angry glare immediately directed at him by Amyra.

"You may be asking yourselves why the Aen-ur should care about such matters," he said forthrightly. "You may think that the world no longer has any awareness of your existence, nor any interest in it. And perhaps you are right, at least in part. The history of your people is not a secret to everyone though. It is no mystery to me. I know that all of the land that is now Rogand belonged to you at the time when the first of Agon's people pushed north two hundred years ago. The people of Lestanor resisted their passage ferociously, and they hurried on until they found themselves in the broad and fertile land of your predecessors. The Aen-ur received them peaceably and helped them find places to settle.

"But more and more of them came, and when they grew strong enough they turned on those who had welcomed them. They burned your fields and laid siege to your fortresses. Bitter years followed, and the songs of joy gave way to dirges lamenting the long, slow defeat of the Aen-ur.

"The remnant of your ancestors retreated at last to Ishitar Ataye, the mightiest and most magnificent of their strongholds. Their resolve was strong as the final siege began, but hope slowly faded as supplies dwindled and the attackers relentlessly wore down their defenses. Two terrible years had passed when Agon's forefathers at last breached the walls and tore down the fortress, slaughtering all who sheltered there. The once mighty and prosperous Aen-ur became fugitives, hiding away in the forests, hoping they would not be noticed."

Some of the men and women before him had gone pale. Others had begun to mutter in anger.

"How dare you speak to them in this way!" hissed Amyra in fury.

Will ignored her, raising his voice until his words echoed back from the surrounding trees. "I make no apology for confronting you with the painful history of your ancestors," he called. "You might believe that these events belong to the distant past, but you know from your own recent history that unfinished business from the past has a way of coming back to haunt you."

He stood tall, summoning every ounce of his authority as he continued. "Nor do I apologize for speaking to you in Rogandan. I know you understand the language well enough, and soon enough it will echo once more throughout your forest refuges—if you choose to turn your faces away from the unpleasant realities of the world around you. All of you here know what to expect, because you are old enough to have witnessed the carnage firsthand."

He paused, fixing his gaze intently on them. "I am aware of Agon's personal history with your people. While he was still a young man he singled out the Aen-ur as the first targets of his cruelty. He hunted your people through the forests of Aen-irac and massacred every man, woman, and child unlucky enough to fall within his reach. Perhaps you think he has forgotten about you. If so, you are wrong. Dangerously wrong."

He pointed at Haldek. "My companion here is Rogandan by birth, although he now lives in Arvenon, and he bears you no ill will. He will readily confirm that Rogandan children are raised on nursery tales of Aen-ur monsters that prey on the unwary at night—demons that will come for them in their beds if they misbehave. No Rogandan will ever sleep entirely comfortably while the imagined threat of the Aen-ur hangs over them. Not while the remnant of your people still linger in the land to lend it credibility."

He glanced at Haldek, who met his eyes briefly before nodding once. Haldek then lowered his gaze, clearly unwilling to meet the eyes of the people around them.

Will turned back to the leader. "Agon was nurtured on the same prejudices. Right now he is heading to Arnost, intent on subjugating the three kingdoms that lie to the west. If he is allowed to crush all foreign opposition, he will remember the Aen-ur. He will come here again, and next time he will finish the job."

Will paused. The people before him had gone silent. He waited, allowing his words to sink in.

He had one final thing to say, and he switched once more to Arvenian to say it.

"I know that, hidden from the world, you have quietly gathered your strength since the dark days when Ishitar Ataye fell. When last Agon came after you, you were able to conceal your true numbers from him. Agon would move against you at once should he ever discover the truth. What has not been hidden from inquirers like me will become plain to him as well, sooner or later.

"Agon will soon pass close to the forests of Aen-irac. Nevertheless, I have not come here to ask you to oppose him directly. I fully understand the wrath you would bring down on your heads."

Amyra translated once more, although he saw that her brows were furrowed in anger as she glanced at him. He saw in her eyes that she considered his bluntness an insult to the Aen-ur. He knew that he had also shown her disrespect in her role as translator.

He had no desire to arouse her displeasure, but what choice did he have?

He fell silent while Amyra translated his words. Then he stood quietly, waiting for a response.

When he finally allowed himself to relax, his shoulders slumped. He discovered that his heart had been racing, and he had been breathing hard.

Finally the leader stood to his feet. "My name is Faluye-Atae," he said, speaking fluently in the language of Arvenon. "You may call me Atae." He offered a stiff bow, and Will acknowledged it with a bow of his own.

"You claim to know a great deal about us, Will Prentis of Arvenon," said Atae. "Why should we pay attention to you and your words? You say you will not call on us to oppose Agon directly. Why then are you here?"

"These are matters I would gladly discuss with you, Atae, although I believe they would be better suited to a conference. First, though, I have promised to convey an offer on behalf of King Steffan of Arvenon. His offer is addressed to you all, and it is not dependent on anything you might do to aid me. This seems an appropriate forum in which to present it."

After a moment's hesitation Atae nodded, caution evident on his face.

Will glanced at Amyra to catch her attention. Then he continued in Arvenian. "You may be aware that the border between Rogand and Arvenon runs along the eastern fringes of the Blue Mountains. It may not seem obvious, but the legal reality is that all of us are currently in Arvenon, not Rogand. I understand your strong historical connection to Rogand, but Rogand has also been the source of your troubles and your persecution. King Steffan extends to you an invitation to relocate to the other side of the Blue Mountains. The land there is almost completely unsettled, and you would be welcome to make it your home. You would be well within the borders of Arvenon, and shielded by a significant natural barrier from any in Rogand who might wish you harm."

As Amyra translated, the listeners began to stir, and a buzz of animated conversation arose.

"Any such relocation would represent a significant upheaval for our people," Atae replied, still speaking in Arvenian. "And it would be of no value to us if Agon succeeds in his attempt to annex Arvenon."

Will waited for Amyra to translate before responding. "That is undeniably true," he acknowledged. "But he hasn't succeeded yet."

Atae considered Will for a few moments. Then he said quietly, "You will have your conference in the morning."

He spoke more loudly in his own language, and people rose from their seats, all of them speaking at once to each other in animated tones. Will could not readily tell from their demeanor how they had reacted to his words.

Amyra turned to him, her eyes still smoldering. He saw plainly that she had no intention of overlooking his offenses, either against her or against the Aen-ur.

"Atae has invited you all to join us for our evening meal," she said coolly.

Then she turned to the armed men who had escorted them to the amphitheater and spoke rapidly to them in their own language.

She turned back to the three men. "You may prepare for the meal in your own way. These men will escort you."

Then she bowed stiffly and turned away.

32

———————

Torchlight flickered around Thomas as he sat with Will and Haldek enjoying the meal prepared by the Aen-ur.

After Amyra had left them, they had been led once more to their assigned dwelling. Fresh water stood beside the dwelling in a large barrel, and after washing themselves they had changed into the cleanest clothing available in their saddlebags. They were now sitting in the hall of a large building, the space illuminated by many torches and warmed by huge fires crackling at both ends of the room.

The meal could almost have been called a feast, except that the mood of the people around him was noticeably subdued.

As they were leaving the amphitheater earlier he had turned the clasp on the chain around his neck to prevent the stone from coming into contact with his skin. It had been an easy decision to leave it that way when they arrived in the banqueting hall. He had no wish to intrude on the thoughts of his two friends, and quite apart from that, the flood of sensations coming to him from the stone would have been overwhelming in a crowd this size. He didn't need magical help to sense the underlying tension in the atmosphere around him though. It had been obvious to him as Will was speaking that his words had touched on a raw nerve. The unease had not diminished; if anything it had grown.

Amyra had joined Thomas and his companions, intending to act as translator whenever that was needed. She made it clear to them that Will's stubborn insistence on speaking in Rogandan earlier in the day—against her explicit advice—had been highly inappropriate. Any repetition would be a serious affront to the Aen-ur.

Thomas sensed that her concerns were well founded. Nevertheless he had the impression that Amyra had been considerably more irritated by Will's action than Atae.

Will had shown surprising insight into the Aen-ur and their history, and Thomas wondered how he had come to know so much. He intended to ask him about it as soon as an opportunity presented itself.

"So you have a wife," Amyra was saying. "You must be missing her."

"Very much so. And my young daughter as well," Thomas replied wholeheartedly. "Are you married, Amyra?"

Her face became suddenly unyielding. "I have not been so fortunate."

He raised a questioning eyebrow.

"Opportunities have arisen," she acknowledged with a shrug. "I have been told more than once that I am difficult to please."

He gazed at her thoughtfully. Amyra seemed very different from his own wife. She did not exude the gentle graciousness of Elena—he had yet to meet another woman who even came close to his wife in that respect—but she was both intelligent and accomplished, and by no means unattractive.

"I'm sure it is obvious to you that I am not of the Aen-ur," she said frankly, "even though they choose to embrace me as one of their own. I suppose the truth is that I'm not entirely sure where I do belong."

He nodded. Most of the Aen-ur seemed sallow of complexion, differing from both Arvenians and Rogandans. Their hair color, though, matched the black tone of the Rogandans. So far he had not seen individuals with hair that was distinctively different.

With her hazelnut brown hair, and skin that was darker than an Arvenian's and lighter than the native inhabitants of Rogand, Amyra presented a marked contrast to everyone around her. Her appearance didn't clearly mark her as a member of any of those races. Her heritage was almost certainly mixed.

Thomas couldn't help being curious about her background. He had caught significant glimpses earlier thanks to the stone, but other people had been in sight at the time and he hadn't felt any need to focus particular attention on her. His main interest had been to discover if she represented any kind of threat to them. He'd seen no obvious sign to suggest it.

"How did you come to be among the Aen-ur?" he asked.

She smiled. "They welcomed us when we came here many years ago and encouraged us to make a home among them. I was a small child, but I know from my mother that we were vulnerable and friendless at the time. Their warm acceptance changed our lives. My mother soon found a role as a healer—she is much respected."

"You seem to have a position of authority here yourself," he noted.

She shook her head firmly. "I have no actual authority here, except perhaps as a senior translator. Most of the Aen-ur learn no languages beyond their own. Rogandan is an exception, although they do not speak it unless absolutely necessary." She aimed a dark look in Will's direction. "They deal routinely with traders of every nationality, including many from Arvenon, Castel, Varas, and Lestanor. Some among the Aen-ur speak the languages of these kingdoms, but few have achieved mastery in them. I am fortunate to have inherited from my mother a facility with languages."

She smiled grimly. "Foreign traders tend to be shrewd in their dealings. A few are unscrupulous—more than willing to exploit anyone they perceive as weak. The Aen-ur have come to appreciate my involvement because I stand up to them."

Her account did not surprise Thomas in the least. She had spirit, and it was already obvious that she was very protective of the Aen-ur. He could easily imagine her negotiating and advocating vigorously on their behalf. Thanks to Will, they had already seen her in action. He threw a quick glance in his friend's direction.

He was confident she meant them no harm, in spite of her prickliness toward Will in particular. And he'd spent enough time with Amyra for her to become a person rather than just another nameless individual. He'd reached a point where he was not willing to use the stone to pry into her mind and memories, at least not without a compelling reason.

Amyra had been conversing at some length with Thomas. She had spoken to him exclusively in Arvenian, and he was grateful for her consideration. His companions had restricted themselves to Rogandan since the ship deposited them on the beach, and he was enjoying a break from the constant effort of translating every thought before he could speak.

When they first arrived for the meal Amyra had initiated a polite conversation with Haldek. Engaging with a Rogandan clearly cost some effort on her part, but she seemed intent on seeing beyond his origins. Nevertheless, it hadn't been long before she turned her attention to Thomas, and she had seemed content to remain locked in conversation with him ever since. Perhaps, having soon discovered that he was already spoken for, she decided she could afford to relax and enjoy his company. Perhaps she simply saw nothing offensive about him.

Will was a different matter entirely. After aiming a frosty nod in his direction when they entered the building, she had completely ignored him. Will had noticed her aloofness, and Thomas caught him shooting occasional glances in her direction throughout the meal.

Will had clearly managed to upset her, and Thomas wondered what exactly had elicited such a strong reaction from her.

Almost at that moment she jerked her head in Will's direction. "It seems your friend—His Lordship, Commander of the armies of the world, or whatever he is—imagines himself as someone very special."

Thomas's brows drew together in surprise. "Will?" He shook his head emphatically. "He's less concerned about his own importance than almost anyone I've ever known!"

"That certainly wasn't how he came across to me," she said disdainfully. "Trumpeting his titles, lecturing the Aen-ur about their own history." Her hazel eyes flashed angrily. "Insisting on speaking to them in Rogandan—after I'd explained they would find it offensive!"

So that was it. Seeing the fire in her eyes, Thomas felt thankful that he hadn't been the one to provoke her.

He gazed at her in fascination. Her face seemed to acquire an elfin quality when she was agitated. She was an intriguing person.

He shot a glance at Will, wondering if he was aware of her displeasure. He caught his friend studying Amyra curiously, although he looked away nonchalantly as soon as he noticed Thomas glancing in his direction.

Amyra shook her head dismissively, sending her chestnut brown hair dancing. "Why should I care?" she asked with a shrug. "He seems to think he can bend the Aen-ur to his will. Let him try."

Thomas decided to change the subject to a less personal topic. "Do the Aen-ur have much contact with the outside world?" he asked.

"As little as possible," she said, "although they are well aware of what goes on around them. All of them learn Rogandan from a young age—they regard it as a necessary concession to the harsh realities of their situation. You have also seen that Atae speaks Arvenian, although he is unusual in that regard."

"Do they trade with the rest of Rogand?"

She nodded. "Indirectly. They trade with visiting Arvenian or Lestanorian merchants, who then sell their products throughout Rogand and beyond."

Thomas knew that Will had grown up with his Arvenian uncle who was a merchant. Perhaps he had traded with these people. That might at least partly account for Will's knowledge of the Aen-ur and their history.

"What do they sell to the merchants?" Thomas asked curiously.

"There are mines in the mountains," Amyra told him, waving a hand vaguely toward the peaks. She seemed unwilling to be more specific.

Shortly after that Amyra excused herself and left the banquet hall, leaving Thomas wondering if he had asked one question too many.

They found their hut strongly guarded when they were escorted there after the meal. Will didn't seem concerned at the implied lack of trust.

"You've upset Amyra," Thomas told him.

"I'm not here to impress her," Will replied with a shrug.

Thomas raised an eyebrow. He had a feeling that Will might care about her opinion more than he was letting on. Whether that was true or not, Thomas was very certain about one thing—Will would never allow such considerations to distract him from his purpose.

"What are you planning?" Thomas asked him.

"I expect we will be invited to a conference tomorrow, with a smaller group of people," Will replied. "I am hoping the Aen-ur will agree to do something to at least slow Agon down for a while. I'd like to get you an opportunity to take a closer look at Agon," he added, giving Thomas a significant look. "Of course that isn't the reason I'll give them for asking them to do it."

Thomas's heart beat a little faster. Getting close enough to see the Rogandan king was certain to be dangerous. But it was the reason he had come here.

"I'm also wondering if there might be an opportunity to examine their oldest records," Will added, "assuming any have survived. They might have an intact copy of your scroll."

Such a prospect captured Thomas immediately. The copy of the scroll that had been read to him and Brother Vangellis at the monastery had been torn and incomplete and offered no detail about either the Stone of Authority or the Stone of Vitality. Knowing more about the Stone of Authority might prove crucial to thwarting Agon's plans. The writer had also promised a more complete explanation of the behavior of the stones later in the scroll, and Thomas had often wondered what he might have written.

THE FOLLOWING morning Will received the invitation he had been waiting for. Atae had promised him an opportunity to explain why they had trespassed on the lands of the Aen-ur. Will was hoping to convince their captors to become their allies, although he was aware that other less encouraging outcomes were also possible. While it was too early to say whether they had found their way to help or to trouble, all uncertainty was likely to be resolved before long.

Amyra came to meet them, greeting Haldek formally and offering Thomas a muted smile. She eyed Will dispassionately, looking him up and down briefly. She was not rude, provided that complete indifference didn't count as rudeness.

Following her to a smaller building, they found Atae and four other men of the Aen-ur waiting for them. A silver-haired woman also stood beside Atae, and Will immediately guessed that he was looking at an older version of Amyra. The woman directed a searching glance at each of them, but reserved her most careful scrutiny for Will.

Atae greeted them noncommittally. "You asked for a conference," he told Will, speaking in Arvenian, "and we are here, although I promise you nothing. We have treated you with courtesy, perhaps more than your bluntness has earned. Whether we come to regret our forbearance will be largely up to you."

He indicated the woman. "I have invited our friend Dahra to join us since we value her wisdom."

Dahra bowed briefly to each of them. "Unfortunately I was not able to join you yesterday," she said, speaking fluently in Arvenian. "I am a healer for this community, and I was called to assist a young woman in her first childbirth. We found ourselves confronted with a number of complications, but I am glad to say that both mother and baby are well."

Will bowed respectfully to her, observing her curiously. As they were seating themselves, his attention was distracted by a sharp intake of breath at his side. He glanced around in time to see Thomas fiddling with the chain around his neck, a thunderstruck expression on his face. His young friend quickly lowered his head to hide his discomposure, but Will saw that Dahra had also noticed his reaction, and she was studying Thomas with considerable curiosity.

The stone had clearly revealed something that startled Thomas. Interested as he was to know more, Will knew he could not afford to allow his focus to be diverted.

"We are listening," Atae said. His demeanor suggested that his patience might have limits.

Will had no desire to waste his time. "I will be frank with you," he said. "At the time we left King Steffan and Queen Essanda, the Arvenian capital Arnost was occupied by mercenaries controlled by an Arvenian traitor, a man who has been financed by Agon and owes allegiance to him. This man took control when King Steffan was severely wounded, and at the same time he also took command of the two Arvenian armies on active duty. We have already regained control of one of those armies, and the king was working to do the same with the other. Meanwhile, although Castel is ruled by the young son of the murdered King Istel, his most powerful advisor is a Castelan traitor who is also working on behalf of Agon.

"King Steffan and Queen Essanda are currently in Varacellan, working closely with their ally King Delmar of Varas. Their immediate goals are to prevent Agon from crossing the border into Arvenon, and to regain control of all Arvenian army forces. Regaining control of Arnost will come later.

"I am telling you this because I do not wish to overstate the strength of the forces arrayed against Agon."

Atae's expression left no doubt about his conclusions from Will's summary. "Given the strength of Agon's support within Arvenon and Castel, it sounds as if he has every chance of succeeding," he said grimly. "He isn't a man to forgive and forget. When he completes his conquests, he will not hesitate to turn the full force of his wrath on anyone who dares to move against him now."

Will was not deterred. "Agon may appear to have everything going his way. He is relaxed and confident, but his opponents are far from defeated. He knows that his assassins struck down King Steffan of Arvenon, and he may well still believe him to be dead. Whether or not Agon is already aware of it, the king has recovered from his wounds, and King Delmar of Varas is gathering forces to resist Agon. King Delmar will stand with King Steffan, and together they will oppose Agon with all their might.

"Meanwhile, Agon's nobles are not pleased at all about Agon's new invasion. They bore the brunt of the losses from the last invasion. Most of their peasants were called away from the fields to bolster Agon's army, and the greater proportion of them did not return. Agon emptied his treasury to fund the invasion, and he has since multiplied the troubles of his nobles by taxing them harshly in an attempt to replenish his coffers. None of the nobles have been bold enough to openly oppose Agon. Not yet. But they are restless."

Will could see that Atae was far from convinced. "And what kind of contribution do you imagine the Aen-ur making toward your cause?" Atae asked. "Before you answer the question, you should know that we see no reason why we should take you seriously, Will Prentis," Atae told him bluntly. "Or why we should believe anything you say."

In response, Will reached into the pouch at his belt and retrieved the tile entrusted to him by King Steffan. He had no idea whether it would have any meaning to Atae, but this was clearly the time to find out. He glanced at it briefly, once more entranced by its beauty and mystery. Then he handed it to Atae.

The leader's eyes narrowed as he took it in. Flipping it over, he squinted as he scanned the tiny writing on the other side. His eyes were wide as he handed it to his countrymen. Each of them examined it before passing it to Dahra. She in turn showed it to Amyra. The young woman examined it almost defiantly before returning it to Atae.

"Do you know what this is?" the leader asked Will sharply.

Will shook his head.

"It is a princely gift," Atae told him. "How does it come to be in your possession?"

"King Steffan entrusted it to me," Will told him. "It was given to one of his forebears by a king of the Aen-ur in return for a service he rendered to that king. I know little more than that. I was given to understand that the details have been lost in the intervening years."

"The ancient gifts of the Aen-ur always had great potential for abuse if they fell into the wrong hands," Atae told him. "For that reason such gifts were always issued with a key. Do you have the key?"

Will looked at him blankly. "I know of no key," he said. He paused for a moment. "King Steffan did tell me, though, that his father pressed him to memorize a phrase when he passed it down to him. King Steffan entrusted the phrase to me when he was bidding us farewell, and I committed it to memory." He closed his eyes and took a deep breath. "Sinowe isakhi wazihe alwa ishae-nixi," he intoned. Opening his eyes, he looked at Atae. "Does that mean anything to you?"

The expression on the faces of the Aen-ur astonished him. All of them appeared stunned. Not one of them said a word.

Atae finally spoke. "You have just provided the key," he replied. Seeing the confusion on Will's face, he added, "The key is not an object, it is a spoken phrase. It is independent of the writing on the stone, and it must be memorized. The writing on the stone is incomplete without the key."

Will was still confused. Perhaps aware of it, Atae added, "You would need to understand our language to fully comprehend the wordplay involved in such messages. But a simple example in your own language might give you the sense of it. Suppose I were to say, 'The food served at last night's banquet was sumptuous.' That might convey the impression of lavish feasting. If I were to add, 'The hungry went to bed hungry,' we might begin to understand that food was not served equally to everyone. The second statement has become a key to understanding the first."

Will nodded slowly.

Atae continued. "Suppose the original statement included both sentences. 'The food served at last night's banquet was sumptuous, but the hungry went to bed hungry.' We might understand a deeper meaning if the key were, 'Those who refused the invitation to the banquet feasted only on their folly.'"

Atae hadn't finished. "We might form a very different conclusion if the key were instead, 'Each person attending the banquet was served exactly what they deserved.'"

Will thought he was beginning to understand, at least in part.

"The tile your king received was originally part of an elaborate mosaic in the floor of the throne room at Ishitar Ataye. The mosaic suffered a similar fate to the fortress. Very few pieces survived, and every one that is still preserved is precious to us. I will not attempt to explain the meaning of the message of the writing as clarified by the key. Suffice it to say that a great debt is owed to your king by my people. As his representative, the debt is owed to you."

Atae handed the tile back to Will. "Keep this, and return it to your king. The debt will not be erased by anything we can do to help you at this time."

Will's mind was spinning as he returned the tile to his pouch. Dahra was watching him with an inscrutable smile playing on her lips. Amyra appeared thoroughly disconcerted.

"Our resources might be limited," Atae told him. "But we will do whatever is within our power to help you."

33

———

W ill stared at the Aen-ur. His prospects had changed in a moment, thanks to a small glazed tile. It was hard to comprehend, but now was not a time for guessing.

"I have two requests," he told Atae. "Are you aware of Agon's column?"

"We are closely monitoring his progress," Atae confirmed, "especially as he draws nearer to our lands."

"Am I right in thinking that he is still some days away?" Will ventured.

Atae had a rapid interaction with one of his countrymen. He nodded agreement. "They are traveling slowly. They are setting up what amounts to a small town every time they camp for the night. The head of the column is not likely to reach this area for another five or six days at the earliest."

Will nodded in satisfaction. "Arvenian forces are moving into position to prevent Agon from crossing the border. Any time we can buy them could prove significant. Suppose a natural disaster were to bring his progress to a temporary halt? A forest fire at a point where the trees fringe the road, for example, or a flash flood caused by the temporary redirection of a river. It could take place well away from your lands to ensure that the Aen-ur come under no suspicion."

Once more the Aen-ur ignored their visitors to converse in their own language. It had more the appearance of a debate this time, and from time to time the participants became very animated. Will glanced at Amyra. She had not joined the conversation, but she was following it closely, a frown slowly deepening on her face. She seemed uneasy with the direction the interaction was heading, and for some reason Will found that encouraging.

Glancing at Dahra, he discovered the older woman studying him intently. He stared calmly back at her, untroubled by her scrutiny. Everything about her radiated gentleness, although he sensed a sturdiness beneath it all.

Something about her made Will think of Brother Vangellis as he had come to know him in the latter days of his life. The monk had been battered by pain and grief, and for a time crippled by his own shame. In Will's experience people were often hardened by such experiences, but the buffeting seemed to have softened the monk. Brother Vangellis had by no means been weak though; a surprisingly tough resilience had underpinned his gentle compassion.

Dahra reminded him of the monk. Will liked the little he had seen of her, and he found himself hoping he would have the opportunity to get to know her better.

He turned his attention back to Atae. The conversation was still in progress, but much of the heat had gone out of it, and heads appeared to be nodding.

After a couple more minutes Atae turned to him. "Any action will involve risk. But there is a place to the north of here where it might be possible to do something along the lines of what you have requested. The location is in the direction of Rog, which means Agon's column will reach the site sooner. Many of my people live in close proximity to it—we can ill afford to act unless our intervention can be made to appear entirely natural."

Will nodded his understanding. "It has never been my desire to expose your people, Atae, and I thank you for even considering my request. I know my king and queen will greatly appreciate whatever help you can give."

"You said you had a second request," said Atae.

"Yes. The Aen-ur have been in the land since ancient times. I have been wondering if any of your older records have survived."

"What is the reason for your interest?" Atae asked.

"There is some suggestion that King Agon is making use of an ancient artifact to enhance his power. I wish to examine your records in case they might mention such an object."

Atae showed no sign of taking seriously any talk of ancient artifacts, but Dahra immediately directed a sharp glance at Will.

Atae once more conveyed the request to the others. After a brief conversation, he turned to Dahra. She glanced at Will before turning back to Atae with a definite nod. He addressed the others, and all of them either nodded as well or simply shrugged. He asked a question of Amyra, and she replied briefly. Will studied her face, but she was giving nothing away.

"Some of our records survived the fall of Ishitar Ataye," Atae told Will. "You may visit with your companions provided you are willing to accept the supervision of one of our number."

Will nodded immediately. "Of course," he replied.

Atae pointed to one of his countrymen, who nodded a greeting. "This is Kaemin. He speaks no Arvenian, but Amyra has agreed to accompany you as translator." He glanced at Dahra. "Dahra would also accompany you gladly if other commitments did not prevent her from doing so."

To Will's eye, Dahra looked very disappointed, but he heard a sigh from Thomas at his side. It sounded a great deal like relief. Will was surprised—he could not imagine that Dahra presented any kind of threat. He promised himself he would pursue it with Thomas once an opportunity arose.

"Our records are located within the ruins of Ishitar Ataye," Atae told them. "It should be possible for you to visit the library briefly and still reach the place where we plan a distraction to delay Agon. But you will need to set out immediately."

Atae was as good as his word. Horses were brought, and Will and his party were mounted within the hour. Accompanied by Kaemin, Amyra, and four armed soldiers, they headed north, led by one of the four men who had joined their party.

Will felt certain that the Aen-ur must have a way of traveling quickly through the forest. He never imagined for a minute that they would be willing to use the main road to Rog. His guess was confirmed after only a few minutes.

Picking their way through the trees they emerged onto what appeared to be an ancient road. Stray leaves blew across it, and the forest had encroached on it in places, but it had survived the rigors of time largely intact. Broad enough for two carriages to travel side by side, it ran as straight and true as the flight of an arrow on a still day. No end to the road was visible to Will. It disappeared into the far distance beyond his sight, rising and falling with the contours of the ground.

As soon as they were on the road they made excellent time. They passed other Aen-ur travelers heading in the opposite direction; during the time they were riding, they passed ten such groups before Will stopped counting. Most of the groups were quite large in number and invariably traveling with heavily laden wagons.

The surface of the road was still firm, and it allowed them to continue riding safely until well after night had fallen. After they had been riding under the stars for about an hour, their guide led them off the road a short distance until a large and sturdy cabin came into view in the moonlight. One of the soldiers disappeared inside and soon reappeared with a burning torch.

A large stack of firewood lay nearby, and the soldiers set to work building a fire in the cabin's fireplace and preparing a simple meal. They shared the food as soon as it was ready to eat.

While they were eating, Will directed a question at Amyra. "Are there other cabins like this?" he asked.

She looked down her nose at him for a few moments before deigning to answer. "Yes," she finally confirmed. "They were built at regular intervals along both sides of the road. People are assigned by the Aen-ur to maintain them for the use of travelers."

"Are the Rogandans aware of all this?" he asked, indicating the cabin and the road.

"They do not come here," she said simply. "They are fearful of venturing beyond the borders of Aen-irac, and we are far from the borders here. Even traders are granted access only to the outer fringes of Aen-ur territory."

Will absorbed this information with considerable interest. Her reply matched his own experience—his uncle had traded with the Aen-ur a number of times in his presence, but their business had never taken them far into Aen-irac.

The traffic on this road had exceeded his expectations. The Aen-ur were clearly numerous and organized. He was beginning to suspect that the full extent of their trade might far exceed the expectations of anyone who didn't know them intimately.

The cabin was large enough to easily accommodate their company, and people began spreading out bed rolls after finishing the simple meal. It was apparent that the soldiers had no plan to post sentries. This remote corner of Aen-irac was apparently regarded as safe by the Aen-ur.

Desiring a few moments alone with his thoughts, Will headed outside. The Aen-ur ignored him. Apparently they had decided he was no threat.

The cabin stood on the edge of a small clearing, and Will moved to the center of it, gazing up at the night sky. He thought of his previous visits to Aen-irac. His uncle's business as a trader had required him to travel widely, and Will had visited many stranger places as a result. His late uncle had certainly hoped Will would follow him in his vocation, and Will wondered briefly if he would have been disappointed with his adopted son's eventual choices. He shrugged off such thoughts. He had learned many useful skills from his uncle, but the prospect of a life as a trader never held appeal for him.

Absorbed in his thoughts, he barely registered that someone had joined him until the lithe figure of Amyra appeared beside him. She followed his gaze into the heavens, and the two of them stood side by side without speaking for a time.

"Your presence in Aen-irac disturbs me greatly, Will Prentis," she finally said. Her tone was pitched somewhere between a purr and a growl, and it made him think of a tigress, poised to pounce.

She stood close enough that they were almost touching. Her presence discomposed him for reasons he didn't understand. He shook his head involuntarily, irritated at his own reaction.

With no response forthcoming, she spoke again. "These people are vulnerable enough already without you putting them at risk. It is clear that their safety and security mean nothing to you. But it matters to me."

He shrugged. "I spoke truthfully to Atae. I have no desire to see the Aen-ur exposed to Agon's attention."

"Then why don't you just leave? It would be the best thing for their sake—for the sake of everyone."

A hint of pleading had appeared briefly through her fierceness. Was it possible that she was finding him a little unsettling?

A sudden desire came over him to say something witty. His life had exposed him to an unusual variety of experiences, and he had never lacked boldness when facing the unknown. Nevertheless, engaging in light-hearted banter with a woman was unfamiliar territory.

He accepted the challenge, his mouth twisting into an ironic grin. "I seem to have occupied more than my fair share of your attention, Amyra. I'd never thought of myself as attractive."

She glared at him scathingly. "Perhaps you've managed to convince yourself that a scarred face and a limp are attractive to a woman, but don't expect me to pander to your delusions."

He winced, surprised by how much her words stung. He'd been a fool—he should have kept his mouth shut.

After an uncomfortable silence, Amyra sighed. "I have no desire to fight with you," she told him. "I just wish you would take your ambitions somewhere else." The cutting edge had vanished from her tone, but she left her earlier remarks hanging.

Standing beside an attractive young woman who apparently regarded him with complete disdain, Will felt uncharacteristically awkward. He'd never possessed the ability to charm women, and for the first time it brought him a twinge of regret. The spitfire standing at his side was equal parts mysterious and exasperating, and he knew himself to be poorly equipped for the challenge of trying to make sense of her. And what would be the point anyway, when she so obviously despised him?

He reminded himself why he had come here. With his mission yet to be accomplished, he had more than enough to occupy his attention. He could not afford distractions.

"I did not come here to further my ambitions, whatever you might think," he said coolly. "If Agon is allowed to succeed, the way of life you seem to find so agreeable won't long survive. The Aen-ur will be swept away, along with everything they value."

He fixed her with a steely gaze. "I am at least trying to prevent that. What are you doing, apart from working against me?"

Without waiting for an answer, he turned and made his way back to the cabin. He made no attempt to disguise his limp.

34

———

A fork in the road took them deeper into the mountains. They had been riding for almost an hour when the trees parted. All of them simultaneously drew their horses to a halt.

Ahead of them lay a deep gorge. The noisy roar of a rushing river carried clearly on the morning air. On the far side of the gorge lay the shattered remnants of a once mighty fortress. Most of its walls had been torn down, and only the broken fragments of towers still climbed skyward to hint at its former glory.

There was something eerie about its whispered grandeur, but even in its ruin Ishitar Ataye was still magnificent.

A broad bridge had once spanned the gorge, but surviving pieces of its crumbling stonework were now visible only on the far side. Glancing downriver Will noticed a flimsy rope bridge suspended across the gulf.

Amyra's voice sounded over the tumult of the water. "We must leave our horses on this side," she called.

She had been avoiding him, and Will was thankful. He had felt more awkward than ever in her presence after their exchange outside the cabin.

Two of the soldiers remained with the horses. Haldek accompanied them to the bridge, but it was obvious he had no interest in joining them. Will knew he had no fear of heights after his years patrolling the battlements of Agon's castle. It seemed more likely that he was reluctant to view more closely the ancient destruction wrought by his countrymen. Either way, Will was content to leave his friend in peace. Haldek would no doubt rejoin the two soldiers if he found himself alone for any length of time.

Flimsy as the bridge appeared to be, Amyra climbed onto it without hesitation and began crossing, placing her feet carefully while holding on firmly with her hands. One of the soldiers was not far behind her, and Will quickly followed their example. When he was halfway across he looked back. Thomas and Kaemin were already on the bridge and the other soldier was poised to take his turn.

With multiple people crossing at one time, the bridge began to sway alarmingly, and Will was forced to focus all of his attention on finding the next place to plant his foot. When he finally reached the end he looked up to find that Amyra had been staring at him. She glanced away before he could meet her eye.

As each person reached the end of the bridge she leaned forward, holding out a hand to steady them as they stepped once more onto solid ground. She hadn't offered him the same courtesy, although he decided not to dwell on it.

Kaemin now took the lead. The older man wended his way through the ruins until he reached a small section of ground that had been cleared of the rubble strewn everywhere. Following him behind a fallen column, Will came upon the cleverly concealed entrance to a low building. Anyone not already aware of the entrance would have been fortunate to find it.

As he entered, Kaemin called out a greeting. An answer sounded from somewhere inside the building, soon followed by a face fringed with gray hair. The man emerged and greeted Kaemin warmly.

After a brief conversation, all of them were invited into the building, and they followed him down a flight of steps into an underground room of vast size covered with shelves. Scrolls and parchments could be seen everywhere.

Their guide turned to them with a friendly smile. "I am Inyaet," he told them, speaking in Arvenian, "and I am the chief librarian here. I normally have two other helpers, but they are currently away visiting family."

Will introduced himself and Thomas.

"I understand you are looking for old scrolls that speak of ancient artifacts," Inyaet continued. He led them to one end of the room and pointed to a single shelf covered with old scrolls. "I have spent many years sorting through our older documents and records," he said. "This shelf contains everything we have that could be categorized as myths, legends, and fantastical stories. Personally, I find such tales fascinating and often informative as well. From the limited range of documents, though, you might reasonably guess that content of that kind was not granted a high priority by past librarians."

"May I?" asked Will, pointing to the shelf.

"Perhaps I can hand you documents for your perusal," Inyaet replied. "Some of the older scrolls are extremely delicate and require special care."

"I will treat them with the greatest respect," Will assured him.

"Shall I begin with documents written in Rogandan or Arvenian?" asked Inyaet.

Will shrugged. "I'm not sure."

"Perhaps we will start with our Arvenian collection, since there are fewer of them."

The librarian carefully selected a dozen scrolls, glancing at each of them in turn before handing them gingerly to Will, one at a time.

Will opened the first. "Reliable lore concerning draggonnes and other winged serpenttes of fearsome mien," he read aloud. He glanced at Thomas, who rolled his eyes heavenward.

Most of the other documents contained similar nonsense. Inyaet had almost reached the end of the Arvenian documents when Will unrolled the latest scroll and read out, *"Three talismans of great potency are abroad in the world, uncelebrated, unrecognized, and hidden from any certain knowledge."* Even before he glanced up to see the troubled look in Thomas's eyes, Will knew they had found what they were seeking.

He turned to Inyaet. "We would like to examine this scroll more closely if you are willing."

The librarian came to Will's side and bent over the document, scanning it briefly. "Ah, yes. I remember it. The writer seems to imagine a circumstance where tiny objects—objects with magical properties, of course—can be used to influence the destiny of kingdoms. An intriguing fantasy. You are most welcome to examine it, for whatever it's worth."

He straightened again, smiling at Will. "I don't imagine that my services will be needed—you seem to be an unusually capable reader."

Hearing the admiration in the librarian's voice, Will couldn't resist a glance in Amyra's direction. Her face was unexpressive.

Inyaet pointed to a table surrounded by three stools, and Will carried the scroll carefully to it. Thomas and Amyra joined him there.

Will slowly unrolled the scroll until all the writing was visible.

"Is it all there?" Thomas asked breathlessly.

Will ran his eyes to the end of the scroll and nodded. "I think so. It ends like this: '*My account ends here. May the scholar who stumbles upon it derive greater benefit from this lore than I have myself. Randolf of Clerbon.*'"

Glancing at Thomas, Will saw that his face had gone pale.

The librarian apparently felt no need to sit with them as they read the scroll together. Instead he turned his attention to Kaemin, who spoke no Arvenian and was probably much less interested than the librarian in myths, legends, and fantastical stories. The two men were soon engaged in an energetic conversation in their own language.

Will turned his full attention to the scroll. Taking a deep breath, he began to read aloud.

· · ·

'*Three talismans of great potency are abroad in the world, uncelebrated, unrecognized, and hidden from any certain knowledge. Perhaps I alone know their true history, long forgotten with the passing of many scores of years. I once learned of an ancient parchment, lost and mayhap forgotten by all save only an aged hermit. The old man had glimpsed it in his youth, and he described it to me as well as his failing memory served him.*

Long did I search for it, and bitter and fruitless my labor seemed. Dark and tiresome would be the full tale thereof. At last, hope having deserted me, I stumbled upon it, the greatest treasure in my possession. Even now I have it before me, a faded manuscript, crumbling with age and arcane in script. Many candles burned to naught ere I found a way to decipher it.

Hear, then, the testimony of a scribe whose witness has been silent for many an age:

Long years have passed away since Goodman Tomas walked upon the earth. A poor farmer and simple he was, yet greatly beloved by all who knew him. He lived in a rude hut in but a small village.

One day his fortunes turned. Though his back had been bowed down with much labor, yet was he seen to stand again straight and tall. Tales grew up around his wisdom, and people journeyed from afar to seek his counsel. His insights failed him not, and his sayings gave birth to a bountiful supply of proverbs.

It came to pass that his village became a town, and the town a city, and he the mayor. His family prospered likewise.

Late in life offered he a gift unto the king of his country. Rude in appearance was the gift but great in effect, and the king, who was a good ruler, handled it wisely. His fortunes likewise changed, and he became powerful even as his kingdom prospered.

The story sprang up and spread abroad that Tomas had received a star from heaven that fell from the sky and landed in the form of a rock beside his hut. Great and manifold were the gifts bestowed by this rock upon its owner—gifts of insight, good health and influence among men. And behold, having received it freely from Tomas, the king rejoiced also in the selfsame gifts. Nor were the benefits denied to Tomas when he yielded up the rock. He continued as before until he had attained a great age.

So Tomas died, full of years, and in time the king also slept with his fathers. The son of the king prospered, too, and increased yet more in power. A subtle, but alas, not a wise king was he, and many enemies gathered themselves against him. The neighboring kingdoms rose up, bound together in hatred for the king and desire for the rock. Nevertheless, try as they might, they could not overcome him, such was his might in arms and his shrewdness in council. Finally, by treachery alone was he brought low, slain by the hand of one he trusted.

Thus lost the son of the wise king his kingdom and his life, all through foolishness and pride. The ruler who wrested control of his kingdom laid hands upon the rock, lusting to command every virtue of which he had heard so much. It benefited him nothing. Years of bitter fortune and failing prosperity passed, until in anger he caused the rock to be smashed into a thousand fragments and cast outside his palace.

And lo, it came to pass that certain peasants, chancing upon the pieces, found them pleasing to the eye. Taking them up, they bore them unto their dwellings. Anon it was seen that some of the virtue of the rock had passed into three of the pieces. One brought health and vitality, a second, great authority, and a third, insight into the hearts and minds of men.

Long and illuminating would be the history that chronicled the fortunes attending those who found the stones. Time revealed that the stones, as likewise the rock vouchsafed to Tomas, lost their virtue entirely when taken by force, at times remaining dormant for a generation. Only when a stone was gifted freely, or found by chance, was the virtue bestowed. The stones together were like the original rock in every respect but one—once a gift had been made of a stone, its virtue was thereafter withheld from the giver.

Some stones passed as heirlooms from father to son or mother to daughter. In time the gift was always squandered through pride or folly, or lost through violence or misadventure.

None can say where the stones are today. Long years have passed since last I heard aught of them. Many say they are lost forever, and some rejoice in their vanishment. Some say they are a gift from God to the wise. Others say they are a tool of the Devil to curse and ensnare all who receive them.

There was a time when one of the stones lay in my hand for a moment. Young and foolish I was, and greatly desirous of possessing it, though every opportunity was denied me. Now I am old, and wiser, and content with my lot in life. Who could envy those who bear the burden of such a gift?

THE WITNESS ENDED THUS. My account concerning the ancient manuscript is accurate in every particular and my translation faithful and true. I, Randolf of Clerbon, swear it on my life.'

'In the unrelenting passage of years since the scribe lived and breathed, many things have changed, and some remain the same. The role of the rock in shaping kingdoms, revealed in the manuscript, has never ceased. The true history of Arvenon and the surrounding kingdoms is incomplete without reference to the stones of power.

Such fateful talismans—how they haunt my dreams! Ever have I sought them, but alas, thus far to no avail. Much lore have I gathered concerning the three—the Stone of Vitality, that grants well-being and life beyond the span of other men, the Stone of Authority, that bestows power and influence for good or for ill, and the Stone of Knowing, that lays bare the hearts and motivations of others. I record here but a small part of this lore, in order that my labor shall not prove entirely vain, that my research shall not crumble to dust with my mortal body.

What, then, can be said of these stones? They respect neither rank nor status. They surrender their power impartially to saint and sinner alike. Certain boundaries do, however, encompass those who bear them. The potency of a stone is diminished by afflictions of the body or the spirit, especially when a stone is new to the bearer. Familiarity increases their virtue, though bearers assume fearful risks with overuse.

Such is the witness of those who lay greatest claim to discernment about the stones.

Nevertheless, overuse has never been chief among the perils confronting those who bear a stone. The principal danger has ever been the lust of others who desired the stones for themselves.

A stone fails of its purpose if a bearer has been killed to acquire it, no matter who carried out the murder. The same failure ensues if a stone is taken without consent.

Such limitations have never deterred the unscrupulous, though. The most cunning among them have ever recognized the futility of force, and sought instead to obtain the stones using fear and intimidation. That history must needs be told.

First, though, it is necessary to faithfully chronicle the properties of the stones. I will describe each in turn, for though their lineage is common, their likeness and behavior vary considerably.

The Stone of Knowing is said to be little bigger than a man's fingernail, smooth to the touch, and colored brightly with azure and magenta tones. The stone grants admittance—full and unfettered—to thought, intent, and motivation of every person upon whom the eye of the bearer falls. Certain parchment fragments, perplexing in nature, hint that even animals and birds lie within its reach, at least in small measure.

No memory from the past is safe—every secret buried deep must be surrendered to its power. The stone may offer glimpses of what is to come, but with no certain assuredness, since many a fork in the road awaits the traveler who journeys to the future.

An extraordinary weight bears down upon the hand that cradles this stone. It is said that, of the three, the Stone of Knowing holds the greatest potentiality for good or evil, depending only on the character of the one who bears it.'

WILL PAUSED, shooting a glance at Thomas.

"The other scroll ended there," Thomas told him, his voice taut with emotion. "It had been torn."

Will didn't respond. Bending down to the scroll once more, he continued to read aloud.

'THE STONE OF AUTHORITY, likewise tiny in size, is reported to be colored gray with flecks of red, and in shape round like the sun and flat like a thick strip of leather. The stone bends all created things to the will of the bearer. Of things living, humans are most to be feared, and they have ever been the chief targets of its power.

The human will can gradually be bent by the stone, shaped to the will of the bearer. All are susceptible, though none can be compelled to act against their deepest beliefs or their own character.

No fool is made wiser, nor do the wise become fools. Leaders lead, workers toil, and soldiers fight as ever before. The will alone is affected. The will is neither expunged nor obliterated, rather it is tutored to new purposes. A crowd is impervious to influence; wills must be tutored one at a time. Most claim that two weeks is sufficient.

The Stone of Authority is a perilous stone to possess. The tight link between the bearer and the person influenced by the stone is broken if the bearer dies or loses the stone. Where this is understood, the bearer of the stone quickly amasses enemies among those determined to release the ensnared.

The Stone of Vitality is unremarkable in appearance, dark gray in color and resembling a crescent moon in form. Unlike the other stones it has no direct or indirect impact on anyone but the bearer. It conveys long life, good health, and extraordinary vigor, although it cannot offer protection from death or disfigurement by violence. Such strange tales surround this stone. Rumors of improbable healings and even resuscitations abound, to the point where it is impossible to separate fact from hearsay.

Having described the stones, a final task remains. I undertook to record a history of the dangers faced by those who possess a stone, and I do so now.

At first, those who possessed the stones made no attempt to keep them secret. They perceived no cause for nervousness, since reports had spread abroad that to take a stone by force was wasted effort. A stone becomes available to another only when received as a gift from the bearer, or when found after the bearer has lost it or died. As already noted, the bearer's death must not have resulted from an attempt to acquire the stone.

Thanks to these protections, anyone fortunate enough to possess a stone openly enjoyed its benefits without consideration of consequences, just as the wealthy have always flaunted their riches in full sight of the poor. This state of affairs could not long persist. The stones awaken a hunger that is fiercer and far more dangerous than any lust for riches.

Taking a stone by force was impracticable, but incidents arose to test the boundaries of the forbidding. I learned of a father who gifted a stone to his son. After witnessing the use to which the gift was put, he repented of his decision and wrested the stone away, wholly against the will of his son. As expected, the stone thereafter failed to work reliably on his behalf. Nevertheless, at occasional moments of particular need it did indeed function as before, even if in lesser measure. Outcomes were alike for other individuals in similar circumstances. Such reports encouraged the unscrupulous to probe every limit with ruthless fervor.

Men and women without conscience, perceiving they had nought to lose, multiplied threats and intimidation in their lust to gain possession of a stone. In time it was seen that almost any abasement could be visited upon stone bearers to induce them to yield up their prize, without compromising the power of the stones. The solitary constraint was one of volition—the bearer must be allowed to retain the stone until they wearied of duress and handed it over willingly. If the bearer was stripped either of the stone or of their life at any moment before agreeing to relinquish it, then the transfer proved of no more value than an extraction by force.

Not surprisingly, any bearer possessing the tiniest ounce of wisdom soon went to considerable lengths to conceal their possession of a stone. The effect of the stones, though, is surpassingly difficult to disguise. How can such power be reliably hidden? None with insight could mistake the obvious signs, provided only that they were acquainted with the history of the stones and their behavior.

In time it became impossible, even for those with wealth and power, to long possess a stone with any expectation of security. Such conditions must persist until the stones are altogether lost to memory, forgotten by the world.

Surely that situation has arisen even now. Where are the stones today, and who among the living remembers them still? Though I yet seek them with unwavering fervor, hope has long abandoned me.

My account ends here. May the scholar who stumbles upon it derive greater benefit from this lore than I have myself.

Randolf of Clerbon.'

WHEN HE HAD FINISHED, Will put down the scroll and took a deep breath. It was obvious to him that he had barely begun to understand the complexities resulting from possession of the stones.

Thomas sat silent, lost in his thoughts.

Will's musing was interrupted by Amyra. "Such nonsense!" she scoffed. "I hope we came here for a better reason than this." When neither of her companions responded, she stared at them strangely. "Surely you don't take this seriously!"

Will and Thomas exchanged glances. The expression on Thomas's face seemed unusually guarded, and Will guessed that he was anxious to avoid his secret being exposed.

A frown slowly appeared on Amyra's face. "Even my mother wanted to hear anything we discovered about small stones," she said, apparently speaking to herself. "She can't have meant fables—she would never be taken in by such idiocy!"

Thomas directed a sharp look at her, but she didn't notice. Pushing herself purposefully to her feet, she shook her head in disgust. She marched out of the building, her chestnut brown locks dancing furiously about her face.

Carefully rolling up the scroll, Will returned it to the librarian, thanking him politely for his help.

Realizing that his guest was preparing to leave, the librarian ceased his conversation with Kaemin abruptly. "Surely you cannot have finished!" he exclaimed to Will in dismay. "We have so much of interest here to a scholar like yourself. Some of our historical records date back hundreds of years! They are more valuable by far than the fables you have been studying."

"I'm afraid I am not the scholar you imagine," Will assured the librarian with a smile. "Arvenon does have true scholars and librarians, and I don't doubt they would gladly explore your treasures for as long you would allow them to. I'm sure they would be pleased to return the favor, too, if you were willing to travel to Arvenon."

After waving Thomas out of the building, Will quickly followed him. The librarian was still pressing them to stay as they emerged into the sunlight.

It was painfully obvious that Inyaet was starved of human companionship. Will wasn't surprised. He would have gone mad this far from human habitation, perched on the edge of a ravine, and spending every day among the rubble of a ruined citadel.

Inyaet looked on glumly as they climbed once more onto the rickety bridge. They inched their way out across the void, trying not to look down at the raging torrent below.

As soon as he reached the other side Will looked back for a final glimpse of Inyaet. The librarian seemed small and pitiful standing alone at the base of the derelict fortress, surrounded by the debris of a forgotten age.

Raising his arm, he sent a farewell wave. When Inyaet's arm rose in response, Will turned away.

Haldek appeared before they reached the horses. "I'm sorry for not joining you, Will."

Will didn't mind at all. The fewer people who knew about the scroll the better. "Don't concern yourself, Haldek," he said, smiling and slapping his friend lightly on the back. "The bridge was already rickety enough without you on it as well."

Will's thoughts were racing as he swung into the saddle. The scroll had given him plenty to think about.

He pulled his horse alongside Thomas. "Based on what you and Elena learned from Tarestel before King Delmar executed him, it seems likely that Agon has the Stone of Authority," he said.

"I agree," Thomas replied. "I've always believed that Drettroth saw a copy of the scroll. If Agon has seen it too, he will have been using the information to full effect."

Will nodded. "It did offer one potential encouragement. If Agon loses the stone, whatever he's done to Pisander and Eisgold will immediately be undone."

35

The soldiers led Will and the others back to the main road. When they reached the junction, Kaemin bade them farewell. After they had thanked him he rode away with one of the soldiers, returning to the place where they had met.

The remaining three soldiers then led them in the opposite direction.

Amyra preempted Will's question by announcing, "We are heading to the location where a diversion is being prepared."

Her tone made it clear that she wasn't at all pleased about the Aen-ur placing themselves at risk in response to his request.

Will held his peace. It was hard to suppress a wave of irritation at her attitude though. None of this was intended to benefit him personally. Why did she continually feel the need to resist him?

They rode until daylight faded slowly around them and the trees were reduced to dark masses. Then the soldiers spotted a marker that pointed to another of the wayfarers' cabins, and they turned aside from the road to find it.

Thomas had been noticeably restless since they left Ishitar Ataye. After the soldiers had shared around some food, Will invited Thomas to join him outside.

"Did the missing section of the scroll answer any questions for you?" Will asked him.

"It completely explained what I experienced after taking the stone from Simon," Thomas replied.

Will decided to be direct. "Something's bothering you, Thomas."

Thomas stared into the dark. "Hearing the scroll in full wasn't easy. It's clear that things didn't end well for anyone who had one of the stones. There was nothing vaguely hopeful about it."

It wasn't hard for Will to guess what his friend might be feeling. Thomas had a family now. He wasn't responsible only to himself.

"And the stone has brought you to Rogand. You're in danger again because of it," said Will.

Thomas said nothing.

"I'm the one who's responsible for putting you at risk," Will acknowledged.

"No," said Thomas, shaking his head, "I'm responsible. I'm the one who's always insisted on keeping it." Thomas met his eyes. "You're not asking me to do anything you're not doing yourself. You've faced danger more than anyone."

It was Will's turn to shrug. "There have always been compelling reasons."

Both of them fell silent.

Will wanted to promise that he'd never call on Thomas again. Just as soon as this crisis was over. But he couldn't do it. He knew better than anyone that another crisis would always be lurking around the corner.

"Let's get some sleep," he said. "We'll be glad of it in the morning."

Thomas nodded, and they headed back into the cabin.

No road had ever been built to connect the ancient road of the Aen-ur with the current main road from Rog. Accordingly the pace of Will's party slowed painfully once they left the ancient road and headed into the forest. From time to time they came upon animal trails heading in the right direction, but for the most part they were forced to pick their way through the trees. Many dreary hours lay behind them before they eventually broke free of the forest.

After a brief consultation with the soldiers, Amyra came to them. "The main road is not far to the east. We will head north for a while until we reach the bridge."

It was the first time Will had heard any mention of a bridge, and he wondered if the Aen-ur were planning to use it as their way of slowing Agon's progress. With no further information forthcoming, Will decided to hold his questions until they arrived.

The riders traveled along the tree line, staying out of sight of the main road. The day was almost spent by the time they finally came to a halt. One of their number rode forward until he disappeared from sight. He eventually returned with another man.

Amyra translated as the new arrival introduced himself to Will. "I am Rhillyon. I have been tasked with slowing Agon for you."

Will dipped his head. "I am Will Prentis. How far away is Agon's column?"

"They are not likely to arrive tomorrow. It will be the following day."

Rhillyon indicated that they should follow him, and the whole group set off behind him, heading north.

The riders didn't stop until they came in sight of a large stone bridge spanning a river.

The source of the river lay in the mountains away to the south. After flowing east through the forest, it bent north, skirting the foothills of the mountains. Agon was traveling in the opposite direction—south from Rog along the main road, heading toward the place where the river bent toward its origin.

For many leagues the road and the river ran side by side—the mountains on one side, the river on the other, and the road in between. As the road continued south, the ground between the mountains and the river became rocky and impassable. At that point the road followed the bridge across the river.

South of the bridge, the road continued beside the river, although the river now lay between the mountains and the road. The road and the river eventually diverged, with the road continuing south beyond the source of the river.

Rhillyon led them to a ridge among a stand of trees where they could clearly see below them the road and the bridge. The position allowed them to observe traffic on the bridge without being visible to prying eyes.

"Where is Agon positioned within the column?" asked Will.

"A large group of soldiers is leading the column," Rhillyon replied through Amyra. "Agon follows close behind. We are planning to collapse the bridge before any of them arrive. Agon will be trapped on this side of the river, so we will need to be careful."

"Who is traveling behind Agon?" Will asked.

"Mostly servants. Another large group of soldiers is bringing up the rear."

Will thought for a moment. "Could we disable the bridge after the first group of soldiers has already passed? It would make our task easier if Agon could be temporarily separated from a large proportion of his guards."

Amyra didn't immediately translate the message. She glared at Will. "You are asking these people to put themselves at great risk!"

Will gazed back into her flashing eyes, trying not to notice how attractive she was when animated. He recaptured his focus with difficulty. "I'm not expecting them to take all the risks. I'll do whatever I can myself."

Both Thomas and Haldek looked alarmed at his statement, but Will was not moved by their concern. He had never been inclined to ask others to face danger on his behalf.

Amyra's eyes narrowed, but she translated his original message. She spoke for long enough that Will was left in no doubt that she was adding plenty of her own thoughts as well.

"It might be possible," Rhillyon replied. He seemed more fascinated by the suggestion than alarmed, apparently seeing it as a challenging problem to be solved.

Will liked Rhillyon already.

The bridge was built with stone and featured a single arch. "It looks very old," Will said after studying it closely.

"It is," Rhillyon replied. "Almost three hundred years old. My people designed it."

Will pursed his lips and gave out a low whistle. "It looks different from bridges I'm accustomed to," he said.

Rhillyon nodded. "It uses a segmental arch design. The arch is curved, but it doesn't form a complete semicircle."

Will nodded. "It stands much higher above the river than bridges in Arvenon."

"The design allows the span to remain clear of the water even when the river is heavily in flood," Rhillyon told him.

Will nodded in appreciation. "How badly will it damage the interests of the Aen-ur if the bridge becomes unusable?" he asked.

"It will have no real effect on us," Rhillyon replied. "We stay within our own territory. It isn't safe for us to travel in the open, so we avoid the road. That also means we don't use the bridge."

Will raised his eyebrows. "So your people built it, but the Rogandans get the benefit."

Rhillyon acknowledged his remark with a shrug of resignation.

"How can you collapse it?" asked Will. The bridge looked very solid—it must be since it was still in good condition after three hundred years. He wondered how anyone could possibly manage to collapse it.

"We will need to remove a few of the key wedge-shaped stones that support the arch," Rhillyon replied.

Will was impressed. "You seem to know a lot about bridges."

"Our skills have not been entirely lost."

"Is the bridge going to collapse immediately once you remove the stones?" Will asked.

"Not if we are careful. We will attach metal hooks to the bottom of some of the stones. Then we will loosen the stones and tie ropes to the hooks. We will need to do it at night when there is no traffic on the bridge, so no one observes us."

Will nodded.

"Pulling on the ropes will remove the stones. They will fall into the river and sink to the bottom with the ropes. The bridge should quickly begin to collapse. The challenge will be to conceal both the ropes and the people pulling on them. If we can do that, it might appear that the stones fell out as a result of age and wear, and that the bridge collapsed naturally."

He peered down at the river. It was broad, and it was surging rapidly under the bridge. It would be dangerous to slip into the water after the bridge collapsed, but he could see no obvious place to hide nearby.

"It's going to be risky," Will acknowledged. "I will help with the ropes."

Clearly it would be much safer to remove the stones before Agon's column arrived. But the confusion would be greatest if the bridge came down just before the king crossed it. Agon would then be separated from the leading group of his soldiers by a swiftly flowing river. Thomas would probably never find a better opportunity to take a close look at Agon with less risk.

Figuring out a way to avoid detection was a challenge, but they still had time to do it.

The sun set not long after they arrived, and a cold wind sprang up. Clouds covered the moon entirely. It was not a night to be abroad, and traffic on the road gradually ceased as travelers found somewhere to camp for the night.

After posting men to keep watch for unexpected arrivals, Rhillyon directed his engineers to start work on the bridge. Ropes were secured to the sides of the bridge, and men were suspended on them. Soon the sound of hammers and chisels rang in the night.

On two occasions a sentry hurried in to warn them that someone was approaching, and all went quiet for a time. Work quickly resumed the moment the travelers had gone.

Will perched himself on the bridge to allow him to observe the work closely as it progressed. It wasn't easy to see what was happening in the dark, but he saw enough of the energy and effectiveness of Rhillyon and his men to be enormously impressed.

As dawn approached they moved off the bridge and hid themselves among the nearby trees.

"The work is almost completed," Rhillyon told Will. "We'll rest during the day and finish it after the sun sets again." He glanced back at the bridge. "We've completely removed some of the wedge stones already. Not enough to make the bridge unstable, but it will make our task easier next time."

"I'll join you under the bridge tonight," Will told him. "I want to be clear about what I need to do to remove the wedges."

Rhillyon nodded as Amyra finished her translation. Then he yawned widely.

Will gave him a friendly slap on the back, and both of them moved away to rest. Almost the moment Will lay down he fell asleep.

It was late afternoon when he woke once more. Rhillyon and his team were stirring too, and all of them gathered to look down at the bridge. No sign could be seen of their work the previous night, and people were crossing the bridge as usual in both directions.

"Are you sure the bridge will be weak enough to collapse?" Will asked Rhillyon.

The man grinned back at him once the question was translated, contenting himself with a single emphatic nod.

Will moved away and found himself some food and water. Then he sat down to enjoy it. Looking up after a few minutes, he found Amyra standing nearby staring at him. She didn't look happy.

"What have I done now?" he asked.

His question seemed to discomfort her momentarily, but she quickly recovered. "Are you determined to go through with this?" she demanded.

"I've explained why it's necessary," he said reasonably.

She didn't respond.

"You seem to have convinced yourself I'm doing this for my own sake. That isn't what's happening here."

She still offered no response.

He sighed. "Do you think I enjoy putting people in danger? Do you think I enjoy putting myself in danger?"

"You seem to live for it," she told him decidedly.

He stared at her for a moment, then he burst out laughing.

She frowned back at him, her face flushed. "Why is that so funny?"

"I'm just struck by the absurdity of our situation. Here I am, in the heart of Rogand, about to attempt something that might cost me my life. These might be my last few hours. I'm spending them with you, and neither of us can think of anything better to do than argue."

She didn't seem at all amused. She took a breath and opened her mouth, no doubt intending to tell him what she really thought. Then she seemed to think better of it. Turning on her heel, she swept away from him.

He watched her go with undisguised admiration, unable to deny any longer that he found her both extremely attractive and utterly fascinating.

He shook his head. There was no point in entertaining daydreams that involved Amyra. Even if he survived this latest venture, he would be wasting his time directing attention to her. She had made it perfectly clear what she thought of him.

It took an effort, but he dragged his mind back to the problem at hand.

***

Amyra stood among the trees, peering down at the bridge. She could make out very little in the dark.

Will Prentis and Rhillyon stood somewhere beneath it, no doubt fingering the ropes that lay in their hands. More wedges had been removed throughout the night. Rhillyon's engineers were satisfied that the span, while still safe to cross, was almost at the point of collapse. The removal of a few more wedges should destabilize it completely.

Rhillyon had decided that two men should be able to complete the task at the right moment. He insisted on being one of them, and

Will Prentis had insisted on being the other. They would need to remain in place until the king had almost reached the bridge.

She knew that the road was visible from their position below the bridge. They had been told that the king was traveling either in a carriage or beside it. As soon as any of the royal carriages came into sight, the two men would tug on the ropes and remove the loosened blocks.

As soon as the bridge had collapsed, they were planning to slip into the river and swim away in the confusion. Some of Rhillyon's people would be waiting to retrieve them downstream.

Amyra had protested that any number of things could go wrong with this scheme, but she had no better plan to offer. Will had told her that if something unexpected happened, they would respond to the situation as it developed.

He was clearly accustomed to being in command, and it didn't seem to greatly trouble him that his actions put others in peril. That irked her.

The Aen-ur had been dragged into an extremely risky plan that had enormous potential to rebound on them. All because Will had called in an old debt. He believed the price was worth paying, and she could only hope it was truly as necessary as he claimed.

She had to at least admit that he didn't shy away from danger himself.

Of late she had taken to resisting him at every turn. She invariably reacted to him with annoyance and often sarcasm. He would never have guessed it, but she was expressing irritation with herself as much as with him.

Her own reactions baffled her. She had never met someone like Will Prentis. He was annoyingly sure of himself—far more so than could possibly be reasonable under the circumstances. He'd been like that from the moment she first clapped eyes on him. She'd always thought of self-assurance as a good thing, but in his case she found it irritating. And yet as much as she wanted to simply dismiss him as over-confident, she had a nagging feeling that he might still prove to be right.

His restless energy astonished her. He was so driven—he seemed unable to rest. He always seemed to be pursuing something pressing, and she felt constantly off balance as a result.

His drivenness wasn't the only reason she found it unsettling to be around him though. It was obvious that he admired her, and she was aware that he'd noticed and appreciated her abilities and self-confidence. There was nothing new about that—plenty of other men had admired her in the past. But there'd always been a catch. Sooner or later every one of them had begun to feel threatened by her. It wasn't her they wanted—it was a dumbed-down version of her.

Not Will Prentis. He didn't seem at all intimidated by her. He didn't seem the kind of man who needed to reduce her so he could feel good about himself.

She had no idea how it had happened, but somehow he'd managed to get under her skin. He was constantly on her mind, and of late she'd frequently caught herself staring at him. Alarmed at her growing obsession, she'd decided to stop thinking about him entirely. That hadn't been working at all. The previous night she had even dreamed about him. And such dreams—her cheeks warmed at the memory.

There was nothing especially attractive about him. Well, not his face, anyway. Even with a limp, his physique was not lost on her. He seemed oblivious to the rippling muscles beneath his tunic. But she had noticed.

She had even been reduced to quizzing Thomas and Haldek about him. It shocked her that she could stoop so low.

After they left Ishitar Ataye she had cornered Thomas. "So is it true that Will Prentis commands an army?" she asked skeptically.

Thomas had looked affronted. "He doesn't just command *an* army," he corrected her. "He commands the entire Arvenian army. And he commanded the combined armies of Arvenon and Castel during the Rogandan invasion. Everyone who knows anything about military strategy gives him most of the credit for defeating the Rogandans. Their army was much larger than ours!"

Once she'd got him started, Thomas warmed to his subject. "You should see the way his men respond to him!" He shook his head in wonder. "Just a few weeks ago I was with him after a battle. His men almost worship him. I've never seen another leader vaguely like him."

She turned up her nose. "No wonder he's so full of himself. They undoubtedly think he's so wonderful because everything has always gone well for him. And he's a noble, too—noblemen grow up expecting to be in charge."

Thomas had frowned at her. "No! You're completely wrong about him, Amyra! He's forever facing situations that everyone else sees as hopeless. His luck is certainly legendary, but he's never relied on luck. His decision making is uncanny. He seems to find a way of turning situations around, no matter how bad they are. And he might be a noble now, but he was born a commoner. King Steffan only made him a nobleman out of gratitude after he defeated the Rogandans."

Amyra was more than a little taken aback by this account of Will Prentis.

Thomas was a countryman of Will Prentis though. A Rogandan might be expected to form a more realistic assessment. Choosing a moment when Haldek was riding apart from the others, she positioned her horse alongside him.

"How did you come to know this Will Prentis?" she asked him, speaking quietly in Rogandan so as not to offend any of the Aen-ur.

Haldek gazed at her narrowed eyes, and for an uncomfortable moment she wondered if he guessed more about her motives for asking than she wanted to admit.

"He rescued me," he replied. "I was with a group of Rogandan soldiers fleeing Arvenon after we lost the battle at Torbury Scarp. Will and his men came upon us. He let the others go, but he kept me with him. Somehow he saw that I had nothing to go back to, and he asked Thomas and his wife, Elena, to take me in. The years of living with them and Elena's father have been the best years of my life."

Haldek had glanced ahead at Will, riding near the front of the group. "He is undoubtedly the greatest general of our times. But he is also one of the most compassionate people I have ever known."

Amyra frowned. "If he's so compassionate, why has he led you here?"

Haldek had shrugged. "He has never put his own interests before his responsibilities. Perhaps that's one reason why others are so willing to follow him into danger. His men will do anything for him. He's unlike anyone I have ever met."

Shaken by these assessments, she could think of nothing to say in response. Nodding to him, she had moved her horse away.

If these men were to be believed, almost every one of her initial impressions of Will Prentis had been entirely mistaken. He constantly managed to surprise her.

She gritted her teeth. She had no desire to become infatuated with him, yet thinking about him had almost become a compulsion. It was maddening.

After her conversations with Thomas and Haldek she reminded herself that she had decided not to think about him anymore. This time she was determined to follow through with it.

Now, a couple of days later, she found herself standing above the bridge waiting for the dawn and thinking about him again. She frowned in frustration at her own weakness.

A voice spoke softly beside her, speaking in the tongue of the Aen-ur. "The dawn—it comes."

She raised her eyes to the heavens. The speaker was right. The sky was indeed beginning to lighten slowly.

As she watched, the light grew stronger. The bridge was now clearly visible. She could see no sign of the two men beneath it.

King Agon's tent city had not been visible from their current position, but the previous evening scouts had informed them that it had been pitched not far away. It must have taken a couple of hours for the tents to be taken down and stored, because the morning was well advanced before Agon's horsemen appeared on the road to the bridge.

Amyra held her breath as they rode closer. Soldiers on foot followed them, hundreds strong, and she watched anxiously as the seemingly endless stream poured across the bridge. Their tramping feet did not appear to affect the span in any way, and for the first time she wondered if Rhillyon and his men had done enough to destabilize it. What if Agon's whole column simply crossed the river and disappeared up the road? She noticed that she had begun to sweat.

The irony of her own reaction was not lost on her. She had been so adamantly opposed to Will Prentis's plan. Now she was worried that it wouldn't succeed. She shook her head, unable to comprehend herself.

The seemingly endless stream of soldiers finally came to an end, and several carriages at last appeared behind them. Agon himself was approaching. Her heart began to race.

As the carriages drew closer she tried to picture Will and Rhillyon pulling at the ropes. She strained her ears for the sound of wedge blocks falling into the river, but she was too far away to hear, and the marching of the soldiers would have blotted out the sound anyway.

Finally she noticed what appeared to be a puff of dust near the top of the bridge. The soldiers marched on, oblivious to it. More dust appeared. A low rumbling sound reached her ears. The top of the bridge appeared to tremble. Then the entire span collapsed, disappearing into the river with a mighty splash. Cries carried to her as soldiers were plunged into the raging river. She saw heads bobbing as men were swept away by the current.

She tried to peer down through the confusion. Were Rhillyon and Will Prentis swimming to safety as they had planned? Frustration rose within her at the impossibility of finding out anything that was happening.

A part of her was tempted to get up and run down there—to help them, or even just to observe the situation for herself. Recognizing her impulse for the folly it was, she restrained herself.

Not all of the soldiers had crossed the bridge before it fell, and men were now lining both banks of the river. A small number of soldiers had been pulled to safety from the water, but most had probably either been swept downriver or drowned.

She could see no sign of either Rhillyon or Will Prentis. She could only hope they had managed to swim away in the confusion as planned. They would surely be discovered if they lingered under the remains of the bridge—there was nowhere there to hide.

The thought of Rhillyon falling into the hands of the Rogandans filled her with alarm. It would be a disaster if Agon's people suspected the Aen-ur of an attempt on the life of the king. He had to find a way to escape.

As for Will Prentis, she felt certain he would be captured, and the very idea of it chilled her to the bone. The force of his personality might have provoked and aggravated her, but, perverse as she might be, she had come to eagerly anticipate the latest clash of their wills.

The world she had known before he appeared had always seemed rich and full to her. Now it felt strangely routine and colorless; his arrival had added unexpected spice to her life. She had come to count on him being around, and the likely future that stretched out before her now seemed unaccountably bleak.

Her mind became numb as she fully acknowledged the truth for the first time—she could not face the thought of losing him.

36

Catching his first glimpse of a carriage on the road, Will touched Rhillyon's arm and pointed. Both men had positioned themselves on the near side of the bridge to simplify their escape. Rhillyon nodded, and both of them shifted focus to the ropes beside them.

Will picked up a rope and began to tug with all his might. After almost a minute, the first wedge began to slide. As he continued to strain, he had the satisfaction of seeing the wedge pull loose and plummet down into the river.

The sound of the splash made him wince, but there was no indication that it had been heard by anyone on the bridge.

Another splash immediately followed, and Will saw Rhillyon toss the rope into the river and grasp another. Soon both of them were pulling and discarding, pulling and discarding, as fast as they were able.

Another wedge-shaped block pulled free, and Will saw the first sign that the span above was beginning to give way. A spray of dirt came down as an adjoining block fell into the water of its own accord. Looking up, he saw other blocks poised, ready to fall.

Then abruptly the span collapsed. Stones and men came crashing down together to disappear into the boiling water. Heads began bobbing in and out of the water downstream as soldiers were carried along by the current.

Men were already gathering along the banks of the river, and it was immediately obvious to Will that their position was now exposed.

Rhillyon must have seen it, too, because Will saw him hastily throw the last of his ropes into the water. He did the same, aware of the importance of discarding all evidence of their interference.

A splash sounded as Rhillyon dived into the water. When his head bobbed to the surface again, he was already far downstream. He was now far enough away that Will was hopeful that he would escape capture entirely. For Rhillyon's own sake, and for the sake of the Aenur, such an outcome was crucial.

Will quickly followed him into the water, allowing the current to take him.

He had barely begun to swim when loud cries alerted him to a woman who had just pulled herself from the river downstream. She was searching the torrent, calling out frantically for her daughter. Almost immediately he spotted the child nearby, struggling helplessly in the water.

He groaned. He hadn't noticed a family approaching the bridge, but they must have been crossing at the moment it collapsed. Striking out vigorously, he headed for the girl. He barely reached her in time. She coughed and spluttered feebly as he held her head clear of the water.

Will swam her to the bank, and hands reached out to pull them both in. The mother appeared and clutched the girl to herself, tears of joy streaming down her face.

Rogandan soldiers had hurried to the riverside to help, and several of them now clustered around Will. "Who are you?" one demanded roughly.

"He's no Rogandan," another growled accusingly. "Look at his hair!"

Will had carefully renewed the black dye in his hair and recolored his skin before joining Rhillyon under the bridge. Now he noticed black dye dripping from his head, staining his garments. The water must have rinsed away the dye and exposed his red hair.

"He's a filthy Arvenian," a soldier spat. "I skewered enough of them during the war."

Men quickly crowded in and began striking him. He was hard pressed to keep his feet, and he knew if he went down he would be kicked and trampled to death.

A voice suddenly rang out with authority. "Move away from him immediately! We need him alive. Lady Ona will want to question him."

The pummeling came to a reluctant end. Hands grabbed him roughly, and he was dragged away and thrown down beside a tree. Several men with drawn weapons gathered around him.

Will's body felt like one massive bruise. As far as he could tell, none of his bones had been broken. That was something to be grateful for.

People were milling aimlessly around the road now that their progress had been blocked. He imagined that Agon's men would be trying to decide how best to get across the river. No suitable fords were located anywhere nearby, and the terrain was difficult to navigate on this side of the river. They would need to somehow find a way to repair the bridge. That wasn't going to be completed anytime soon, and the knowledge gave him considerable satisfaction. How Thomas might contrive to get a glimpse of the king he didn't know. But the king would certainly be here for some time.

Several hours passed before he saw any sign of order emerging. Tents were starting to appear beside the road, stretching back along the way the column had come. Agon's tent city was appearing before his eyes. It would undoubtedly be situated here for however long it might take to repair the bridge.

Before nightfall his guard was changed, and he was led to a different location. He now found himself well within the camp, almost certainly inaccessible to anyone who might want to rescue him. Two iron stakes were driven into the ground, and the guards chained him between them. After tossing him a water skin and a small lump of bread, they ignored him completely. It was becoming clear that he was being left to spend a cold night in the open.

WHEN THE DAWN CAME, Will greeted it without enthusiasm. Throughout the night the cold had gnawed away at him, and his bruises left his entire body in a state of constant pain.

He wondered if Thomas would find a way of getting close to the king. It wasn't easy to see how it might happen, but the disruption might offer at least some kind of opportunity.

Amyra was not far from his thoughts either. She had warned that their escape plan could easily go wrong, and she would no doubt feel completely vindicated by what had just happened. He could well imagine her disdain when he failed to appear and it became obvious that he had been captured.

Dubious as his own prospects might be, it would be a disaster for the Aen-ur if Rhillyon had been captured. That outcome seemed improbable to Will. Rhillyon's chances would undoubtedly have been good as long as he survived the river. His own people should have been on the lookout for him, and after the drama of the bridge collapse, Agon's men had been completely disorganized and distracted. It seemed unlikely that the Rogandans would have reached him first.

The morning was not long advanced when a group of guards came and unchained him from the stakes. After tying his hands roughly, they led him to one of the larger and more elaborate of the tents. Four guards stood on duty outside the tent, and their leader instructed his escorts to wait with the prisoner until he was summoned.

A succession of people came and went from the tent, and Will could occasionally hear snatches of conversation from inside the tent, especially when the voices were raised. The most easily distinguished voice was that of a woman. Sometimes she purred, and sometimes she growled, but from the demeanor of people leaving the tent, he was left in no doubt that she was a force to be reckoned with.

Eventually his turn came, and he was unceremoniously dragged into the tent. Before him stood an unusually attractive woman.

She might be attractive, but he couldn't help noticing that she didn't have flashing hazel eyes and restless brown locks dancing carelessly about her face.

"Bow before Lady Ona, you dog!" exclaimed the guard, and rough hands forced Will to his knees. He was left wincing at the pressure on his bruises.

Lady Ona's beauty was real enough, but Will saw at a glance that she was also exceedingly dangerous. She had the look of a person not accustomed to having her will thwarted.

"And who might you be?" she demanded.

"Just a humble merchant, My Lady," he replied respectfully.

"You were near the bridge when it collapsed. What were you doing there?"

He bowed his head humbly. "My business partner and I had just begun crossing the bridge when it collapsed, and we fell into the water. My donkeys and my business partner were swept away in the river. I had just reached the bank when I was apprehended by your guards—I have no idea why they seized me. I have been left with nothing, and I am worried about the fate of my friend."

Will had adopted a worried tone, and he was not entirely faking. He allowed his concern about the fate of Rhillyon to flood his thoughts as he was speaking, and he felt sure that he sounded convincing.

Lady Ona, though, was studying him closely, a shrewd look on her face. "What is your name?" she asked in a silky tone.

"I am called Ronald, My Lady," he replied.

"Well, Ronald, I want you to come for a little walk with me," she said.

Her delicate hand swept out, indicating the entrance to the tent.

He headed outside with Lady Ona following close behind. Several guards swung in beside him, maintaining a respectful distance from their mistress. They apparently had few concerns about her safety, and Will was left in no doubt about her ability to handle herself.

She pointed toward the remains of the bridge, and he headed obediently in that direction.

They had gone no more than a few paces before she appeared to change her mind. "That's far enough!" she called, pointing back toward the tent.

Will shrugged, and retraced his steps.

When they were inside the tent once more, Lady Ona turned to the guards. "Untie his hands," she ordered, "and then leave us." Seeing their uncertainty, she added, "You need not concern yourselves. I'm well able to handle him."

Bowing, they cut Will's bonds and left as she commanded.

"Take off your tunic and your top," she ordered Will.

A frown of determination came at once to his face. Seeing it, she waved a hand dismissively. "Don't be ridiculous. It's obvious that you're covered in bruises. They need to be treated."

After a moment's consideration, he shrugged and complied with her request. She pointed him to a stool, and he positioned himself on it while she opened a trunk and rooted through it. Eventually retrieving an expensive looking white container, she removed the lid to expose a fragrant smelling paste. Scooping large dollops of it onto her fingers she gently smoothed it over his skin.

The soothing effect was immediate.

"Thank you," he said noncommittally when she had finished.

"It's my pleasure," she purred, a coquettish smile on her lips. "You're so strong." She ran a finger across his shoulders, setting his skin tingling and his face glowing.

"It's a strange thing," she told him, shaking her pretty head. "Sometimes we see only what we expect to see. We can completely miss the unexpected, however obvious it might be."

She smiled daintily. "Take yourself, for example. For many months I've been longing to meet the famous Will Prentis in the flesh. But he was the last person I expected to be brought to me in my very own tent this morning!" She gave out a laugh of pure elation, a sound overflowing with triumph and with relish.

Will looked at her with narrowed eyes.

"I can imagine you must be surprised. It was the scars on your face that first alerted me, along with your distinctive red hair under the dye. I simply had to take you for a little walk, just to confirm that you had the characteristic limp I'd heard about."

She smiled. "It's so good to meet you, Will. Or should I call you Lord Torbury?" She paused for a moment, musing. "No, I think it has to be Will," she finally concluded. "The title is much too formal, too stuffy. Not at all appropriate between friends. And we *are* going to be friends, Will—very special friends."

She looked at him in a way that sent heat flooding into his cheeks and up into his forehead. His reaction to her brazen provocativeness seemed to please her enormously.

Coming up behind him, she ran her fingers through his hair. "It's obvious that you have yet to be tamed by a woman," she breathed. "That is so much the better—for me as well as for you. You will not be disappointed, I promise."

Leaning over him, she ran a finger along the scar on his right cheek. Her perfume flooded his senses, and he felt his face glow hot once more.

"I know exactly what's going through your mind," she said softly. "You can relax. Your bruises are looking very angry right now. Your education can afford to wait a while."

She smiled sweetly. "Cases like yours can be surprisingly delicate, and I've never been one to ruin the moment with over-eagerness. I want to make sure you're fully able to appreciate the adventure," she crooned.

He swallowed. He had no intention of being seduced by Lady Ona, but he was painfully aware that he had very little experience dealing with women, and none at all dealing with a woman like her.

Amyra had presented him with more than enough of a challenge. He might have responded clumsily to her, but he sensed that he was stumbling toward the opening movement of a timeless dance. He would have been willing enough to be drawn in if she had ever allowed it, for all that it felt awkward and unfamiliar.

Lady Ona was another matter entirely. She was dancing to an very different rhythm. He couldn't pretend he didn't feel its allure, and he could see from the look in her eye that she was more than confident she had his measure. He was determined never to yield to her, but he didn't doubt for a moment that she intended to make it very difficult for him to resist.

She tossed her head, allowing her lustrous hair to fall forward across her shoulder. Every movement was enticing. She seemed well aware that men found her irresistible.

He tore his gaze away. Seeing it, her full lips formed a smile. It was a predatory smile, and she flaunted it.

Then she sighed, and the spell was broken. "I do have one small obstacle before me. One way or another, the king will soon learn of your existence, and he will be furious if he believes I have tried to withhold you. The problem is that once he finds out who you are, he will undoubtedly want to kill you. He will see your arrival as an ideal opportunity for a spectacle. If I can forestall that, he may over time be persuaded to change his mind. The king is very unpredictable though."

A look of determination came to her lovely face. "Never fear, Will Prentis. I will do whatever it takes to save you." She slowly eyed him up and down, a smile of eager anticipation playing across her face. "I have the feeling that you will be well worth the effort."

Will felt unaccountably exposed and vulnerable.

"Dress yourself," she commanded.

Calling for the guards, she jerked her head toward her prisoner. "Bring him. We are going to the king."

She set off toward the largest of the tents, with the guards pulling Will along behind.

The sound of angry yelling reached Will's ears even before they reached the tent. He saw Lady Ona wince slightly, then she made her way to the guards outside the royal tent. Singling one of them out, she spoke quietly into his ear.

He nodded, before directing a hard glance at Will. Then he seemed to steel himself before stepping inside the tent. He soon emerged, a new round of shouting chasing him outside.

Taking a deep breath, he nodded to Lady Ona.

She came to Will and took his arm. "Leave the talking to me," she said firmly, guiding him into the tent.

King Agon was sitting on a small throne within the tent, and he glared balefully at Lady Ona as she approached. She bowed low before him. He then switched his gaze to Will. Will contented himself with a nod of the head. He saw alarm flash across Lady Ona's face, and perversely it gave him at least a small measure of satisfaction.

Curiously, the king did not react. "Who is this bold fool you have brought before me?" he demanded.

"Great King, may you live forever," she replied. "This man was found near the bridge when it collapsed. The soldiers suspected him of involvement and brought him to me."

The king's eyes narrowed. "His head will not be long on his shoulders if that is true," he said. "Perhaps even if it is not true," he added with a nasty smile. "Who is he?"

"His name is Will Prentis, although he is also known as Lord Torbury. He is Arvenian."

The king's eyes went wide with surprise. "*The* Will Prentis?" he demanded. "The man who presided over the destruction of Drettroth's army?" A gloating look came into his eye. "And here he is, completely in my power."

"I am willing to interrogate him, Your Majesty," said Lady Ona. "I have ways of uncovering the truth. If you will give him to me for two or three days, I am confident I can expose his true intentions."

The king turned his gaze on her. Then he threw back his head and laughed. "My Lady Ona, you are so boringly predictable! All this talk of uncovering and exposing—you think of nothing but your unbridled lust." His face turned suddenly cold. "Your appetites mean nothing to me," he spat. "I will do as I please with this prize."

He returned his gaze to Will. "Will Prentis! What an unexpected opportunity you present me with. What a messy spectacle I could arrange, with you as the centerpiece. Sweet revenge! It has been far too long coming, and I would be able to savor it to the full."

He paused, and went silent for a full minute. "Delicious as it might be, I have a far better idea. A man like you offers unusual potential. You and I are going to become very well acquainted. You have served your king loyally, I'm sure." His lips peeled back in a vague semblance of a smile. "Who knows, though? Perhaps even the most loyal of subjects can undergo a change of perspective. I dare to imagine that you might gradually find yourself coming around to my point of view."

Agon gazed at his captive, a smirk of satisfaction on his lips.

Will kept his face impassive.

Agon laughed. "I see you are skeptical, but you may yet surprise yourself."

"Guards!" he called. Several men clustered around his throne snapped to attention. "Tie this man's hands behind his back. Tie them securely but loosely, and don't harm him. I merely want to ensure that he can't interfere with me in any way."

He turned to Lady Ona. "You are dismissed," he said coldly, flicking his fingers toward the entrance of the tent.

Lady Ona looked as if she was sorely tempted to speak, but she held her peace and withdrew.

It was perfectly obvious to Will what Agon had in mind. As he looked at the king he noticed his hand straying to a hidden fold in his clothing. No doubt the Stone of Authority lay secreted there.

He had escaped the web of Lady Ona, only to fall into the hands of a ruthless tyrant with the power to magically bend the wills of other people to his own.

What could he do to resist? The scroll had offered no insights whatever, but there had to be a way.

He wasn't going to stand by and allow himself to be transformed into the compliant puppet of a monster. He would rather die.

37

———

After four harrowing days in close proximity to the Rogandan king, Will had long since learned to stay well clear whenever Agon worked himself into one of his rages. It happened all too frequently. Ennawi usually bore the brunt of it.

Agon's eyes bulged, and the veins in his neck stood out as he harangued his mute slave. "I should have reached Arnost long ago. Why am I thwarted at every turn?"

In spite of his fury, he kept his voice low, apparently well aware that he could expect no privacy in his royal tent, surrounded as it was by dense clusters of the tents of his servants.

As usual, Ennawi showed no reaction to the tirade. Will had long since ceased to be amazed at the slave's ability to remain unresponsive.

Will had observed that Agon spoke to Ennawi as if they were holding a conversation, and that the king seemed to say whatever was on his mind. Sometimes when Will was standing nearby, Agon whispered conspiratorially in the slave's ear. Ennawi apparently suited the king perfectly—he was the ideal listener, and he was the soul of discretion. The king's secrets were safe with a man who could neither speak nor write.

Will had met Ennawi on the first day of his imprisonment with Agon. It was far from obvious how a slave without hands managed to feed himself, and Will was not surprised when he caught his first glimpse of the slave's carer. The king had disappeared off on some errand, and Nistinaa soon arrived to feed and tend to Ennawi as usual. Seeing Will in the room, she had observed him doubtfully for a while before apparently deciding she had little choice but to take the opportunity presented by the king's absence.

Since then he had contrived to speak to her several times, and she had gradually relaxed in his presence. Ennawi's situation appalled him, and he told her so directly. It left him speechless when she told him the slave had been enduring such abuse from Agon for years.

The king spoke, attracting Will's attention once more.

Agon had finally mastered himself. "For all the frustrations, a new source of delight will soon present itself," he told Ennawi. "As I have already told you, I have at last found a use for the Aen-ur. I won't need to wait much longer now." A gloating smile played across his lips.

Will had heard no previous mention by the king of the secretive people who had offered their help, and Agon's words made him uneasy.

Some part of him recognized that even a couple of days ago this information would have chilled him to the bone. Others before him had come under the influence of the Stone of Authority, and he wondered how many of them had understood exactly what was happening to them. Perhaps his situation was unique. But it made no difference. He had been resisting the power of the Stone of Authority with all his might, but nevertheless he knew he was slowly succumbing to it. The process was already well advanced. Agon's agenda, not to mention his moods and attitude, still seemed sour and distasteful to Will, but he felt vaguely aware that everything about the king should be inspiring a much stronger negative reaction from him.

Through the fog that seemed to be clouding his volition, Will sensed that Agon's reference to the Aen-ur was significant, and that something needed to be done, and done quickly, to protect them.

If Thomas could get a glimpse of Agon, all would be revealed. It suddenly occurred to him, though, that there might be another way.

It hadn't taken long for Will to decide he could trust Nistinaa, and they often conversed quietly whenever they found an opportunity. Eventually he gathered his courage.

"Is there any way you could get a message to my friends?" he whispered.

Immediately she became guarded. "I will do nothing to put Ennawi at risk," she told him firmly.

He made no attempt to press her. He would need to choose the right moment.

There was little he could do other than to bide his time.

HALDEK HAD POSITIONED himself as near to the royal tent as he dared, contriving to look busy while surreptitiously observing the people who came and went from Agon's presence. To a casual observer he was just another Rogandan soldier. Thanks to Rhillyon's men he had been clad and equipped appropriately—everything he was wearing had been pilfered from unwary guards.

He had taken fearful risks to get near to Will. After watching the area for some time he had boldly claimed the guard duty for a supply tent located quite close to Agon's own. His years of sentry duty allowed him to put in a very creditable performance. So far he had not been exposed.

He soon came to recognize Nistinaa as a frequent visitor to the royal tent. He often caught glimpses of her through the entrance to the royal tent, and more than once he saw her whispering with Will. Their body language suggested they were comfortable in each other's presence.

Mustering his courage, he decided to speak to her next time a suitable opportunity arose. In the end he didn't need to wait long.

She had been hurrying past when he called softly to her. "Excuse me! Can I speak with you?"

Startled, she paused long enough to peer in his direction. When it became obvious that she wasn't planning to stop, he decided to fall in beside her.

"Could you give a message to the man you were talking to in the tent? His name is Will Prentis."

She looked at him mistrustfully.

"I'm a friend of his." Conscious of the risk he was taking, he nevertheless decided he had little choice but to trust her. "All I want you to do is to let him know that I'm nearby. Could you do that please?"

The suspicious look on her face gave him little hope that she would follow through.

"Just tell him that Haldek spoke to you," he said.

Then she was gone.

Haldek returned to his guard duty. Knowing that the woman could turn him in whenever she chose, he found it almost impossible to relax. It was therefore an enormous relief when she quietly approached him the next evening, jerking her head toward a quiet corner behind a nearby tent.

"I told him," she said. "He wants to know what you're planning."

Haldek exhaled in relief. "We want to get him away from here as soon as possible. Come to me again tomorrow—I'll let you know the details then."

She left after giving him a brief nod.

That night and the following day were extraordinarily tense for Haldek.

The king's camp was surrounded by sentries, but with no one expecting trouble the guards were unusually lax. Before Haldek first entered the camp, he'd carefully monitored the approaches from the forest, finally selecting a location where the guards appeared to be especially inattentive. Since that time he had been safely using the same entry point to come and go from the forest.

In preparation for getting Will, Haldek first returned to the forest and arranged for a party to be on hand to spirit them away. He then returned to the camp and found his way to a cluster of supply tents.

The supply tents were more heavily guarded than the camp itself. Knowing the reputation of Rogandan soldiers, Haldek didn't find it particularly surprising.

To extract Will he needed to get one of the sentries drunk, and to achieve that he needed a wineskin. Wineskins were the most desirable of prizes for thieves, so the penalties for anyone caught stealing them had always been severe. Nevertheless, he decided to steal more than one to allow for contingencies.

Two hours stretched to three as he stood near the supply tents watching for an opportunity. By the time the afternoon had almost worn away, he was reaching a point of desperation.

He began to wonder if he should have instead asked the Aen-ur to supply him with wineskins. There wasn't time to go back now though, and their wineskins might be very different from the ones supplied to the Rogandan army. He couldn't afford to rouse suspicions.

He was almost ready to abandon hope when a large group of men came to collect supplies for the evening meal of the king, Lady Ona, and other senior leaders. They rummaged through the tents noisily, eventually leaving with a large quantity of food and alcohol.

Once they had gone, Haldek decided to risk everything on a gamble. Waiting until they were well out of sight, he hurried toward the supply tents, approaching from the direction in which they had gone.

"They didn't get enough of the good wineskins!" he told the guard. "The king will have our hides if we don't get it right!"

After looking doubtfully at him for a moment, the guard shrugged and waved Haldek to one of the tents. Wasting no time, Haldek dashed into the tent and carefully selected the three most expensive looking wineskins he could find. Then he hurried away, waving his thanks to the guard as he headed back the way he had come.

The moment he was out of sight he came to a halt. His heart was pounding, and he was panting from nervous energy.

It was too soon to relax though. His next task was to steal a couple of dark cloaks with hoods. Fortunately that proved much more straightforward. After hiding the cloaks near the king's tent, he returned to his guard duty and waited for darkness.

Not long after sunset, the woman appeared again, just as he had requested. Having instructed her to send Will to the same current location in four hours, he slipped away.

His final task was to deliver the wineskin to the guard at the perimeter of the camp. He knew from experience which guard should be on sentry duty that night. Haldek had previously spun him a yarn about hunting in the forest, even returning with a small boar on one occasion to support the deception. After a few days Haldek had come and gone often enough that the sentry simply ignored him.

On this occasion Haldek wanted to make sure the man was thoroughly inebriated when the time came to slip out of the camp with Will. One wineskin should be more than enough to do the job.

When he approached the sentry post, Haldek was shocked to find no sign of the regular guard. Another soldier was there in his place. Dismayed at the setback, he backed away to consider his options. Time was not on his side.

A bold approach had secured him the wineskins, and he decided to risk a final gamble.

Staggering up to the sentry with the three wineskins clutched to his chest, he peered at the sentry through blinking eyes. "Wheresh the king's tent?" he slurred.

The sentry snorted. "That way," he pointed. "From the state you're in, you'd better stay well clear of it."

"Thank you, sho much," he replied.

Spinning unsteadily in the direction indicated, he lurched forward, apparently failing to notice that one of the wineskins had slipped from his grasp and fallen to the ground.

Haldek stumbled on until he was out of sight, then he crept back to observe the sentry. To his relief the man had already started on the wineskin. It was now simply a matter of time.

Hope began to stir for Will when Nistinaa told him about meeting Haldek. He assured her that Haldek could be trusted, and after some initial hesitation, she agreed to meet with him again.

Time seemed to crawl while Will waited for the next contact to take place. He sensed that his independent will was slowly ebbing away, and the urgency of escaping from Agon had become pressing. It needed to happen soon if he expected to leave with any of his volition still intact.

At the same time, he found himself increasingly struggling with any idea that required him to go behind Agon's back. A part of his being had slowly retreated to a hidden inner sanctuary, and that hidden core affirmed the importance of removing himself from the presence of the stone. But another part of him was bent toward Agon and his priorities, and that part had been growing ever stronger.

The war within him continued to rage unchecked, but his independent core somehow managed to rise up to assert itself. It allowed him to reach an agonizing decision.

The next time Agon left the tent, Nistinaa appeared again. "I met with Haldek again!" she whispered excitedly. "They're going to try to get you away from here—tonight. They told me the details. You need to..."

"No!" he replied, cutting her off. "Don't tell me any details. It's important that I don't know them."

As she stared at him in bewilderment, he dug deep, drawing upon every reserve he could summon, willing himself to respond only out of the inner core of his being, weakened though it was.

"I'm going to explain to you what needs to happen," he told her. "You and Ennawi will be the ones going with them, not me. Follow their instructions. As soon as you are safe, find Thomas Stablehand

and let him spend time with you, and especially with Ennawi. Thomas Stablehand—don't forget! Nothing else matters."

She looked back at him wide-eyed.

"Do you understand?" he insisted.

She nodded.

"We must not speak of this again."

She opened her mouth to protest, and he shook his head emphatically. "It's already too late for me," he told her with a frown, turning away.

The hidden core of his will had chosen to abandon his own interests, favoring instead a path that might save the Aen-ur. And the remnant of his independent self was not idle even now. Working tirelessly, it positioned the interaction with Nistinaa as a matter of no relevance to Will's conscious awareness. *I am not responsible for these two people—they don't answer to me. Whatever they might be doing is none of my business. I must be careful to ignore them. Any involvement from me would be an intrusion.*

Nistinaa slipped away, and Will felt a sudden need for fresh air. Following her to the entrance of the king's tent, he paused, peering out with uncharacteristic timidity.

Lady Ona stood nearby, watching the tent. Her eyes narrowed at once when she saw Will.

He groaned. The king had banned Lady Ona from both his tent and his presence as soon as he had Will in his power. Agon had no intention of sharing his prize with anyone.

She had obeyed, but more than once he had seen her prowling nearby like a lioness, ready to pounce the moment her prey came within reach.

In his reduced state he simply couldn't face her—he could no longer summon the resources.

His head began to pound, and reaching up unsteady hands, he ran them through his hair. Then turning away from the relative freedom of the open air, he stumbled back to the suffocating confinement of his prison.

38

———

"Where's Will?" hissed Amyra. She had barely been able to restrain her eagerness as the moment of his escape approached. Now there was no sign of him. Her brows were furrowed in vexation.

The nearest sentry was drunk and snoring loudly. Haldek had slipped past him without difficulty, and not one but two people had followed him—a woman and a younger man. There was no sign at all of Will.

The woman stared back at Amyra anxiously. "He wouldn't come. He insisted on sending us instead. I am Nistinaa, and this is Ennawi." The man she pointed to was completely unresponsive.

Amyra glared at her suspiciously. "Did you pass on Haldek's message?"

Nistinaa nodded, but Amyra wasn't at all convinced.

"She's telling the truth," Thomas whispered insistently. "I know why Will sent them."

Rhillyon drew closer. "We can't stay here," he told them. "We'll need to find a way to rescue Will later."

He led the little party swiftly away, toward the safety of the forest.

They didn't pause until they were far from Agon's camp. Ennawi had to be helped every step of the way. In the end a soldier stood on each side of him and took an arm, guiding him forward and even carrying him at times.

When they finally stopped, Nistinaa faced them, tears glistening in her eyes. "Thank you," she said. "I never dared allow myself to believe this day would ever come."

A look of determination came over her face. "I made a promise to Will. He wanted us to meet with Thomas Stablehand. He said that nothing else mattered."

Amyra glared at the woman. How could meeting with Thomas possibly be more important than freeing Will?

Thomas did not seem at all surprised. He approached Nistinaa. "I am Thomas Stablehand," he said gently.

He studied her for a few moments, then his face grew grave. He turned to Ennawi next, and his eyes quickly grew wide with alarm.

"Thank you," he said to Nistinaa. "I will meet with you again soon."

He turned to Amyra. "I must speak with you. It is extremely urgent."

She frowned at him, still struggling to overcome her frustration at the outcome of their attempted rescue.

Seeing her hesitation, he reached out a tentative hand.

She pulled away instantly. "Don't touch me," she snapped, more irritated than ever. She glared at him, refusing to budge.

Thomas sighed. "I wanted him back as much as you did," he said quietly. "I'm truly sorry about what happened."

She felt a flush rising to her cheeks at the implication of his words. If he thought this approach would win her over, he was badly mistaken.

His face hardened. "There was a reason why Will sent them instead of coming himself. He decided that the reason was more important than his own safety. Do you want to hear what it was, or not?"

She glared at him for a long minute. "Very well," she said sullenly. He'd have been wasting his time if he appealed to anything except her curiosity. Perhaps he was smarter than she'd thought.

Thomas turned and headed away from everyone else. She followed him, although she didn't do it with any grace.

He didn't stop until the others were well out of hearing range. Then he turned to face her. He stared awkwardly at her for long enough that she began to feel uncomfortable, then he shook his head and slowly released a long breath.

She frowned at him in bewilderment.

"I have something to tell you," he said. "You won't want to hear it, and you definitely won't like it. But I'm doing it for Will—he would want you to know. If you care about him at all, you'll hear me out."

She glared back at him defiantly for a moment. But she nodded. She was skeptical about what he was going to say, and she made no attempt to hide it. But he had succeeded in getting her attention.

"I need you to promise you won't tell anyone what I'm about to reveal to you."

"If you insist," she said.

"I do."

She shrugged. "Get on with it, then."

"I'm sure you must have wondered why the three of us came here," he began.

"I've never made any secret of that," she snorted.

"And you must have wondered why Will brought me in particular."

She didn't bother to deny it.

"You were there when Will read the scroll aloud," he said.

She frowned. "Are you talking about that old scroll at Ishitar Ataye?"

He nodded.

"That was utter nonsense," she scoffed.

He sighed. "You agreed to hear me out," he reminded her.

She scowled at him, but she subsided.

"The scroll talked about three stones of power. One of them was the Stone of Knowing. Will knows where that stone is, Amyra. He knows that I have it. He sent Nistinaa and Ennawi to us for one reason—so that I could use the stone to discover everything they know about Agon and his plans. Ennawi can't speak, and he can't write, so the king has known he's safe. He's been confiding in him for years. Will knew that I could use the Stone of Knowing to find out everything that's passed between them."

She rolled her eyes and shook her head. "Surely you don't expect me to believe any of this."

He ignored her reaction. "I don't use the stone to pry on people I know, and that means I've avoided using the stone to discover your thoughts. But I can use the stone anytime I choose. If you want proof, I can offer it right now."

Amyra's eyes narrowed as she considered this. She didn't believe him of course. But even the idea of having her thoughts exposed gave her pause. "Are you claiming you can find out something I'm thinking?"

His eyes bored into her. "Not just *something* you're thinking, Amyra. Everything. Past and present. Your hopes and dreams, your memories, your secret desires. All of it."

She blushed scarlet, unable to prevent herself.

"Choose any topic you like," he said boldly. "I'll pick you clean. You can try to hide your thoughts if you want. It won't make any difference."

She stared back at him, and he didn't blink. She faltered, suddenly unsure what to think. She reached a decision very quickly though. It wasn't a risk she was willing to take. Not under any circumstances.

"Go on," she said warily. "I'm listening."

"I've done what Will wanted me to do. I examined their thoughts, and now I know what Agon is up to."

Her eyebrows drew together. "Come on, Thomas! You can't have looked at either one of them for much more than a minute!"

"I didn't need longer than that," he told her. He took a deep breath. "Look, I can well imagine that you don't want me poking around in your mind. But if it's the only way you'll believe me, I don't see that we have much choice."

"Go on with whatever you were going to say next," she said stiffly. "Like you would if I believed you."

He looked at her hesitantly for a moment, then he shook his head. "It won't be useful to continue if you don't believe me." He took a deep breath. "I told you that I've avoided using the stone on you, and that's the truth. But I did use it when we first encountered you."

Her shock turned to anger before she could blink.

"Why should that be a problem?" he asked pointedly. "You don't believe any of this is true." His tone was mild, but she saw the intensity in his eyes.

"What did you see?" she asked breathlessly.

"That you were no real threat to us," he replied. "That was my main purpose in checking."

"And what else?" she insisted.

He gazed at her hesitantly for a moment. "Your father," he finally offered.

Her eyes narrowed. "What about my father?"

"You feel abandoned by him."

She didn't respond.

"He loved you, Amyra. He died to protect you and your mother."

Tears came unbidden to her eyes. "How dare you?" she asked furiously. "How could you possibly know anything about my father?"

"You don't remember him—you were too young. But the memories are there, locked away in your mind. I saw him when he left you for the last time. You were wailing, and he kissed you on the forehead. He had tears running down his cheeks."

She was sobbing now. "It can't be true. I wasn't thinking about him when I first saw you."

"You didn't need to be thinking about him. It stood out, because it's such an important issue in your mind."

He was trying to be gentle, and she could see he was feeling wretched himself. It didn't help. She shook her head in angry denial.

"Let me try again," he said with a sigh. "When we first met the thing uppermost in your mind was the man who had been trying to woo you. He'd been pestering you for weeks, and you find him intensely annoying. He tried to give you a valuable gift—a horse—and you refused it. He thinks you need to become submissive."

Her tears ended abruptly. She stared wide-eyed at him. "What was his name?"

"I don't remember. But there was something about a pig."

A snort escaped her lips. She wasn't sure if it was laughter or astonishment. "That is his name. It sounds a little like the Aen-ur word for boar." She screwed up her face. "Far too close for comfort in his particular case."

She ran a trembling hand over her eyes, and her breath hitched as she mastered herself. Then she faced him. "I believe you, Thomas."

He looked shamefaced. "I'm sorry I did that to you, Amyra. I'm truly sorry. I know it's a violation, which is why I avoid using the stone around people I know." He glanced up at her face apologetically. "My wife is much better at this kind of thing. I mainly rely on the stone to find out people's motives and intentions. She's able to use it to help people. She's a lot like your mother..."

"What about my mother?" she asked sharply.

"Never mind," he said, his expression suddenly guarded.

He seemed to recover himself. "That isn't all. There's more you need to know."

"I'm not sure how much more I can take," she said unsteadily.

He shook his head. "I don't mean like that. The scroll talked about another stone—the Stone of Authority."

She'd been so ready to scoff at the scroll before, but her ridicule had dissolved like the morning mist. "It supposedly lets you control other living things, especially people."

He nodded. "Agon has it."

She looked at him in alarm, hoping he could somehow be mistaken. "How do you know?" she asked.

No hint of sarcasm remained in her tone. Impossible though all of it was, she no longer doubted him.

"From Ennawi's thoughts and memories."

She frowned, more from surprise than skepticism. "It's hard to imagine anything meaningful going on in the mind of that one."

Thomas shook his head firmly. "Don't let appearances deceive you. He's both intelligent and aware. He's only like he is because Nistinaa drugs him."

Her eyes narrowed in disapproval.

"There are reasons why she does it. None of that matters though," Thomas insisted. "The scroll suggested that it takes two weeks to completely bend someone's will. Will has been with Agon for almost a week now, and the stone has begun to have an impact on him." He eyed her uncertainly for a moment, then he seemed to reach a decision. "You might as well know the truth. I was able to witness his interactions with Nistinaa in her memory. He's already been badly affected."

Her eyes grew wide again, this time with horror as the implications began to sink in. And she wasn't alone in her concern about Will—Thomas looked pale enough to be ill.

"What's worse is that Will knows what's happening to him," Thomas continued. "That's why he sent them instead. Even if we could get him away from Agon right now, he wouldn't be himself. He'll never be himself again—not until Agon loses the stone or dies."

Her heart had begun to pound. She stared at him, speechless.

"It doesn't end there either," he told her miserably. "Agon is planning to attack the Aen-ur. And he'll soon be in position. Once he crosses the river he'll be very close to Aen-irac."

"But why attack them? Because of the bridge?"

"No! He has no idea who's responsible for collapsing it. He hates the Aen-ur for reasons that aren't important right now. His motive is that he believes he's found a way to live forever. He intends to do a deal with the dark gods. His end of the bargain is to provide rivers of human blood, and he's planning to start with the Aen-ur. He'll have them rounded up and slaughtered. That will only be the beginning—the people of Arvenon will be next."

It was all so much to take in.

Thomas continued with barely a pause. "Will went to great efforts to make sure we would find out. The Aen-ur need to be warned!"

A look of determination came to his face. "Somehow we need to stop Agon and find a way to free Will."

39

The column stretched far ahead of Will and even further behind as he rode beside the king. The enforced delays lay behind them at last.

A makeshift bridge had been erected over the river, allowing horses and their riders to continue the journey. The wagons filled with provisions were another matter. The column had been obliged to wait while an endless line of new wagons, all of them fully laden, were assembled on the other side of the river. It had been enough of a challenge to replace the food and drink and other supplies left behind on the other side of the river. Replacing the tents was going to take much longer. The king, Lady Ona, and a small number of others would sleep under cover that night. Everyone else would be camping in the open.

As was frequently the case, Agon was restive and disgruntled. Both the delays and the disappearance of Ennawi had contributed strongly to his irritation.

Ennawi's disappearance was especially baffling. An exhaustive search had failed to find any trace of the slave. He posed no threat, but he was Agon's property. Whether he had wandered away or fallen in the river and drowned, he had no business doing it without the king's permission.

None of this troubled Will. Although the circumstances of Ennawi's departure were known to him, he was firmly convinced that it was not his business to intrude in the matter. As for the king's moodiness, that wasn't his concern either. His purpose was only to further the king's interests.

His current state of compliance had not been reached overnight, and he knew that even now a part of him still fiercely resisted any notion of bowing to the will of the king. It wasn't as if his objections had gone from his mind—it was rather that his former reasoning no longer seemed compelling.

The king guided his horse alongside Will's. "It is a glorious day, is it not?" asked the king, a savage smile creasing his lips. "Very soon I will carry out final judgment upon the Aen-ur devils," he said. "My soldiers will burst upon them unawares. They will be herded together, and I will watch with delight as they are slaughtered."

"How will such bloodletting further your cause?" asked Will bluntly.

The look on Agon's face turned rapidly from astonishment to anger. The anger soon faded, though, to be replaced by a smug smile. "You cannot imagine how satisfying you are, Will Prentis," he said. "At last I have someone capable whose only goal is to further my cause." Then his face grew harder. "I will be lenient this time, but never question my plans again. It is enough for you to know what I wish to do."

Will nodded. It was true that he didn't need reasons. As long as he understood the king's will, nothing further should be necessary.

At the same time, the king's plan raised uncomfortable questions for him, questions that would persist even when the resistant part of his will had finally been suppressed. He had never countenanced the indiscriminate killing of non-combatants, and he could not stand by while women and children were slaughtered. Yet if he had under-stood Agon's words correctly, the king was planning exactly that.

Will shook his head in confusion. Not having ever been

confronted with a conflict between his duty to his sovereign and his convictions before, he had yet to decide how he should handle it.

A BRUTISH SOLDIER was ushered into the king's tent, and Agon bared his teeth in a semblance of a smile.

He turned to Will. "Will Prentis, I want you to meet the commander of my soldiers," he said. "This is Wannyk."

Wannyk bowed stiffly. Will greeted him with a non-committal nod. He had already encountered enough Rogandan army commanders to last a lifetime.

The king addressed Will. "My commander has been considering how to respond should my enemies attack us on our journey. He would like your thoughts and opinions."

Will stared back at the king cautiously.

"Do you hesitate to take any necessary measures to protect your sovereign?" snapped Agon irritably.

After a moment's hesitation, Will shrugged, nodding his acceptance. What harm could there be simply in protecting the king?

Wannyk pulled out a parchment, and Will saw that it was a crudely drawn map. No writing appeared on it anywhere, so it was impossible to tell which region it depicted.

"Suppose our forces were deployed here, and the enemy here," began Wannyk. "What would you do?" He eyed Will skeptically.

Will glanced at the map for a moment. He pointed at a particular location. "They would expect you to deploy your main defenses here." He pointed again. "And they would attack here."

Wannyk was unimpressed. "That is obvious," he grunted.

Situations like this were child's play for Will, and he found himself rising to the challenge. "You would instead carry out a preemptive attack here," he said, stabbing a finger at a different location. "They would be forced to move soldiers to that location to counter the attack. It would only be a feint. Your main attack would be carried out here." He pointed once more.

Wannyk's eyes went wide.

"Well?" demanded Agon. "Get onto it immediately!"

Wannyk scurried from the tent.

Will frowned. "What just happened, Your Majesty?"

"Don't trouble yourself, Will," said the king loftily. "It was nothing more than a training exercise." Agon's smile seemed even more false than usual.

Had Will just given Agon's commander a strategy for attacking the Aen-ur?

He gritted his teeth in annoyance. Acting against his convictions had never been an option for Will. But he wasn't used to working with a sovereign who deviously manipulated his subjects, and he couldn't escape the feeling that he had just been played.

He would need to be doubly on his guard, because it surely wouldn't be long before he faced a similar situation again. And he had no doubt that the stakes would be higher next time.

THE ROAD along which the column was traveling still ran parallel to the foothills of the Blue Mountains. Outliers of the forest that covered the slopes stood to the right of the road. No trace of the river remained; it had long since bent sharply away from the road, stretching up into the mountains where it had its source.

To the left of the road lay a series of rolling hills leading to vast expanses of grazing land.

A distant rumble caused Will to glance upward. No storm clouds had gathered in the sky, and he drew his horse to a halt in bemusement as the rumble continued to grow in volume. The column moved on, but others had also noticed the sound, and many of them were beginning to peer around nervously.

The noise grew abruptly to a deafening roar as the hills to Will's left burst suddenly into life. A vast mass of stampeding cattle thundered across the nearest ridge, charging straight toward the column. Long horns flashed ominously, picked out by rays of the late afternoon sunlight.

Panicked screams filled the air as men and horses fled for their lives. Any semblance of order vanished in an instant as the column descended into a chaos of fleeing forms and flashing hooves.

In the confusion a cart was overturned just behind Will. Fighting for control of his horse, Will somehow managed to steer the terrified animal behind the cart. The cattle flowed around them, trampling everything in their path.

Peering around in the dust and the turmoil, Will spotted the king and half a dozen of his guards sheltering behind the royal carriage. As he watched, the carriage began to wobble under the strain of pressing cattle. Abruptly the carriage came crashing down onto its side, the king and his men barely scuttling back to safety in time. The fugitives quickly hurried forward again to shelter behind the overturned carriage.

The flow of cattle slowly began to diminish, but before it ceased entirely a lean figure dressed in black rode up. Leaping from his horse, he landed on the overturned royal carriage, a sword flashing in his hand.

By the time the startled guards had drawn their own swords, two of them lay dead. The remaining guards outnumbered their attacker four to one, but they were soon fighting for their lives.

The king watched the battle with wide eyes, bellowing for more guards. He had picked up a fallen sword and was preparing to defend himself, but the ashen appearance of his face suggested he wasn't optimistic.

By the time Will finally managed to reach them only one of the guards was still fighting. Will's weapons had been taken away when he was made a prisoner, so he reached down for a discarded sword.

A quick glance at the king suggested that Agon was not entirely sure what his captive would do now he was armed. Will ignored the king, facing the intruder instead. He wasn't a moment too soon. The last guard finally went down.

The attacker engaged him without hesitation, and Will marveled at the stamina of the man. The black clad fighter had been battling without pause for several minutes, but he moved as if he had just begun.

A couple of minutes were all it took for Will to wonder if he had finally met his match. The man was simply too skilled, too fast, and too determined.

More of Agon's guards arrived before the attacker could finish Will off. A lucky jab by one of the guards took the intruder in the leg, distracting him enough that Will was finally able to penetrate his defense with a thrust to his torso.

Reaching for his belt, the attacker withdrew a knife and threw it at Agon. Out of the corner of his eye Will saw the king twisting to one side away from its path.

Throwing the knife was the final act of the dark clad intruder. Thrust through by several swords, he fell to the ground and lay unmoving.

Will saw at a glance that the king had survived the attack. Apart from nicking Agon's arm and drawing blood, the knife had missed him entirely.

A piece of cloth lay nearby on the ground. It appeared to be relatively clean. Will tore off a couple of strips and moved to bandage the arm of the king. Agon glared at him while he worked, but made no comment.

If Will had been expecting gratitude from Agon, he would have been disappointed. Certainly King Steffan would have responded differently. Having never been motivated by the need for praise, Will ignored Agon's stony silence.

"Call for the royal physician," Will told a guard calmly. The man hurried away to do his bidding, apparently choosing to ignore Will's status as a prisoner.

Agon appeared to be slowly emerging from shock. "Who was he?" he demanded, pointing at the body of the attacker. The king moved closer, poking at him with his foot. As he did so, Will noticed what appeared to be a parchment tucked within the man's clothing.

Bending down, Will pulled the parchment free.

"Give me that!" demanded Agon furiously. Stepping forward he snatched it from Will's hand. A frown came to his face as he scanned its contents. "Impossible!" he finally snorted, before thrusting it back into Will's hand.

Will read the parchment. His brows furrowed together. He turned to the king, lowering his voice. "So this man was an assassin? And Drettroth hired him to attack you?" He shook his head, glancing at the chaos around them. "I imagine we have the assassin to thank for the cattle."

Agon glared back at him. "Drettroth always hated me. I should have killed him myself instead of leaving you Arvenians to do it for me!" He scowled. "Drettroth was a failure when he was alive." Then he gave out a mad laugh. "Now he's failed again!"

Before the king could say any more, a guard arrived, accompanied by the royal physician.

Seeing the flustered look on the physician's face, Agon snapped at him. "Well, don't just stand there! Get on with it!"

The physician bowed briefly before unwrapping Will's strips of cloth and examining the wound. His brows knit together in a frown. "This wound..." he began tentatively.

"Stop fussing!" Agon snapped.

"But Your Majesty," sputtered the physician.

"Bandage it!" roared the king.

Fumbling awkwardly, the physician rewrapped the wound with fresh bandages, his fingers trembling. Then he hurried away.

The king watched the retreating back of the physician for a moment, then he took a breath and cast his eyes around. What he saw caused him to shake his head in anger.

Will followed his gaze. Most of the cattle had vanished in the direction of the forest, although a few still wandered nearby, lowing mournfully. The devastation left behind them was staggering.

The column would be delayed once more, and this time the king had the long dead Drettroth to thank for it.

Agon would not be happy. Having seen more than enough of what that looked like in practice, Will turned aside, allowing his feet to drift. He saw no reason to be around to witness the storm.

Wandering back down the column he noticed the first signs that order was beginning to emerge from the chaos. Men were scurrying about, righting upended wagons and rounding up horses. Supplies were being retrieved from the mess and placed in orderly piles. Curious, he stepped behind a wagon to observe.

It quickly became clear that the driving force behind the efforts was Lady Ona. Will had never seen the king lift as much as a finger to organize anything, yet somehow the practical needs of the column were met each day. Tents were set up, food was prepared, horses were provided for, supplies were replenished, and everything ran remarkably smoothly. It seemed likely that the king largely had Lady Ona to thank for it.

Being himself an organizer by nature, Will watched with considerable curiosity as she went about the task. There was much to admire about her approach. She was clearly an effective communicator as well as a skilled manager, and she didn't entirely neglect little compliments and words of encouragement.

As he watched, a young servant approached her carrying two heavy bags. He appeared extremely tentative as he put them down in front of her.

"Where have you been?" she demanded, her eyes flashing dangerously. "You're late—as usual! I expected you long before this."

The servant bowed his head, but didn't dare to reply.

Pulling open the neck of one of the bags she peered into it. "This isn't what I told you to bring!" she shouted.

She stood with her hands on her hips, glaring at him for a moment. "Take off your tunic and your shirt," she commanded, her voice now controlled and even.

He obeyed, trembling violently.

She approached him, casually running a finger across his bare back. "It upsets me when my people disappoint me," she said smoothly. Then she turned to one of the soldiers. "Flog him. Twenty strokes."

Soldiers took each of his arms and dragged him away.

"Don't dare to disappoint me again," she yelled after him.

Will looked on, appalled by her behavior. Perhaps her servant had failed to bring what she wanted in a timely fashion, but she made no attempt to explore the reasons. She had simply erupted.

Perhaps this was how she relieved her own tension. Perhaps she used such opportunities to keep her subordinates alert and responsive. Either way, after the demonstration he had witnessed, her underlings would undoubtedly work doubly hard to satisfy her demands. Every servant in sight was certainly scurrying about frantically.

Lady Ona's cruelty left Will cold. Unwilling to watch her any longer, he slipped quietly away.

He wandered aimlessly, going wherever his feet happened to take him. How could he find his place in this new environment?

By a strange sequence of circumstances he had become attached to King Agon's column, and serving the king's interests had become his main focus. He had a new purpose, and he would find ways of fulfilling it. Being fully committed to Agon's cause, he intended to follow through with all of his energy, in whatever ways the king permitted him.

Nevertheless, other changes had crept into his life, sneaking in behind his new focus. The changes disturbed him, and he had no desire to pretend otherwise.

Satisfying reasons for his change of purpose had never presented themselves. But his new commitment was not founded on reason, so what was the point in trying to understand it?

One issue weighed heavily on him. He already knew how he would respond if asked to do something he didn't believe in. But he had an uncomfortable feeling that his principles had already been put to the test and that he had been found wanting.

Unshakable though his commitment to King Agon might be, it felt profoundly wrong. A new and unfamiliar fault line had opened inside him.

Difficulties and challenges weren't new for him—throughout his entire life he had been confronted by adversity. Yet he'd somehow discovered what he was made to do and found a satisfying way of doing it. Since reaching his adult years he had been given almost unlimited opportunity to fulfill his calling, always in support of a cause he believed in.

With that had come an underlying sense of contentment, a serenity that sustained him through the darkest times.

He was contented no longer. He wondered if he ever could be again.

40

———

Thomas huddled with Amyra, peering out at Agon's camp. Fires twinkled in the night between the tents that now straddled the road.

The havoc wreaked by the cattle was obvious even from a distance. The observers had no idea what to make of the stampede. Did it have a natural cause, or did others besides the Aen-ur have a motive for disrupting the king's progress?

Whatever its origin, the disruption had given the Aen-ur valuable breathing space.

They had taken seriously the warning delivered through Ennawi. The most vulnerable among them had already been removed from the area likely to be targeted by King Agon's soldiers.

Those trained to fight were another matter. Their leaders had decided that the Aen-ur would no longer allow themselves to be lightly pushed aside. They were ready to do battle for their homes as well as their lives.

Aen-ur soldiers had taken up positions facing a river, and they did not intend to make it easy for the Rogandans to cross the natural barrier. If Agon's men succeeded in spite of their best efforts, they planned to lead the attackers away from their dwellings and into an ambush.

Thomas and Haldek had been invited to offer suggestions for the defense. Haldek had excused himself from the discussion, and the Aen-ur respected his unwillingness to fight his own countrymen. Thomas had declined simply because he knew he had nothing to offer.

Amyra had told the Aen-ur she was willing to fight alongside them. She had been rebuffed. They insisted that the fighting be left to those trained for it. The defensive preparations of the Aen-ur were well advanced, and it seemed Amyra had little more to contribute toward them than Thomas.

The person the Aen-ur really needed was Will, and Thomas found himself hoping fervently that Agon wasn't planning on using Will's strategic genius for his own purposes.

Thomas returned his full attention to Agon's camp. Amyra crouched beside him, restless and agitated.

"How are we going to get him out of there?" she asked fiercely.

With little else useful to do, it was not surprising to Thomas that her attention was now fully absorbed with Will's predicament. Crucial as the information delivered via Ennawi had been, it still rankled with Amyra that their careful plan to extract Will had failed. She had been especially baffled by Nistinaa's assertion that Will himself had refused the rescue.

Thomas guessed that Will believed himself to be already ensnared by the Stone of Authority. Amyra understood the implications of that as well as Thomas did. Nevertheless, the logic of switching the rescue to Nistinaa and Ennawi failed utterly to satisfy her.

"I'm going in there," Amyra abruptly announced.

Thomas stared at her in alarm. "What do you mean? You'll end up captured yourself!"

"I don't care. I'm not going to just sit here waiting for something to happen."

She got up purposefully. "Where's Haldek?"

Thomas jumped up himself. "Wait! Let's think this through!"

But it was too late. She had already gone, looking for Haldek.

It left Thomas with a huge dilemma. Should he go with her?

Will had brought him here so he could use the stone to discern Agon's plans. Thanks to Ennawi, he'd already been able to do that. He could think of no further compelling reason to venture into the Rogandan camp with the intent of using the stone. And he had no skill with weapons, so he would be of little use if it came to a fight.

Taking the stone within reach of Agon would be a huge risk, and it didn't take him long to conclude that the risks far outweighed any likely benefit he could offer Will.

His decision was made. If Amyra did go to the camp, he wouldn't be going with her. He could only hope that his decision truly had been based on common sense and not simply on cowardice.

Before long his self doubts were interrupted by the arrival of Amyra. Haldek was following in her wake, but he didn't look comfortable.

"Are you sure you want to do this?" Thomas asked Amyra.

"Yes," she said impatiently. "And don't try to talk me out of it."

"I won't be coming with you," Thomas said awkwardly.

She frowned at him. "Of course not! What would be the point?"

Seeing his reaction, she softened immediately. "I didn't mean it like that, Thomas. Both of us know there are plenty of reasons why you shouldn't even consider a risk like that."

He nodded his agreement, but she had already turned away.

"Haldek is going to get me past the sentries."

"I will *try* to get you past the sentries," Haldek corrected her. "I want to see Will rescued as much as you do, but I need to say again that I think this is a bad idea!"

"I fully understand that," she replied, waving a hand dismissively. "But the Aen-ur can't help—they're distracted planning their defense —and neither of you have any better ideas. I'm going."

"What will you do if you do find Will?" Thomas asked.

"I'm taking a couple of cloaks." She showed them a dark bundle she was carrying. "We'll put them on and wait for an opportunity to slip past the sentries."

It sounded more like a rough idea than a plan to Thomas. "They'll be on high alert, especially after the stampede. And they're expecting to go into action soon as well," he protested.

"They won't have fully recovered from the chaos of the stampede," she countered. "There will never be a better time."

She was determined, and Thomas could see no way to persuade her otherwise. Nevertheless, he made a last ditch attempt. "What does your mother think about you doing this?"

Amyra immediately became guarded. "She isn't here to ask. But it's my decision."

Thomas could think of nothing further to say. He wondered if little Tammi might one day grow up to be a firebrand like Amyra. He had mixed feelings about such a prospect.

And then they were gone. Thomas stared at their departing backs with deep foreboding.

DAWN HAD BARELY BROKEN when a group of guards appeared at Lady Ona's tent calling for her attention.

"What is it?" Lady Ona asked irritably. The effort of organizing the clean up after the previous day's stampede had kept her up well into the night, and even when she did go to her bed she had slept badly.

Two of the guards stepped into the entrance of her tent. A young woman was struggling between them, but they held her firmly in their grasp.

"We found her snooping around the camp, My Lady," one of the men reported. "She can't give any account of what she's doing. She was carrying these." He held up a couple of cloaks in his other hand.

The young woman had now transferred her baleful gaze to Lady Ona, and the noblewoman examined her thoughtfully.

"Do you understand me?" Lady Ona asked in Rogandan.

The young woman hesitated before nodding once.

"Are you prepared to be sensible if I tell these men to release you?"

Once more she paused before nodding.

"Release her," she told the men, "but remain outside the tent. If she leaves without my permission, kill her."

The young woman's eyes went wide, indicating clearly that she had understood. She stood there quietly enough when the guards released her.

"So who might you be, and what are you doing here?" Lady Ona asked her curtly.

No answer was forthcoming.

"Do you have a tongue in your head? Or are you mute like Ennawi?"

At the name of the missing slave a flicker of recognition passed across the young woman's eyes before she could prevent it. So she knew something of Ennawi. Lady Ona betrayed no indication of having detected the response, but she noted it with considerable interest.

Apparently her captive had little ability to hide her reactions. Lady Ona decided to take a gamble. "I suppose you've come to rescue Will Prentis," she said casually.

A deep blush came instantly to the face of the young woman.

Lady Ona burst into delighted laughter. "You're adorable!" she said. "You must surely be the most satisfying person I've interrogated in months. Your answers are written all over your face, even without you uttering a word."

Once again the young woman's face was flushed, this time with anger.

"Why should we be enemies?" Lady Ona asked soothingly, beaming her most charming smile. "I'll tell you my name—I'm Lady Ona. What's yours?"

Her initiative was greeted with disdain by the young woman.

"Very well, then," Lady Ona said coldly. "In that case I might as well have you executed immediately. Guards!"

"Wait!" the young woman called hastily.

The guards had appeared at the entrance to the tent once more, and Lady Ona held up a finger indicating they should wait.

"My name...is Dahra," the young woman said hesitantly.

Lady Ona dismissed the guards with a flick of her bejeweled finger.

"That's better," she purred. "There's no need for unpleasantness between us. So, Dahra, what brings you to King Agon's camp? And before you answer, I already know you've seen Ennawi, and you're here looking for Will Prentis. So don't imagine you can treat me like a fool."

"I do know Ennawi, although I can't imagine how you might know him," she replied. "We grew up together in the same village. It's true that he doesn't have much to say, although I certainly wouldn't call him mute."

Lady Ona watched her performance with real admiration. She was smooth. "And what about Will Prentis? Did you grow up with him too?" This time she spoke in Arvenian.

'Dahra'—it almost certainly wasn't her name—answered fluently in the same language. "No. I met him on the road. My family are traders. I heard he was somewhere here in the camp, so I came looking for him."

"And is he a trader too?" This time she had switched to the language of Lestanor.

The girl followed the language switch without missing a beat. "So he told me." She shrugged. "In case you were wondering about my language skills, traders need to be fluent in many languages."

She was smooth indeed.

"And who is Dahra?" asked Lady Ona. "Your best friend?" No response. "Your sister?" She paused again. "Your mother?"

Once again the girl gave herself away.

"So your mother, then. And what's your real name?"

The young woman sighed in resignation. "It's Amyra."

This time she was telling the truth. "A lovely name," affirmed

Lady Ona with a smile. The poor girl had no idea who she was dealing with.

The nature of the girl's relationship with Will Prentis was not yet clear, but there were ways to answer that question too.

"How friendly have you become with Will Prentis?" she asked innocently.

The girl did not respond, which was itself telling.

"I found him to be a good lover," Lady Ona offered breezily. "At first, anyway. I soon tired of him."

Amyra had almost gone purple. She was barely containing her rage.

This situation was becoming more interesting by the minute. Lady Ona had failed to get access to Will Prentis, and she never satisfied herself with failure. The more she pondered it, the more promising the girl's arrival appeared.

"You came to see Will Prentis," she said. "Let's go visit him."

The girl still hadn't recovered from Lady Ona's earlier announcement. The noblewoman ignored the wide-eyed look that came to her face and headed to the entrance of the tent. "Follow us," she told the guards. "Kill her if she tries to get away."

Turning back to Amyra, she beckoned with a hand. "Follow me."

Then she set off toward Will's tent. She knew exactly where to find it.

Normally his tent was pitched beside the king's, but since the cows appeared nothing could be said to be normal.

Lady Ona herself had survived the stampede as much by luck as anything. After her carriage had been overturned, a couple of hefty cows crashed into it, breaking it apart. Somehow managing to avoid their writhing bodies, she had crawled free of the carriage and cowered between its rear wheels until the danger had passed.

Amyra caught up to her as they walked. "Where did the cows come from?" she asked boldly. Lady Ona smiled to herself, guessing that the girl was attempting to recover her poise before they reached Will Prentis.

"An assassin arranged it," she said matter-of-factly. "He planned to take advantage of the distraction to kill the king. He failed."

The look on Amyra's face made it clear this was news to her. She clearly had no awareness at all of the plot.

"Will Prentis defended the king himself. In fact he was the one who eventually killed the assassin," she added.

Lady Ona couldn't resist a self-satisfied smirk when she saw Amyra's reaction. There was little doubt that any remaining poise had now deserted the girl completely.

Will Prentis had already risen when the two women arrived, but he hadn't left his tent. His eyes went wide when he caught sight of Amyra, and both of their faces turned scarlet. Will's reaction in particular was more delicious than Lady Ona had dared hope. It was plainly obvious that he would do nothing to put Amyra at risk.

She couldn't resist gloating. The situation promised to be very interesting indeed.

"I believe that you and Amyra are good friends, Will," she began.

He tore his gaze away from the girl with difficulty, his eyes narrowing when he turned his full attention to her captor.

Lady Ona's heart skipped a beat when their eyes met. Will Prentis was not her usual helpless conquest. This was the man who had overseen the destruction of the Rogandan army. She realized abruptly she'd needed a reminder of that. She would need to tread delicately.

He would become a dangerous enemy, the more so if she was ever foolish enough to let him conclude he had nothing to lose. She couldn't threaten his life either—Agon would never tolerate her having him killed.

At the same time danger was not a deterrent to Lady Ona. High risk behavior had always excited her.

"I'll have her killed in a heartbeat," she told him casually. "Whenever it suits me. You know I'm not bluffing."

She paused to let her words sink in. "I'm willing to give you an opportunity to save her though." She gave him her best coquettish smile. "Let me have you for the night, and she'll still be alive in the morning." Then she let her face go hard. "Refuse and she dies right now."

Will Prentis stepped toward Amyra, his face calm. "I'm sorry, Lady Ona," he said, "but any decision about her fate is not in your hands. The king alone will decide."

With that he took Amyra's arm and led her away, heading for the tent of the king.

Lady Ona watched them go, too stunned to respond. It had never occurred to her that Will Prentis would risk taking Amyra before the king. Apparently he intended to do just that.

AMYRA HEAVED a sigh of relief as they walked away from Lady Ona. "I was a bit worried back there, Will," she admitted with a shudder.

"You had good reason to be," he replied. "Lady Ona is a dangerous woman."

He glanced back over his shoulder in the direction of the noblewoman. "I've seen enough to know she is also a self-serving liar. Don't believe anything she told you."

She stole a glance at him, hoping it was true.

Will seemed so normal. And he had rescued her from Lady Ona. "What will we do now?" she asked.

He eyed her sternly. "That depends on why you came here."

She grinned back at him. "To help you escape of course."

"I was afraid you might say that," he replied sadly.

She stared at him, struggling to grasp the import of his words. Her eyes grew wider as she saw the look on his face and began to fully understand at last how the Stone of Authority had changed him.

"You're not committed to the interests of King Agon," said Will. "You've come here to undermine him."

Her heart began to pound in her chest. She opened her mouth to speak, but no words came out.

"I'm taking you to the king," he told her, "and he will pronounce judgment over you. I will plead on your behalf for leniency, but you will have no choice but to submit to his decision, whatever it might be."

41

———————

Amyra followed Will with dragging steps, overcome by the horror of his transformation. She paid no attention to where they were going, and she dared not imagine what the outcome might be when she stood before the king.

Barely a few minutes had passed when an elaborate structure rose up before them. Guards stood outside at attention, and there could be no doubt that they had reached the royal tent.

The guards ignored Will, and he walked in without waiting to be announced. That simple act set the seal on Amyra's despair.

She lifted her chin defiantly, determined not to go meekly.

King Agon stood before her, but he was not what Amyra had expected. He appeared afflicted.

Seeing Will, he managed a wan smile. "Ah, Will Prentis. I have just issued the order to finally destroy the Aen-ur. You were not here to witness the moment!"

The king's words snapped Amyra completely out of her misery. Fierce anger rose up in her as she thought of the fate in store for the peaceful men, women, and children of the Aen-ur—people she had come to love and respect.

Agon's voice had slowed as he spoke. He appeared exhausted, and when he spoke again his speech had become slurred and erratic. "My men have already moved into position," he said, "and the local barons have added to their number. They have been waiting only for their commander, Wannyk, and he has now ridden away to join them. The attack will begin...a little before noon."

The king finally seemed to notice her. "You have brought someone. A woman. She must wait...I am ailing." He passed a shaky hand across his brow.

Amyra's brows drew together as she peered at the king. He had been swaying unsteadily, and he sank abruptly onto the small throne positioned behind him.

"What is happening to me, Will?" he asked. "You must help me. There are so few I can trust."

Will bellowed immediately for the guards. One of them quickly bustled into the tent. "Fetch the royal physician! Urgently!" Will commanded. "Hurry, man!"

The guard bolted.

Will approached the king. "Your arm, Your Majesty?"

Agon held out an arm that appeared swollen almost to twice its normal size. Will began unwrapping the bandage that covered the arm. Careful as Will was, the king cried out in pain more than once before the arm was released.

Amyra gasped when she caught a glimpse of what had emerged. Black and blue flesh surrounded an enormous weeping sore. The king blanched at the sight of it; only Will appeared unshaken.

A man hurried into the tent. The look of relief on Will's face suggested he was the royal physician.

The king's head had begun to loll drunkenly from side to side.

The physician went pale when he saw the arm. "It was the assassin's knife," he murmured to Will. "I fear it was tipped with some kind of slow-acting poison." He raised his arms in frustration. "I wanted to treat it at the time, but he would only let me bandage it."

Will nodded reassuringly. "What can you do for him?"

The physician checked the king's vital signs carefully. Then he stepped back and slowly shook his head. "Nothing," he whispered. "Nothing at all. It won't be long now."

Agon took a shallow breath then released a slow sigh. His head sank to his chest, and his arms slumped by his side.

Amyra looked on in stunned amazement. From her earliest memories, the very name of King Agon of Rogand had struck terror into the hearts of his enemies and his subjects alike. Absolute ruler, dreaded tyrant, persecutor of the Aen-ur—he lay dead before her. Once all-powerful, he had suffered the same fate as the most wretched of his subjects.

Everything seemed to happen at once. The physician reacted first, turning on his heel and scampering out of the tent.

Two of the guards peered curiously inside to see what was happening. Seeing Agon slumped on the throne, they ventured further into the tent. Amyra saw their eyes go wide when they saw his arm.

Leaning toward them, Amyra said in a tense voice, "The plague has taken the king. It is highly contagious! The physician has fled."

The men looked first at the body of the king, then at her. Then they dashed from the tent in terror, shrieking at the top of their voices. "The plague! It's the plague! Run for your lives!"

The growing commotion outside suggested that chaos was spreading quickly.

Oblivious to it all, Will stood unmoving, holding his head. A stricken look had appeared on his face. He looked up into her eyes. "Amyra!" he said shakily, as if he had just noticed her. "I've just woken from a terrible nightmare."

Ignoring him, she hurried to the king and began running her fingers over his clothing. She tried hard not to notice his bloated arm.

"Whatever are you doing?" he asked. He sounded as much dazed as bemused.

"I'm making sure none of this happens again," she replied tersely.

Several anxious minutes passed before she straightened again, a triumphant look on her face. "I have it!"

In her hand she held up a thin gray stone colored with flecks of red. She didn't doubt for a moment that it was the Stone of Authority.

It suddenly occurred to her that Will might put it to better use. "Would you like to have it?" she asked him.

He shuddered. He didn't need to speak to make it clear what he thought about that idea.

"We need to go!" she told him firmly. "Agon might be dead, but his soldiers are still planning to attack the Aen-ur. We have to stop them somehow."

Amyra strode purposefully from the tent with Will trailing along behind her. It was apparent that he had yet to fully emerge from his stupor.

No guards remained at their posts outside the tent, and few people were visible anywhere nearby. Then a familiar figure swung into view around the side of a nearby tent. It was Lady Ona, shadowed by four guards. Amyra's hand closed instinctively over the stone.

"What's this about the king dying of the plague?" Lady Ona demanded suspiciously.

Amyra jerked her head in the direction of the royal tent.

The noblewoman's guards looked decidedly restless. She glared at them. "Wait here. And don't let these two out of your sight!"

The guards dutifully clustered around Will and Amyra. Lady Ona disappeared into the tent.

"It's highly contagious!" whispered Amyra to the guards. "The royal physician fled in terror, and so did the royal guards." She pointed into the tent. "If she goes anywhere near him, she'll catch it, and you will too. None of you will see another dawn."

That was enough for the guards. All four of them turned and ran.

Amyra saw no reason to wait around either, and she grabbed Will's arm to urge him forward. Before they had gone more than a couple of steps, Lady Ona reappeared. Amyra turned to face her.

She regarded them coolly. "It was the assassin, wasn't it? I have some experience of poisons myself."

Amyra stared back at her impassively.

"So where did this story of a plague come from?" the noble-woman asked, her eyes narrowed.

Amyra didn't bother to answer.

Lady Ona's gaze flicked over Will, still trying to master himself after his sudden reawakening, and settled on her. "I see," she said.

A knife appeared in Lady Ona's hand. Amyra flushed with anger when she saw that it was her own weapon, taken from her when she had been captured. She glared at the noblewoman.

"This situation is by no means a disaster. It raises such interesting possibilities," said Lady Ona, advancing toward her. "The king has no offspring of course. Someone entirely different will need to ascend the throne. Someone energetic and capable. Someone like me."

Amyra peered frantically around for a weapon to defend herself. A discarded shield caught her eye, and she grabbed it, slipping her arm hastily through the straps. She barely managed to raise it before Lady Ona reached her.

The noblewoman clearly had extensive training with a knife, and Amyra saw that even if she'd been armed herself, she wouldn't have survived for long. The shield was all that saved her in the first frantic moments of the struggle.

The shield was almost certainly a ceremonial item—each of the guards had been carrying one when Amyra arrived at the royal tent—and it was lighter and smaller than the shields carried by regular soldiers. Nevertheless, it had been fashioned from metal and was solidly constructed. With it she was able to keep Lady Ona at bay, and even to push her back. But she could think of no way to disable her opponent or finish the fight.

The noblewoman abruptly turned aggressive, thrusting forward in a series of lunges that forced Amyra back. Unable to risk looking anywhere except at her attacker, Amyra tripped on something behind her and fell heavily to the ground.

Before she could move a muscle, Lady Ona was standing over her, one foot firmly planted on the shield to prevent her from raising it.

A cruel look covered the noblewoman's face. "You were pathetically easy to manipulate," she gloated. "Your interference was beginning to annoy me, but it ends here."

She raised Amyra's knife for a killing stroke.

Waiting helplessly for the end, Amyra heard a dull thud. Lady Ona slumped senseless to the ground.

Will appeared in her place, his eyes clear at last. Reaching down a hand, he helped her to her feet.

Amyra stared down at her enemy. "Is it safe to simply leave her?" she asked, making no attempt to soften the hostility in her tone.

Will shook his head. "No, it isn't. She's a dangerous woman, and she could do a great deal of harm if she did manage to ascend the throne."

"Is that likely?"

He shrugged. "She's immensely capable, and I've met few people so devious." He stared down at her prone form. "But even so, I couldn't bring myself to knife her in the back when I could easily disable her. And I won't kill her now when she's defenseless."

Unable to think of a suitable response, Amyra reached down for her knife and wrenched it from the noblewoman's hand. She felt anything but satisfied, but she was no more willing than Will to kill a person while they were unconscious.

She shot an awkward glance at Will as she turned away. "You didn't, did you?" she asked.

"Do what?" asked Will, a puzzled frown on his face.

"Bed her. She told me you did."

"Never!" he replied vehemently.

The revulsion on his face answered her question as plainly as his words. Embarrassed at having asked, she felt her face coloring deeply.

Will didn't notice. "We need to find horses," he said, his eyes roving among the tents.

In their haste to escape the plague someone must have released the horses, because a few of the animals could be seen nearby. Approaching one of them, Amyra found it already saddled. Having secured the reins, she reached forward to shorten the stirrups.

"Amyra!"

The warning shout caused her to spin around. She found herself confronted by the vengeful face of Lady Ona, her hair matted with blood and a crazed look in her eye. Once more she held a knife, raised high and ready to strike.

The killing blow never came. Her eyes went wide with surprise as the knife dropped from her fingers. Blood seeped slowly through the clothing below her ribs.

Amyra stepped nimbly aside as Lady Ona pitched forward. She lay still with a knife protruding from her back. The horse threw back its head and stamped its feet in alarm.

Will sprinted up. "I would never let her kill you," he said breathlessly. He stared down at Lady Ona for a moment, then knelt to examine her. "She's dead," he reported.

Amyra gazed at him unsteadily. One of her hands still enclosed the Stone of Authority, and the other tightly gripped the reins of the horse. She was leaning heavily on the horse for support.

She wanted to throw herself into his arms, but an uncharacteristic timidity paralyzed her, and she couldn't move.

His brows drew together tightly as he stared at her. "Did she harm you?" he asked fiercely.

She shook her head.

He gazed into her eyes. What was he thinking and feeling?

Her heart knew what she wanted, but her limbs had let her down. She stared helplessly at him, desperately hoping he would take the step for her.

He was the one who looked away first. "I'll find a horse," he said at last. "We don't have much time."

42

———

Amyra and Will rode as fast as they dared, skirting the fringes of Agon's army as they headed for the river where the Aen-ur intended to make their stand.

Amyra's thoughts were a confused jumble. Everything had started going wrong almost from the moment she blundered into the Rogandan camp. And yet—impossibly—she had achieved her goal. Will Prentis was free, and riding beside her. More than that, King Agon, the scourge of the Aen-ur, was dead, along with the manipulative schemer Lady Ona.

The Stone of Authority disturbed her the most. She had glimpsed its terrible power—she remembered vividly the despair she had felt the moment Will decided to turn her over to Agon. The look in his eyes still haunted her.

Now he was free of it.

She had every reason to feel exhilarated. Instead she felt strangely deflated.

The stone now rested in a tiny leather pouch she had discovered at Agon's camp. She had tucked the pouch into her bodice. Apparently she was the stone's new guardian. What did that mean? She tried hard to remember anything at all from the scroll read to them by Will, but details eluded her. She hadn't taken the scroll seriously enough to commit any of it to memory.

Thomas had believed every word, and so had Will. How must it have felt for Will to know he was coming under the power of the Stone of Authority, knowing he was slowly being bent to the will of a man like Agon?

Stray thoughts came unbidden to her mind. Could the bearer of the stone use it to compel someone to love them? She blushed at the thought, immediately rejecting it as the dangerous fancy she knew it to be. Whatever she might do with the stone, she knew she could never use it on another person. Not for any reason. She had seen the effects all too clearly.

The sound of water could be heard ahead, and Amyra's thoughts were drawn back to their immediate circumstances. She was leading them to a location upriver from the place where the two armies would confront each other. It wouldn't be possible to cross the river at her destination of choice, but the elevation would afford an excellent outlook of the entire area.

Only a few minutes passed before they emerged at the top of a series of rapids. Below them they could clearly see Aen-ur soldiers spread out on the opposite side of the river.

They had apparently arrived barely in time, because horns sounded, and the first of the Rogandans came into view across the river from them. It took no more than a glance to see that the Rogandans far outnumbered the Aen-ur.

"I recognize this place," Will said grimly. "Agon tricked me into giving his commander a battle plan."

"What can we do?" she asked miserably.

He studied her quietly for a moment. "You have the stone," he suggested.

"How will that help?" she asked.

"You won't be able to influence any of the people," he replied, "it takes too long. But the scroll did say that the stone bends all created things to the will of the bearer."

"What does that mean?"

He shrugged helplessly. "I don't know."

"Does *created things* only mean things that are *living*?"

He raised his eyebrows. "You'll have to find that out for yourself."

Retrieving the stone, she held it in her hand, trying to imagine how it might be possible to use it.

As she glanced down at the rival armies, it struck her that something wasn't right. Amyra knew that cheers and battle cries could usually be heard as men prepared for battle. Both armies were completely silent. She knew this fight was deadly serious for the Aen-ur. That might account for their silence. But the Rogandans?

She looked at Will quizzically. "Why are they so quiet?"

"The Rogandans haven't come for a battle," he replied grimly. "They're here to carry out a massacre."

As he spoke, the Rogandan lines began to move forward, quickly reaching the river. The first of the soldiers were already wading in.

Something rose up inside her. The Aen-ur did not deserve this. They were a people of peace. She and her mother had come to them vulnerable, and the Aen-ur gave them a home and a future, pointing them to hope.

This must not be allowed to happen. She shook her head in denial.

The water below her lurched and swayed in response to her agitation, and she stared at it in amazement. She raised a hand, and water sprayed into the air.

Clearing her mind, she moved her hands about randomly. Nothing happened. As soon as she focused her will on the water once more, it responded to her intent.

She was painfully unpracticed, and there was no time to experiment. Gulping in great breaths of air, she tried to steady herself. Then she thrust out both hands as if holding back the river. The flow slowed at once to a trickle, water welling up as if a dam had suddenly appeared in the river. Water was soon spilling out over the riverbank, splashing around their legs.

Downriver the Rogandan soldiers paused, peering upward to find out where the water had gone.

Amyra abruptly dropped her arms, and water thundered down over the rapids in a flash flood that swept down the river.

The Aen-ur fighters were far enough back from the river to be largely unaffected. The Rogandan soldiers were forced to scramble to safety. She could only imagine what they must be thinking. Swooping her hands toward them, she sent a howling wind that pushed them further from the river. The Rogandans must have withdrawn immediately, because none of them at all were now visible along the river. Stilling the wind abruptly, she began to wave her hands back and forth, focusing on the trees.

She had no way to see what was happening, but if she was achieving her purpose, the trees were waving their branches violently, slapping at any soldiers who wandered within reach. Creepers would be winding across every path, tripping the soldiers as they fled. Even the wild creatures of the forest would be haranguing the soldiers as they passed, snarling or howling as if demented.

After half an hour of this she collapsed in total exhaustion.

Returning her attention to her surroundings with an effort, she noticed that water was flowing normally across the rapids as if nothing had happened. Her wet feet, though, still provided a tangible reminder of the climactic events that had taken place.

Glancing at Will, she saw open awe on his face. "What have you been doing since the water and the wind?" he asked.

She closed her eyes and took a few unsteady breaths before responding. "I've been using the trees, the bushes, the creepers, and the animals," she said wearily. "To eject the Rogandans from the forest. If I did it right, all of them will have survived. But they'll be convinced the forest is haunted. I'd be amazed if they're ever willing to go anywhere near the Aen-ur again."

Admiration shone in his eyes. "You're remarkable, Amyra!"

She returned a weak smile, too spent to respond.

He shook his head in wonder. "You routed an army with nothing more than the Stone of Authority."

She was no less bemused. How was it even possible?

"We need to find Thomas and Haldek," he said. "And Rhillyon. They'll be worried about us. As soon as you think you're capable of riding, I'll help you onto your horse."

"CAN I SPEAK WITH YOU, DAHRA?" Thomas had been dreading this moment, but he knew he could put it off no longer.

The older woman looked at him curiously before nodding and leading him to a quiet place among the trees. She sat down on a fallen log and gazed up at him.

The laughter of children and the sounds of normal life penetrated faintly to their location, but Dahra had chosen a setting that seemed to radiate tranquility.

With Agon dead and the Rogandans repelled, the Aen-ur had celebrated wildly for a couple of days. Since then everything had quickly returned to normal.

For some, nothing would ever be the same.

"You've been working with Ennawi," he ventured.

She nodded. "He's a sad case. His spirit was broken a very long time ago. Nistinaa has been trying to help, but there is only so much I can do for him."

"You were able to help people in the past," he said. "Much more than you can now."

She gazed at him in her quiet way, but she didn't speak.

"I think you've guessed, haven't you?" he said. When she still didn't reply, he added, "Would it help if I call you Sheylha, the Seer?"

Her face went pale.

"I have the Stone of Knowing now—the stone you once called your own."

He took a deep breath. "I didn't know you existed before we came here. I was touching the stone when I first saw you, because I wanted to understand people's intentions. I saw that you'd held the stone for many years. Until you got rid of it."

She didn't seem able to speak.

"I tried to tell Amyra, you know," he said awkwardly. "Ahnya as she was. I tried to tell her that her father didn't abandon her. I'm not sure that it helped."

The anguished look in her eyes made him wince.

"I'm not very good at this kind of thing," he said remorsefully. "My wife Elena is much better at it. It's remarkable how much she's achieved, even with so little practice." He shook his head. "But she isn't here."

He took another deep breath to steady himself. "You, though—you are here, and you're a master. You worked with the stone over many years, and it's astonishing how much you were able to do for people."

All trace of expression had vanished from her face, and her eyes were guarded.

He sighed. "I'm not using it right now," he assured her. "When I first found it I abused it badly. Eventually I decided not to use it on people I know. Everything I discovered about you was from our first meeting—I haven't used it on you since."

He passed a hand over his eyes. "What I saw shook me to the core though," he admitted. "I haven't been able to get it out of my mind."

Her face had grown calm again, but still she found nothing to say.

He knew what he needed to do. For so long he had felt trapped by the stone, bemoaning his inability to ever break free of it. Now the opportunity had come, and he felt like he was about to lose a vital organ.

He shook his head and set his jaw. This wasn't about him. He had seen into Ennawi's mind, witnessed the full extent of the abuse the slave had endured over the years. No one apart from Dahra had even a chance of helping him. Thomas could never live with himself if he refused her the opportunity.

The choice was clear—he could play his part in repairing a lifetime's worth of abuse, or he could selfishly hoard the stone, to use or not use as he saw fit.

He sighed deeply. Reaching for the chain, he withdrew it from beneath his clothing and pulled it over his head. As his hand closed over the stone he was careful to look away.

Heart pounding, he opened his hand and held it out.

Out of the corner of his eye he could see that she hadn't moved.

"Take it!" he insisted.

After an agonizing delay she slowly stretched out her hand.

He took one more deep breath in a futile attempt to calm himself. "It's yours," he said firmly. "I want you to have it."

As she took the stone from his hand, his eyes found their way to her again. He felt suddenly naked, and heat rose up to cover his face.

Her eyes had closed briefly when she took the stone. Opening them again, she stared directly at him. He steadied himself under her gaze, finally managing to bring his racing heart under control.

After a long moment she abruptly dropped the stone into her lap. A flush came to her face.

"You can have it back now," she said, although she made no move to return it.

He shook his head. "You know why I've given it to you. You need to help Ennawi."

Slowly her face grew calm again, and she nodded her head.

He opened his mouth to explain how she could rotate the clasp to control the contact of the stone with her skin. Then he remembered that she didn't need to be told.

"I didn't entirely believe you, Thomas," she admitted. "About not using the stone once you got to know someone." Her face briefly reddened once more, and she wouldn't meet his eyes. "You've been much more respectful of others than I ever was. But then you already know that."

He shook his head. "You only ever used it to help people. You never abused it the way I did."

Her face was noncommittal. "Perhaps not. But I intruded constantly on people's thoughts without their knowledge. I didn't even spare my own husband. Almost until the end he had no idea what I was doing."

She shook her head. "It was still a form of abuse, for all that I tried to use it for good. I've had many years to reach that conclusion for myself, but until you came along I couldn't see it. Perhaps I wasn't willing to."

Her face set in determination. "I will try to help Ennawi. But starting from now, I won't knowingly intrude on people again."

<hr>

HAVING RECEIVED a request from Dahra to join her at her hut, Will made his way there with considerable curiosity. She met him at the door and ushered him inside.

He studied her furtively as he followed her in. Her daughter's resemblance to her was striking, although he decided that Amyra had fire and she had grace. If Dahra had ever been as fiery as her daughter, she had long since mellowed.

"Please!" said the older woman, waving him to a seat.

He obediently sat where she directed him.

"Tell me about your limp, Will," she said.

He shrugged. "It's an old battle wound. The lower half of my body was crushed under a horse."

"Does your back cause you pain?"

He nodded.

"Constantly?"

He shrugged again.

She rolled her eyes. "Men! Some of you seem to think a battered body is a virtue. The more damaged, the better."

He didn't respond.

"Can I examine you?"

He gazed at her uncertainly for a moment, then nodded.

"Take off your top, and lie face down on that table," she told him, pointing to a flat surface covered by a blanket. It stood just below waist height.

He hesitated for a moment before doing as she requested. The situation brought back uncomfortable memories of his introduction to Lady Ona, and he felt unusually vulnerable.

A large pot of steaming water stood by the fireplace, and she gingerly drew a blanket from it. After folding the blanket many times, she placed it into an empty tub between two thick pieces of wood and squeezed out the hot water.

After a couple more minutes she brought the still steaming blanket over to him. After touching it to her face to test the temperature, she placed it carefully across his back. After the initial shock, the warmth felt very soothing.

She lifted the blanket to expose the lower part of his back. "This is going to hurt," she warned. "Probably quite a lot. Rest assured that I won't be doing you any damage."

She was soon prodding and pressing around his lower spine. Her warning was not overstated—some of the probing left him clenching his teeth to manage the pain.

Eventually she slapped him lightly on the back. "You're a tough one," she told him jovially. "You can dress again. I want to see you again in three days."

She spent a few minutes describing some exercises. "Do each of them once a day. And don't come back with excuses about why you didn't find the time!" She gazed at him with an eyebrow raised threateningly.

"Thanks," he said. "I think." He nodded to her, then turned to go.

"Will!" she called softly.

He looked back over his shoulder.

"Follow your heart," she told him, an unreadable look on her face.

He faced her again, frowning. "What does that mean?"

A wry smile came to her lips. "You do know what your heart is, don't you?" she teased.

When he didn't respond, she sighed. "You lead men, Will Prentis, and you devise strategy. You're very good at it. But a different kind of skill is needed for matters of the heart."

He felt himself blushing like an awkward youth. Was it possible she'd somehow guessed his feelings for her daughter?

She looked at him seriously. "You're actually much more capable than many men. You know how to build effective partnerships with difficult people, people who have very different backgrounds and purposes from your own." She grinned knowingly at him. "That particular skill happens to have very broad application."

He didn't know what to say.

"There's just one other thing you need to master," she told him, serious once more.

She had his full attention, and he tried hard not to look too eager.

"You need to learn to say what you're feeling. Women like that."

He stared at her wide-eyed.

"It isn't exactly *what* you say that matters," she assured him. "The fact that you're making the effort will count for a lot."

He stood unmoving, his thoughts whirling chaotically.

"Off you go!" she ordered firmly, waving her hands to shoo him out.

Jolted unceremoniously back to reality, he spun around and hurried out of her hut.

Back pain had been part of Will's daily experience for years. Like his limp, he had come to accept it as normal. Although Dahra's efforts had left him wincing, he didn't actually feel worse when he left her. And after a day or two he began to feel noticeably better.

After his second visit he began to catch glimpses of a quality of life he had long forgotten, one he had believed gone forever. And her efforts had already begun to improve his limp.

She was changing his life.

"Dahra, I don't know how to repay you," he told her seriously.

"Nonsense," she replied. "No repayment is necessary." She paused. "There might be something you can do for me though."

He gazed expectantly at her.

"I'll let you know when the time comes," she told him vaguely.

He left her with a shrug.

Spending time with Dahra inevitably set him thinking about her daughter.

He had completed everything he came to Rogand to do. Far more, thanks to the contributions of Rhillyon and others. Amyra, too, had played a key role at the end.

No Rogandan army would be attempting to force the border with Arvenon now. No further reason remained to delay his return to King Steffan.

No reason except Amyra. He would not leave Rogand without making an attempt to win her. He couldn't pretend he felt confident, but he had never been one to shy away from difficulties. And he wasn't entirely without hope. She had pursued him into Agon's camp, almost with disastrous consequences for herself. Did that mean anything?

He knew one of the biggest challenges of his life lay before him. Dahra could say all she wanted about following his heart, but he had more basic problems to overcome first. From his first meeting with Amyra he had succeeded in alienating her, ignoring her advice and bypassing her as translator. Opportunities for irritation had only multiplied from there. And while he found her hopelessly appealing, she had made a point of telling him to his face that she found him unattractive.

A much bigger problem had been weighing heavily on him though. Almost immediately after taking the Stone of Authority, she had discovered how to bend it to her purpose. She made it appear effortless—the memory of her mastery still filled him with awe. With the stone she had rallied nature to end a battle before it began.

The invaders had been routed without loss of life on either side, and her achievement confronted him with a difficult truth. If he had been the one to awaken nature, he would not have hesitated to turn it against the Rogandans.

He was a man of blood. Multitudes had died as a result of his mastery at war. Not just his enemies—his own men had drunk deeply from the same chalice.

It wasn't that he thought he should have acted differently in the past—he could see no other options. But Amyra, faced with the destruction of the people she loved, had conceived of a different way and imagined it into being.

How could a man like him ever hope to win such a woman?

43

———

For better or for worse, the time had come for Will to find out if he had any hope of a future with Amyra. He knew she liked to spend time alone in the forest when she could, and having once glimpsed her horse in the distance tied to a tree, he thought he had a rough idea where he might find her. Mounting his own horse, he gathered his courage and headed for the location.

Her horse was exactly where he expected it to be. After securing his mount beside it, he picked his way through the trees in search of her.

Not far in he came upon a small clearing. The sight he saw there took his breath away.

Amyra stood on the far side of the glade. One of her arms was raised high, and a host of brilliantly colored butterflies filled the air around her.

He watched wide-eyed as she slowly weaved her arm back and forth through the air. Glimmers of blue, red, purple, and every color of the rainbow danced before his eyes as the fluttering insects swirled about her in a delicate cloud, imitating her every movement. She swept her arm majestically in a circular motion, down and up again, and the butterflies dipped and soared smoothly in response. He stood entranced, oblivious to all else.

How long it went on he couldn't say, but a wave of disappointment washed over him when the spectacle finally came to an end. She dropped a small object into a leather pouch; he didn't need to be told what the object was. Then she stood quietly, watching as the colorful cloud slowly dispersed.

All this time he'd scarcely dared to breathe. As he shifted position she finally noticed him. A delicate blush tinged her cheeks when she realized he'd been watching her.

Stepping into the open, he approached her slowly. "How did you learn to do that?" he asked in wonder.

Her slender shoulders lifted in a shrug, setting her hazelnut brown tresses swaying. "It was a chance discovery. The stone seems to have a gentler side," she said with a faint smile.

In her hands, the stone was presiding over creativity rather than coercion. It came as no surprise to him.

His breath hitched as he gazed down into her face. He'd always seen the fire that flashed in her hazel eyes, but how could he have failed to be captivated by how beautiful they were?

She was no ordinary woman. Could he really do this?

He checked himself. He needed to stay focused. A challenge lay before him, but he would find a way through it. He always did.

"What brings you here, Will?" she asked quietly.

He sucked in a breath, telling himself it couldn't be that hard. "I want to speak with you," he finally managed.

She raised her eyebrows questioningly, watching him far too intently for his comfort.

In an attempt to collect himself he looked beyond her, into the trees. "I've been thinking," he began. "About a lot of things. The stone —in Agon's hands—it got me to do things. Things that made no sense."

He looked back into her face and almost lost his way again. Diverting his eyes once more, he tried again. "It got me wondering— are there other things I've been doing? Things that make no sense?"

Had he repeated himself? This wasn't working. He needed to change course before it turned into a complete disaster.

He thought he had rehearsed what he was going to say when he talked with her, but the words had become a jumbled mess in his mind. Releasing a heavy sigh, he gave up any attempt at delivering a speech.

In the heat of battle he had sometimes been forced to abandon caution entirely and follow his instinct. He decided now to do something he couldn't ever remember doing before. He would just talk—about himself.

He began at once, before he could change his mind.

"I never knew my parents," he said. "I was raised by my uncle and his Rogandan wife. I think my uncle cared about me in his own way, but from the beginning my aunt never liked me, and she took every opportunity to abuse me. I had no siblings, and they never had children of their own. I was their only child, but it never felt like we were family."

She stood completely still, her big eyes fixed on him.

Now that he was underway, the words were welling up inside him. "There was no reason for me to stay. I had no idea where I belonged, but I knew it wasn't with them. All I wanted was to make my mark in the world, and I decided the best way to do that was to become a soldier. I don't see it that way now, but it was all I knew at the time. Things just happened after that. I think I ended up in the right place at the right time."

He had no idea what she was thinking. But it was too late to stop. He'd set his course, and he would follow it to the end. "Once I started leading the army, life became overwhelming. I never found time to think about anything else. After the invasion, the king made me a nobleman and granted me holdings in Erestor—I have no idea why. But I can see now I was being given a chance at a new beginning. I didn't take it. The idea of settling down never even occurred to me.

"So here I am, years later, still wandering the world in a vain attempt to fix it." He smiled, but there was no mirth in it. "You already know how that's been working out for me. If it hadn't been for the assassin, I'd still be under Agon's power." His chin dropped to his chest. "I even turned you over to the maniac," he added miserably.

Amyra gave no response.

How could she remain silent for so long? He'd hardly known a woman to be lost for something to say.

"I never thanked you for coming to rescue me," he blurted. "It was incredibly brave!" He frowned at her. "Incredibly foolish."

Still she held her peace.

He threw up his hands in frustration. "I'm no good at this," he exclaimed, shaking his head. "There's a reason for it, too—I grew up without a woman's influence. It's left me tongue tied when it comes to feelings. I care about things, and about people. I truly do! But I don't know how to talk about it. I always thought it's the way I was made. But maybe it's just another thing I've been doing that makes no sense."

He heaved a deep sigh. For better or for worse, he'd managed to get something out.

"Thank you," she said, her voice gentle. "That can't have been easy. It means a lot that you've shared it with me."

He stole a quick glance at her. "My face will always be scarred," he said awkwardly. "But my limp is gone at least."

She stared at him blankly.

"It was your mother," he explained. "She's been working on my back."

Her eyebrows twitched together in a puzzled frown. She clearly had no idea what he was talking about.

He shrugged in resignation. "You told me that a scarred face and a limp are not at all attractive to a woman."

Merry laughter burst out of her. "And you took me seriously? Oh, Will!"

He stared back at her, completely nonplussed.

She took a step closer, and his heart began to pound.

"There's a lot more to you than your scars, Will Prentis. From the very beginning, it was obvious to me what you have up there," she told him, delicately placing a finger on his forehead. His whole face tingled at her touch. "You have a sharp mind, and you use it to great effect."

She paused for a moment. "You're self-sacrificing, too—I've seen that for myself."

A delicate flush tinged her cheeks. "You need to know that I quizzed Thomas and Haldek about you," she confessed. "You're a strong leader, but I'm well aware that you're also humble and compassionate."

She nodded solemnly. "Yes, Will, I'm afraid your secrets have been exposed." Her hazel eyes twinkled mischievously.

"But until today I hadn't glimpsed anything at all of what's going on in *here*." Amyra touched a finger to his heart, setting it pounding even harder. She lowered her voice almost to a whisper. "I must say, I like what I've been seeing."

Her beautiful eyes settled on his, and he swallowed, barely able to think straight.

She stepped closer. "Did you come here today to woo me, Will Prentis?" she asked him softly.

She was beautiful, she was beyond amazing, and she was everything his heart could possibly desire.

He could bear it no longer. Reaching out, he swept her into his arms, clasping her to himself almost with desperation.

Her face turned upward to him, and he bent down instinctively, pressing his lips onto hers. She kissed him back with a passion that sent fire racing through his veins. He cradled her head tenderly in one hand, and in response she stretched up her arms to send fingers snaking through his hair.

Time seemed to stand still as he lost himself in the miracle of her embrace.

When eventually they drew apart he stood breathing heavily, holding her at arm's length and gazing into her eyes. He couldn't speak—his heart was too full. It was more than enough just to soak her in. She gazed back at him in silence, a smile playing across her lovely face.

Dahra had been right about what he needed to say. He hadn't

planned what had come out though—he'd simply done the best he could, and somehow they'd found their way together.

"I had no idea what I was saying," he finally confessed. "I've faced major battles feeling less nervous."

"The fearless commander, quaking before a woman?" she teased.

"I've never met a woman like you," he said. "I never dared to believe I had any hope of winning you."

"You underestimate yourself, Will," she said with a shake of her pretty head. "My heart has been in your keeping almost from the day I met you, even though I stubbornly refused to admit it to myself."

He gazed at her in wonder. Then he drew her close once more, heaving a sigh of complete contentment.

When at last they walked hand in hand from the clearing, he discovered that the whole world had changed. The birds sang more brightly, the snatches of blue in the sky above were more brilliant.

Will stole glances at her as they walked, unable to keep the smile from his face. Then they mounted their horses and rode to the settlement side by side.

Will wasted no time seeking out Dahra, Amyra at his side. The older woman didn't need to be told what had happened between them. She took one look at their faces and burst out laughing.

"You look like you've figured out the meaning of the word 'happy,'" she told Will. "As for you," she said, turning to Amyra, "you look like you've finally discovered how to relax. Not before time!"

Will glanced self-consciously at Amyra. She treated him to a beguiling look intended for him alone.

Dahra raised an eyebrow. "I do hope you realize what you've taken on, Will," she warned. "She might be all smiles and sunshine now, but she's feisty enough for the two of you."

Then she grinned at them. "Your lives will never lack drama. But I have to say I'm confident you're going to make each other very happy."

44

———

The following day Will found himself heading to Dahra's hut with Amyra once more. Amyra would have nestled comfortably into his shoulder if he'd let her. He wanted it as much as she did, but Thomas had joined them, and Will was feeling extremely self-conscious.

In spite of Will's self-restraint, Thomas was clearly aware that something was up. Will turned to Dahra, eager to divert attention elsewhere. "I'm sure I'm not the only one who would like to know how Ennawi is," he said.

He chose the right topic, because Thomas immediately redirected his full attention to Dahra.

"I'm happy to tell you," said Dahra. "Before I begin, it might be helpful for you to know that Amyra has told me all about the scroll. I know how Thomas was able to discover Agon's plans through Ennawi. And he has been a great help in my attempts to better understand Ennawi."

Will nodded. He glanced at Thomas, who for some reason appeared to be carefully studying the floor at his feet. Will guessed he must have used the stone to study Ennawi, and passed on to Dahra whatever he learned.

"So how is Ennawi?" asked Will.

"I feel more hopeful than I would ever have imagined," she said. "He has a long road ahead of him, but he has taken some promising initial steps."

"What have you discovered about his background?" asked Amyra.

"It wasn't easy to get to the bottom of it," she sighed, "but between us we have been able to dig it out in the end. Nistinaa helped too, of course," she added hastily.

Her eyebrows drew together. "His situation is so complex and so incredible you could be forgiven for refusing to believe it. Lord Drettroth was the one who organized for him to be placed with King Agon, although the king had no awareness of who'd done it."

She waited for the expressions of amazement to fade away.

"It was also Drettroth who arranged an abundant supply of the potion that enabled Ennawi not to react to Agon's abuse. The supply never failed, even after his death. The potion is the only thing that kept Agon from killing him—that and Ennawi's inability to pass on anything he heard the king say. Where the potion came from I don't know, but apparently Drettroth made quite a study of poisons and their effects. This seems to have been one of his more unusual concoctions. What made it hard for Ennawi is that the drug allowed him to remain fully aware of everything that was happening, even though he never showed any sign of it. The abuse has been wearing away at him for years."

"And Ennawi had no way of striking back," said Will.

"No," agreed Dahra. "Ennawi had plenty of reason to want to harm Agon, even without the abuse. The king was the one who ordered his hands and his tongue to be cut off. I'm sure Agon wasn't aware of that when Ennawi joined him, though. Sooner or later he would have said something to Ennawi if he'd known."

Ignoring their astonishment, she pressed on.

"It happened when he was young. Word reached Agon that Ennawi's father had spoken against the king, so Agon ordered in a rage that the tongues of everyone in the family should be cut out. He demanded to be told if any further trouble surfaced in the region.

Some time later he was told that a child had repeatedly been caught stealing bread, and he apparently ordered the child's hands to be cut off.

"I imagine that Agon had no way of knowing that the same child had been affected by both actions. He probably forgot even giving the orders. But the first punishment led directly to the second. Once the family had been marked, the father couldn't work. All of them began to starve, so the young son turned to stealing.

"After the second punishment was carried out, Drettroth somehow found out about it. He took the family in and arranged for them to be cared for, perhaps wanting to make himself look good in comparison with Agon. Then he had Ennawi placed with Agon. A drugged Ennawi would have made for an ideal listener—one with no way of passing on anything he heard. Drettroth had known Agon since childhood, and he must have guessed that Agon could never resist blurting out all his secrets to such a person."

A look of horror came to Amyra's face. "So Agon was abusing Ennawi every day. And the whole time Ennawi knew that Agon had been responsible for his condition, but Agon didn't?" she asked.

Dahra nodded. "That's a good summary. You can imagine how much Ennawi has been damaged by everything that's happened."

The revelations appalled Will. His own newfound happiness seemed almost obscene when seen alongside the relentless and seemingly endless blows that Ennawi had endured.

"How did it benefit Drettroth to place him with Agon?" asked Will.

Dahra turned to Thomas.

Thomas sighed. "It's one of the first things I discovered from Ennawi," he said. "Drettroth was quite open about his reasons. One of his greatest ambitions was to acquire the Stone of Knowing. He was anticipating a day when he had taken possession of it. He would be able to read Agon's thoughts himself through direct contact, but if Agon ever refused to see Drettroth for any reason, Ennawi would provide an alternate way of discovering Agon's plans. Ennawi did eventually prove useful in exposing Agon's thoughts and plans, of course, even if not in the way Drettroth intended."

Will frowned. "And that was all there was to it?" he asked.

Thomas shook his head. "There was more. Drettroth was a subtle and devious man, and I'm not sure I fully comprehend all of his reasons. But the depth of his hatred toward Agon came through clearly in what he said to Ennawi. Agon was cruel to Drettroth from their earliest years, and it came to a head when Drettroth stumbled on the Stone of Authority while they were both still young. Neither of them realized what the stone was at the time, but Agon tricked him into handing it over, and Drettroth never forgave him. When Drettroth later learned about the true value of the stone, he hated Agon even more.

"After that incident, the young Drettroth decided to devote himself to bringing Agon down. He was canny about it. To all appearances he was Agon's strongest supporter. All the while he was making sure he strengthened himself through everything he did for the king."

"What did that have to do with Ennawi?" asked Amyra.

"Drettroth told Ennawi all this," Thomas replied. "He also told him that he was going to arrange for Agon to be killed, but he didn't provide details. If Drettroth failed and Agon got the Stone of Knowing, Agon would have discovered Drettroth's intentions from Ennawi. Agon would always be wondering what Drettroth might have planned. And Drettroth arranged that the assassin wouldn't be hired until well after his own death. By then Agon might have thought he could relax."

"It sounds bizarre," said Amyra, a baffled look on her face. "Why would he go to so much trouble for a reason like that?"

"I think I can guess at the answer, at least in part," said Will. "Drettroth captured me during the Rogandan invasion of Arvenon when I tried to infiltrate his camp posing as a priest. He had plenty else to do at the time, but he found time to taunt me. I think he derived pleasure from taunting his victims."

Thomas nodded. "I'm sure you're right."

"Ennawi might not have known what Drettroth was planning, but we do now," said Will.

"The assassin," said Amyra.

"Yes," agreed Will. "Drettroth might even have made other plans as well that we don't know about."

They all fell silent, musing.

"Drettroth must have hated Agon with a bitter passion," said Amyra finally.

"Yes, he did," Thomas agreed. "His hatred lasted a lifetime and beyond."

Dahra shook her head in disgust. "The two of them were as bad as each other," she said. "Both men were responsible for the years of abuse Ennawi suffered at the hands of Agon. They hurt him so much, and he needs to find a way to forgive them, or he'll be eaten up with bitterness for the rest of his life."

Will couldn't help but be relieved when the conversation gradually turned to less harrowing topics.

Eventually Dahra addressed herself to him directly. "When will you be leaving?" she asked.

"Soon," he replied. "King Steffan and Queen Essanda need to know what's happened here."

Dahra glanced at Amyra. "I imagine you'll be accompanying Will," she said.

Her daughter nodded. "We're planning to get married in Arnost. Once control of the city returns to King Steffan, of course. You will come for the wedding, won't you?" she asked anxiously.

Dahra grinned. "Nothing could keep me away," she assured them.

"Would you ever consider relocating to my holdings in Erestor?" asked Will hopefully.

"There's only one thing that could possibly induce me," Dahra replied.

"Grandchildren," said Amyra, rolling her eyes.

Dahra laughed, but she didn't deny it.

Thomas had been listening to the conversation with open astonishment on his face. Will leaned in close to him. "If you don't close your mouth soon, Thomas, a bird might decide to make a nest in there," he whispered. Then he clapped Thomas on the back with a wink.

As they were leaving Dahra's hut, Will turned back to her. "You said there might be something I can do for you," he reminded her.

"You've already done it," she assured him with a smile.

THE DAY of their departure had finally arrived. After so long away from his family, Thomas was impatient to be reunited with Elena and Tammi and Rubin. He was also aware that Haldek was barely less eager to see them again, even though his return to Arvenon might well mean his final farewell to the land of his birth.

As for Thomas, his own future was uncertain. He was planning to suggest to Elena that they join the community at Newhaven, along with Rubin and Haldek. They should be able to remain safely hidden there. He also thought they could invite his parents to join them.

It had briefly occurred to him that without the stone there was little reason to hide away anymore. But the people who had been searching for him wouldn't know he had given it up. Even without Agon paying them, they might decide to pursue him anyway in the hope of robbing him of whatever the king had been searching for. He concluded that Newhaven was a good choice even without the stone.

Now Will and Amyra were to be married, and Thomas imagined they might locate themselves on Will's holdings in Erestor. Newhaven wasn't impossibly far away from there; perhaps the two families could visit each other from time to time.

Will had told Thomas that Amyra now held the Stone of Authority and had described what she'd done with it. He also spoke openly of his love for the young woman. Thomas still hadn't decided which revelation astonished him the most.

Thomas had never glimpsed the vaguest hint of a romantic side to Will, and he was still coming to terms with the relationship between Will and Amyra. It seemed all the more remarkable given the way Amyra had appeared to despise Will. Appearances could certainly be deceptive.

Thomas was delighted for them both, and he had been trying to tell himself that nothing was more important than Will's news. As they prepared to leave, though, little else occupied his mind except the missing chain around his neck. He hadn't yet found a way to tell Will that he no longer had the Stone of Knowing. He had decided to wait until they left Aen-irac.

Atae, Rhillyon, and others among the Aen-ur had assembled to wish them well on their journey, and especially to bid their final farewells to Amyra. Thomas noticed more than one young man among the crowd directing dark looks at Will.

At that moment Dahra and Amyra were locked in a tearful parting embrace. Dahra had finally opened up to Amyra, revealing the details of her life before she met her husband, Kalvor, describing their years together, and recounting the events that led to his death. The two women had talked far into the night with many tears on both sides.

Dahra herself had told Thomas about it later. He wondered if he had precipitated the interaction by his comments to Amyra about her father, and he apologized to Dahra for raising the subject. She assured him that he'd done both of them a favor.

Dahra and Amyra might be parting now, but their separation was expected to be short-lived. Dahra intended to travel to Arnost as soon as it was safe to do so, and Will had promised to send an escort when that moment arrived.

None of the travelers had any idea what they might find across the border. Will expected Rellan and Lord Burtelen to be stationed there with an army. The status of the other Arvenian army was still unknown, but Arnost was almost certainly still occupied, and Castel remained to be freed from the influence of Eisgold. However, Agon's death meant that no further support would flow to either Pisander or Eisgold, and Will was confident that a way would be found to deal with them both. They would be dealt with permanently this time.

Amyra finally mounted, and all of them waved their farewells. As

Thomas was about to ride away, Dahra hurried up to him, beckoning him to bend down to her.

Dahra reached for his hand as he did so and pressed a folded piece of cloth into it. Something firm lay hidden within the folds.

"I'm giving it back," she whispered, a sober expression on her face. "It belongs to you again."

Thomas was too astonished to reply.

"I never really wanted it," she told him. "I've done what was needed with Ennawi, and I want to be rid of it. After all these years without it, the insights have felt oppressive. You and your admirable wife will be much better guardians of it. I'm very much looking forward to meeting her, Thomas!"

She stepped back into the crowd, giving him opportunity to do no more than wave an acknowledgment.

The moment Thomas found himself riding apart from the others, he opened his hand and unfolded the piece of cloth. Inside he found the chain and the clasp with the stone. Slipping it back over his head, he concealed it once more beneath his clothing.

He took a deep breath, then released a long sigh. With the stone around his neck once more, the familiar feelings of ambivalence had returned in full force.

The situation had changed, though. It somehow comforted him to know that the Stone of Knowing was no longer the only arcane influence in his world. The Stone of Authority was also heading to Arvenon, and in safe hands at last.

And he was going home. With Elena's help he had always found a way to deal with the unnerving predicaments presented by the stone. New challenges would not be long in coming, of that he was certain. When they did, he and Elena would face them together.

***

Thomas was startled out of a dream by a weight that squeezed the breath from his lungs. A rag covered his mouth, and a knee was pressed hard against his chest. Thomas struggled to open his eyes.

"Get up! Quietly!" whispered a harsh voice.

The knee was removed, and he was hauled to his feet. The fire at their campsite flickered low, and everything around him was quiet. He glimpsed the motionless forms of Will and Haldek, apparently soundly asleep. He couldn't spot Amyra, but he knew she was sleeping nearby, on the other side of the fire.

Bustling him away from the firelight, his captor pulled him to a halt among the trees.

"Agon wanted you badly, Thomas," growled the voice. "Badly enough to drag me to Rog to put some kind of spell on me. And you actually left Varas and went to him! I never reached him in time to tell him. And now he's dead."

Thomas's heart raced as a blade pressed against his throat, cold on his skin.

"I'm my own man again now," the intruder continued. "And I didn't go through all this for nothing. You've got his heirloom, or whatever it is, and I'm not leaving without it. Hand it over without a fuss, and I might even decide to kill you quickly."

"Let him go!" commanded a woman's voice. Thomas's eyes flicked up to see Amyra poised at the edge of the campsite.

"Come a step closer and he dies immediately!" warned Thomas's captor. The pressure of the knife increased at Thomas's throat. "Hand it over, Thomas," snarled the voice, "then I can go kill her too."

Thomas's mind spun, his body frozen.

Before he could respond, a screech shattered the night. Something dark glided above them, descending rapidly toward the two men.

The intruder cried out in alarm as dark wings beat about his face. "What *is* that?" He crouched low, slashing his blade wildly above his head.

Finding himself suddenly free, Thomas stumbled hastily away from his captor.

A knife flew through the air, burying itself in the body of the writhing man. He went down hard, falling directly onto the knife. He didn't get up.

Haldek appeared, rolling the intruder over to retrieve his knife. He grimaced as he examined the body. "He was going to kill you," he said to Thomas. "And her next," he added, jerking his head toward Amyra.

The young woman stood rooted to the spot, her face pale.

Will hurried to her side, not relaxing until he had assured himself she was unharmed. "You used the stone," he said softly.

She nodded unsteadily. "There was nothing nearby I could call on apart from the owl."

Thomas was struggling to master the trembling that shook his body. "You saved my life," he breathed. "Thank you."

Amyra shook her head. "It was nothing," she protested dully.

Haldek had returned to the fire and built it up again, and soon all of them had gathered around it, staring silently into the flames.

They were still huddled there when dawn broke. Working distractedly, Thomas helped Will and Haldek pile rocks over the body of his attacker. Even with the threat behind him he couldn't relax. Not with the fresh memory of the knife at his throat.

His would-be killer had been sent by Agon, and he had even known Thomas's name. The man's words echoed hauntingly in his mind.

"I imagine there's a story behind him," said Will.

"I don't want to know it," Thomas returned emphatically.

He felt nothing but relief when they mounted up once more and rode away from the campsite, continuing their journey toward Arvenon.

Thomas's mind was numb. Once again the stone had almost cost him his life.

Would it never end?

45

L ord Mardone watched covertly as Lord Eisgold stumbled along a corridor of Castel Citadel. Hidden in the shadows beside Mardone stood Count Gordan.

"Something's happened," Mardone ventured. "Eisgold is blundering about as if he's in a fog."

"The time has come," Gordan responded. "It will be too late for the king if we don't act soon."

"How many of the others are with us?" Mardone asked.

"We can count on two or three of them," Gordan told him. "The rest are still wavering. We're wasting our time pursuing them further."

They continued to observe Eisgold until he disappeared from their sight.

Mardone turned to his friend. "So we move tonight?"

Gordan nodded. "Tonight."

KING RUPERT LAY in his bed, groaning softly. The pounding in his head and the twisting in his gut had prostrated him once more.

When would it end? He was only seventeen years old, much too young to die.

At first he failed to notice the four men who burst into his bedroom. He became aware of them when they appeared at his bedside and began lifting him bodily from his bed. When he opened his mouth to protest, they thrust a gag into it.

Every fiber of his being cried out, "Treason!", but the gag in his mouth prevented him from uttering a sound, and he was too weak to struggle. They bustled him out the door of his bedchamber—a door that should have been secured by his royal guards. No guards were anywhere to be seen.

He was hurried along an empty corridor, only to scramble down another corridor and another, until he had lost all sense of direction. All he knew was that they were traveling through rarely trafficked corners of the castle.

He had the presence of mind to recognize that they could have knifed him at any time, with no one to witness it. He could only conclude that they didn't intend to kill him. Not yet, anyway. That was some consolation.

Eventually they turned into a dark room, and the motion stopped. The youthful king was placed into a chair and his gag removed. A man bowed low before him, although he couldn't recognize him in the dim light.

"I apologize for the abduction, Your Majesty," said a voice he knew. "We have done it only for your protection."

"What is the meaning of this treason, My Lord?" he demanded.

"Have you ever had reason to suspect me of disloyalty to the crown, Your Majesty?" Mardone asked, bowing respectfully again.

Rupert frowned. After the events of this evening, he wanted to answer in the affirmative. But he couldn't honestly do it. "Before tonight, no," he replied.

"You have no reason to doubt me now, Your Majesty! I am fiercely loyal to you, as I was to your father. Would you be willing to trust me, just for a few minutes? I want to invite you to observe something."

Annoyed as he was, Rupert was at least a little curious. Why had Mardone risked everything to bring him here?

"Very well," he grunted. "It had better be worth my while!"

"We must be very quiet, Your Majesty." The nobleman led him to a wall and uncovered a couple of peepholes. Rupert found himself staring down into a section of the royal kitchens. A maid was preparing food on a tray. He recognized the tray and some of the dishes. The food was intended for him.

Two men approached the maid. "Move aside, woman!" one of them ordered.

"Not so, sir! This is the king's meal. You cannot tamper with it!"

The second newcomer delivered a stinging blow to the maid's face, knocking her to her knees. "Don't talk back," he spat. "This is the king's medicine, prescribed by the royal physician. Don't interfere if you know what's good for you."

He pulled a vial from within his clothing, and shook a few drops into the king's wine.

The first man pulled the maid to her feet. "Now take this to the king, and don't make a fuss if you know what's good for you."

The second man shook his head as the maid hurried away. "Where's the usual girl?" he growled. "Eisgold will have our heads if word of this gets out."

The king looked on, too stunned to speak.

He continued to watch wide-eyed as royal guards appeared in the kitchens and dragged both men away.

"As Your Majesty can see, the traitors are being dealt with," said Lord Mardone with satisfaction. He covered the peepholes once more, and candles were lit in the room.

"I'm sorry you had to witness that, Your Majesty," he said. "The usual maid is in the pay of these men. We arranged for her to be replaced tonight so that you would see them in their true colors."

Rupert stared at the nobleman, aghast at what he had seen. The rumors that he was being poisoned were nothing new, but he had steadfastly refused to believe them. And yet all of them were true.

And the poisoners had named Eisgold as a conspirator.

Some of his noblemen had tried to warn him about Eisgold, and he had turned on them. A flush of shame came to his face as he recalled the rage he had directed at Count Gordan when the count dared to assert that pardoning Eisgold was dishonoring the memory of his father.

"Please read this, Your Majesty," said Lord Mardone, handing him a partially burned parchment. "One of our people rescued it from the fireplace in Lord Eisgold's apartments."

He skimmed through the scorched remnants of the parchment, barely able to believe what he was reading. The document was addressed to Lord Eisgold and signed and sealed by Agon of Rogand. It reminded Eisgold forcefully that Agon expected an early return on the generous payments he had advanced to Eisgold.

Rupert looked up into the concern on Lord Mardone's face. He knew he did not deserve the nobleman's sympathy. He could only be appalled by his own blindness and ashamed of his foolishness.

"Eisgold must be arrested at once!" he said.

Lord Mardone nodded to his men, and two of them left the room at once. "It will be done, Your Majesty. In the meantime, it is safest if you remain here with us."

Several hours passed before Rupert heard a knock at the door. The person admitted was none other than Count Gordan. The count came and knelt before him, kissing his hand.

"I owe you the most abject of apologies, Gordan!" the king told him.

"Your Majesty was deceived and imposed upon," Gordan replied.

"What of Eisgold?" Lord Mardone asked.

"He is dead," Gordan replied. "When we arrived we found that he had poisoned himself. He must have had hints of what was coming. Perhaps his end was fitting in view of his actions toward the king. He lived long enough to insist that he had been bewitched by Agon, and that he never intended harm either to Castel or to the king."

"How could he have expected such a story to be believed?" asked

Rupert, shaking his head incredulously. "And what of his lackeys? My blindness seems to have been lifted at last, and it is now apparent to me that he has been spreading his parasites throughout the capital."

"The traitors will be rounded up, Your Majesty," Lord Mardone assured him. "When it becomes known that Eisgold is dead, any waverers will quickly fall into line."

"I don't know how to thank you both," the king told them. "You have saved my life and restored my kingdom to me."

"No thanks are necessary, Your Majesty," Count Gordan replied. "We are doing no more than our duty as loyal servants of the crown."

PISANDER PACED SULLENLY in the castle's main reception hall, waiting impatiently for his deputy.

When Lygell arrived, he was nervous and fidgeting. "Armies are approaching the city from two directions! The one from Varas is almost at the gates," he said, his voice quavering.

Pisander stared at him contemptuously, slowly shaking his head. "Yes," he agreed, "the king is coming to reward his loyal subjects."

Lygell just stood there, wild-eyed.

"I hear you've been arguing with your lackeys," Pisander growled.

"Some of them dared to question my authority!" Lygell replied, his face petulant. "At a time like this!"

The former earl just stared at Lygell until his deputy began to be indignant. "Why are you looking at me like that? You appointed me as your deputy—I deserve your support!"

"You deserve to be hanged!" spat Pisander. "This is a time for decisive action, not for squabbling over the scraps left on the table." He shook his head again. "What did I ever see in you?" he wondered aloud.

"Jarah!" he called. Jarah stepped forward and bowed. Pisander jerked his head toward Lygell. "Hang him in the market square. Do it now."

Jarah waved over four of the guards. They surrounded the panicked deputy and grabbed hold of him tightly.

Lygell's struggles forced them to lift him bodily as they carried him away. "No! Wait! You can't do this!" The screams grew ever fainter as they dragged him from the castle.

Pisander put it out of his mind. Everything was rapidly falling apart around him. He had seen it coming from the day his mind had suddenly cleared. He'd been acting on Agon's behalf under compulsion; he understood that clearly only when the compulsion ceased.

Pisander had never been a man who readily succumbed to pressure, so how he had been coerced was a great mystery to him. But his thoughts returned again to his abortive search for the youth who'd intruded on the council meeting so long ago. Jarah had made real progress before Pisander called a halt to his search. It was regrettable, but he had needed the hunter in Arnost.

His investigations hadn't been limited to the youth either. He had also sent an agent to Rog in the hope of gaining insight into Agon's persuasiveness. Having heard nothing further from the man, he sent another agent with no better success. After that he'd become too distracted to pursue it further.

His thoughts were interrupted by the arrival of one of his aides. "I've been asked to pass on a message, My Lord," the aide told him, bowing low.

"I am expecting no message," Pisander told him with a frown. "Who was the messenger?"

The man bowed again. "I don't know him, My Lord, and he didn't wait around."

"Well? What's the message?" Pisander asked impatiently.

"He's heard that you are looking for reliable men, and he believes he can help." The aide hesitated. "He said he would sign on with you for the right price. He claims he knows where to find plenty of others as well. A man is waiting outside the city gates to guide you to a meeting place."

Pisander frowned at the aide. A meeting location outside the city sounded very suspicious.

"The messenger said if you weren't sure whether to trust him, you should bring as many guards as you thought you needed," added the aide. He looked at Pisander uncomfortably. "Those were his exact words."

So the invitation had come from someone who was either extremely bold or had nothing to hide.

Pisander couldn't ignore the truth—he needed all the help he could get. Executing Lygell only highlighted the problem. And he had never been in the habit of turning away mercenaries willing enough to hire out their services. If Agon was no longer in the picture, the flow of resources had already ended, of course. But he had plenty in reserve.

Pisander hesitated only for a moment. He had never hesitated to take the main chance, and it had carried him further than he could ever have dreamed. Now was not a time to begin playing it safe. Nevertheless, he was no fool—twenty men rode with him when he headed for the city gates.

The man waiting outside the gates was unknown to Pisander.

"My Lord," he said with a bow that bordered on the insolent. "Could you all please follow me? We don't have far to go."

The man's brazenness didn't alarm Pisander. He would have been more suspicious if the man had feigned respect.

After only a few minutes their guide turned aside and dismounted. "Follow me," he said.

One of the men stayed with the horses. Pisander and the others followed along behind.

A second man was waiting for them, and he bowed obsequiously as Pisander approached. "My Lord," he said.

"Well?" Pisander asked. "If you want to join me, well and good. But make it quick. Two armies are about to arrive on our doorstep."

"I have a slightly different proposition," the man replied with a sneer.

Fighting immediately broke out all around him. He should never have come without Jarah at his side.

Men swarmed around Pisander's guards, so many of them—fifty at least. Whoever set up the ambush had not skimped on resources.

The struggle was over in a few minutes. Only Pisander was left standing.

"What do you want?" he asked the man facing him.

"I only ever wanted what was due to me," growled a different voice at his back. "If only one royal died in the barn, that was on your head. You wouldn't pay me what was needed to get the job done properly."

Pisander felt the knife go in as he twisted his head to confront the speaker. Even through the agony he recognized the face of his attacker.

A voice whispered in his ear. "Remember me, Count Nothing? I attacked the kings in the barn for you, but when I came to collect you cheated me. You were so very, very pleased with yourself. No one cheats Alfic and gets away with it."

The knife twisted in Pisander's back, and pain flooded over him. Everything went black.

———

THE MAN who remained with Pisander's horses frantically remounted and galloped back to the city the moment the fighting started. As soon as a large enough group of armed men could be assembled, he led them back with Jarah at their head.

The bodies of Pisander and his men were still lying where they had fallen. No trace of the attackers could be found.

"What now?" asked one of the men.

"Pisander and Lygell are both dead, so who's going to pay us?" asked another.

"Don't look at me," Jarah retorted, "I won't be paying anyone."

"The army from Varas is getting close!" another voice piped up. "Rumor says it will reach Arnost in a matter of hours. And there's another army almost as close, coming from the direction of the Rogandan border."

Jarah mounted his horse. "I'll be long gone when they arrive," he assured them.

He threw them a parting glance as he rode away. "Do whatever you want," he called. "You're on your own now."

46

———

Lord Krasmir, Acting Regent of Rogand, stood with his wife Deka staring out at the city of Rog beyond the palace grounds. Krasmir had chosen a small set of apartments within the palace for his use as regent, and he did so partly for the view. He had always found the squalor of the capital city confronting, and he didn't want to lose sight of it.

Deka studied him with a concerned eye. "How are you coping with the role of regent, my beloved?" she asked.

He smiled at her. "I've been finding it surprisingly manageable. I expected unrelenting opposition, and it's been a pleasant surprise to discover how many people are willing to be reasonable."

"It's no shock to me," she replied, one eyebrow lifted ironically. "You're standing in for a heartless monster given to violent rages."

"Be careful what you say, my dear," he chided. "I won't hear you speak badly of the king. I fully support him, which is no doubt the reason he appointed me."

Deka shook her head in bewilderment. "It's a complete mystery to me how anyone can fully support him, much less you." She threw up her hands. "It isn't as if you've ever lacked opinions about how the kingdom should be ruled."

"I have priorities of my own," he acknowledged. "I'm making it clear to anyone who asks that my focus is the stability and economic well-being of the kingdom." His brows furrowed. "I'm hoping we don't have a repetition of Drettroth's invasion."

"Especially since the king's done nothing whatever to ease the burden the invasion placed on every family in Rogand," she grumbled.

She ignored his dismay at her continued disrespect. "Do any of the barons want to keep the war going?"

He frowned at her for a moment longer before giving up with a sigh. "No," he said. "Thankfully not. None of them see any benefit in attacking our neighbors. As long as the Arvenians don't attack us, they'd prefer to let them be."

She said nothing for a while, but he could see she was eyeing him sternly. "What?" he eventually asked, throwing up his hands in exasperation.

"The fact that you're agreeing with the king now is bad enough. When are you going to abandon this ridiculous pretense about being no better than an animal?" she asked him bluntly. "You might have been able to get away with it when you were just Lord Krasmir, but you're the regent now!"

He snorted. "I've had my reasons. None of the factions among the nobility have ever bothered trying to recruit me."

"I know," she said with exaggerated patience. "It means you don't owe favors to any of them." She sighed. "You're certainly odd, but I won't deny that you're canny. These people don't know how well off they are. One day the nobles, the administrators, the priests, the common people—the whole lot of them—will wake up and discover you're the most even-handed and reasonable ruler Rogand has ever seen."

He grinned at her, blowing her a kiss.

KRASMIR STUMBLED about his apartments in a daze, groaning loudly.

"Whatever's the matter?" asked Deka in alarm. "Shall I call for the physicians?"

He ignored her question, continuing to moan.

"What is wrong with you?" Deka demanded. Her tone made it clear he needed to respond, and he needed to do it immediately.

"Something happened," he said. "It was like I woke up from a nightmare. Except it was full daylight."

He held his head in his hands. "I don't understand it!" he wailed. "How could I ever have thought that anything about Agon made sense? I must have been mad!" He paused, scowling. "Either that, or he used some kind of sorcery on me!"

She stared at him wide-eyed, probably convinced he had gone mad. He didn't care.

"A lot of things are about to change!" he said, a look of unshakable determination on his face. "If Agon was fool enough to make me regent, he'll have no one but himself to blame for the consequences. He isn't going to recognize his kingdom when he gets back."

Krasmir felt weary beyond words when he finally dragged himself back to his apartments. Deka was waiting for him there, concern in her eyes.

"You need to sleep!" she told him.

"How can I sleep?" he asked. "Rogand hasn't faced a crisis like this in generations! The king is dead, and there's no heir. The situation is unprecedented!"

"There's a simple solution," she said calmly. "One of the nobility needs to be anointed as king."

"Who? None of them will tolerate a king from a rival faction. We'd end up with a civil war on our hands!"

"Of course," she said reasonably. "Everyone understands that. The solution is obvious. They need to crown you as king."

Seeing the look on his face, she planted her hands on her hips impatiently. "Why must you be the last person to see what's obvious to everyone else?"

Then she relaxed, gazing at him smugly. "The wives are in complete agreement, which means there's no doubt it will happen."

***

Jonas shifted uncomfortably in the saddle. After another day of riding he felt hot and dusty.

From the moment Will offered him the position of steward on his holdings in Erestor, the appeal of life as a soldier had diminished greatly for Jonas. Already thinking ahead, he had approached Breysen about joining the estate as the blacksmith. When he made it clear that Breysen's family would be welcome to relocate permanently to the holdings, Breysen accepted at once.

Breysen understood that the offer was conditional both on Will returning safely from Rogand and on King Steffan and Queen Essanda being restored to undisputed control of Arvenon. No one could say with any confidence when either of those events might take place.

Considerable progress had been made toward the goal of restoring the kingdom to its rightful rulers though. The western army camped outside Steffan's Citadel on the border of Erestor had already been restored to the control of the king. That army had been placed under the leadership of Rellan and Lord Burtelen, and sent to the border of Rogand to prevent King Agon of Rogand from entering Arvenon.

The northern army, originally camped outside Deadman's Pass on the border of Castel, had been moved by Pisander and his henchmen to Varas to block a short-lived Varasan invasion of Arvenon. Once this second army came within reach, Rufe and Count Ranauld managed to induce the soldiers to turn on the leaders appointed by Pisander. The situation was resolved only after a vicious battle, but Rufe and Jonas prevailed with the help of loyalists in the army along with several units of Varasan soldiers.

With both armies now firmly under King Steffan's control, only Arnost remained in the hands of Pisander. The second army was marching south for Arnost, led by Rufe and Jonas. A strong detachment of Varasan soldiers from King Delmar's army was marching with them. Messengers had been sent to the first army under Rellan and Lord Burtelen to inform them of King Steffan's plans.

Arnost was now no more than a couple of days' march away. Scouts reported that Arnost was shut tight and still under the control of Pisander.

Jonas sat daily in conference with Rufe and King Steffan, and he knew that the idea of attacking his own capital did not appeal to the king at all. The only alternative was a siege. Starving out the defenders would spare the besiegers at the cost of everyone in the city.

Neither option was attractive. Nevertheless, the hour of decision was fast approaching.

ARMED SOLDIERS APPEARED abruptly on the road ahead, startling Amyra into sudden watchfulness. She had felt especially tense since the attack on Thomas.

"Who are you, and why are you entering Arvenon?" demanded a rough voice. It appeared that Will's party had reached the border at last.

Hearing the challenge, all of them reined in their horses.

Will stepped his horse forward. "I am Will Prentis," he called.

"Did he say Will Prentis?"

"Is it really him?"

"Will's arrived!"

Soldiers appeared from everywhere, racing forward and surrounding Will eagerly, all of them talking at once. Somehow word spread, and soon they found themselves at the center of an enthusiastic crowd of milling soldiers. One of the men began chanting, "Will! Will! Will!" The others quickly took it up until the air rang with their shouts. The noise was deafening.

Will held up a hand, and the din gradually faded away. "It's good to be with you all again," he said. "Thank you for defending the border for the king!"

"Are the Rogandans coming?" someone called. "We're ready for them!"

"No," Will replied. "I won't be needing to ask you to fight. King Agon has just died, and none of the Rogandans seem to be looking in this direction right now."

Cheering erupted, and Will had to hold up his hand again.

"Where are Rellan and Lord Burtelen?" he asked.

"I'll take you to them, Will," one of the soldiers offered.

Amyra had been looking on in awe. Now that she had witnessed for herself the adulation with which Will was greeted, she felt completely confounded. How could she ever have imagined herself worthy of him?

Then he rode close to her, and she saw the love in his eyes. "I need to go for a while," he said. "You'll be safe with these men. One of them will lead you back to their camp."

He turned to the men. "Can you please take care of my friends? This is Thomas, and Haldek," he said, pointing to them in turn.

"The horse master!" someone called as Will pointed at Thomas, and she saw Thomas color.

"And this is Amyra, my betrothed," he said with a grin. A mock frown came over his face. "Treat her well, or you'll answer to me!"

At Will's reference to his betrothed, more cheering erupted. Every eye turned in Amyra's direction, and some of the men began to whistle noisily. Will aimed a wink at her as he rode away.

"I'm one of the captains of this rabble," a cheerful voice called over the din. "Let me lead you to our camp. We'll find some warm food for you there."

Amyra saw very little of Will over the next couple of days.

He came to her one evening just after nightfall. "I'm sorry I haven't been able to spend time with you, Amyra," he said apologetically.

She smiled at him in the dark. "I completely understand—you have a job to do. There'll be plenty of time for us later."

"I'm going to be distracted for the foreseeable future," he told her. "But once we're married I will take you to my holdings in Erestor. We can build a life for ourselves there."

"It sounds very cozy," she said, leaning in to him. "Just you and me."

"And the Stone of Authority," he added wryly. "I've seen enough to know that the stones have an uncanny way of attracting trouble."

"Whatever comes, we'll meet it together," she promised with a smile.

He left her after stealing a kiss, and he went reluctantly.

The following morning the soldiers packed up the camp around them, and the army set off marching in the direction of Arnost.

Will himself stopped by in person later that day.

"We've received a message from King Steffan," he told them. "He's left Varas with Rufe and Jonas. They're leading an army to Arnost."

"Are they expecting a fight when they get there?" asked Thomas.

"No one knows exactly what to expect," Will replied. "We're planning to link up with them outside the city. We'll do whatever it takes to arrive at Arnost roughly at the same time."

———

WILL WAS LED to the tent of King Steffan, with Amyra, Thomas, and Haldek close behind him.

With the two armies already beginning to merge, confusion reigned supreme. Will had been overseeing the process of coordination before turning aside to seek out the king.

When they were announced, King Steffan himself appeared at the entrance to the tent. "Will! You've arrived at last! It is good to see you. Please, come and join us. Thomas and Haldek, you are very welcome too, and your lovely friend."

After sending a soldier in search of Rufe and Jonas, the king stood aside to usher the new arrivals into his tent. The tent was spacious, and it needed to be. Will knew that the king routinely used it to host conferences while on the march.

Will caught a glimpse of the queen at the far end of the tent, attended by Elena and Brother Ander.

The moment Elena spotted Thomas, she ran to him with a glad cry. After embracing him eagerly—much too briefly if the look on Thomas's face offered any indication—she turned to embrace Haldek as well. Elena called over a servant, then whispered in Haldek's ear. At her words he brightened immediately, setting off after the servant without delay. Will guessed that Elena had arranged for Haldek to be taken to Rubin and little Tamara.

Elena turned to Will, greeting him warmly.

"I'm glad you traveled with the army, Elena," he said. "Thomas was becoming very restless."

Thomas raised an eyebrow ironically. "Will has barely seen us in the last few days, so don't believe a word he says," he retorted with a smile.

Rufe and Jonas arrived in the tent just as Queen Essanda appeared at Elena's side to greet the new arrivals.

"And who is this?" asked the queen, turning to Amyra with a smile.

Will bowed. "King Steffan, Queen Essanda, Rufe, Jonas, Elena, Brother Ander, this is Amyra, my betrothed."

The occupants of the royal tent greeted his announcement with no less enthusiasm than Will's soldiers had shown and with equal astonishment.

Amyra had dipped into a curtsy when he introduced her, and Will saw that she was blushing furiously as she rose. Taking her hand, he gave it a gentle squeeze for moral support.

"Thank you for your kind welcome, Your Majesties. And Rufe, Jonas, Elena, and Brother Ander," she said. Her face might have betrayed her, but she demonstrated admirable command of her voice.

Congratulations flowed freely, and Will felt both delighted and humbled at the warmth of their response. Several of the men were unable to resist wisecracks at his expense, and several minutes passed before the laughter began to die away.

"There is a tale worth the telling here," said King Steffan with a pleased smile. "We will defer it until we can give it the attention it deserves. In the meantime, what news do you bring us from Rogand, Will?"

"King Agon is dead, Your Majesty—killed by an assassin hired by Lord Drettroth if you can believe it. We no longer have reason to expect a Rogandan army at our border. I imagine that the Rogandans will be distracted for some time by the question of the succession. What will happen when a new king emerges in Rogand remains to be seen."

Astonishment greeted his report.

"Did you have a hand in what happened, Will?" asked the king.

"Each of us played a part," he replied, "including Amyra. But none of us can rightly claim credit for the final outcome. And that is undoubtedly a good thing. I imagine the Rogandans would not take it well if their king had been assassinated by an Arvenian."

Will pulled a small object from the pouch at his belt and handed it to the king. "This tile played a key role," he said. "Keep it safe, Your Majesty. It is exceedingly valuable."

The king took the tile, shaking his head in surprise. "Once more, we must wait to hear the full details," he said regretfully. "The immediate task before us is to retake Arnost from Pisander."

"Pisander's days are numbered," Will replied. "His plan always depended on killing you both, Your Majesties. If he'd succeeded, we would have had no one to rally behind."

Rufe nodded. "We were able to retake control of the two armies because the soldiers were still loyal. They just needed to be shown the truth."

"Now that Agon is gone," added Will, "the supply of resources—to Eisgold in Castel as well as to Pisander—will come to an end."

"The reach of these traitors is greatly diminished," agreed the king. "Once Arnost has been freed, their day will be over in Arvenon. I'm confident they won't long survive in Castel either."

The king's voice took on an expectant tone. "Agon's schemes and manipulations are almost at an end, and a new day is about to dawn," he said. "All of us have endured a time of peril and grief. That time is almost behind us, and we will emerge stronger and more resilient than ever."

EPILOGUE

U ndisputed master of its domain, the eagle soared high on the currents above Arnost.

Serene and majestic, it ignored the clanging of the cathedral bells and the little figures that swarmed around the city gates. The monarch of the air glided effortlessly over the city, pursued faintly by the sound of cheering as the king and queen of the surface dwellers rode in astride their mounts.

The noise and commotion fell swiftly away in the wake of the hunter's silent wings. Climbing the thermals, it wheeled westward in search of prey.

The saga will continue in
The Stone of Vitality
(The Stone Cycle Book 5)
by Allan N. Packer

LIST OF CHARACTERS

- *Agon* - king of Rogand
- *Aiden* - prince of Arvenon, son of King Steffan and Queen Essanda
- *Amyra* - young woman living with the Aen-ur; daughter of Dahra
- *Ander* - Arvenian soldier who traveled with Will and later commanded soldiers at the Battle of Torbury Scarp, before becoming a monk following the death of Brother Vangellis
- *Ashar* - Rogandan fighter willing to accept dangerous assignments for the right price
- *Atae* - leader of the Aen-ur
- *Ava* - handmaid to Queen Essanda of Arvenon
- *Axel Stablehand* - master of the royal stables at Arnost and the father of Thomas
- *Alfic* - mercenary leader
- *Anneka* - former noblewoman who leads a community hidden away in the forest near Erestor
- *Belac* - mercenary under Lord Redfass
- *Bottren* - high-ranking Arvenian nobleman and close

confidante of King Steffan; liaison to Will Prentis at the battle at Torbury Scarp

- *Breysen* - member of Hazor's mercenary force
- *Burtelen* - high-ranking Arvenian nobleman from Erestor who is a close confidante of King Steffan; played a crucial role in bringing an army from Erestor to the battle at Torbury Scarp
- *Carnwill* - tracker in the pay of King Agon of Rogand
- *Carpis* - well connected Castelan fisherman
- *Chalno* - mystic and former priest of the Rogandan dark gods
- *Dahra* - healer living with the Aen-ur; mother of Amyra
- *Delmar* - king of Varas, a neighboring kingdom to Arvenon; ally of King Steffan of Arvenon
- *Drettroth* - high-ranking Rogandan nobleman who commanded the Rogandan army during the invasion of Arvenon; known as Vilkami during his childhood
- *Duke of Erestor* - King Steffan's uncle, and the regent during the king's absence during the Rogandan invasion; the senior member of the nobility in Erestor
- *Dunnridge* - nobleman who later became the Earl of Pisander (see *Pisander*)
- *Eisgold* - Castelan nobleman formerly commanding the Castelan army; exiled after the Battle of Torbury Scarp for ignoring orders at a crucial moment in the battle
- *Elena* - young woman living in hiding with her father Rubin in the forests of Arvenon
- *Elias* - abbot at the Monastery of St. Rodrig the Martyr where Brother Vangellis was hiding away
- *Ennawi* - slave of King Agon of Rogand
- *Eravitt* - Castelan nobleman who survived the assassination attempt in the barn at Paradise Valley
- *Essanda* - Queen of Arvenon, formerly a princess of Castel
- *Gareth* - mercenary leader
- *Gerome* - monk originally at the monastery led by Brother

Elias, later living at the Newhaven forest community; close friend of Brother Ander

- *Gordan* - Castelan nobleman and confidante of the late King Istel
- *Haldek* - former Rogandan soldier who unwittingly helped Will on more than one significant occasion; living in a tiny forest community with Elena, Rubin, and Thomas
- *Hazor* - mercenary leader
- *Inyaet* - chief librarian of the Aen-ur
- *Istel* - king of Castel, a neighboring kingdom to Arvenon, and father-in-law and ally of King Steffan of Arvenon
- *Jace* - assassin with an unequalled reputation
- *Jarah* - mercenary and hunter in the employ of Pisander
- *Jaxin* - retainer of the Duke of Erestor familiar with the dockside district of Maranelle
- *Jonas* - senior army leader and close confidante of Will Prentis; fought at the Battle of Torbury Scarp
- *Kaebon* - nobleman commanding the Castelan army at Deadman's Pass
- *Kaemin* - elder and senior member of the Aen-ur
- *Kantor* - member of Hazor's mercenary force
- *Karevis* - Varasan nobleman and commander of the Varasan army; played a key role at the Battle of Torbury Scarp
- *Kernon* - mercenary leader
- *Krasmir* - wealthy and powerful Rogandan nobleman
- *Kuper* - Arvenian soldier from Erestor who led a cavalry force to the battlefield at Torbury Scarp with his twin brother Rellan; killed at Torbury Scarp; son of Rellan and Anneka, named for his late uncle
- *Lygell* - deputy to Pisander and most senior nobleman in Arvenon
- *Mardone* - Castelan nobleman
- *Marya* - wife of Axel Stablehand and mother of Thomas
- *Namor* - mercenary leader

- *Nistinaa* - slave who cares for Ennawi
- *Ona* - Rogandan noblewoman and trusted associate of King Agon of Rogand; proficient in multiple languages
- *Pisander* - earl and former head of King Steffan's foreign spy network who remained in Arnost during the Rogandan siege; imprisoned for treason during the siege, but bribed his way out of prison before his execution
- *Petar* - hunter and bowman living at the Newhaven forest community near Erestor
- *Ranauld* - Arvenian count and a senior leader in the army at Torbury Scarp; a close confidante of King Steffan and a friend of Will Prentis
- *Redfass* - self-styled Arvenian nobleman; mercenary leader
- *Rellan* - Arvenian soldier from Erestor who led a cavalry force to the battlefield at Torbury Scarp with his twin brother Kuper; husband of Anneka
- *Rhillyon* - leader among the Aen-ur
- *Ronya* - member of the Clan
- *Rubin* - father of Elena
- *Rufe Sarjant* - respected and physically imposing Arvenian soldier; a close friend of Will Prentis and a key leader in the army
- *Rupert* - king of Castel following the death of his father, King Istel; brother to Essanda
- *Scar* - respected leader in Anneka's forest community
- *Steffan the Second* - king of Arvenon
- *Tamara* - daughter of Thomas and Elena
- *Tarestel* - Varasan nobleman who became puppet ruler of Varas after the Rogandan invasion; exiled after the defeat of the Rogandan army at Torbury Scarp
- *Thomas Stablehand* - possessor of the Stone of Knowing
- *Torbury* - title granted to Will Prentis by King Steffan; Will Prentis was elevated to the Arvenian peerage as Lord Torbury in honor of his efforts in defeating the Rogandans

- *Vangellis* - Arvenian monk who became a key mentor to Thomas; killed at Lord Drettroth's stronghold
- *Vilkami* - noble-born Rogandan who became Lord Drettroth
- *Viggor* - leader of the Clan
- *Will Prentis* - commander of the Arvenian army, greatly respected by his soldiers as well as King Steffan due to his remarkable qualities; fluent in Rogandan and widely traveled
- *Yordin* - captain of the Nomad Lady

NOTE FROM THE AUTHOR

Thank you for reading *The Struggle for Authority*—I hope you enjoyed it. Please consider leaving a review on Amazon for the benefit of other readers. I also very much appreciate feedback from my readers.

The Stone Cycle saga continues in *The Stone of Vitality (The Stone Cycle Book 5)*, described below.

When the abduction of an imperial princess sparks a tense standoff between Rogand and the distant Empire of Ahr, the dispute threatens to engulf Arvenon and its allies.

Hurrying to the Rogandan capital with an Arvenian delegation, Will joins the kings of Rogand, Castel, and Varas to plan a response. The upheavals that overtake them quickly thrust all else aside.

While the Grand Vizier of Ahr ruthlessly pursues his secretive agenda, mystery and suspicion swirl around the long-lived High Priest of the Rogandan Dark Gods.

No one is prepared for the emergence of the Stone of Vitality.

Note: The Stone of Vitality *is Book 5 of* The Stone Cycle, *a multi-*

part saga. The story will continue and conclude in Book 6, The Hope of Vitality.

In case you haven't already read it, *The Seer: A Prequel to The Stone of Knowing* is a short novelette that provides useful background to Dahra and Amyra in the story you have just read. See below for more information.

To be kept up to date on new releases, sign up to my mailing list at *www.allanpacker.com*. New subscribers will receive an exclusive bonus novelette—a prequel to *The Cost of Knowing*. The novelette, *The Rending: A Prequel to The Cost of Knowing*, is a complete story four chapters (13,000 words) in length. It provides background information on Anneka and her community. The novelette is described below. A paperback version is also available from Amazon and other online bookstores.

Endings may be beginnings in disguise

Anneka is comfortable and confident, a noblewoman of consequence living a life of privilege. Until the day her world is torn apart.

After losing everything she most cares about, she must abandon her home and her way of life in an attempt to secure the future of those who depend on her.

No one, least of all Anneka, could anticipate a deeper significance to her struggle. Yet her journey will one day influence the fate of kingdoms.

Where was the Stone of Knowing before Thomas found it? The answer can be found in a prequel to *The Stone of Knowing*.

The Seer: A Prequel to The Stone of Knowing is a novelette, 5 chapters (13,500 words) in length. It is a standalone story, and as such can be read independently of other books in *The Stone Cycle* series. The novelette is described below.

Eyes see no more than a glimpse

Sheylha is a seer—a woman with unique and extraordinary abilities. Powerful men want to control her, to use her to dominate others.

Kalvor is a warrior of unusual tenacity, a hunter who never gives up. Driven by his past, he has become a dangerous enemy.

When Kalvor is sent to find and capture the seer, each of them will be tested in ways they could never have imagined.

In time the outcome will determine the fate of kingdoms.

The Seer: A Prequel to The Stone of Knowing is available at Amazon's Kindle store.

ACKNOWLEDGMENTS

This book is dedicated to my sister, Julie, and brother-in-law, Chris. I've been blessed to share life's journey with them, and I hope I never take them for granted.

As always, I owe a huge debt to my wife, Merilyn, who is not only my most enthusiastic supporter, but has become increasingly effective as my alpha reader. It's no exaggeration to describe her role as that of a developmental editor. Her patience is awesome, and her feedback unfailingly valuable.

My heartfelt thanks to Andrew Menzies, Jen Neal, Cherilyn White, Ray, and Stephen, for their encouragement and constructive feedback as beta readers, to Brian Plush for his wonderful map, and to Karri Klawiter for her outstanding effort with my latest cover.

My official developmental editor, Mary Novak, came through again. As always, I have very much appreciated her insights. They invariably result in improvements to the story.

Special plaudits to Deborah for her usual thorough proofread, just weeks after giving birth to her third child.

2020 has been a challenging year for us all, wherever we might be living in the world. At a time of great uncertainty and social upheaval, I am grateful to God, my rock and my place of safety.

ABOUT THE AUTHOR

Allan Packer writes epic fantasy. *The Struggle for Authority* is his fourth novel.

Allan grew up surrounded by books and became an avid reader during his childhood. In his university years fantasy displaced science fiction as his favorite genre, thanks primarily to J. R. R. Tolkien. He later shared this love with his four children by reading *The Lord of the Rings* to them aloud—a three-month marathon he completed twice during their formative years.

Born in Australia, Allan has lived and worked on three continents, and spent one quarter of his working years abroad. Having worked as an IT professional throughout his career, he was first published as a technical author.

Today he lives with his wife in Adelaide, South Australia, near their children and a small but growing band of grandchildren.

Allan is currently working on the fifth novel in his series *The Stone Cycle*.

www.ingramcontent.com/pod-product-compliance
Lightning Source LLC
Chambersburg PA
CBHW030344200726
48286CB00013B/76